# The Shade

## by Judy Hogan

BLACK OAKS PUBLISHING

Permission requests for reproduction should be mailed to:
Permissions Department
Black Oaks Publishing
1310 11th Street
Port Townsend, WA 98368

Library of Congress Catalog Number 96-086179
Hogan, Judy
The Shade / by Judy Hogan - First Edition
ISBN 0-9652673-0-X


Printed in the United States of America

Layout, Proofing and Technical Assistance by Jackie K. Parrett
Computer Systems, Software and Services, Inc. - St. Louis, MO

Cover Design by Stephen Streett
Streettworks, St. Louis, MO

Cover Photography by Bob Bullivant
Bullivant Photography, St. Louis, MO

# FEET OF A DANCER

I hope you find the feet of a dancer,
I hope you can sing in the rain,
I hope you find all the easy answers
To your pain.

It won't be easy,
But what can I say?
There will be trouble on the way.

And around every corner,
Every terror and tear.
But always remember,
That we're here.

And I hope you find the feet of a dancer,
I hope you can sing in the rain,
I hope you find all the easy answers
To your pain.

And I hope you find love and affection,
I hope you find someone who cares,
I hope you find all the right direction
Everywhere.
Everywhere.

A shoulder to cry on, whenever you're low,
You know you can rely on us you know.
'Cuz there's nuthin' too crazy, and there's nuthin' too dear.
But always remember that we're here.

Even when the rain comes fallin' down,
You know it's fallin' down on you.

Always remember that we're here,
That we're here.

Feet of a dancer.
Feet of a dancer.
Feet of a dancer.

*Maura O'Connell is the singer of this opening psalm. She is an Irish performer. You read books only once, but you sing a song over and over. Let this one enter your heart, and if the words don't cause you to stop, it might be better to just close this book and ask for your money back.*

*Black Oaks Publishing*

This book is dedicated to

The Reverend Dr. Martin Luther King, Jr.

and

Yitzah Rabin

*Not to their memory, for they still live in each of us.*

*Thank you to the following people for taking the time to work on my book. Your encouragment and suggestions brought it from just a story to a finished work.*

*Dennis Terrill*
*First Reader and Publisher; he believed the story was true and spent his Christmas Day, 1995, in Pond Ridge*

*Lucille A. McClelland, Ph.D.*
*Chief Editor; she sleeps with a copy under her pillow*

*Drs. Scott and Mary Landau-Levine, Dr. Rahul Singal*
*Technical Advisors; they overlooked what was wrong for the sake of the possibilities*

*Josh, Sean, and Greer Hogan*
*Relentlessly, they proved that a child can teach a parent*

*Dona M. Burnett*
*Avid Reader; whose valuable suggestions assisted in the final revision of The Shade*

*Jermaine Wider*
*The final word*

**Thank you to the following supportive people whose lives are testimony that we're closer to fulfilling the dream.**

*Althea and Robert Allen, Maxine Clarkson and Jeffrey Allman, Warnetta and James Bonner, Marilyn Baker, Christina and Herbert Becton, Alfredo Belez, Calvin Jean and Maurice Bembry, Benny Bend, Gloria Beard, Deborah Ann and Terry Louis Billups, Gloria Bogan, Dennis Boresow, Carla Bort, Daniel Bowen, Robert, Annie, and Shawn Boyd, Goldine Boykin, Nathaniel Branch, Millie Brim, Carol Brookins, Elisha and Delores Brown, Vernice and Willie Brown, Cornell Cannamore, Lisa Holton and Mark Scott Carroll, Walter Carroll, Pastor Daryl Carson, Joyce Channel, Irma Childres, Ruby Groves Clay, Alvinette and Walter Collie, Cheryl and Dereck Clerkley, Adrienne Linette Crenshaw, Curtis Cross, Melvin Davis, Pastor Toney Davis, Myrtle and Roger Dickson, Jim Dobernic, Roderick Donald Dotson, Murry and Lisa Du Bose, Dorlene and Doris Dunne, Sen. Thomas Eagleton, Mattie Edwards, Yolanda Edwards, Velma D. Erwin-Fulks, Frances Gerlach, Mary L. Giles, Evelyn and Leevert Gordon, Gavin Grace, Arlisher Guss, Gregory and Rochelle Haines, Harry Hamell, Edward J. Hanlon, Jill Harper, Earlene Harper, Forrestella Harris, Drs. Jennifer Wetmore & Derek Hausladen, Deborah Henderson, Patricia Jean Henderson, Carolyn Banks Hill, Delores and Horace Henry, Nancy Moss Hollingsworth, Garie and Norman Holman, Walter Holman, Cheryl Holt, Rosie A. Ivory and Johnny Lee Hopson, M. Shane Mills and Scott Jackson, Barbara and Henry Jefferson, Glenda Jehle, Alma Johnson, Arthur Jones, Carol Jones, Jeri Kincade, 'Kon-tiki' Kohler, Dean R. Koontz, Petina Kostos, Randall Lang, Christine Lim, Renee Logan, Lishele Love, The Late Great Maureen Luh, Valeree Marion, Carla Mathis, Gynda and Venus Mathison, Frances Massey, Amos McClure, Rosalie Meert, Susan Green Miller and Daniel Miller, Eric Mink, Evelyn Mize, Joe Morgan, Barbara J. Mosby, Janet and Glenn Mueller, Penny and Vito Napoli, Diane M. Neal, Lou Hazel Nelson, Andrew Newbern, Linda Padfield, Francine Harris Page, Sha-shi Partee, Carolyn Payne, Marvin Perkins, Aaron Petty, Dan Poynter, Susan Pratt, Tim Purvis, Herschel Randolph, Alonzo Reed, Vicar Timothy Renstrom, Erma Robinson, Frances and Alfred Robinson, Linda Shaw, Daniel Schene, Annette Shores, Herman Smith, Mardie Sonnier, Paulette Stanley, Darral Stith, Pat Sweet, Kim Taylor, Gloria Thomas, Dwayne, Linda, Joshua and Jeremy Tubbs, Willie Andrew Turner, Jr., Diane & David Vojta, Audrey & Charles Vreeland, Pastor Sam Walter, Sharron Washington, Doretha Washington, Christina White, Michelle Wilks, Teresa & Joseph Williams III, Paul Zerr*

It isn't often that one man can make a difference, a difference felt in history, in the now, and in his own mind. He only speculates that he can do it, dreams of the feelings of suspense and wonder as his dream finds a foothold, a certain cringing fear that his dream will not end as he hoped it would. But to have the dream at all, to boldly step into it, push it, analyze it, perfect it: the dream must live. Whether it's a worthwhile dream doesn't matter. Whether it will become something different, he cares not about that. To have it, to plan it, to think it through, to have it actually work, a-a-h! There's the dream fulfilled, even if it turns out a nightmare for someone else. His is the scientific approach: if it breathes, it has life. If it has life, it has mobility. If it has mobility, it has a purpose. And he has decided the purpose, he has set the format, he will enjoy watching it unfold. It is destined.

For what is destiny but the dream we hold before our eyes, the goal we have set forward; what is it if not the bracing feeling of setting a destined goal and making it come true?

Is the joy in the setting or in the achieving? Is it necessary that the dream be a singular one or does it only manifest its goodness and viability if it embraces mankind?

What if the goal, the destiny, could do both? Could such a dream be possible that meets both goals? What if the goal was to make enough money to never be hungry again, as in Poor Scarlett, but accidentally, everyone was fed? What if the goal was to set aside anger at a neighbor over a fence line, only to find that all fence lines, all over the world, were no longer argued over, as if by one stroke? If by one action we could set aside all world hunger, all worldly greed, all injustices against women, men, children, all of mankind: A-a-a-h, such a pleasant dream.

And for some, it would mean setting away all people of another color, another culture, different religions. For some, it would mean setting aside all fat people, all thin people, all marathon athletes, who hurt them to the very quick, because they achieved something only dreamed of by a poor runner.

We need to sit and rest here a moment, think of our dreams, think of what we would do if by one magnanimous sweep we could change something. What would we change? What would we redesign to fit the mold of our dream?

It is the dream. It happened to Martin.

# Chapter One

*You say you want a revolution, well, you know,*
*We all want to change the world.*

*John Lennon "Revolution"*

The morning was cool, but not ready for fall. The flowers still bloomed along the sidewalks leading to the buildings housing the great thinkers on campus. Martin struggled with an unwieldy stack of books, and barely saved one from falling to the cobbled walk. It was an awesome responsibility, this getting up and going to class, this struggling with strangers, who didn't realize from whence he came, or where he was going. How should they know? He, as yet, didn't know. He only knew he was a Jew going to college, his religion standing out in his long face and green eyes, in his dark curly hair and his small stature. He was Martin Schoenfield, and he was here to succeed. There was no question of his ability to do so. SATs don't lie: they project the potential, and his was one of the highest scores that Cornell University ever recorded. He hid from this fact himself; he felt overburdened by the brain he carried behind his eyes.

If it would only go away, let him breathe for a while without the papers to write, the lectures to hear, the diagrams to draw, the microscopes to pore over. Damn them all for being stupider than he was; damn the majority of them for being Protestant. He hated the Protestant thinking even more than the ancient Catholicism that rankled in his bones. His early religious training had brought him to the amazingly simple conclusion that in spite of all protests, more atrocities had been committed in the name of Christianity than that of Judaism. What atrocities had the Jews committed? They had worked hard over the centuries, only to find themselves without a land, without an undivided religion, without attack on others as warriors, reviled because they had succeeded financially, socially, organizing their assets into a cohesive effort to establish a homeland, one they had been deprived of us as no other people had been deprived.

His own father, Micah, now answering to the name Michael, to be more agreeable to the Protestants, had forsaken his name only to find he could not forsake his genes. He was a Jew. Using this name meant nothing to anyone. Such a big step for him; no step at all in being accepted. The life he chose was a hard one: a large box of slats and skids, tied together with sheets of metal scrounged from the docks, provided him with a magazine stand. The age at which he became a father left him little time or patience to spend with the daughter his wife, Amelia, bestowed on him in their fourth year of marriage. A devout and talented seamstress, she rose each day and took the over town bus to the warehouse district near Seventh, where she poured over designer patterns and exhibited her needlework by being the only one allowed to add the pearls and sequins around the necklines of the gowns and dresses passing under her nimble fingers. She beamed with hidden pleasure when her work was examined by the floor director, Cecile, who only smiled at her and went off with the gown to the hemming room. She anxiously awaited a pay day with a bonus. Such excellent work, she reasoned, would not go unrewarded. The skimpy check never changed. Nothing ever changed. She was a drone, spending her eight hours in a stooped position that bleached the color from her face and the bloom from her body.

With her meager salary, paid every week, she handled the grocer and the landlord, and proudly presented to Micah the balance, after carefully deducting carfare for the coming week. Micah beamed his pleasure at her, stroked her hair, told her how much her efforts meant to him. He was stooped at thirty-eight; she was bent at thirty-two, but on they worked.

From sundown on Friday night to sundown Saturday, Micah and Amelia observed their Sabbath. No doorbell was answered; no light turned on. They ate a simple meal, which required no cooking, mostly leftover cold soup and crackers. One passion they shared was the fruit Micah would bring home, having traded some back issues of magazines with the man who ran the fruit market near his magazine stand. Late at night, after all the buyers and browsers would leave, he would place the aged plywood over the front of his stall, clearing the counter first of his secondary sales items, cigarettes and candy bars, and clasp the padlock through the iron loops, snapping it neatly closed. Then off he would hurry, carrying the last issues of *Mademoiselle* or *Fortune* or *Atlantic Monthly* to Evon, who would gratefully set the stack aside and wave his arm generously over the fruit he had set aside in the back as a little too soft to sell to the busy office workers strolling by during business hours. Micah took a small paper bag, and picked up the better looking plums and a nectarine with the blush still glowing. He looked up as he saw Evon watching him, but Evon nodded, so Micah added a lightly browned banana and a firm looking grapefruit, a ruby red-fleshed one from California, the sticky little seal told him. He looked again to Evon, to assure himself he was right in taking so much, but the back had turned and Evon was waiting on a customer. Micah took one more thing, a nicely rounded soft lemon and put it in his bag. As he passed out of the tarp hanging over the back room, he held up the bag for Evon to see, and Evon nodded. How much could you get in a child's brown paper lunch bag after all?

Micah scurried up the street, passing his own locked little warehouse of magazines, and he felt grateful he had such a friend as Evon, who never questioned what he took for an exchange that would have been more bother to Micah then turning it into a trade. For the magazine distributors were always fair when Micah returned unpurchased merchandise, giving him ten cents on the dollar for every copy he couldn't move in the allotted five days. The figures he kept in a small green notebook, adding and subtracting every day, so he would not lose track, and they always took his figures for the truth when they adjusted his accounts and carried off the unsold copies.

The copies they bought off Micah were resold through Hymie Goldstein on 53rd Street, a thriving little businessman, who supplied reading material for colonies of nursing homes, dentists' offices, and retirement communities, who never knew one month from the next, much less one week from the one before. The television kept them distracted from reality, and the everyday news went in one ear and stayed there.

His passage home left him tired, but contented, his steps only dragging as he reached the fourth floor and slid his key into his apartment lock. Even though it was late, always near midnight, Amelia would have a small pot simmering, and a salad made, and a glass of port ready for him. She smiled when he entered and hung up his sweater or coat, depending on the New York weather, but he never rushed to hold her, nor did she expect it. He nodded. She nodded.

He went to their bedroom, stripped off all his clothing and went across to the bathroom to run a shower. Standing under the warm spray, he rubbed the washcloth in lavender soap to wash away all that had sullied him that day. He knew she did the same when she came home from her needlework. They both smelled of lavender, and after their soup and crackers, or meat balls and gravy, and leafy vegetables touched with olive oil, they would smile at each other over the white cloth and gather the dishes and wash them, side by side, wiping up the sideboard, shutting off the kitchen light, and moving together toward their resting place.

As they fell into a tired contented sleep, following a connecting between them that swam and lulled and exalted them, Evon, at his place, was filling the back yard waste can with the rest of the fruits too old to be sold the next day. His clientele was very particular. His wife would enjoy the magazines. Friends were very good to have, even Jewish friends.

The child born of the love between Amelia and Micah was a six-pound black haired angel with long fingers and a gentle disposition. They settled on Amy because they wanted her to be accepted and American, and those were the only reasons. Cecile from the shop knew a woman in the neighborhood, who would watch over Amy while Amelia was at work, so after a futile try at nursing, she gave the child reluctantly into warm black arms and fled for her bus each morning.

# Chapter Two

The door swung open before him as two classmates slipped into the lecture hall, and he slid in behind them. Two coltish looking, well-fed girls, silly and side glancing at all the male students, sized this one up with a sigh, let out a low groan at one they wouldn't consider (both were destined to spend Friday night alone). They moved into their student seats, pulled up their note taking boards, and slumped back to scan the room as if they were twins with one mind. Martin hunched behind them in his seat, gazing over their fluffed and gauzy hair to see the lectern below. He felt sure he had caused at least one of the groans. He didn't care. He didn't like them either. Nothing about them did he like.

The lecture was on Kant's philosophy, a subject Martin enjoyed because it caused him to set aside his scientific bent and analyze the thinking, non-productive side of him. He considered it a luxury to simply study the way another man thought out a philosophy of life, its origins, its meaning, its end. He felt convinced that the philosophers didn't get their daily bread by selling magazines or kneeling over sequins too tiny to see until four were sewn together expertly. He stored the memory of his mother and father's sacrifice to get him to school as something he would need to pay back in the future, the sooner the better. Plato, Socrates, Nietzsche: all noodles in a thin soup broth. For in his Jewishness he could not think of it as a rich broth, only a liquid that would sustain life until his real life began.

The chair, being uncomfortable from the moment he sat in it, became his foe. The arms were too close to his neighbor on the left, a pharmacy student overburdened with additional poundage, and to his right, a small redheaded girl whose large horn-rimmed glasses seemed to need constant adjustment. He was stuck for now; his goal to get through these four years, then be accepted into medical school, seemed a far reach. But he remembered Amelia and Micah and their joy at his success and promotion, and the seat didn't pinch as much.

The paper rated an "A," and the assistant professor, who graded the paper, suggested to Martin that he might rethink his major, move over to philosophy, for, as he phrased it, Martin "jolly well" had the feel of it. Martin agreed. The whole field was a grand joke to him. Everything was jolly. But a doctor he wanted to be, not to treat patients. He had realized this shortly after his decision to become a physician, but because he liked the contemplative part; he preferred the silent laboratories of research. Time was not a problem to him. There was no hurry to decide, but the costs of continuing his education were becoming an overwhelming burden on his parents. He had to find a way to finance the rest of his education, and he was struck by a poster in the education hall claiming the Army was looking for good doctors. He couldn't see himself in the Army, for some unknown reason. Yet if the Army needed doctors to train and serve their four years, Martin knew the Navy would need people, too.

After class, he looked up the number of the Navy recruiting office in the hall outside his rented rooms, and dropped a dime into the slot. The answerer confirmed the need of enlisted men and college graduates in the medical corps and asked when Martin could come by to fill out a few simple forms. The appointment was kept; the forms were filled out, and the miraculous answer to his insolvency was provided. Thereafter he would be in graduate school for the U. S. Navy, Lieutenant Martin Micah Schoenfield, get his training, and serve his four. Then the Navy would see the last of him.

The news of the imminent wealth of the elder Schoenfields, due to the absence of further expense in educating their son, came as a welcome relief. Amy had grown and prospered and left the nest early, to try a marriage based on love, and that failing, had gone on to become a very independent and accomplished artist. Her paintings were circulating slowly in the smaller galleries in Boston and New York. No great deal of money, but her friends supported her talent, and her gracious manner made her a welcome guest. She never asked anything of Micah and Amelia, and quietly resented her younger brother, the male, getting financial help when she herself had never asked for anything after high school.

Amelia Schoenfield had just passed her sixtieth birthday, and Micah was in his first year of retirement. He had always paid into the Social Security program, knowing it was his only retirement package, being self-employed all those years. The monthly check of $1,024.00 supported them both, and for some time now they had lived in the upper story of a two-family flat in the Bronx near a synagogue. They heard often from Amy, quick notes dashed off at a luncheon or opening, always optimistic about the future. They rarely heard from Martin, but he was engrossed in his studies, they knew, and had little time for idle chatter.

The landlord was a man named Hymie Goldstein, the same man who purchased the unsold copies of magazines from Micah's distributor, who collected his rents in person and cautioned the two about bringing animals into the house. Fear edging on panic caused this man in his eighties to detest anything four legged. Being chased haunted his dreams, and the wealth he had accrued over the years gave him little pleasure after his wife died of ovarian cancer in her forties. After her death, the family broke up. His only daughter left the United States to marry a Brazilian and never returned. Josh Laurent, the lawyer, had discussed writing Hymie's will again, but this time there was no one to leave the properties, the business, the savings to. It panicked Hymie that the State of New York would get all of it, but for the life of him, even though he had relatives and organizations he could have dutifully remembered, even an endowment to the Synagogue, it grieved him so to think of parting with his money that he could name no one. So Josh sat back on the affair and urged him no longer to decide.

Money was what the four-legged chasers were after in his dreams, and he worried lest they strip him of it, if only in his dreams. To his added torment was the fact that the four-legged animals in his dreams resembled crouched down Blacks, who, because they were so like animals, he thought, only appeared to run on all fours. This fear, added to his knowledge that he could not legally turn away these Blacks, who wanted to rent his units near Hill Road, nearly drove him mad in his waking hours as frantically as the night dreams pursued him in sleep.

The lower half of the flat resided in by the Schoenfields was vacant for more than a month, and no prospect in sight. Hymie always found tenants by word of mouth, and it was just by chance that he met a woman through the magazine distributor's office who was looking for a place to live for herself, her husband, and college-age son. Not actually met her; only spoke with her on the phone, and she sounded delightful, well educated, and her husband owned his own business. The location suited them as it was near a bus line to the college where her son was in his second year and on the Dean's list. Hymie needed to hear no more. The lease would be ready for them at seven. He would show them the flat, give them the key, and accept their check for $1,000, $500 deposit and one month in advance. Claire Hauk was delighted. She knew Luther would approve. He operated independently as a heating and cooling contractor, and where he lived didn't matter when he spent almost all the time in the van anyway. Dwayne, the son, would be glad there was a bus so close to the school and his home, with no transferring this term.

A model of deportment Hymie was, waiting in the street before the flat at 6:45 P.M., rubbing his wrinkled hands together in earnest readiness for the feel of the check. Small beads of perspiration ran down his neck and soaked into the yellow-rimmed shirt collar. Never a meticulous man about his appearance, he had become downright slovenly in his advanced years, bearing his filth like a badge of honor his age provided him.

Amelia pulled back the curtain to peer down at the landlord pacing in the street.

"Micah, come look," she said softly. He was reading in his chair with his slippers on, enjoying a letter from Amy, but he sighed and struggled up to his feet. Shuffling over the rug to her side, he gazed over her shoulder and down at Hymie. He stifled a chuckle; the window was up a few inches to catch the breeze, and he didn't want old Hymie to spin about and look up at the two peering down.

"It must be a tenant for downstairs," he guessed. "Old Hymie wouldn't be wasting all that hand rubbing over a bar of soap. Must be money coming in and very soon."

"My mind agrees with yours," she whispered. She let the curtain fall back, but the two continued to peer through the sheer lace. The tea kettle sang out its chirp of ready, and she slipped away to the kitchen to turn it off, hurrying back to see the minor drama unfold.

They had not long to wait, for as they were pulling up chairs and settling their teacups on the sill, a black sedan pulled neatly into the parking place in front of the flat. A tall well dressed Black woman got out of the car and reached back in for her purse. She waved jauntily at Hymie, who had stopped his stroll in mid-stride, and put his hand out to lean against the boulevard tree. His back was to Micah and Amelia, but they imagined the look on his face. He had shared his nightmare with everyone.

The elegant Black woman's smile seemed to fade, and then her mouth closed into a single pursed line. Her voice drifted up to the teacup sitters.

"You are Mr. Goldstein, I presume?" She stretched her hand out to him, but he kept his firmly on the tree; his eyes looking some place above her head.

"The apartment's not available after all," he said in a cracking voice.

"And why is that, when it was available only this morning? You assured me over the phone it would be held for me. I came as soon as my work was finished, and I could get to the bank. You did say seven, and surely it's not much past that. Why have you changed your mind, Mr. Goldstein? My supervisor assured me he thought you a man of your word. He'll be disappointed, along with me, if we have to . . . inquire further . . . into your change of heart." She bit her lower lip in distress. How she hated scenes, especially this type of scene, for she guessed the reason for his unwillingness to honor his promise. He remained silent.

"Look, Mr. Goldstein, if it's the law to let people live where they can afford to live, why stand in the way? Why not just understand that Luther and I are good people who need to rent until we can get Dwayne through college, then we'll be buying our own place. It won't be for long." She realized she was practically begging, to avoid a clash of wills. He slowly turned his back and stared at the building he owned.

Amelia and Micah shrank back from the window, knowing they couldn't be seen, but fearful that their listening ears would not let them be quiet. They looked at each other, and then, as if of one will, they reached forward and picked up the teacups. Eyes searched the beloved face of the other, the teacups clinked slowly together, and Amelia laughed.

Down the stairs they hurried, but not so fast as to spill the contents of the cups. Throwing open the front door, they saw the startled face of Hymie staring at them with the tall woman standing back slightly, still in the street in front of her car.

"Welcome, welcome," Micah shouted, starting down the steps and across the shaggy lawn. "A face for downstairs. We were just saying, weren't we, my dear?" and he turned back toward his wife, "how very dreadful it is to live over an empty nest. No sounds coming up, and no helping heat in the winter." He winked at Claire.

"Just our words," sang Amelia, handing the cup of tea to Claire, who stood stock still in disbelief.

"This is for you, Hymie," offered Micah graciously, settling the china cup into the old man's hands. "Sip away, it'll do you good. Always drink hot things in the heat. It'll make you cooler. And today's been so warm, the evening breeze will help. You'll be keeping your windows open, too, Miss . . . uh, Miss?"

"Claire Hauk," she breathed out.

"Like the bird?" questioned Amelia, touching her fingers lightly in the air.

"The sound is like hawk, but we spell it 'H-A-U-K' not 'H-A-W-K,'" she answered, and took a sip of tea for lack of something else to do.

"They won't be staying," interjected Hymie.

"For long, is that what you meant, Hymie? 'Course none of us knows how long we'll be staying. This is a short life, but our God tells us we better live it right the first time. We won't be getting a second chance, like the Protestants." He nudged Hymie in his waistcoat, the teacup wobbling in its saucer ever so slightly.

Hymie cleared his throat, and handed Amelia the cup and saucer. He moved away up the sidewalk, and Micah narrowed his eyes as he watched the man rudely exit.

"Well, Hymie," he called out. "Better not place too much hope that we'll be here next month, either." Hymie's body froze on the spot. He slowly turned and faced the company brandishing teacups as weapons, or that's how he saw it.

"You say?" he inquired, moving back to them. "You say you'd leave, over this matter?"

"In a heartbeat," said Micah, hoping his tone conveyed a confidence he didn't feel.

Hymie turned to Claire. "The check, can I see the check?" She set the saucer and cup in the grass, unclasped her purse and quickly drew out a blue bank envelope. Hymie hastily tore it open, and extracted a certified check payable to Hymie Goldstein, and his heart melted. A mellow safeness surged through his body, the world was in the hollow of his hand.

"The key's in the mailbox. I collect rent on the first of the month. Fifteen dollars late fee after the first." With those parting words of farewell, he quickly moved up the street to catch the bus. All that money and too tight to buy a car.

The three stood by the tree, and Micah spoke first. "I'll be running up and getting another cup of tea, seeing you've snagged mine, and then we'll give you the cook's tour."

Amelia lightly took Claire's elbow, and steered her toward the steps of what was to be her next home, her home of light colors and beautiful ferns on the long porch, her place for her husband and son, won so easily because of Christian goodness. But as she looked at the back of Micah scurrying up the stairs in his slippers after a fresh cup of tea, and turned to gaze at the smooth knot of grey hair piled on Amelia's head, she knew she had found a greater force.

# Chapter Three

*One day we'll laugh, yeah, and we'll look on the bright side,*
*But that's no consolation for the moment at hand.*

*Vance Gilbert "If These Teardrops Had Wings"*

The moving van backed against the curb on the following Wednesday, guided by the gloved hand of the main man of the day, Luther Hauk. He told the driver when to stop, to avoid running up over the curb. He cautioned the movers to be careful with the furniture, and to especially watch for the armoire, an antique from an estate they had sheltered since their marriage. Someday it would stand in the parqueted entry of a home in New Rochelle, but for now it was ensconced between a washing machine covered in blankets and a tile-topped table made by Dwayne in the eleventh grade as a shop project. He got an 'A'.

Women were all right, in his mind, when it came to finding, but to get it done, you needed a man. He had always been just the man to carry out his wife's bidding. Their marriage worked.

Micah, in his retirement, had plenty of time to sweep out the lower rooms and polish the bright work in the bathroom. He hung up a wreath on the door, a wreath of welcome, but Claire spotted it and knew it would find a place other than the front entry. She, too, knew her mind, and although she dearly loved the humble couple above, she wanted it known that her place was her palace.

Full of the mastery of his position, Micah drew Luther aside and informed the Black man that he should consider himself lucky that no lease was offered.

"You, see, Luther, with that lease over your head, you give up your freedom. He can find a reason to break it if he locates another tenant. This way, as long as he gets his rent, you've got a thirty-day stranglehold on him, and he can't break what isn't there. You follow?" Luther nodded. Micah moved closer.

"And he'll never break it as long as you keep paying. What gripe has he? You have the upper hand. Never lose the upper hand." Luther nodded, keeping his eye bent on the movers moving his goods out of the van.

"Always, before," Luther started, "I could get in with the landlord, do him favors that would help him out, like fix an air conditioner or an icebox for little or nothin'. They held me in high esteem over that. You say I can't work off some of this rent with this man?"

"Don't smile with him at all," warned Micah. He somberly shook his head. "He has dreams, my friend, and you're in them."

The moving in was the simple part. Many boxes, full of Christmas decorations and school book treasures from Dwayne's childhood, were stored on skids, provided by Micah, in the cellar. The house was so old that to call it a basement, with a hope of becoming a rumpus room, would have been bestowing upon it an honor it didn't deserve.

"The skids'll keep the dampness from seeping into your stored things," wisely directed Micah. Luther nodded in appreciation. The last apartment had no basement at all, so he was glad for the extra space. He looked carefully into Micah's face.

"You're a very smart man, Micah Schoenfield, and I'm proud to call you my neighbor and my friend." He pulled off his leather work glove and extended his hand to the older man.

"Ah, you don't owe me no compliment, Luther, but a neighbor I'll be. Old Hymie isn't long for this world, but you and me, the likes of us, we'll be here forever." He held the man's hand for a moment before he squeezed it gently. The two men stood in the cellar, deliberating the placement of a large box of athletic equipment from Dwayne's high school days, shoving it first on top of the Christmas decorations, and then remembering those would be needed first, moved it below and soundly placed the decorations on top. They paused at the printing on the carton.

"Now, that's not an offense to you, is it, handling Christmas decorations? 'Cuz if it is, we're in for some real hard goin', long 'bout the first of December. Hard as I've tried to get her to stop, that Claire of mine starts in every December One with a carol in her heart and a song on her lips." He pulled his gloves on and looked at Micah for a response.

"And you don't agree?" asked Micah. "Isn't the man the head of your household? If your wife's celebrating is not in tune with your own, let her know and she'll step back."

Luther laughed, a hearty deep laugh, rumbling inside his chest. "Step back? You ever know my Claire to step back? She took your wreath off the front door, didn't she? And how'd she 'splain that to you?"

"She said she had a place for it, but it wasn't right for the front door. She has a right to place my wreath wherever she likes, Luther." Micah had forgotten, momentarily, that the wreath he had placed had been switched for a garland of white babies breath, dried pink roses, swirls of frozen ivy, and a turquoise colored ribbon. He loved her wreath.

"But how'd she 'splain it to you?" Luther grinned.

"She didn't have to explain it to me," Micah stammered. "It's her house, and I welcomed her, and she put up what she wanted, and I don't know what she did with my wreath."

Luther let out a loud hoot, and he wiped tears of laughter from his eyes. "My man, that's what I been tryin' to tell you. Claire's got that wreath of yours, and she hums over it, and she worries about it, and she moves it from the bafroom to the kitchen, but she's got no place to put it that looks right to her. Now, you tell me, how'm I gonna tell this woman what to do?"

Micah stopped, wondering where this had started, where it would end. He shrugged his slender shoulders under the weight of it all. "A man is a man in his own house. You need, Luther, to tell Claire what to do with Micah's wreath." It had been so simple before, now the complications began. He, Micah, after raising his family, had to do his paternal role and advise this man of his rights of household.

Luther laughed again. "I'll be doin' it, yessir, Mr. Micah. I'll be going upstairs this minute and demand to know what's become of the welcomin' wreath." He chuckled softly, moving toward the stairs.

Micah followed slowly, lifting his slippers up, one step at a time, following the sturdy air conditioner installer into his kitchen.

"Claire!" Luther hollered. "Where you be?" Luther turned and winked at Micah.

She came around the corner between the dining room and the kitchen, setting one hand on her long hip, and said, just as loud, "Who you be calling?"

Luther faced his wife, the grin wide on his face, and knew she was into the game. "Your upstairs neighbor here, Mr. Micah, want to know what you done with his wreath."

"His wreath? That wreath? I plumb forgot about it." She turned away, straightening some dishes on the table.

"Now you be lyin', 'cuz you just held it yesterday, and said, 'What's a body to do? The man's so kind and I got his wreath and I want mine and, Luther,' you said to me, 'what should I do?'"

Micah shrank back a moment, not knowing all the rules of this game they were playing, not knowing that some people play games in their marriages, not hurtful con games, but games they know, dialect games, games that remind them of their heritage, word games that feel like fun, get them ready for love. He thought of Amelia waiting for him upstairs, waiting with supper and warmth and love in her still.

Claire glared at Luther for taking the joke so far. She hurt, in a way, that he would mention the wreath to Micah. Why had this gone so far? She knew she would find a place for Micah's wreath. Just not on her front door.

# Chapter Four

*See the curtains hanging in the window*
*Summer breeze, makes me feel fine*
*Blowing winds of jasmine in my mind.*

*Seals and Crofts "Summer Breeze"*

The sons returned, one by way of bus and a short stroll up the elm lined street, the second in a taxi cab from the airport, paid for nicely by the U. S. Navy. Stepping spic and span in his R.O.T.C. blues, Martin Schoenfield gazed up at the two story duplex where his mom and dad were waiting for him. Not waiting, exactly, but practically dying for a look at him. The tea kettle had been off and on since two, and now, approaching four, it was time for a light snack for their only blessed son, coming to see them in their dotage, or that's how they saw it. For they could hardly claim to be his benefactors, supporters, any longer. The Navy had done that for them. Instead, they hoped to glimpse him, kiss him, hold him for a while, and then let him loose again, to follow his path.

They parted the curtains many times that afternoon, watching for a sight of him. Each one hoped they would be together at the curtain when he arrived. They had been together when he came; why not now on his return?

It was only by coincidence, or a weird stroke of fate, that the first person who saw Martin stepping from the taxi cab was Dwayne Hauk. He moved his books to his left arm, hoping to have a greeting that would end and begin in a warm handshake. His large athlete's body bore down on the smaller Schoenfield, but when Martin turned to look at the approaching man, his eyes bore a softness, friendliness, and warmth he couldn't explain. Perhaps his own shone the same way.

"So, the student returns," Martin called, guessing the young man was the Hauks' son. His telephone calls in the past few months had been long recitals of the evenings the couples spent playing cards, betting dimes and nickels, laughing together over Luther's skill at outguessing all the others. Luther always came up fifteen dollars to the good, but he always found a way to pay it back, in a small repair, an errand for Amelia, a bush for the yard, and extra close trimming on the yard, which he prized above everything else. Had he been a gardener, he would have thrived. Everything grew under Luther's big pressing thumbs once placed around the base of a newly planted bush. Claire did it with the dried flowers; Luther had it for the living.

The two young men stood at the base of the stairs, shaking hands and checking each other out. Yes, the story Claire had told over and over, about Hymie, and the lease, and the teacups, and the wreath had not escaped the studious Dwayne. He knew what pleasure his mother had found in the Jewish couple upstairs, and only hoped he would find the same friendship in their college age, Navy-bound, son. Martin looked into the eyes of Dwayne, and found a light of intelligence and humor, a bond from the first time they touched hands. The man towered over Martin, but the way he looked at him, the warmth and kindness in his handshake, dispelled any hint of setting him aside. They both belonged to this extended family, and they moved up the stairs side by side, the muscular athlete-scholar, the finely chiseled Jew with the dark close cut Navy haircut under his cap.

"You're here!" Amelia shrieked out the upstairs window. "Micah, he's here!" Her hand brushed the curtain back as Martin looked up to see his father joining his mother at the open window. The two faces, wide in smiling, looked down at the two men below.

"And where else would I be if I had a choice!" He doffed his cap to them, spun around in his uniform like a model, and slapped it back on, pretending to salute them. They crowed with pleasure at the sight of him, jostling each other to crane for a closer look.

"You're coming up then, son?" called Micah, putting his arm around Amelia's shoulder. Her face, flushed with a rosy glow, beamed with happiness as she gazed down at Martin.

"Nah, I don't think I'll be coming up. Me and my buddy Dwayne here, we think we're going to go down the street and shoot some pool and try to pick up some girls." Martin nudged the other man and laughed. Dwayne laughed back, good naturedly, just as the lower front door swung open. Claire stood in the open door, looked at Dwayne laughing, turned her gaze on Martin, and she fairly ran down the steps to him.

"You're Martin," she said, beaming at him, stretching her long arms with the lovely hands out to him. He stared at this woman, the one he had heard so much about from his mother, and wondered why his mother had never told him that she and dad lived over an African queen. For that was what she was, Martin knew it immediately: a dispossessed, disenfranchised queen who should have had jewels and coaches and palms waving over her in sleep. This was a mistake, her being here, a mistake in time, in placement, in the true order of the universe. There had been an error.

"Hi, Mom, remember me? I'm your son, you know, the one who lives here, goes to school nearby, comes home every day at this time. Remember me?" Dwayne interjected over the handshake of Martin and Claire.

Claire laughed, withdrawing her hand. "Yes, I seem to remember you, but only faintly. Are you sure you're mine?" She looked at Dwayne with merriment in her eyes.

Dwayne looked at his wrist. "Well, same color, same eyes, same great legs." He gave Claire a slight kiss on the cheek. She pushed him away.

"Same as yesterday, Dwayne, but this is the Schoenfields' day. This is their son!" She stepped back and looked hard and long at Martin. "You look not at all like I pictured you. Your father said you were seven feet tall and blond, but your mom said you were little and trim. They both lied. You're just perfect." She stepped forward. "May I?" She put her arms around him and kissed him gently on the cheek.

Now anyone passing and observing this scene would have looked twice. The African queen kissing a darkly tanned Jew in a Naval uniform, fit very close over his trim muscles. The athletic looking man, who could only be a hand servant of the queen, was standing to one side smiling, holding what must have been the books of the kingdom.

The door to the upstairs burst open, the screen slamming back against the bricks alarmingly, and Micah hurried down the steps in his slippers. Amelia trailed behind, stopping only briefly to check that the door was still intact.

"Martin, Martin, Martin!" Micah shouted. He crossed the few feet between them and grasped his son in a bear hug. He kissed him on both cheeks, bent his head forward and kissed him again and again on the back of his neck. "Amelia? Where are you?" He turned to his wife, following behind, regally holding back the tears she felt forming behind her eyes.

"Mama." Martin tried to hold back the pressure of love he felt for them both. She held her hands out to him, touched his face, murmured, "Oh, oh, the joy." She stood before him and touched his face, removed his hat, touched his close-cropped hair, pulled him down to her, and kissed his ear.

"Enough, now, enough, I'm home, I'm here, we're all here." He glanced at Claire and Dwayne, standing in rapt attention. "We need to watch what the neighbors will say about our love fest here in the street." He reached down for his luggage, but found Dwayne's hand already on the strap.

"Allow me, sir," said Dwayne, lifting the case and moving

toward the upstairs entry. Just as he loped up the stairs with the bag, Claire blew a kiss of good bye, and wafted into her home. Martin hugged his mother as they walked up and Micah followed behind, stopping to check the screen door. How bent it looked all of a sudden. Well, Luther will take care of that. And where was Luther at a time like this? Luther should have been here. Wasn't perfect without him.

Dwayne stayed for a few more minutes, chatting about the neighborhood, and watching out for dogs who might bite, then looked out the window and gestured to Martin where he should be especially careful.

"They got a Shepherd that'll make you think twice," he pointed, looking at Martin's attentive gaze out the window. They were standing close together, framed in the lace curtains, and Dwayne felt a rush of compassion, maybe even affection, for the trim green eyed man in the uniform. Maybe it was the uniform, maybe it was the eyes set in the lean face, but he recognized a common element between them. He felt it strongest when he let the lace slip from his hand.

Dwayne headed through the living room and down the stairs. His walk was jaunty and filled with life. He felt good, felt happy in this house with the Schoenfields upstairs, knew they were part of him, knew they had a son who deserved them, and he was happy. He bounded down, waving good byes over his shoulder, only pausing to try to close the screen door.

# Chapter Five

Amelia felt contented watching the two men in her life, bent over the checkerboard. It was great fun for her to see Micah win when it meant so little to Martin. Luther always won when he and Micah played. He never cheated; he was just good with checkers. He brought up a chess set one night when Amelia was just going to bed, her face scrubbed and her woven cotton gown in place, and she let him in to stay for the game that would go on until two in the morning.

Her job at the dress manufacturer had turned more golden as she advanced in experience. Now she found Cecile coming to her first with a new pattern, a new flounce, asking her how it could be done and how inexpensively. Amelia could now afford the luxury of pursing her lips and holding the sample away from her fading eyes, bringing it close to examine each detail, and setting aside the ones that would work, and the ones no one would be able to execute, she haughtily discarded. Cecile always nodded, agreed, moved away to the pattern room, carefully thinking about what Amelia had said. The small checks had grown larger, but the price Amelia paid with her eyes and her hands, in sewing on the appliques and the sequins, would never compensate for her loss. She was growing blind, she knew it, but she faked very well, knew by touch and feel what there was to know, knew the way to the bus by heart, felt in her purse for the change of the right size, carried the lunch Micah prepared for her to her work station; never left during the day, and then only to return to the home she shared with her husband. Her husband. What a husband. A lover. A friend. Ah, the lover part.

He was still her fond and attentive lover. Whatever else she had missed in not staying home with Amy as a baby, or with Martin as a toddler, she had been more than compensated for in the bedroom. Her Micah was the total eclipse of the sun, the gentlest nurturer of her deepest feelings of being a woman. He had to know what being a woman was: the way he touched her and stroked her feet, kissed her thighs, long after the tone of her muscles had left. Ah, Micah . . .

Her yawns turned to sighs as she watched the two men in her life battling a quiet mental game over the checkerboard; some moments passed while she drifted into sleep and shook herself awake, like the feeling of stepping off a curb and being startled, knowing she had to work tomorrow while these two could sleep in until noon if they chose. She got up from her chair and set her mending down, the sock she had tried to put together for the last two hours, and said she was going to bed.

"Ah, so early, Mignong, so early," Micah intoned, reaching out with his hand. She held it warmly in hers.

"It'll be early for me, but late for you, and my old bones are tired. Go on with your game, you two. Your stomachs are full and your pastime is pleasant. I'm heading for sleep, and none too soon." She kissed Micah's hand and moved to Martin. "Good night, my son, and welcome to your home."

He reached for his mother's hand, and found his arm around her bending neck, her cheek held to him in offering. He kissed it gently, brushed her hair with his hand, and said, "Mama, it's good to be home." She stood back, smiling at the two of them, and moved quickly and quietly to pick up her teacup and leave them alone. She hesitated at the doorway, touching the frame, and moved more deliberately toward the kitchen. Her steps sounded as they padded to the sink, water was heard, she reentered the living room, and touched the wall as she went toward the bedroom. Martin watched and shut his eyes against the thought.

"Your move, Martin, you're dawdling over my last move. Kind of got you cornered, have I?" He rubbed his hands on his thighs, hoping Martin wouldn't notice the very intricate move he had made, placing Martin in a double jump situation. He hoped Martin wouldn't see it, the very same move Luther had gotten him boxed into just last week. If Luther were here, the game would have been over. Luther would have done him in. But his son was not as good at checkers as Luther had helped Micah become. Tonight Micah was king.

"Dad?" Martin turned away from the departing Amelia. "Dad, when did Mom start to touch the walls when she left the room?" He reached over and picked up a cigarette, lighting it carefully and thoughtfully, only four a day and he measured them out.

"Ah, it's her home, she loves it, she touches it. Your mother is a very touching woman. Why the walls? Why not the walls?" The move, Martin, make the move I want you to. Let me do a Luther on you.

"Dad, I think Mom's not seeing real well. Has she had her eyes checked recently?" He leaned back in the chair, blowing the precious illicit smoke out, watching his father's face. The old clock on the wall ticked away, the room slightly misted by the smoke from the cigarette.

"She's fine, I tell you. Never said one word about not seeing so well. We all don't see as well as we get old, Mr. Student. You watch. You won't have the eyes of a child forever." Micah was anxiously awaiting the next checker move, slightly on edge that the delay may cause Martin to look more closely after the interruption in play.

"Papa, I think Mom's work has tired her eyes. She seems to be uncertain unless she touches the walls." Martin stubbed out the cigarette, leaving half of it in the ash tray. He pondered his next remark.

"Dad, I want you to take Mom to a doctor, an eye doctor, and let him look at her eyes." His father shook his head. "But why not, Papa? I'll pay for it, if it's the money you're worried about."

Micah twisted uncomfortably in his chair. It wasn't the money, that he knew. It wasn't anything except finding out something he would rather not know. Besides, checkers was on his mind, not Amelia's imagined eye problems. Just make the play, Martin, he thought, let me have my great moment.

"You think that your mother wouldn't tell me if her eyes were bothering her? You think we haven't shared everything, everything, even the smallest troubles? Eh? You know so much, Mr. Navy student, but you don't know that much," and he snapped his fingers in front of Martin's eyes, "of what we know about each other. No eyesight problems, no, now just make your play, I think you're stalling." He settled back, rubbing his thighs again in anticipation of his great jumps.

Martin got up and stretched. He suddenly felt tired, bored with the game. "Could we finish tomorrow, Papa? I really do feel like turning in. The travel and all." He picked up the ashtray to carry it to the kitchen. Micah felt crushed.

"You're quitting? How can you quit when it's just getting good? I have some things I want to show you so you'll be a better checker player," he called as Martin went to the kitchen.

Martin reappeared and nodded toward the bedrooms. "Same old room?"

Micah nodded. "Your mother freshened the sheets, and put flowers in there for you. You haven't seen them, but they were pretty this morning." He sat back, defeated. He watched his son in the blue Naval shirt and pressed trousers wave good night and move toward the bathroom.

The room was quiet except for the tick of the clock. 11:48 P.M. The great play, the one he wanted to make, the two jumps that only he knew how to block, pressed into his eyes. What a shame to waste them. He wanted to make them, and he knew Martin wouldn't know how to block that move, only Luther had showed him. But only one time, late at night, and maybe Luther didn't remember he'd shown him.

An idea brightened his outlook, and he sprang to the stairs, shuffling down quickly. He went out the door and pushed back the screen, now readjusted and fitting perfectly, and slipped across the porch to the lighted doorway of the Hauks. He pressed the bell.

"Who's there?" came Luther's protective voice. Micah could hear him put down his paper and move across the floor to the door. He saw Luther's face in the door window, a small five inch square of glass. The eyes changed to a twinkle when the intruder was recognized.

"Well, what have we?" began Luther, opening the door, standing in his clean slacks and undershirt. "Air conditioner actin' up?"

"Air conditioner's fine, had a guy up the street look at it just last week," Micah said solemnly. "My son's home. Did Claire tell you?"

"Sure, she tol me, she said he's not seven feet tall and blond, not that I believed that for a moment. I missed the homecomin', didn't I? I'll see him tomorrow, I hope. Didn't want to bust in on your first evenin' together."

"Well, our first evening together went well, yes, very well. He's an excellent checker player. You'll have to sit down with him, but just now when things were going along nicely, he decided he was tired and wants to go to bed, but I hate to leave a board half done. You understand?"

Luther scratched his chin, paused, looked over his shoulder, and said, "Wait one minute. Do you want to step in?" Micah shook his head, stayed on the porch in his slippers. Luther moved through the living room, straightening the newspaper as he passed the footstool, and went down the hall. He was gone maybe two minutes, but came back, broadly grinning.

"She says okay, ain' that grand?" He grabbed his pipe and pouch of tobacco and came back to the door. "Wait. My keys." He grabbed the keys off the entry table, and came out on the porch, locking the door behind him, testing it twice to be sure it was locked.

They came back across the porch, and went through the readjusted screen door and up the steep stairs, being quiet not to disturb the sleepers. Micah's head felt light with the play ahead; he could see it plainly. Luther just didn't know what he was in for.

They pushed the door open into the living room, and everything was just as he had left it. The clock kept its quiet measure of time; the lamp was still focused on the play table, the ashtray would have to be brought back from the kitchen. These things took a few moments. He came in with iced tea for both of them, the ashtray balanced on his arm. Luther relieved him of the ashtray.

"Thanks, my friend, thanks." He held the icy glasses, looked at the table, could see the rings before they appeared if the glasses were set on the oak. He glanced for coasters, and finding none, he motioned to

Luther to get the socks on Amelia's sewing basket.

"These?" Luther asked, standing by the basket.

"Yes, yes, they will do." Micah was anxious, more than anxious as Luther put the clean white socks at either side of the board. Micah set the glasses down. The clock chimed midnight, a bewitching hour, an hour for his first triumph over the fabled Luther.

"You really did stop, dint you, right in the middle?" Luther scanned the board with a practiced eye.

"The son just got tired, you know, the travel," said Micah.

"Which side was he on?" asked Luther, touching the chair nearest the door, the one Martin had been sitting in.

"When a son comes home, in a righteous home, he is given the seat of honor. He sat in my chair," intoned Micah.

"Fine with me, all's play the same." Luther sat back in Micah's favorite chair, tamped his pipe, lit it with a kitchen match, and slowly puffed until the barrel glowed. He blew out smoke once before the tobacco died.

Micah sat down in Martin's vacated chair, the play already repeating in his mind. Now he would know how to stop the double jump: Luther had shown him.

"Take a minute now, Luther, to see where we were in the game. Let me give you a minute," Micah offered generously.

Luther ducked his pipe into the ashtray, leaned forward and looked at the board, carefully running the checkers through his mind. He looked up at Micah.

"You say this was his play, or your turn?" he questioned.

"My turn," said Micah, holding his breath.

"Ah," said Luther, picking up and drawing on the dead pipe slowly.

Micah held his breath, held it one moment longer as he moved his hand to block the double jump, just as Martin came down the hall toward the kitchen, maybe for a drink of water. He stopped in his skivvies to stare at the two men at the table, and Luther rose in the same moment.

"Papa?" his voice asked. The game had gone on without him apparently, a substitute coming in nicely. All the pieces fit.

"Martin! I thought you were tucked in. This is Luther, came up to fill in for you, being up at this hour." Micah felt his voice sliding into a dark place.

Martin stepped toward Luther, extended his hand in friendship, and Luther gripped it gently but firmly. The young man and the Black installer of air conditioners stared into each other's eyes. A feeling of understanding ran between them.

"Papa, why'd you take my side of the board? If Luther's to finish my game, shouldn't he be on my side?" Martin asked this innocently, standing there in his underwear, saying it not out of meanness, but out of concern that he left Luther a mess to piddle with, and his father was going to try to win for him.

"Go on to bed, son, we'll handle this." Micah waved his hand impatiently toward Martin, who felt dismissed. He nodded to Luther, went into the kitchen, got his water, and carried the glass down the hall.

Luther sat back down in Micah's usual chair, reached for the pipe that had gone cold, and tentatively struck a new match to the tobacco. He shook out the match, puffed a moment, and looked long and hard at Micah. He leaned forward again, over the checkers, and sat back again, puffing slowly on the pipe.

Beads of perspiration ran down Micah's forehead. His hands didn't rub his thighs at all. They felt limp and useless on the chair arms.

"Micah," Luther started, "maybe it's later than we thought. Maybe we should start fresh, a new board. A new game, a new day, what d'ya think?"

Micah only nodded, saddened by the turn of events. Luther tamped the dead tobacco and tried to light it again, but the flame flickered and died over the bowl. He stood in one movement, and his hand extended to Micah.

Micah looked up at him, towering over him, and felt ashamed, ashamed for the play he had been going to make, the move he knew would stop Luther's two jumps, the move he had learned from Luther, but somehow, somehow, Luther knew, too. Micah felt ashamed for the first time in his life. He felt a real shame.

"It's later than I thought," said Luther, moving toward the door. His shoulders sagged in a way that made Micah want to jump up and hold him.

"Luther, wait, I can explain," stumbled Micah. "And I didn't shake your hand."

"No need," said Luther, starting down the stairs. He didn't turn back.

"Luther," Micah called after his retreating back. "I just wanted to win!"

Luther turned, five steps down, and his glistening black skin shone back to Micah. "Winning's not everything. Screw what Lombardi said. It's how you play what counts."

As it turned out, it wasn't as big a deception as Micah imagined. Yes, he had tried to win, but Luther had seen the play as soon as he sat in the chair. Had seen it and known it for what it was: a chance to beat him. Luther found it sadly ironic that the Jews and the Blacks, two of the most spit upon peoples of the earth, should try to cheat the other. He found it deliciously ironic; he found it too personal to tell Claire about. His pride stopped him there. He planned to stay friends with Micah, for in the end, all Micah had shown him was his own humanness.

The days of Martin's visit slipped by like leaves on a river, moving away to a distant place, not to be brought back. No, you don't gather the leaves sticking against the log downstream and haul them back for another day. Only Christians believed you could do that, do it all over. For Martin, he knew the leaves went by only once. And for him, once would be enough.

He had liked being home, wanted to stay longer, but knew the beginning of the last semester was fast approaching. Books to buy, schedules to memorize, new buildings and classrooms to become familiar with. What new buildings could they come up with? Hadn't he been in them all in the past four years? He was a senior this year, and it would be over and out in May. Then the four-year stint with the Navy. He had agreed to New London Groton Base in Connecticut, close to New York. He planned to live off base, maybe find a roommate with a car so he wouldn't have to buy one. Maybe start dating, just to please Amelia.

The thought of dating gave him the shivers, the very thought of touching a woman and kissing her and taking her to bed left his brain completely empty of a plan of how to do it. How are these things executed, he pondered? Does the woman do the guiding? Does she get aroused and then invite him in? Inside, in the warm wet red lips, the monthly lips, how does that work, he thought. Why have I not wanted to find out? All the delicious stories he had turned away from hearing, the many times when a campus hero was retelling for the fifteenth time how the coeds tore his clothes off and he had to make it with at least three of them before they'd give him back his cashmere sweater, and he had to have it back, that's the only reason he did it, because it was a gift, a gift from his mother.

The medical books helped him very little to understand a woman. The pictures showed the parts, all laid out and neatly named, and he knew all the Latin names, all the stems and derivatives. The names he understood, their function was lost on him. The breasts, he knew, were glands to supply milk for a nursing infant. That he knew. That they bobbed and jiggled gently under blouses he noticed. A picture in a centerfold of a naked woman fingering herself only made him look away. Why would a woman do that? Make fun of herself.

It was confusing, Martin agreed with himself once again. So much easier just to be a man, ease the old hand down when the nerves got on edge, the backlog of unreleased emission pressing him to have a glass of wine and slip into the dark bathroom and kneel over the toilet. Maybe it would always be that way for him, but maybe he'd meet someone at the hospital, maybe a nurse, maybe a male nurse. That image stopped him. Not the nurse image, not the male image, but the image that flashed in his mind was of Dwayne. Now where the hell did that come from?

ɚ

Dwayne turned the key in the lock, knowing he was the first one home today. Luther would be out on calls and his mom was at the magazine distributor's office, kowtowing and smiling and running errands for Goldstein's cronies. God, he hated that, his mother working outside the home. Why his dad allowed it, he couldn't say. It may have been her pride in pulling her own weight; it may be the college bills that loomed over them. Maybe the new shiny car she insisted on driving. His dad should be making good money on his job, but Dwayne had the gnawing feeling that his dad worked for free a lot of the time, doing favors for people who were having a tough go of it, raising a family on minimum wages, both parents working to bring in the rent and groceries. How else could Luther explain the sweet potato pies he would bring home, or the almost new end table, or hardly used shirts. Even a mantle clock, someone's heirloom, was brought home by Luther, and sheepishly given to Claire. She only sighed and went about fixing dinner. One thing he had to hand to her: she wasn't a shrew. She never nagged Luther about his business. His business was his.

Once a month she sat at the kitchen table, made a neat stack of the bills, took a tablet and divided up the means between the creditors. She never spoke out loud when she was doing her figuring, and Luther would only watch her over his newspaper, feet up on the hassock he'd gotten for loading a refrigerator to the dump (paying the fifteen-dollar dumping charge himself). He might get up once or twice, to get a piece of sweet potato pie Mrs. Harris always paid him with, and he'd glance over Claire's shoulder to peek at her addition. She always moved her hand over the tablet, shielding it, and eyed him coolly. He retreated to his chair and paper, waiting for the final outcome which he knew, without a doubt, would be good news. Claire never brought him bad news at the end of the bill paying evening.

"Well," she'd say, pulling off her glasses, and rubbing her nose where they pinched, "we've made it another month."

"Yahoo!" he'd exclaim, tossing his paper on the floor, and getting up to come to her. He'd always kiss her forehead, then each of her hands, and stand like a love-struck schoolboy.

"Claire, what would I do without you?" He waited patiently while she put away her tablet, and the freshly stamped envelopes were set on the end table by the front door, ready to be dropped in the mail in the morning. The checkbook went back in her purse, and the pen went back in the cup on the window sill, near the flowering violets. Dwayne could hear them murmuring on the way down the hall to their room, and he sometimes thought he heard them making love after the hall light went out.

They were adults, after all, and his mother was a beautiful woman for her age, and his dad probably was as gentle as a lamb and . . . why was he thinking these thoughts? What did his mother and dad in bed together have to do with him? It was hard for him to imagine the two people he loved the most in the world making love, sticking together in sweat, moaning softly, rolling in waves of rapturous love. The pleasure he could only pretend would be there for him someday. But not like his parents. No, that was for sure, not like his parents.

# Chapter Six

*Livin' on a razor's edge.*
*Sharper than a knife.*
*Surrender to the power of wedge,*
*Keep running for your life.*
*You won't need no periscope,*
*You won't need no second sight.*

*Emerson, Lake, & Palmer "Paper Blood"*

The softness of the fabrics moved Dwayne first, then the fresh smell of skin and perfume, mixed in with warmth and closeness enveloping him as he slipped in and out in his mother's closet. He stood at the doorway again, and started over, slipping in between her silk shirts, and waved back gently through her skirts, weaving slowly as if guided by a stick over his head, a magnetic silver baton, weaving him this way and that way, leaving him breathless and sexually excited at the doorway after his tour.

It wasn't that he loved his mother in the wrong way; he knew that wasn't the reality of his dilemma. He never wanted to be in Luther's place, throbbing and clinging over his mother, he knew he wanted that love to stay separate from him as if it didn't exist. He loved the smells and feelings in his mother's closet because it made him feel safe with himself. He came out of her closet feeling safe. The smells seemed to stay on his skin, the feel of the shifting fabrics became one with him. His bunched up muscles and erect penis seemed only an extension of the joy of being alive. He carried his erection like a sword, back to his own room in the flat, and he never touched himself, to ease the tension and the pressure. He only sighed as he sank onto his bed, and covered his head with his pillow, to shut out all the bad things.

Dwayne's early introduction to sex had been both unexpectedly early and demeaning. He had been caught away from the group on a Cub Scout outing by a counselor with habits favoring little boys. The young man had taken Dwayne into the woods and disrobed him, telling him they were going to be naked Indians, but the naked Indian didn't do any dancing or war whoops, not with a belt around his hands and a tee shirt stuffed in his mouth. Dwayne's tears of confusion and fear only fed the fantasy of the counselor, who dragged his body over the helpless boy, rolled him over and bit his legs and bottom, spread his legs and kissed and fondled the child to his first erection, then smiled happily as he fell over the small boy with his mouth open.

"You like, huh? Feel good, huh?" The young man darted glances over his shoulder, sensing someone approaching. He pulled on his tee shirt and pants, bent quickly to undo the belt binding Dwayne's hands, and pulled his tee shirt out of his mouth. Dwayne gulped great breaths of air, felt a rush of oxygen hit his lungs, and he screamed. The counselor laughed, then he, too, screamed. "Hey, we're Indians, right? Indians doing the war dance. Let another one rip, Dwaynie, howl like an Indian." He slipped the tee shirt over Dwayne's head and tossed him his shorts. Dwayne tugged them on quickly. He stared at the counselor and started to cry. The man carefully picked Dwayne up and carried him out of the woods, back to the trail back to camp. They passed several other Scouts and a counselor with fishing gear.

"Got a problem, Mick?" The other counselor patted Dwayne on the head.

"Na, just a little homesick, I guess. We tried to play Indians, but he's not ready yet."

"Is that what that yelling was all about? Thought somebody was getting killed." The three moved off and Mick continued to carry Dwayne down the trail. He held him loosely in one arm, but his free hand clamped down on Dwayne's, twisting it very hard. He whispered. "Killed? Did you hear him say he thought you were getting killed? Now, wouldn't that be a shame, little Black boy, you gettin' killed. But that doesn't happen to good little Black boys who keep their big mouths shut, you understand me?" Dwayne nodded quickly, feeling pains shooting up his arm. The counselor relaxed his grip. He put Dwayne down, and watched as the boy ran away. Dwayne looked back once at the counselor, standing in the middle of the trail, laughing and slapping his thighs. Dwayne ran to his tent and crawled into his sleeping bag, zipping it up to his neck. His bottom stung from the bites, but he dared not look at them. Someone might see. He touched his pee-pee and it felt tender and sore. His eyes closed against the memory of something he knew had happened, but he could not understand why. The fear of staying here with Mick being around filled him with terror. When the tent flapped opened, he cringed and slipped deeper into the bag. It was only Petey, his friend from school, not Mick.

"Why you in bed?" asked Petey, staring down at Dwayne.

"I doan feel so good," answered Dwayne. "I think I'm gonna be sick." And with that, he rolled to one side and vomited on the tent floor. Petey jumped back to avoid getting splashed, saying over his shoulder as he ducked out of the tent, "I go get somebody."

Dwayne pulled his head around quickly. "Doan get Mick!" he shouted.

He knew it was wrong, these feelings tearing through him as his body relaxed and his erection was lost, gone flaccid and still upon his leg. The memory of Mick when he was only eight made him groan audibly and hug his pillow closer. Tears swam in his eyes, spilled over and he wiped them with the pillow case. The scene with Mick played over and over in his mind, and the scenes he put in their place only made him angry with himself.

It had only been play, only been an extension of reaching toward manhood that had made him play the games in the back of the fields near their apartment. All the boys played, sometimes with each other, sometimes to the noise of happy toddlers on the swings nearby, out of sight of the unconcerned babysitters and mothers watching their own. No one watched the boys in the woods, and the young boys frolicked, and kissed each other, and held each other tenderly, watching the mystery between their legs sprout and grow large and sometimes, if they were lucky, a warm squiggle of juice would reward them.

These hidden times almost ruined his summers when he was nine and ten, ruined them because he felt dirty about them, didn't understand why he felt he was doing something he shouldn't, but he had no one to turn to, no one he could confide in. He was so young and uninformed that he thought he and his friends were the only ones doing these things with their bodies. Not old enough to know why, and not wise enough to know they were simply preparing their bodies for the future. No shame there, but the knowledge of knowing he looked forward to the games, and the touching, and the squiggle of juice excited him. Their bodies excited him, their lean buttocks and strong young backs, their skin, smooth and satiny in the humidity of the summer day, their half-closed eyes, moving from one boy's fondling to the next boy's soft caress of his testicles, moved him to a height of exaltation he knew he loved to be feeling. The erections came more easily now at eleven and twelve, and by thirteen his group met more frequently and not always in the woods. Sometimes it would be two or three only, not the usual ten or twelve, and it might be in the basement of someone's home before the parents came home from work, or at school, in quick little get togethers in the locker room or in the boys' bathroom.

School became his outlet, and he excelled, striving to bring home good grades and do his chores without comment, hoping to salvage something of himself when he felt burdened with guilt over his sexual life. Had someone sat down with him at that juncture and explained to him about the raging hormones and the nocturnal emissions, that everything was normal, that he was very, very normal, he might have passed this period without guilt, becoming a player. But no one did. Claire was busy with work, her dried flower arrangements, and Luther was forever on call, just moving off as Dwayne would try to talk to him man to man.

In junior high, when his height was a formidable five ten and his weight was one hundred eighty, the football coach came to see his parents and suggested he might like to try out for the team.

"All brains, that son of yours," the coach began, "but you know, a scholarship for Dwayne's athletic ability might not be too far away." He sat back on their couch and winked, and Claire and Luther looked at each other and agreed to disagree with the coach.

"What Dwayne does athletically is really up to him. To be truthful, we think a lot of young Black men, and, don't take this wrong, but a lot of Black men have given up their minds because they didn't believe in them. They only believed what the white men told them: you got to make it on muscle, cotton-built muscle. We really don't want Dwayne to give up his mind for his body," Claire pointed out, setting her long hands on her knees. Luther nodded in agreement.

"Now you don't want me to preach about what great athletes Black men are, no, you don't want me to do that, but just let me say: a mind like Dwayne's in a uniform would be outstanding, yes, outstanding. Let the boy fly, Mr. and Mrs. Hauk, let him find his own roost. Who knows? He might just be the next O.J. Simpson." He sat back and let that wonderful image sink in: Dwayne running through films, running through airports. Marrying a white woman. Did they want Dwayne to marry at all, much less a white woman? What was the prize there?

Were they that far ahead or drifting slowly behind? Would their son need their blessing to be an athlete? They sincerely hated to hold him back, so they agreed: if Dwayne wanted to play football, then Dwayne could play football.

And play football he did, an All-State halfback, running more yards than any previous player, white or black, had ever run in the past forty years. His name was in the papers, his prospects for the future were extolled by coaches statewide, and, by his senior year, everyone thought Dwayne Hauk was the next star player in the pros. Who would get him? Who could be so lucky? Why play college ball when the pros were already astonished at his ability? Those hands, that finesse, that swiftly shifting hip move, the astounding running ability. Dwayne Hauk. The name smelled of success.

Everything smelled like success; even his teammates begrudgingly admitted that Hauk had it all. Some were mildly jealous, some were delighted for him, but for one second string quarterback, Hauk didn't smell right to him. He hefted his leg up to untie his practice cleats, and spotted Dwayne headed for the showers. He kicked his feet free of the shoes, peeled off his stinking socks, and followed the muscular Dwayne into the mist of the showers.

"Hey, old Draino, you got a minute?" asked the second string quarterback.

Dwayne turned slowly in the mist and spotted Johnny Melton, naked as a jaybird, in the doorway to the showers. His mind pulled out the image from the past, Johnny-o being one of the white boys on the ongoing fun circuit of premature explorations into erections, but now they were men in their late teens, men with purpose, direction, and future.

"Man, I gotta hand it to you, you were beautiful out there today, completely beautiful. That run against Cotter, perfect. Knocked him for a loop, and him all primed for big league. God, you were great!" Johnny stepped under the shower and Dwayne took the next one. The water flowed over them both, and Johnny reached out and said, "Can I scrub your back? It'd be an honor, just to touch you again, like old times."

Old times. And didn't Dwayne feel a wave of relief that his old friends were still with him. He swung his arms around Johnny and gave him a big hug in friendship, and Johnny let loose of the soap, and stepped back.

"Hey, man, I didn't mean that close. You got a problem you ain't outgrown?" Johnny stood under the drizzle and eyed Dwayne.

"No, I ain't movin' on you, if that's what you meant. What the hell did you mean, washin' my back?" Dwayne turned away from Johnny, and Johnny turned his back to him, studiously scooping up the soap bar and rubbing the soap over his arms and legs and lavishing special attention to his buttocks. He bent to inspect his feet, and Dwayne, moved by an impulse he couldn't control, stepped closer and held the man tight between his legs. They were alone in the shower, all the other players making the four thirty call had showered and left, and the only two left in the silently echoing locker room were Dwayne and Johnny. The aspiring pro halfback and the second string quarterback who might have been first string if he didn't play the ponies and ride every woman and man from Pelham to Co-op City.

"Hey, some of the old tricks still there, big boy?" Johnny winked through the shower of water spraying over his head and bent further to the floor. An open invitation. An excited and happy Dwayne found a bottle of baby oil and rubbed it on himself, over and over, an abundance of smoothness, a softening of the effect of his size, a diminishing element between them, a ruse, so to speak, a way they could be joined without hurting the other, a communion.

"Go for it, big boy, I'm ready," piped Johnny-o, bent over and ripe for the game. Dwayne thought one moment and let it slide: let it feel the sides, let it rub the way he knew it would feel inside him, the marvelous ripples of pleasure, the feeling of having the man under him, letting him know what it was to be Black over white, it came as a shudder, the final explosion, expulsion, the spent feeling as he withdrew, the feeling of not being what he was, a Black man in a white man's game.

"Yo, man, that's power, you stoke, man," gasped Johnny-o. He shook his head under the spray, clutched his privates in joy, and strode away on the tiled floor, tight but not too tight. His butt hurt.

Dwayne, relaxed and relieved, scrubbed himself down, shut out the worries and the tension, felt tentatively pleased at the release this moment had given him, for he never could do it alone. And with an old buddy, he reflected, it would stop there, or maybe Johnny-o would try again for the prize bull, the one he had allowed entry to his magnificent rear end. But it wasn't something you needed broadcast news over. He had good press; he didn't need any mess like being gay to complicate his future. For, what the devil, was that what he was? Was he gay? Did he prefer men over women? He didn't know. He just knew he wasn't a jack-off kind of guy, couldn't feel right with himself if he fondled himself into an erection and exploded on the sheets Claire washed. No, he would never bring his mother down that low, to accept a degenerated jack-off.

# Chapter Seven

*Big boys don't cry*
*Big boys don't cry . . .*

*10CC  "I'm Not in Love"*

Martin adjusted his uniform shirt, tucking the tails in as flat as possible by himself, turning to check the creases in the mirror. He slid the tie around his neck and flipped it through the knots and pulls that were becoming second nature to him. The freshly pressed uniform jacket went over the shirt and he quickly buttoned up. Today was his induction into the Navy for his four-year stint, and he seriously wondered if the Navy would make a doctor of him. The unswerving line of his education had brought him to graduation from Cornell, just a week ago, with summa cum laude honors, and all the hours of study and dedication to his mind had left him tired, emotionally spent. He had lost some weight, but he knew he would pick that up again as soon as he got settled at New Groton and started cooking for himself. Cooking had been a hobby as a boy, learning how from Amelia, and then later from Micah, who could make biscuits that would melt in your mouth.

And how proud they had been at the graduation, walking beside their wonderful son, nodding at others as if to say, Come look at our boy. Isn't he grand in his graduation gown? Sons of bankers, daughters of tycoons, parents of mediocres, who barely got through, all swept past the Schoenfields, not realizing the stooped man in wire spectacles and his wife, who needed help seeing the steps and curbs, were standing next to the most important person alive, their son, Martin, soon to be a doctor. Soon. Very soon.

Martin took a cab to the Navy office and waited in the ante room until a crisp young woman in a uniform ushered him into the office of the Navy's inductor. Instructions . . . books . . . when camp will begin.

It had been worth it, he felt, to relieve his parents of his responsibility, to pay his own way, to be like Amy; his thoughts raced to Amy. Just when he was starting his sojourn into the next phase, he knew his sister, who never wrote to him, was struggling with her own career, her own acceptance. The friends they had been, growing up, the times they'd shared their ice cream and their dreams, only floated in the memory of his mind, a  remembrance of what had been.  He remembered her tucking him into bed; he liked the way she straightened his covers, and said to him, "Ah, little Martin, go off on a dream boat, fly the skies, ski the slopes, keep sharp for the antelope." But why the antelope? He had never thought about the great herds, thundering in shoulder-to-shoulder movement over the icy tundra up north; now why would she interject antelope? He puzzled over this in his small five year old mind, and the remembrance of that came back to him now, a graduate, an honor student, a man destined for the great things beyond the Navy's helping hand.

And so it was done. He'd taken the oath, signed the papers, shook the hand before him, giddily walked out into the sunshine and said to himself: I'm me, and nobody's going to take me from me, and I'm going home for awhile, and I'm going to be happy, and I'm going to be a great researcher, and I'm going to clear up all the disease in the world, and I'm going to be the Midas touch for the world, and ... I'm going to be poor, but I'm not going to care that I'm poor, but I don't want a new car, anyway, I don't even know how to change oil on a car, so I certainly don't want a car. I'll be like Hymie, with no car. Hymie. What a sad excuse for a human being.

The lights were dim when he entered his room and started packing his books and accumulation from the last four years. He shuffled his papers into files and stuffed those into boxes and the boxes covered the floor and his bed and left little room for him to curl up that night. But curl up he did, in his last night on campus, and sleep did come to him, even though the herds of antelope ran over and over his body in the dream he succumbed to, leaving him breathless and worn out when the sun jerked him awake in that first morning as a graduate.

❧

The Navy had a way to build men, he knew it as he stood in line to get his packet of clothes and shaving kit and first aid box; knew it like he had memorized everything he would need to know to survive the basic training. It all had to do with breaking him down, taking that part of him he treasured most, his identity, and reshaping him into a Naval officer. He had a way to go to face the physical task before him, he had never been more than average in athletics, but he calmly surveyed the expected results he had to achieve, and he quietly took his vitamins and did extra exercises along a different course. Late at night, when the dead tired recruits were snoring or grumbling over sore muscles, put to the test, Martin would slip out of his bunk and put himself through an extra hour of knee bends, and stomach pulls, and leg lifts and holding books over his head until he thought his arms would die from the effort.

But die he didn't. He began to see a change in his body, more muscles building on his arms, a trimmer waist, legs with a shape he never thought he could achieve, but achieve he did. He even ate every starchy plate of macaroni and cheese, doubled up on meat and potatoes, munched salads with bean sprouts and no dressing, skipped desserts and ice cream, his long ago passion, and settled for low-fat yogurt. He gained ten pounds, all muscle, and he began to like the new little Jew boy he was; the re-sculpted Martin Schoenfield. He even forgot the pleasure of his four-cigarettes-a-day habit, if a habit that small could be called one. He became an active member of the growing checkers group, slumped on their bunks before bedtime, reaching over and tentatively moving pieces until the lights-out call, but he was getting better, he knew he was, when he picked up tricks from the guys from Jersey and Los Angeles. He looked forward to his next match with his father and maybe even Luther. Did Dwayne play? His mind stopped for a moment, remembering Dwayne, the hulk of the man, the gentle eyes, the hand on the curtain, warning him about the dogs.

Lights out. Snores beginning. Martin rolled off his bunk and started his hour of extended workout. He crawled back in, exhausted, only wanting tomorrow to begin, to end, to be over, to have these eight weeks behind him, to leave here, and begin studying again. The books sounded so good. He missed his books, his time alone, completely alone; missed the feel of the wheel on a microscope, the clean smell of laboratories, the white smocks, the gloves. He knew he was going to be a doctor now, a real doctor, maybe a Navy doctor for a while, until they'd chewed up a part of their expense, but soon, he'd be his own.

The basic training passed, remarkably fast; knowing his mind set, he couldn't have endured one day more. He hated the regimentation of his time, the control over even his bladder, the time for this, the time for that, the hurry up and wait. He knew it was discipline they strived to drill into him, but his scientific mind, thoroughly encased in creative exploration, resented anyone telling him the time to do bodily functions.

The last day of basics, the hand shaking and heartfelt hugs from all the men who'd endured, who hadn't been shipped home at the first call of duress, the ones who had made the grade. Martin Schoenfield shone as one of the top five men in his group. Graded well above average at all skills, especially good as a Marksman, earning a ribbon in free shooting and correct aim on target. A prize he would wonder at after all the years had passed: he hated guns.

Many goodbyes, and see ya' soons, and off each went to his next designation: Martin to a hospital training unit in New London Groton. Before they were to be assigned to the Navy life, each man was given a two-week leave, to visit parents, friends, relatives. Drink beer and party hearty. They had earned it, this respite.

Martin slung his gear over his shoulder, ran his hand over his shortly clipped hair, admired his tanned face in the mirror on the locker door, before slamming it, soundly and finally. His footsteps down the barracks hall sounded empty and alone, he was the last out, or almost the last. His feet dragged at the end as he turned and looked down the rows of bunks, all empty now, the mattresses turned and the sheets wadded up neatly on the floor, all waiting for the cleaning, and the disinfecting, and the new recruits soon to land.

He jumped on the shuttle bus to the airport and slung his gear under the seat, between his legs. The engine noise drowned out conversation of any depth with his fellow passengers, all in a mood lighter than his. He had no girl to come home to, no wedding plans, no involvement with anyone besides his parents, probably waiting even this early by the window with their teacups. He wondered if his dad had finally given in to having Amelia's eyes checked. Probably not.

The transport left him at Early Airport for the transfer to O'Hare, then the last run to New York's La Guardia. His hands felt elastic and smooth on the straps as he shifted the pack onto his shoulder, shook hands with the men nearest him as they disembarked the bus, and quickly found his way to the next shuttle to the exit field. Flight 456 was leaving in about fifteen minutes, so he washed his face and wiped a wet paper towel under his arms before donning his shirt again and setting out for the terminal exit. The flow of the people, the girls and guys, the passengers coming and going, some with kids in tow, in strollers, some getting warm embraces, others simply smiling, "I'm home," made Martin feel sad that he had no one special in his life. Oh, his parents were special, and he liked the Hauks, but someone special. Someone . . . like Dwayne.

There! It had dared to jump in front of him again. Why, why did Dwayne Hauk always jump up when he got into this wanting mood? He had exchanged no more than a nominal few words with Dwayne, but the touch of his hand still left an impression on Martin. Foolish, foolish. All this is foolish. I'm not even gay, Martin consoled himself, at least I don't think so. I'm not really very, well, sexual.

The plane lifted off from O'Hare, and in a few moments he was asleep, sliding into a dreamland framed with giant sunflowers and tufts of clouds, small bushes with berries which he gobbled as he ran through the dream, stopping finally as his hand reached through snow. Yes, it was snow, in the dream. And he heard the sound of pounding hooves, large strong flat hooves hitting the frozen ground, running toward him as he held the berries. He saw they were antelope, many, many antelope, all glassy eyed and intent and coming straight at him. Even in the dream, he carried the pack, and it became heavier and heavier as he turned to run and finally he dropped it, letting it lay there in the snow, his hand smeared with blue juice from the berries. He hesitated when he saw the juice, thought for a moment that it was the juice they were after, not him. But the juice was on him and they were almost on him, the spray of fine snow spinning up behind their hooves, driving down hard, swirling the snow, blinding him in the sparkle and lift and spin of it. Martin sank to his knees in the dream, felt the cold hit him right before the first hoof struck him. He rolled with pain, even in the dream he knew he was hurt, the blue on his hand ran with fresh red blood from his shoulder, his marksman's shoulder, he remembered, then his whole world spun and the drumbeat of the hooves faded away. He was alone in the snow, completely at rest in the white soaking with red. He rolled onto his stomach and pressed his face into the cooling white drifts, and he started to melt into it. He sank deeper and deeper and finally he came against a force of heat and light, which stopped his descent and left him in the middle of a cold nowhere. Where was he? How to get back out? He flailed in the snow, felt something ahead, like a silver baton, and he reached for it and it warmed his cold hand and pulled on him as he found he couldn't let go.

"Hey, buddy, you got a bad dream there or what?" The man next to him in the plane seat tapped on Martin's shoulder, not the marksman's shoulder; that he knew would be too bloody to touch. He jerked upright in the seat, restrained by the seat belt, but if it hadn't been for that, Martin Schoenfield would have been in the aisle and down the row of passengers, warning them about the antelope. He shook himself completely awake, recognized the dream for being a dream, a nightmare, and sank back in exhaustion.

"Sorry, didn't mean to startle you. Just got through eight weeks of basic, and I think I've bottomed out." He turned to see himself, a perspiring Martin, in the oval window.

"Man, don't I remember the feeling," the older man in the gray suit said, loosening his tie and sipping on his cocktail. "I was in the Marines, did a stint overseas, and never want to go back to that. Man, what a drill. Hope all you get is nightmares for a while. I can still see flames and smell bodies burning in my sleep. My wife, she's really cool about it, but it sure doesn't just get up and leave you the day you're discharged. Been seventeen years, and I still wince when I see a fire. I'm not very romantic about fireplaces, not at all. And you say you've just done basic?" The man turned to look more closely at Martin.

"Yeah, just basic, eight weeks of it," Martin responded. He really wished the man would keep talking about himself, and not look at Martin like he didn't have what it took.

"Look, don't mind me, I'm just an old has-been veteran," the man said quietly, confidentially, glancing over the seat to see if anyone was listening, "but war sucks like nothing else. If you got a chance to get into something else real soon, get into it. Family business, anything. Just don't be a soldier. It kills you for life, I mean it, nothing is the same for me, nothing." Martin turned and examined the chunky man with graying hair more closely. He turned in his seat and set his hip against the back to peer more closely at the man.

"So what do you do now?" Change of subject, forget the dream, wipe the forehead, and smile graciously like it was something not to worry about.

The man stared at Martin straight on, never let his blue eyes stray from Martin's face, and said, softly, "I don't know. I sell something, I guess I sell something, I get a pay check every two weeks, but my wife handles the money, and irons my shirts and packs my bags and I start out again, from O'Hare to St. Louis to Omaha, and I guess I'm working, that's what it is, I'm working, I talk to people, I shake hands, I attend meetings, I pay for lunches on a MasterCard, but for the life of me, you caught me off guard . . ." he fumbled in his jacket. "Here it is, Diamond Steel and Construction, see? That's what I do. I was salesman of the month in February." He got silent then, shoving the card back into his jacket. "Don't know why I forgot that. I remember everything else." He got quiet again.

Martin thought of an answer, but it didn't seem right. He wanted to respond, support the man in his vacant and long ago grief, but the words wouldn't come out. Martin debated answering at all, then the quiet got to him. He felt he had to respond.

"I'll bet you're the best damn salesman every month."

The man turned to him again, slowly closed his eyes a moment as if to rest them, then said, "Maybe, maybe not. It really doesn't matter. After your eyes get filled with shit you can't forget, your life is changed forever." He opened his eyes, his face close to Martin's, the man's breath lightly tinged with gin, the smell of his aftershave pleasantly masculine and desert-like. He smiled professionally, patted Martin's good shoulder, and tipped his glass as he waved at the stewardess for a refill.

Martin turned on the overhead light, beamed the little spotlight toward his lap, and reached for the magazine in the seat holder ahead of him. He pulled out the standard trade magazine, perfume at a third the price, tours over Paris and Amsterdam, sunglasses absolutely guaranteed to refract any danger from the light of the sun, but he barely glanced as he flipped through the slick pages. His seat partner had the drink brought to him, and on an impulse Martin spoke up.

"Let me pay for that for you." He pulled out his leather wallet, churned out three dollar bills, and handed them to the stewardess in front of the surprised and grateful seat mate.

"Well, that's darn considerate of you, friend, mighty white." He beamed as he accepted the glass and nodded once more to Martin. "Damn white."

Martin reflected a second, turned to the man in the gray suit sipping his free cocktail, and asked, "Fill me in. What's that mean, 'damn white'? Give me a meaning of that term. I've never heard it."

The man smiled, feeling a little superior at that moment, set his glass down before a last quick hefty swallow. "It just means that white folks do nice things for white folks, and it's a way of saying we know how to do things. It's a way of acknowledging we got an edge, you know what I mean?"

"What edge do we really have?" asked Martin, leaning forward in his seat, setting the magazine back in the seat holder. He knew he was getting into the subject of black-white relations, but this man had been a Marine, and he knew a lot of Marines were black men, and many had died for this country, just like the poor white high school boys from Tennessee, so he actually wanted to know what this man had observed about black-white in the Marines.

"Oh, the boys try hard, they really do, and two of them were like my brothers when we were in, but when we came home, I never saw them again. One was going to be a teacher, maybe he did get to be one, he was smart, really smart, reading all the time, never drank or smoked, a nice guy, really. But you know what's going to happen to them when they get back, that old game starts all over. They're never gonna make it, that's it." He sipped his drink. "You know, the damn fool part of it is they agreed to all that affirmative action shit, they never should have let themselves get sucked into that hole. If you're equal, stay equal. Fight like hell, but don't let anyone tell you that you got to be a token, because, grand slam, they're gonna dunk you again, war heroes or not. That's the fucking shame of it. I wouldn't be alive today if a black man hadn't saved my sorry ass." He sipped again, laid his head against the seat.

Martin waited for him to continue, but it seemed he had nodded off into a memory lane and wasn't talking for the moment. He finally turned, and said quietly, conspiratorially, like they had to be really careful with this, and he nodded to Martin to come closer. Martin shifted and set his ear near the man's lips. "I was not too good at what I did, but I did the best I could, what with the shelling and the wet feet and the stink of my own body near me. I like being clean, you know, but you can't be clean 'cuz there ain't no water all the time, and very little soap, and anyway, war's shit." He stopped. He slipped out of his seat belt and shrugged his jacket off, laying it neatly across his lap as he sat down again. He re-buckled the belt, reached for his glass, took a sip, and said, "I was fucked up, man, really zipping fucked up. I'd done a couple of prostitutes and come back with a bag of hashish that took my whole month's pay, but, shit, I didn't care. I was twenty-four and probably gonna die in that hole anyway; I wanted to die happy, you know that feeling? No, maybe you don't, but sometimes just living a little is better than living a lot. You follow?"

Martin nodded as if he knew. He knew nothing of what this man had seen and done, knew nothing of watching people screaming in flames, in napalm, their children dying in front of them, a normal day turning into hell with their straw huts being torched and the soldiers crawling over their daughters, raping and cutting their hair off, the pigs running wild and screaming with the knowledge that they alone might make it if they were swift of foot.

"I was zoomed out, barely moving, crawled into my sack about three when the alarm went off: Charlies on the perimeter. I dragged myself into my clothes and lifted my rifle, but I forgot the damn clip. I carried an empty gun out of that bunk, and sorrier than hell I discovered my stupid mistake. I was running and dodging with the best of them, trying to get my head cleared up, when a jet flew over, and the sky was lit up like the Fourth of July. I almost peed in my pants. I thought it was the fuckin' Fourth. And the next thing I remember was a hand on my belt, and it grabbed me and shoved me down, and I was looking, honest to God, into the face of a Charlie, a gook, a slant eyed scared kid with a knife in his hand bigger than he was. I froze, I know I did, and he just looked into my eyes under the lights from the fireworks overhead, and he said, 'Goodbye.' Just as nice as you please, no thank you, no I'm sorry, just an old American term he'd picked up. 'Goodbye.'"

The gray haired man in the suit minus the jacket, tipped his drink for a swallow, and finding only ice, waved his hand for the stewardess again. "I'll pay this time," he said. He shifted his bulk and pulled out his wallet. Flipping the stewardess three ones, he stared at the glass as she refilled it for him.

"No tonic," he said, covering the glass.

No mention of breathing at this point. Martin Schoenfield was in that pit with this man, feeling the dread, the cold-knifed fear, the absence of any refining quality that would make this whole scene come out right. He didn't want this man to die, nor did he want the slant eyed young Charlie to die. Why have to die at all, like that? His breath halted as he waited for the man to continue.

"Well, it came down to this. I was cooked for sure, I could barely stand, what with the shit in my system and no bullets in my clip, but for some strange and unknown reason, God must have smiled at my stupidity and maybe didn't like slant-eyes, shit! I don't know, up comes a buddy, a crawlin'-on-his-belly buddy, a die hard Marine wacko named Duel Mannes, and by Jesus! He leaped like an orangutan; he came off that turf like he had steel springs in his legs, and he came down on that mother fucker, and the damn knife meant for my throat went screaming into the Charlie's heart. Couldn't have been purer. Straight into the heart, ripped through any protective ribs, and he was gone like a slithering pile of material off a table. Shoved him off the face of the earth."

Martin was unaware at this moment that he was breathing at all; his breath must have come in and out without his knowledge. He adjusted his seat belt, looked out the window, found some reason to cough, but all he could do was sit and stare, finally, into the man's ashen face.

"So that's how old Duel saved my skinny butt. He shoved me in front of him towards the perimeter, laid on top of me when the Charlies walked out, missing us because they thought we were dead. And goosed up as I was, on all that hash, I would've screamed, 'Here I am!' if he hadn't held my mouth closed in the mud. He was something." He stopped, lifted his glass.

Martin sat back in the seat, watching the approaching lights of New York's airport rising before him, and he forgot for a minute who he was and what he was doing and why he was doing it. He felt drained of the emotions he normally felt on being home, heading toward warmth and food and the caresses of family. He felt lonely somehow, somewhere in the jungles with the man in the gray suit, the man who had to carry his memories onward each day in a job he remotely remembered as a salesman for Diamond Steel and Construction.

The plane lowered its landing gear and joggled along, settling into a smooth landing. The swoosh of the backup engines cutting down the forward momentum tugged them slowly to a surface speed, and the ground crew ran out in the dark with their flashlights flicking up and down, left and right, the guiding hand moving the plane into its resting place. The passengers moved to gather their things, but Martin sat back and waited. He'd had enough of hurry up and wait. The last passenger could leave, then he would walk out alone, unencumbered, no pausing in the aisle, no shifting his pack carefully to avoid bumping someone.

Whether someone would be there to meet him, he did not know, but he had sent a telegram ahead, compliments of the ever present efficient Navy, that his flight would be arriving at 10:10 P.M. on the sixteenth. The days had worn on him as his arrival became more immediate, but now, after the talk with the man from Nam, the best salesman in February, he really didn't care if someone was there or not. The address was in his mind, the taxi driver would deliver him and take twenty for his trouble, but so what? No big deal. No checkers would go on that night, only comforting sleep in his soft familiar teen-age bed, the pillow smelling like he remembered a pillow should smell. His mom, she was good with scents. Lovely lavender, lovely lace, something smooth, always something to taste in her warmly glowing kitchen. Or was Micah, his dad, now the chief cook? Into his retirement, and Amelia still working, at least he thought she was still working. He'd lost track. And what about Amy, he reflected, not one word from her while he was in basic, and he felt he had to talk to her sometime soon, at least to tell her about the dream and the bloody shoulder and the glassy eyed antelope ready to run him over.

He tripped down the plane's runway quickly, following the last passenger ahead. He noted it was the gray haired man with the Diamond Steel and Construction Company business card, his seat mate for the past few hours. Martin slowed, so he wouldn't catch up, but the man slowed too, and turned as Martin caught up. He stopped Martin in mid-stride, and held his arm firmly. Martin stopped, let his pack slide to the floor of the gangway, and the man, a little shakily and maybe slightly drunk, pushed Martin against the curved walkway wall.

"Now, son, I don't mean to get in your face, but what I just been telling you, that's personal shit, you understand? I don't want it to go no further. Yeah, it was rough, but I was there, and you weren't. By the looks of you, you won't ever get there. You strike me as smart, son, too smart to get sucked into a mess like I was stuck in. You follow?" He shifted his weight between his feet, trying to stabilize on an exact center.

"I got you, captain, got you right on. Nothing you told me will ever get repeated to another soul, so help me God." Martin reached for his pack and the man relaxed a little, swung his arm around Martin's shoulder, the good one, not the bloody one, and he smiled in relief.

"'Cuz I do know if fellows aren't straight with me. I do know when someone's not telling the truth, and, so help me God, you shoot off to my wife or Duel about this, I'll come after you, I swear I will. Don't want no one to know a Black man saved my ass." He sucked his stomach in and flexed his arm, which even now was surprisingly large in his jacket. "You follow?"

Martin only nodded, hoping the scene would end now, on the steps out of the walkway, the steps to the tarmac, and the few remaining steps before he could get away from this man forever.

The rain had started just as they struck ground level, and the man shielded his eyes with his hand, and zig-zagged off quickly in the dark toward the door of the terminal. Martin held back a moment, not wanting to come near him again, and he counted to ten, shouldered his pack, and moved across the slick tarmac to the door.

The door was being held open for him, and Martin, just for an instant thought the man was waiting for him, but it wasn't the ex-Marine holding the door. And it wasn't Micah. It was Luther.

"Well, bless my eyes. You're a sorry sight. Those uniforms don't hold up to rain, do they?" He shut the door after the dripping wet Martin entered the carpeted lounge area, and Martin shook his head in relief that the ex-Marine was gone. He slung his pack down one more time, and offered Luther his hand. The man shook it with both of his and smiled indulgently.

"I'm your chauffeur tonight, son. Amelia and Micah are at a new showin' of your sister's work, and it was tug and war there for a while, which they was gonna do, but me and Dwayne felt you needed men to come home to, not a family battle, so Claire's got supper waitin', it should be good and dried out by now, but, hell! I'm hungry. Let's move on it." He grabbed the pack and lifted it in one hand as easily as if it were a marshmallow. Martin again was reminded of his limitations. Even Luther, thirty years his senior, was stronger than he was.

The two men chatted about the trip, the length of it, the time he'd last eaten, all the details one asks a fellow traveler and Martin was lulled through the claims check and showed his pack and the attendant smiled and nodded him through. She looked questioningly at Luther, standing to the side waiting, and Martin couldn't resist the temptation. He stepped back to her, and softly admitted, "An old family retainer." She looked slightly miffed when he said that. He doffed his wet cap and hurried to catch up with the fast-paced Luther.

Rain pelted down everywhere outside, and the two men hurried to find the truck with the wide lettering on the side: Hauk Heating and Cooling. Luther was sure it was on the roof level but he wasn't positive it was the Lion aisle or the Giraffe. "They all look the same to me," grumbled Luther, finally locating the van high above the other parked cars. "Should get myself a ribbon to put on the antenna."

New York expressways have a certain eerie feeling in the dark of early night, especially in the rain. Martin wasn't sure where he was, but Luther knew every byway and side street as if he'd memorized them. The van sped along, well tuned and ripe for the plunge through the six-inch water flooding over the street.

"You think they'll ever figure out a way to open those grates big enough to grab these belly gulchers? They only been comin' down now for the past two hunnert years, but you'd think the boys in charge would know how to handle the run off by now." He chuckled to himself as he drove along behind the sloshing wipers, hurriedly trying to keep up with the deluge.

Martin sank back in the seat, feeling the wet uniform reshaping itself into his slump, nodding softly into his shoulder as he fell fast asleep. Luther glanced over once at a stoplight, and smiled at the young man's earnest face set in sleep. Let him sleep, he thought, as he gunned the engine into first and started ahead on green: let the innocent sleep.

# Chapter Eight

Dwayne slouched in the doorway to the flat, looking out at the rain. It was past eleven P.M. and he knew his father would not fail in this call. If he could make it to Mrs. Harris and her frantic late night calls, when she damned well didn't even need air conditioning, then his father could surely make it to the airport and back in a reasonable amount of time. Where were they, he pondered, looking up and down the sparkling rain-sogged street. A car slowly approached and its headlights illuminated the fog and rain for about twenty feet. It slowed, did a U-turn, and started back the way it had come. A cop car, Dwayne noted, staring after the retreating taillights. Claire called from the kitchen.

"Any sign of them?" She was checking the meat loaf and added a half cup of water over the drying top and set it back to stay warm in the oven. Her biscuits were laid out under a towel and the lima beans and ham simmered away on the stove, off again, on again in their delicious ham juices, never to be bad, no matter how mushy. The salad of greens, turnip tops, and radishes, with a few alfalfa sprouts thrown in for Martin's well-being, held safe in the refrigerator, ever ready for the blue cheese dressing she whipped up with no effort, and she did have a way with herbs and oil. She sliced a large red onion and fingered the rings apart, contented to be at home for this overdone midnight dinner.

"Ma, do you think they got lost? Dad's not been to the airport much." He kept looking up the street, half-crouched in the open screen door. He turned when she didn't answer and saw her standing in the archway between the kitchen and the living room. Her neatly sculpted hair, almost recently done, swept back from her forehead and framed the face he knew so well, but he couldn't see her features with the light behind her. She came up by him at the opened door, and glanced once up the street and then directly into his face.

"Is it your father you're worried about, or could it be Martin?" She asked this softly and gently, her hand on his shoulder.

"I think it might be Martin," he admitted, turning to her in a moment of recognition, holding her against him, and the tears started falling as if she'd willed them to come. Claire touched his face, a man's face, and it took all her will to recall the boy she'd held so dear these long years, the troubling years of moving and rejection wherever they went, until now, this safe haven in spite of Hymie Goldstein's renewed efforts to oust them. Only Micah's pledge to also leave and live with them, wherever the two families could stay together, kept Goldstein at a stalemate. He hated the idea of losing one thousand a month, a sure thing, every first of the month. And Amelia's ever failing eyesight only made the four more determined to keep her near the walls she knew now by touch. Her happy smiling face, just this morning, reminding Claire that her boy was coming home tonight, did Luther really mind, oh, how grand it was for him to be a father to pick the boy up, they could only be parents to one at a time, how lucky Claire was to have just Dwayne, and such a son he was, Amelia clucked, love that son of yours.

"Did you know, Claire, that he's been doing my dusting for me, and I think he's found spots I've been missing for years. Though he never tells me, but he does go out on the porch and shake that cloth many, many more times than I would need to." Amelia tottered back up the stairs, touching the wall, and left Claire to go to work, come home, wait for the evening meal that didn't arrive until nearly midnight.

By the time the two dispirited and soggy men pulled to a stop before the flat and turned the lights off, the rain had slackened to just a drizzle. The pack got slung under one arm and Luther guided the tired steps of Martin up the walk. Claire met them at the door.

"We're here, Claire, late, but here. The transouth route was blocked and we had to come around thirty-third street, you never saw so much water in those gutters." He set the pack down and settled Martin on his feet. Claire reached to hold him, and Martin was aswim in the smell of her hair, the hint of powder, and if gold could have a scent, here it was. He smiled and said, "My new parents. Mom and Pop not back yet?"

"No," Claire said, "they'll probably stay with Amy tonight. Said they were sorry, the timing got messed up, but Amy wanted them there. This is her big showing, you know, lots of her acrylics; boy, I bet she's excited. You hungry?" she added, turning toward the kitchen. "I hope so. Cook this food one minute longer and we'll have hog swill."

"And I'm just in the mood for hog swill, Claire, how'd you

know?" boomed Luther, shoving off his damp coat and settling it over a kitchen chair. He pulled up to the table and sat waiting for his plate. Claire eyed him coolly.

"You might change your shirt, Luther, and wash your hands. We're not in the sty yet."

Luther moved off the chair, went into the bedroom, and came back in a clean shirt. He moved to the sink and used a little brush to go at his nails as if they carried the filth of the earth. He showed her his pinkened fingertips and she nodded approval. Drying his hands, he sat down again and laid the towel in his lap for a napkin.

"Where's Dwayne?" he asked, for the first moment realizing the absence of his own son.

"He's got to get to school in the morning, he tried to wait up, but I gave him supper about an hour ago and I guess he read awhile, his light was on, but last time I looked in, he was asleep, wrapped around that pillow like it was a football." Claire spooned out the food onto three plates and set the men's plates down before she reached for hers. It was almost midnight and she thought about the food weighing on her all night, she never ate this late, but something heavier had seeped into her mind to weigh on her, and this thought she found more disquieting.

Martin washed his hands, neglected the nail brush set on the sill, but examined his fingers nonetheless in fear of Claire reprimanding him. He became fully awake after his short nap, awakened to the dark faces sitting across from him, beautiful faces, carved in features he had become closer to at basic training, but just now took more time to explore: the wonderful whites of the eyes, the flash of the white teeth around the food, the good natured bantering between Luther and Claire, the delicious if slightly soft lima beans he had never tasted before, the salad served last as if it were the main dish, and he sopped up the sprouts in the blue cheese, wanting to lick the plate. He sat back, burped, and apologized. They both laughed, Claire clutching her napkin to her lips.

"I remember when I was a child, that my mom said that in some parts of Africa, apparently our home country, that unless you belched at the end of a meal the host was sure you had not enjoyed the food. And he would set about beating his wife, who had prepared the bad feast, and the youngest and most comely daughter, a virgin, was sent to the guest as an offering and a penance, and the poor confused tourist, probably European, would get his first glimpse into darkest African cultural tribal behavior." She wiped her eyes of the tears of laughter and began to pick up the plates.

"Allow me, Mrs. Hauk, I'm really awake now and I'd like to do this. Perhaps by the time I've cleaned up, you'll be fast asleep, and I'll slip up the back and into the sack. Please, let me."

"Well, it by no means would hurt if we left them for morning, but if you really want to . . . " she paused, resting her hand on the plate that he slipped out of her hand.

"My pleasure, ma'am, and I do real good on dishes."

"I'll just bet you do," she winked, and she moved to take off her apron, and stifling a yawn, she tapped Luther on the back, and he stood as if already asleep and followed her down the hall.

Martin scraped the dishes into the newspaper by the sink and folded it neatly, tucked in one end and dropped it in the trash. He started the sink of hot water and noticed a slow flow then a full spurt and then slow again as the Hauks were using the water down the hall. He smiled, leaned on the faucet for a moment, turned it off and slowly turned to the hall. He imagined all sorts of things, but as he pushed open the unlatched door on Dwayne's bedroom, he never imagined that the light from the kitchen would spill so directly on Dwayne's smooth chocolate face and closed lids, that the moonlight coming in over the window sill would encase his head in a rainbow of colors, that he would gleam, but gleam is what that figure did, it gleamed in its sleep.

He shut the door quietly, settling the latch to a firm closure, deciding not to look in again even if desiring to do so. He suddenly felt like an intruder in the home, the quiet clock in the living room ticking away the dawn's sleepiest hours, but he felt awake, surely the most awake he had ever felt. Maybe it was the food in his satisfied stomach, maybe the dreamy quality of washing the china plates slowly, cloth swirling over stuck on food then gone, then rinsed and stacked in the wooden tray. His movements were dreamlike, his mind already resting on a place next to the pillow in the room nearby. Housewives' dementia, he scolded himself, happily drying the knives and forks and spoons and laying them on the table, not sure into which drawer they went.

His uniform, although shapeless, had dried by now and he felt warm and tidy as he wiped up the crumbs and shook the tablecloth into the sink, spraying the tiny bits down the drain. He turned to admire his handiwork when a jarring noise struck his ears. The phone. A damn phone at this hour. He leaped for it, lunging for the white plastic on the kitchen wall, hefted it up, and said, "Yes?" Oh, please, God, not now. Not Amelia and Micah in a car accident. Not Amy crying over not one painting sold. Please, God, nothing bad for the Hauks, they didn't need bad.

The voice on the other end sounded disjointed against a

background of hard rock n' roll music, a juke box or live band, who could tell, but the voice, young and male, sang out, "Drain, you there? Man, we got a party going, you got to get down here. Things are stokin', man, if you get my drift. You coming?" The noise in the background filled in when the voice stopped.

"It's late," Martin managed to say.

"Hey, that's cool, baby, okay, it's late, but tuck mom and pop in and stop on down at Johnnie's tonight, man, you will not be sorry. There's even straws on the table if you'd like to dabble, though I know you're too clean and wholesome for all that fun. But it sure does jam it up your ass higher if you catch my drift . . . " The voice trailed off. "You know, sweet Draino, you're good on the givin', but you sure should take a look at the takin', and there's some guys here tonight, outta Detroit no less, that would love to give it, and give it, and give it." The voice stopped, but the background music blared through the receiver.

"What's the address?" Martin answered, casually glancing toward the refrigerator for a notepad he knew Claire would have handy. People like Claire always had a pad handy. His eye caught the announcement of Amy's showing, grandly printed and embossed on heavy cream paper. He dragged the cord toward the window sill for the pen he saw by the violet plant, spilling its petals over the ceramic edge.

"What the hell do you mean, the address? My address, baggo, the same one you've been using for the past six months. Don't shit with me, Dwayne, I got no time for shit. I got action to get back to, I'm only calling you 'cuz these guys want some black ass, and yours is prime if I remember, prime, so what the fuck game you playing? Dwayne? Answer me!"

Martin held the receiver away from his face, held it at a steady twenty inches before he bellowed into the phone, "You got the wrong number, fucker. Ain't no Dwayne here!" He slammed the phone into the wall, and turned slowly and reeled onto the kitchen counter. He steadied himself and felt a wet dishrag under him. He slowly picked it up, wrung it over the sink, and spread it to dry on the faucet. One last look around the kitchen: everything in place, Claire would be pleased, and he let himself out the back way, up the shared rear entry, and slowly moved down the hall to the bathroom, conveniently placed where he had left it, for tonight, if it hadn't been there, he would have not even noticed. Everything was screwy, he analyzed as he splashed water on his face, peeled out of the uniform and left it on the bathroom floor. Everything was screwy and he wasn't in on it.

The familiar light switch under his hand, the light bringing up the clean corners and neatly made bed, even flowers on the nightstand. Had Amelia done that or was it Dwayne's long fingers that had set the blooms in place for his enjoyment? He sat on the bed a minute, wondering how he would sleep after that phone call, so he decided not to try. Flinging open his dresser drawer, he pulled out a navy blue long-sleeved jersey, some jeans, and scrambled into fresh socks. The hunt for his moccasins took a minute: they were stored neatly in a shoe box. Grabbing his wallet, he went down the dark hall, flipped on the living room light, and headed down the front stairs. Maybe he could catch Amy, even this late.

è&

Amy was a success. The news rippled through the artsy-fartsy community of gays and lesbians, the straight art lovers and the ones who wished they knew a de Kooning from a Cassatt, all agog over something they knew was a phenom. Amy Schoenfield, new young artist, had captured strong bold dreams in her painting, had swirled a landscape of lines for the following crowd, lit a new beacon of creativity in the local art scene. She had come full round. Fourteen of her paintings had sold at the showing, ranging in price from $190 to $3,400. She quietly wept in the arms of the gallery owner, richer by thousands by the takings in the last few hours.

"How can I? How can I go on?" she pleaded, her eyes smeared with eye shadow and mascara. "Please, tell me. This is all a dream. How could this have happened?"

Mr. Antoine Dupres, the flamboyantly gay and successful owner of Arts Currente, Inc., only held her calmly in his hands and smoothed the wet hair from her face.

"You are tres chic, mi amore`," and he kissed her forehead. He wished with all his might that he felt more than kindness for this slim young Jewish girl with the talented hands, but his mind was elsewhere. He was already mentally in bed with Claude, his roommate of ten years, and he longed to separate himself from the distraught and talented artist before him. "Sleep, little one, you have smelled success. Go back to the canvas! Create anew! You are charmed. You are also, by my reckoning, a bit richer than you were yesterday." He lifted her hands from his shoulders, and set his glass of cognac, half finished, on the round table separating them. Claude hated a snootful.

Watching his back end, large and robust, leave her in the

darkening rooms of the gallery, she felt shut down. No one here now, no one to encircle her as she walked aimlessly through the gallery, looking at her paintings lighted by starlight and streetlight though the windows. She should call Jane and ask for a ride. Jane had been kind enough to take Amelia and Micah home with her. She had a roommate, who was out of town, and it really was simpler to have them gone. Amy felt foolish that she had left this final detail of the day to chance. Where was her purse? Did she even have any money?

The wine, the cheese squares, the melon balls: all gone, only the melting ice chips sinking into water as she walked past the formerly gaily encircled table. Where were all the people now, the people with the money to buy her pictures? What did it matter? She had created her pictures, so they would be admired and sold, wasn't that the point? She had made her point, she had only forgotten that after the point was made, after Micah and Amelia were safely set aside for the evening, not to embarrass her with their shouts of gratitude to the gods for such a daughter, yes. This was respite. But the quiet disturbed her. The ultimate quiet after her well-earned achievement. For that was what it was after all, her ultimate achievement, surviving the years of stupid newspaper ads and interviews for talented secretaries and nobody really wants to know that she, Amy Schoenfield, was really good. And, Martin, yes, sweet Martin, the brother, the male, got all he had coming to him, fit into the Navy, by god, and a college scholarship, as she remembered it. Martin never had to suffer in the draft of a cold sewer, never had to hear a roommate screwing her brains out, so she'd have rent the next month. Martin knew nothing of this.

Martin, the perfect Jewish brother, who never wrote a single word of encouragement to her, the same Martin, who selfishly spent his parents' retirement money, oblivious to the real world, the world she shouldered each day. That Martin. That one. That one now standing beyond the window by the last print, on the street, staring in on her, that Martin of her childhood, the one who finds her with no purse, no keys, no cab fare: Yes, it was her Martin, come to her at last.

She burst though the door, facing him on the empty street, glaring at him, but at that moment not sure why.

"It went well, big sister?" He opened his arms to her and she ran into them and kissed his neck and let herself be lifted up and brought back into the gallery, and she exclaimed, "I am so glad you're here! Martin, they bought my paintings! I can't believe it. They will all be gone tomorrow."

He smiled at her, lifted her head to gaze at her streaked face, and said, "You are talented, Amy. Why do you doubt yourself? I'm amazed that even now you doubt yourself. You were always the most talented of us, always had the flare and lilt to do it, and, by Jehovah, you've done it! I'm proud of you for that!" He swirled her up and spun her around in the air, the lights from the street playing havoc with their spirals, the noise of the air conditioning softly droning out their musings and whisperings as he stopped their swirl and they walked hand in hand around the darkened room. The light from the street set directly over her picture of the antelope running over the tundra, a light that was low and soft, even gray as Martin slowed to look up at it. It was one of her bigger efforts, several feet tall and four feet wide, and Martin's breath was taken with the pure perfection of the painting.

"This is it, then, this is my favorite. Did it sell?" He prayed in his heart that it hadn't. He was ready to trade her anything for the antelope painting,

"Oh, Martin, I don't remember. I really, at this very moment, don't remember if this one sold. It was pricey, mind you know that; I really hated to part with it, but money's money, you know."

It was close to two A.M. as they left the gallery, grabbed a cab, and headed to Amy's shared quarters under the bridgework, a small brick apartment building, the entry lit by greasy field lamps. Someone was just leaving, so Amy caught the door and held it for Martin to slip in. What a dismal hall, he thought, following her up the stairs. Living here must seem like hell. Amy rapped on the door, loudly, and, as Martin interpreted it, groans of pleasure mixed with pain met his ears. The squalor of it all met Martin. The clean eye of the man of medicine had become the man of the hour, here to save his sister, who, somehow, had miraculously surpassed him. She wouldn't need him now. At any rate, she would be moving out of this dump.

The door opened and a face peered at the two. "I lost my key, Peg, sorry to bother you," she mumbled apologetically.

"That's okay. I had to have a break anyway. Sometimes he just gets crazy, that Larry." She tied her bathrobe a little tighter, and stared at Martin. "I'll bet you're the brother who never writes." She grinned at him.

"That's me, the one that never writes." Martin wanted to end this conversation, wanted old Peg to trundle back to Larry and try to keep it down. Maybe they would, now that he was here for the night. Peg ambled back out of the room, blowing a kiss back at him.

"Is she all there?" Martin whispered. Amy giggled.

"Yes, she just can't get her life together. Lost her job because of that dope keeping her up half the night. But she's really a good-hearted person," she whispered back.

"Where's the bathroom?" Martin said quietly, slipping into a chair and pulling off his moccasins.

"We share one across the hall, don't lock the door behind you when you go out." She sat down on the couch and let out an audible sigh. "I made it, Martin, I finally arrived."

"You sure did, Amy, and no one could be happier for you than me." He got up and kissed her cheek. She pressed his hand against it harder. "Thanks, Martin, thanks for coming."

"Wouldn't have missed it. You got a blanket?"

"Will you be okay on the couch?" she offered in a whisper. She moved to the closet while Martin slipped across the hall to use the toilet and wash his hands and face. The bathroom was clean. He didn't know whose towel he used, but it smelled like Amy.

His couch was made up as a bed, even a pillow, when he returned and locked the door. Amy was in her nightgown, sitting hugging her knees on the couch.

"Martin, I'm so glad you're here, I can't believe you're here. Tomorrow's gonna be so much fun, now that you're here. Are you gonna be comfortable?" She patted the couch.

"I'll be fine, go to sleep, sister artist." He pulled her to him and kissed her shoulder and she slipped away, fading in his memory, lifting a curtain he couldn't remember being there, but sleep slipped over him and he rolled over in his clothes and sank into the deepest sleep he could remember.

§

The next day was spent running errands with Amy, stopping at the gallery to find her purse, stuck behind a plant, and the delighted and newly wealthy young woman spotted her brother a good brunch. She admired his tanned face and well-proportioned body, secretly hoping the fellow diners would think he was boyfriend and not a brother. Her freshly scrubbed face looked bright and alive, as alive as he had ever seen her. She wore very little makeup today, and the natural color of her lips and cheeks fit her buoyant mood.

"We've got to get a car and get Mom and Dad picked up. I can't have Jane thinking I've dropped them on her for keeps." She pursed her lips and pondered the car. "I could afford to get one now, but I hate the idea of changing oil in a car, do you think that's strange?" She looked at him.

He laughed out loud. "It must run in the family. I hate the idea of owning one, too, and for the very same reason. You know, I don't think Dad's ever had a car. Does he even have a driver's license?" They looked at each other over their cups of coffee, sweetly sugared, a taste Martin found strange after leaving sugar behind for so long.

"I'd like to think I know them better than I actually do, Martin, but the truth is, our parents are of a different time, a time we probably won't ever see again. They're part of the old way, I think." She set her cup down and inquired with her eyes if he was ready to go. He nodded as he rose. She paid the cashier and ran back to the table to leave a tip, a generous one, and she skipped past him to the street.

She danced around in circles, wiggling with happiness on this her big day, and she happily showed Martin the piece of paper Mr. Dupres had handed her at the gallery.

"Fifteen thousand dollars, Martin, that's how much I made yesterday. Only it took me years to get there, so if I break it down, into hours and sweat and canvas, I guess I worked for about four cents an hour." She winked at him and he caught her hand to slow her down.

"Look, let's forget the car. Let's grab a cab to your friend's and get Mom and Dad and then we can have some time later to talk about your future." It was settled that easily.

*. . . attraction . . .*
*Ice forming on the tips of my wings . . .*
*Unheeded warnings, I thought I'd heard of everything . . .*
*Can't take my eyes from the circling skies . . .*

*Pink Floyd "Learning to Fly"*

"Well, the runaways return," said Jane, swinging open the walnut door of her apartment. "Thought I was about to rename your parents and keep them, not that I'd mind. Man, can your mom ever talk! And I can't get your father away from the TV; he's been playing Tetris for over two hours and he keeps getting better." She ran her hand through her short gray hair, smartly cut and shaved up the back. Her silk blouse looked expensive, and her perfectly tailored matching slacks all looked like money to Martin. The whole apartment looked rich, done in blues and grays with a splash of yellow.

"Jane, you've been dear. How can I thank you?" She hugged her friend who gently patted her back. "Jane, this is my brother, Martin. Martin, Jane." They shook hands. Jane looked squarely into Martin's eyes.

"You wouldn't be the one who doesn't write, would you?" she asked impishly.

"Enough, enough about the not writing!" Amy got in. "He's been busy, running the Navy. Gonna be a doctor, this guy, and I'm just a scribbler. He should get the praise, not me."

"You both should be praised, but it's enough for me to see your work recognized after so long. You richly deserve it, my friend, and it's long overdue. Coffee, or is it too late for coffee and time for champagne? I've got several bottles chilled, just in case you were in the mood to celebrate." She paused and glanced at Amy. "Unless you think you shouldn't . . ." she stopped, wishing those words hadn't fallen from her lips.

Amy glanced quickly at her friend, and ducked her purse into the hall chair, a pale lemon striped with black. "Oh, I think it's safe to say I could handle one glass, with the toast in mind. I have to say thank you once more for everything." She looked past her friend to her mother, just feeling her way out of the kitchen.

"Amy, is that you here? We were just wondering if we should

get a cab and let your sweet Jane have her life back." Jane moved to encircle Amelia and draw her toward her children.

"No, Mom, Martin and I are here, and we're going to stay a few minutes, have a glass of wine, and toast my fabulous luck. Can you do that with us?" Amelia eyes got a little bleary, but she perked right up.

"I'm not much on drinking wine in the daytime, makes me sleepy, but if Micah will, I will, too. So you're back, eh Martin, come here to me, let me hold you." Martin moved to his mother and held her close to his chest. She called out, "Micah! Come away from that set, now, you'll ruin your eyes. Martin's here!"

Micah came in from a side door, a room appearing to be a den as far as Martin could see into it: a desk, a console, several easy chairs in black leather, a bank of phones on a slender sideboard. What Jane did must pay pretty well, he figured. Just the at-home-office-look made him know she had another bigger one downtown.

"Martin, you're here!" He pulled Martin into a bear-hug, kissed his forehead. He gazed back into the den. "You're not gonna believe what Jane has in this room. Every game imaginable, everything to call on, and send people letters on, and she doesn't even have to go out if it's snowing. She's got it all here," he beckoned back into the den.

"It's great, isn't it, Dad? It sure is neat, all this stuff, but we're going to pull you out of there and help celebrate Amy's good fortune last night. You do know that she sold fourteen of her paintings and is now practically rich?"

Micah looked slightly confused, standing there in his baggy black pants, wearing the now wrinkled white shirt he so proudly wore to the gallery. "You mean I have to stop?"

"Yes, Dad, I think it's time for wine and then time to leave. Jane's got things she has to do, and she's been more than accommodating to the Schoenfields today." Martin didn't mean for that closing remark to sound so clipped, but it came out that way. He was suddenly aware that the Schoenfields did not really belong in this custom-draped apartment, maybe not even an apartment, maybe a condo, maybe she owned it. Seeing his father in the wrinkled shirt and unpressed pants, not even wearing shoes, made him uncomfortable. There was a time, not too far back, when a Jew wouldn't even have tried to get into this building.

"Well, then," Micah asserted quietly, "sons know best in a friend's house. Jane, you'll need to shut it off. I don't know how." Jane quickly went in and closed out the game.

"And now the champagne," she said swiftly, eyeing the group watching her move from den to kitchen. "Amy, can you grab those glasses? No, not those, use the good ones. Nobody's ever used them and it's about time." Amy moved to the glass doored sideboard of teak and mahogany, heavily encrusted with panels of birds and fish in flight, and opened the door with a metal key fit in the lock. She set the crystal stemware gently on the lip of the piece, lining up five goblets.

"These really are too nice to use, Jane," remonstrated Amy. "What if one should get broken?" She thought of her mother's failing eyesight, so bad now that a return to work had been impossible; it had been over six months since Amelia had turned a collar or tatted lace. Cecile would miss Amelia, but the small pension would never be missed. That was the garment district for you. Use you and lose you.

"So what if it did? I'd just call up and get two more, just like 'em, that's what things are for, Amy, to use. Everything that's worth anything has to have a use. Except art. Art needs no excuse for being. It is above use. It, it . . ." she stumbled on her little speech. Amy picked up two of the goblets and set them down on the kitchen counter. She returned for two more and Martin carried in the last one. It was heavy, and the sharp edges of the finely wrought piece bit nicely into his hand. A hundred a piece, he hazarded a guess. Easily, a hundred a piece, and that at PX prices.

Each glass was surveyed scrupulously by Jane for dust. Not being satisfied, she whipped out a fresh linen napkin and swirled it around each goblet briskly, checking often for dirt. There was none. Martin was asked to do the honors of uncorking the bottle, the wire was pulled, and the cork moved slightly before Jane could slip the napkin over it. "Just a precaution," she murmured, glancing at the beveled glass doors of the sideboard.

They all waited for the explosion but it didn't come. The cork slipped neatly into Martin's napkin-wrapped hand, and he was glad he hadn't pulled the gaffe of the day by letting it fire across the room. Amy was asked to pour and she did so neatly, wiping the bottle top off between each glass, and the five glasses were meted out equally, just killing the bottle.

"Perfect," Jane crowed. "One more person would have gone dry today. Let's take this out on the porch and see the view that Amy will be seeing very soon." She walked across the deep blush pile and the others followed: Micah first, then Amelia, holding the glass firmly in one hand and holding Micah's wrinkled shirt in the other, tagged by Amy, giggling in the joy of the celebration, and Martin played caboose, shutting the sliding Venetian glass door behind him as he stepped onto the tiled veranda perched off the living room. Not a veranda, that was too Western, he felt; more like an oasis in the sky. A burbling fountain, hidden behind velvety green plants with large pink flowers framed the side to his right, and to the left, among chintz pillows and wicker couches, sat a green-marbled pedestaled hot tub, covered for now in matching chintz fabric. A low round table with hassocks circling it invited the guests to sit down and enjoy the cool breeze blowing in off the Hudson River. The air was clear, and wispy clouds floated past them.

"This is gorgeous," Martin breathed out, "just gorgeous." Jane looked at him with thanks in her eyes.

"Just a little place I like to call Heaven," she answered. "Now, who's going to toast first?"

The group shyly went silent, and Martin, being the last one in, became the first to speak. He lifted his sparkling glass and put his finger in the champagne. He walked around to where Amy was seated, and touched the drop on her nose. She laughed in delight. He circled the table and sat on the last hassock. "Toast finished," he said, raising his glass in the air, and the group laughed and gently touched theirs together over the glass round.

Laughter filled the air, and Jane, enjoying their company and the freshness of Amy when Martin was near, sprang to her feet. "I want to be next, now that I know I'll have to show up Mr. One Liner." She winked at Martin and turned to Amy.

"To my dreams, you have added the joy of finding a friend I needed. You gave me hope, Amy, when I did not see hope. You watched over me and let me find out for myself that I'll never be a painter, but in showing me what I didn't have, and so gently, so gently . . ." and she lifted her glass to Amy, who only stared in wonder, "you showed me what I could do. And I've done it. And now we're all here to say you are great, Amy Schoenfield, and no one, no one, can ever take away from a true talent what God gave them."

Amy caught her breath at her friend's beautiful words, and raised her glass toward the others as they saluted her. The glasses tinkled with a magic sound of lights and ice and crystal. Only quality sounds like that. And thankfully, thought Martin glancing at his mother's wavering aim, not one chip.

The champagne was excellent, a very good year and a very expensive bottle, if the coating on it had meant what Martin thought it did as he remembered the cold feel of the silver blue bottle. Not a brand he knew, but his tastes ran more for ales and bourboned coffees. Some imported dark beers, but not very many or very often. He wasn't a teetotaler, but his mind ran in a different direction than wanting to be depressed by alcohol.

Micah sidled on his hassock, a little disconcerted that he, the father of the artist, had not made his toast sooner. He stood and raised his glass to Jane. "I speak now, and my words are meant for everyone here. Jane, you are our Amy's friend, and you seem to have been behind her when we, her parents, were not able to help. I toast you, for that, as I toast God in thanks for all the talent he gave to our Amy."

"Here, here," chimed in Amelia, staying seated and holding the heavy glass in two hands. She started to rise but Micah laid his hand on her shoulder.

"Mignong, you can't jump in when a man is making a toast. You must wait until I finish, then you can make your own toast." He smiled down on her gray knot of hair, and she settled back. She demurely sipped from the glass. "It wasn't time to drink yet, but go ahead, drink. All of us drink. We are one without the chance of chipping these nice glasses. I'm finished now, but, Amy, I'm so proud of you. Know that," and he raised his goblet to Amy who only smiled and raised her glass toward him.

"I'd only like to say that you were a good baby and a good child and I want you to be happy." Amelia seemed proud that she'd gotten that remark in, and Micah only sat down and shook his head indulgently. The glasses were emptied swiftly and the group rose as one and moved back through the glass doors and sank into the lush carpeting again. Martin took one look back onto the porch, trying to absorb the beauty of it and hold it in his memory. It seemed he was trying to take it in and hold it against a time when he would need that beauty again, to soothe him as it did now. He wasn't an artist, but he knew something wonderful had created the beauty of that porch.

Jane watched him savoring the view and came back to stand by him as Amy helped her mother get their things together.

"It is gorgeous, isn't it?" she asked, loving the way he touched the glass on the door and took in the view.

"Jane, if you designed this area, you're a genius. It couldn't be more perfect."

She sighed, appreciating Martin's approval of her year-long struggle with the light, and the fabric, and the plants. It had been worth it, she realized, but only at that moment. She smiled and touched his arm.

"You must come back, Martin, during the Holidays. I really put on a show then." She winked at him and moved to the others.

Hugs at the door, see you soon, kisses on the forehead between Micah and Jane, and promises to come back for more games in the den. Martin felt himself following along, not the leader of the group, suddenly only part of this small ragtag foursome moving down the silent carpeted hall to the elevators. They swept down to the ground, ten floors below, and moved through the well-appointed lobby, with its marble walls and evergreens in bronze pots. The doorman elegantly opened the door for them, and Martin asked him to call a cab. The man touched his cap and moved to the street, raising his arm in a slow arc, which brought a Yellow almost immediately into the circled drive. He helped Amelia into the backseat, and shut the door to move around to the opposite side for Amy and Micah to enter. Martin opened the passenger door and slid in by the driver.

The dark skinned man swiveled and looked at Martin. "You're in the military?"

Martin glanced at him. The man wore an old bomber's jacket and gray slacks. His face was lined with deep creases around the eyes, and his teeth had been capped in gold. The mild odor of an unwashed body met Martin's nostrils. He responded, "Does it show?"

The driver boomed out a harsh laugh, threw the car into gear, and shot out into traffic without looking. "Show? Does a dog show his balls? Does a cat lick her kittens? Don't a bear shit in the woods?" He seemed supremely pleased at his avid assessment, giggling and burrowing in the collar of his bomber's jacket. He stole a furtive look at Martin as he whipped the car around in heavy traffic. "I'm right, aren't I?"

Martin turned to look at his sister, mom, and dad, sitting quietly in the back seat. He turned back to the driver and said, "1432 Summit, if you please, and if you don't mind, I'm not military. I'm a dental student from Detroit, here on a mission of mercy, a funeral of a close friend, so please, let's cut the commentary and get going, savvy?"

The man stared back at him swiftly, keeping an eye on the traffic stopping for a light.

"Well, you fooled me, and I ain't usually fooled. I read people, and you read military to me. Just so's you know." He pulled himself straighter and studied the traffic intently.

Martin turned to look in the back seat, and Amy had a wide grin on her face. Micah looked confused and Amelia was peering out the window, trying to focus on the buildings and keep her head from swirling with champagne.

The cabbie let them off at Amy's apartment and nodded briskly to Martin. "You know, if you ever change your mind, the Marines are looking for a few good men. If the teeth thing don't work out." He took the fare and tip and shoved it into his pocket, leaving them in exhaust fumes as he sped away. Martin only stared after him.

Amy opened the outer door and the four mounted the steps to her second floor flat. Martin had a horrible flash of what may lay ahead, Larry and Peg in a tumble of entwined limbs, draped over the living room couch where he had slept last night, but when they entered the crowded room, all evidence of Peg and Larry were gone. Martin exhaled in relief, heading across the hall to the bathroom, which was not as tidy as before. Perhaps Amy was the only one who kept it clean. Her towel lay in a pool of water on the tiled floor: a big footprint was pressed into it. He scooped it up and wrung it out in the sink. Dirty water drizzled out as he twisted the cloth, finally leaving it spread on the tub's edge. What else was he to do with it? What else was he to do with the whole mess this day was fast becoming? He longed to be gone, to be away, to be at work, not sucked into this family mess, which held him back, wasted his time. They'd tasted Amy's success, they'd had some champagne, they had the rest of the day to talk, and talk, and . . .

Micah was at the door, tapping gently, when Martin turned from the sink and opened the door.

"You through, son? If not, I'll come back later." His face looked through the half-opened door more in curiosity as to what would keep Martin in the bathroom that long, especially when they all had to use it.

"The floor, Dad, the floor was wet. Wanted to wipe it up, so Mom wouldn't slip and fall. Damn sloppy people."

Micah pushed the door opened and surveyed the clean floor and neatly wrung out towel. "Funny, how some people live, just tramplin' on the things of other people. I don't ever remember a time when that was right." He gazed at Martin a little longer, and Martin blushed slightly and pushed himself off the sink and out into the hall.

"Smart boy, Martin, I like that," said Micah, closing the door.

It was girl time, apparently, as he entered the room he had slept in not too comfortably last night, girl time, as he saw Amelia and Amy seated on the couch, shifting pages of sketches between them, Amy showing Amelia about the first time she'd tried a technique, and the intervening problem with lighting and back lighting and the goal she had tried and abandoned, and then a new sketch, a central theme breaking in, a color change, a new idea forming. Amelia gamely handled the sheets like she had handled the old lace patterns, sifting through them until she found a known she could execute with precision.

Martin sagged into an overstuffed torn armchair. He hesitated to put his hands on the arms. Who knew what had brushed that chair? He compared Amy's surroundings with Jane's, and his heart sank as he felt pity for his happy sister, sifting through sketches that were barely perceptible to Amelia's fading eyes. Amelia touched the paper, drew her finger around the arches and loops and commented, "You could have been a lace designer, Amy. Your lines are beautiful."

Amy hugged her mother and smiled into her face. She was so delighted at the attention and praise, much more than she felt she had earned. Martin cleared his throat.

"Amy, we need to get you out of here, while I'm home, so I can help you pack and move." She glanced up at him.

"Move? Why should I move? I can't just leave Peg and lark off. I can't just do that." She tugged her pictures together, straightening them, and sliding them into a large cardboard holder. "What's Peg to do if I just up and move?"

Martin leaned forward in the chair and clasped his hands together between his knees.

"I think Peg's problems are hers, and you can't solve them for her by staying on here. Maybe your success is meant as a sign that it's time you moved on. I'll bet Jane could help you find a loft with decent lighting and a bathroom to yourself. Don't you want that?"

She sighed, looking first at her mother, then back to Martin, but her answer was interrupted by Micah, coming in from the bathroom across the hall. He shut the door and stopped to listen. Amy's eyes ran to Micah and she asked him, "Daddy, Martin thinks I should move, find a better place, a place where I can live by myself and paint. What do you think?"

"Martin has good sense, little one, he's made good choices. A place of your own might not be a bad idea. We'll all help you move. I'll bet Luther would pitch in and help, too. He has friends in the moving business."

Amelia wiggled in her seat. "We haven't called the Hauks, Micah, they'll be wondering what became of us." She rose and picked up her purse, stood there like a rag doll waiting to be held together and moved by someone else's hand. Micah went to her and put his arm around her shoulder. "Soon, Mignong, soon." He turned to Amy and then to Martin.

"Let's all go back home and have dinner, and see if we can decide what Amy is to do." He turned to the door, guiding Amelia, when Amy fairly flew up from the couch. Tears were in her eyes, tears of confusion and childishness.

"Why is it you think you can direct my life now, when there was never any direction before? Why is my staying here, helping Peg, and going on with my work now of so much importance to you? I got by before, I'll keep getting by. Please, don't tell me what I can and cannot do with my life." Her cheeks flamed pink and she tossed her black hair back with one hand. She settled back on the couch.

"Just let me do what I'm used to doing and we'll see what comes of my own decisions. Please, I'm not angry," she said, brushing away Martin's hand as he reached to touch her arm. "Let's just leave it as it is for now. I'll be in touch, I promise." She stayed on the couch, watching them move to the door.

"I'll call," Martin said, "as soon as I can get a minute tonight. We can talk then. Okay?" She nodded. He blew her a kiss and shut the door. The quiet hit her then, her body slipped over onto the couch and she had the good cry she knew she had been holding back.

# Chapter Ten

The three Schoenfields walked to the corner and waved for a cab, but it took awhile before Martin could get one. When he finally did, it had started to rain again, and a wet knot of gray hair got ducked in first, then Micah in his damp wrinkled suit, and Martin shut them in the back and climbed into the front with the driver.

The cab didn't smell good, he knew something bad had happened in this cab, probably over and over, and he looked back at Micah holding Amelia in his arms, crooning to her, and he turned quickly to the driver and gave their address.

The man, somewhere in his thirties, showed exquisitely pointed teeth and narrow lips in his black face. He said, smiling benignly, "That's a long way. I never go that far." He pursed his lips as if to whistle and flipped the maps on his dashboard. "Oh, man, I never been that far."

Martin knew that lisp, that language slant, knew he was listening to an African, probably an Ethiopian, and he patiently said, "How far can you go?"

"Ah, maybe to the Bronx I could go. I get ya to the Bronx, then you get another driver, okay, okay?" he questioned, fooling with his maps.

"Okay, yeah, okay, go." Just his luck to pick the only driver in New York afraid to go more than ten miles away. Martin guessed he had been instructed carefully in this matter, had been schooled over and over in this foreign culture, about who to give rides to, who to avoid, how not to wander too far away from help from his sponsors. Yes, he knew, this was a "sponsored man," living in a flat with eighteen other immigrants, already newly positioned as cab drivers, these Ethiopians knew how to train and regiment the newcomers, letting them loose to move to other cities to start new receiving centers: Chicago, Detroit, St. Louis. Smart. Someone was just plain smart. Black networking. African networking. Small dollars heaped into big pockets, then carefully distributed where they would do the most good. Smart.

The Jews had done that, mused Martin, settling back for the ride and trying not to breathe in too deeply. The Jews had newcomers coming to these shores daily, staying with relatives, enrolling in colleges, getting degrees, and then, ready to be shipped to other cities to begin the journey of helping others, had dug in their heels and sent money to Save Israel instead. Why hadn't the Jews stayed with the small idea? The Jews could learn from the Ethiopians.

The transfer of cabs was not difficult, and Martin had to smile when they pulled alongside another cab in the Bronx and got shuttled into another cab, driven by . . . oh, my! What were the chances? An Ethiopian.

"My friend, you are in luck," said their driver. "This man can take you to your very doorstep. You are lucky today." He grinned and reached his hand out for the fare, which Martin had noticed as he slipped out. Sixteen-fifty-three.

"How much?" asked Martin, pulling out his billfold. Amelia and Micah stood behind him on the sidewalk.

"Ah, would twenty-five be too much, being I've come so far and passed up many fares in between, more lucrative fares?" He grinned his pointed teeth at Martin.

"Seems a little high, seeing the meter's at sixteen. How's about a twenty and we part friends?" Martin handed him a twenty, which the man sniffed and stuck in his shirt. "Mahn, that's okay, time's are hard, but we keep pumpin'."

He jumped into his cab and waved an arm at his comrade, who opened the doors on the cab; this time resigning himself to no more conversations with cabbies, Martin crowded into the back seat with his parents.

The neighborhoods improved, the streets looked cleaner, the trees provided some decent shade as they approached their own flat. The cabbie seemed lost in finding the right street and Micah leaned forward and told him a short cut, but the man didn't seem to hear, heading out on the main intersecting street three times and cutting back two streets further than he would have had to. Great training, Martin had to admit, great way to run up the meter a few extra bucks.

The sun was high overhead, right on at two o'clock when they pulled in front of the flat. The cabbie leaped out and courteously helped Amelia out, touching her arm gently and with tenderness, and in that flash of kindness, Martin resolved to give the man a good tip. As he stepped out, he noticed the meter at twelve dollars three cents.

He stood on the sidewalk with the cabbie and asked him how much. The man scratched his chin, looked from Amelia to Micah, and said, "Eleven flat, fine. I not listen as fairly good to the man there. He was right. I ran you too long." Martin was puzzled for a moment, then he watched the dark slanting eyes watching Amelia groping for Micah's arm as they moved up the sidewalk. He turned to the cabbie.

"Your mother? She remind you of your mother?"

"Dah. My mother, my aunt, all have the blindness, the light smoothed over their eyes. Bugs they say caused it. Bugs in the eyes.

But I hope to send money home, to kill the bugs that hurt their eyes. Your mother, she has bugs, too, here in America?" He questioned Martin sincerely.

"Dah," said Martin, handing him a twenty. "Big time bugs in America, too, called Bury your Head in the Sand." The man shook his head, not knowing the term, but looked hard at the money held out to him.

"Change, I get change," he said, hurrying around to his box on the seat.

"No change," said Martin, slapping the top of the cab. "Off with you, friend."

The man looked over the top of the cab and smiled at Martin. "You are a good man. I say, the money you give me will go back to Africa and my relatives can kill the bugs, you think?" His child-like face looked at Martin for the hoped-for response.

Martin laughed. "For eight bucks, I'll bet you can kill all the bugs in Africa."

The cabbie grinned again and ducked into his cab, slamming the door, and pulling out into the street. He honked two times at the corner and disappeared.

The sidewalk was empty of people except for a lone roller-blading boy, darting in and out of the sidewalks to the houses. He'd skate up one and come careening back down to the main walk, bending low for his turns, standing straight on the main, swooping low for his turns up the separate walks. He screeched politely to a halt when he saw Martin standing in his way.

"You live here?" he asked, jerking his thumb at the house shared by the Schoenfields and Hauks.

"Just visiting," answered Martin, moving in the direction of the house.

"You know Dwayne?" he called out. Martin turned back.

"Yeah, I know Dwayne. You know Dwayne?"

"Everybody know Dwayne. I gonna be just like Dwayne when I get big." He smiled and struck off on his blades, digging in and pushing hard, building up speed and swooping into a crouch to turn into the next sidewalk. Martin smiled to himself. Dwayne Hauk. Neighborhood hero, but what kind of hero got calls from the likes of people he'd talked to on the phone last night? What was the deal? Who was kiddin' who? Dwayne was mixed up in some stupid game with guys he should be avoiding, in Martin's estimation. How he was going to address this, he didn't know, but from what he had seen of Dwayne Hauk, he was too good to be dragged into that scene.

The living room was just as he left it last night, the only change being the light spilling into the room through the pulled-back lace curtains. His father was seated by the window, into his slippers again, holding a small book of prayers he liked to read on Saturdays. His trips to services had stopped when Amelia's eyes had failed so much that she needed his help with the slightest chore in the evening. He shut the book when he saw Martin, and moved his chair around to face the one across from it.

"Sit down, Martin, sit down, let me take another look at you." Martin sat in the chair and laid his arms on the lacy crocheted covers. His arm felt a small prick, and he glanced down at a pin there to keep it in place. He shoved it further into the upholstery.

"Well, we're back home, at our own place, and you find it good?" He paused, holding his book gently in his hands.

"I find it . . . different. This time, Papa, I find Mother almost blind. I find you as strong as ever, and that I would wish for you, but Mother . . ." and he paused.

Micah tapped the book gently, and set it on the window sill by the flowing lace curtains. "Your mother's eyes have failed, but she is still your mother, eyes failing or not, I stay by her, she is my love, my life. You find offense in that?"

"Papa, I find offense that Mother's eyes were failing the last time I was home. I asked you to take her to an eye doctor, and that, apparently, never happened. She is much worse now, that anyone can see. Why didn't you take her to a doctor, to see if he could help her?"

Micah paused, touched his book on the window sill, and replied, "So much you do not know, little one. You may be a great student, but before you have gotten dry behind the ears, I tell you this: sight comes to us from God, and God decides when you are no longer able to see. The doctors, they know so little. The scribes warned us of doctors. Let God heal, they tell me, and they are always right, those scribes."

Martin closed his eyes for a moment and opened them to stare directly into his father's hooded gaze. "Father, the scribes can only mean that God wanted all men to see with their eyes as far as the light would give them life to do it, but the scribes, the ancient ones, knew only what they knew, they only knew what they believed was true, based on what had been known to that point, but Father, God has also given us new sight, new understandings. We can learn, Papa, we can learn and we can do more, and maybe the scribes didn't know this, but modern medicine has advanced very far, into cataract surgery, into medicines for glaucoma. What if Mama had glaucoma, and only a doctor could help her? Why did you delay? Why didn't you ask, Papa?"

Micah fumbled a minute with his book, finally leaving it on the window sill. "Some things you will know in time, my son. For now, it is as it is."

It is as it is, thought Martin, pulling himself up from the chair, and moving to the kitchen, the sanctuary it was, the place of light, bubbling water, and canisters of tea bags. Why had he thought his mother was there, starting dinner, washing lettuce and slicing tomatoes, dipping gravy over meatloaf, smiling at him as she worked . . . why had he thought that? She was not in the kitchen. He ducked back out and asked Micah where she was.

"Ah, resting in the bedroom. The wine, you know. Your mother is not a very good drinker. Men have stronger constitutions, I think, don't you, about spirits?" He had his book of prayers in his hand again, holding it in the light from the window. Martin came and crouched down by his father's chair. Micah shut the book quickly and stared into Martin's face.

"Papa, can I take Mother to see a doctor? I need to know, before I leave again, that everything that can be done has been tried. I'm going to be a doctor, Papa, and I think someone could help her." Martin laid his hand on his father's arm, and Micah stared at the strong young hand. He laid his hand over it.

"If it will make you rest easier, yes, take Mother to a doctor. I will not tell anyone at the Synagogue that you have done this. They may think my faith is weak. I have great faith, son, great faith, that your mother is going the path that God has chosen for her. But if you want to, then you do it. I cannot."

Martin stood and looked down at his father's graying hair, the wistful glance out the window, the steady easy breathing of life, breathe in, breathe out. "I'll let you read, Papa."

He went down the hall to the bathroom, used the toilet, and washed his hands carefully. The door to the bedroom was open and he glanced in. Amelia was curled on her side in only her slip, the coverlet lightly moving up and down with her breathing. Was it all about breathing, Martin thought, something so natural and unlearned? Was it breathing we forgot to do as life comes to an end? Do we die from disease or disinterest? He touched his mother's forehead, and she moved slightly in her sleep, a little smile moving over her lips. He bent quickly and kissed her cheek. She didn't wake up. He straightened the cover, and smiled down on her.

Retracing his steps, he passed the living room and called out, "I warn you, I'm not much of a cook, but I'm going to put together some dinner for us." Micah looked up from his book and smiled.

"All those lessons from your mother must have sunk in, stubborn that you are. Let's see how you do. Remember to use the left-hand cupboard for dairy, the right for meat." Martin could hardly forget. The separation of the dishes and pans, each getting a separate pan of dish water, the lessons he'd learned from being raised in this family. Why now should they be important? They probably weren't important, he thought, pulling open the refrigerator and scanning the contents. Everything was distinctly clean in that icebox, separate and neatly marked. The lettuce looked fresh, there were two nice Roman tomatoes, a block of Parmesan not yet opened, parsley, one large Porta Bella mushroom sealed in cellophane against the time of use, celery long and pale green, no yellow on it, and four small radishes wrapped individually. Martin smiled at that. God, these people. My parents. He opened the freezer and pulled out a long flat white-wrapped package marked beef steak, sirloin.

"Nice choice," he remarked. "Papa, where are the potatoes? And onions?"

Micah stirred himself and came into the kitchen. "Under the sink, in a basket. We may not have too many potatoes. I haven't shopped this week, waiting to see what you wanted to eat before I went out." The onions were slightly soft in Martin's grip, but the four potatoes were Idaho whites with a firm feel.

"These are fine. I'll whip us up a nice meal. You'll be surprised, Papa. I can cook pretty good." Micah looked at him with a knowing sureness that what he said was true. He washed his hands again, paying careful attention to his nails, thinking of Claire. He needed to slip downstairs later and say hello, try to get Dwayne off to one side. The phone call from last night still baffled him. His feelings for the family below made him seem part of them, not a stranger intruding. He needed to speak to them all, but Dwayne first, he knew. What about the real Dwayne? Lost in his thoughts, Martin didn't notice his father leaving the kitchen and walking down the hall to the bedroom. Half-way through the salad, he moved the defrosting steak over a little, making room for the onions he was chopping; the potatoes he decided to fry up in golden hunks with their jackets still on. He heard the gentle sound of snoring. He wiped his hands and moved down the hall with the towel still twisted in his grip. He paused and looked in. His father had slid into bed and covered himself as well with the cover, resting his arm across his mother's shoulder, and she, tossing in her sleep, had her hand over his, and the two were out like two overfed puppies. Great that spirits don't affect men, Martin remembered, laying the towel over his shoulder and returning to the kitchen.

He tossed the salad and set it back in the fridge, covered, of course, with cellophane. Great hunk of cheese, he noticed, handling the block easily over the grater. He placed the remaining lump into a seal-tight bag and zipped it neatly closed. Someday they'll operate that way, he thought, the surgeons will simply attach a zip-lock baggie over the incision and nature will do what it always was meant to do: heal itself. No more sutures, no more metal staples that need to be removed one week later, the healing flesh festering and red looking, causing the doctor to order another round of antibiotics. And isn't that the worst? All those antibiotics being prescribed for a touch of this, a rash of sorts, a mild inflammation: where would it end? Martin saw the natural body being taken over and then manipulated like a small guinea pig, the antibiotics finding another germ or bacteria they don't recognize and they quietly lie down and the new strain runs rampant. The bodies have already met all the new medicine, and the abuse of the antibiotics has worn them thin. The body needs new ones, new ones, and the industry doesn't have it all together yet; they thought the miracle drugs would last and last, but their time is coming to a fast end. Overuse means a stronger new one must be created, to block the inhibitors, to stave off the old diseases, to warn the folks randomly passing out instant cures, that there is no instant cure. The body must remain strong, no antibiotics will help it forever, the body needs to be strong enough on its own, to fight within itself, not rely on medicine indefinitely.

Now where did that come from, mused Martin, sliding the potatoes into the already heated oven. 350 degrees, turn 'em in ten, lightly brown, and how about some more cheese over them? The grater came out again and three passes made a neatly wriggling kiss of cheese over the oblong chunks of half-baked wedges. This meal was beginning to look edible. Now for the steak. He pondered which pan to use, the heavy iron skillet over the stove looked like it was for meat, but who knew? Maybe they fried eggs in it. How to botch up their whole life in the throw of the meat on top of the dairy? He wondered momentarily if he should ask his father, but the thought of waking him, with the skillet in his hand, asking such an inane question, bothered him.

"Losing My Religion" ran through his mind, the REM tune, currently lighting up their fortunes. "That's me in the corner," he hummed along with the remembered lyrics. He was really getting into it, this cooking, smelling, touching the food, really wanted it to be perfect for his two sleeping friends. Yes, friends, not just the people who copulated and conceived him, brought him up, held him fast in their love, the two friends sleeping side by side, one whiffed by the champagne at Jane's, admittedly so; the other, bound that it had no effect on him, slipping under the coverlet to let the moment pass.

Everything's ready but the meat. Martin held the skillet in his hand, balancing the weight, not sure if it was meant for dairy or meat, but he tossed it into the air and when he caught it, he decided on meat. He slid a pat of butter into it and turned the flame up high, to sear the delicious juices in, to make them grab each other in collective cohesion, sucking them in, holding them near the bone, succulent and tender. Ah, this is a good cut, Martin realized, noticing the marbling running across the meat, not too fat, not too lean. Corn fed, I'll bet, he nodded to himself. He counted to three one thousand, turned the heat down, flipped the steak deftly, and covered the pan with a plate, turning off the heat. Let it just finish quietly, he thought. Creep into the meat. Let it smother itself.

The kitchen was soaked in afternoon light. The four o'clock chime had yet to be heard from the clock, and Martin knew his meal was ready, but his dinner guests were not. He checked in on the slumbering pair under the coverlet, nothing had moved in half an hour, and he set his dinner into a holding pattern and washed his hands again. Will this hand washing go on and on? He wondered if Lady Macbeth shouldn't have been finishing a like supper, for he knew her hand washing was over a much more celebrated affair. His lot was to wash his hands again, and stand before the late afternoon sun shining in the window, wondering what he was to do with all the time left on this leave. There was Amy to consider, the Amy he'd held last night, holding her brilliance up against the view of how she saw herself; of Jane, that very nice friend and comrade on Amy's street of hope and desire, that Jane, who Martin, he remembered at this moment, had stupidly forgotten to ask her for her number, so he could keep in touch, such an elegant and hopeful woman friend, how long a friend? When a friend? Why is she a friend? Martin scrambled for the answers when he heard a voice from outside the kitchen window, a woman's voice downstairs, in the backyard, calling about pot mix, or soil, or some such thing. The words wrapped themselves around his brain. He moved to the backstairs, swiftly going down, down, and alighting in the little vestibule shared by the duplex that entered the back yard. He pushed through the screen door, and saw Claire sitting on a cushion, pulling up weeds and laying the pluckings on a newspaper. She turned quickly when she saw Martin, laid her gloved hands down on her thighs, and swung around to face him.

"Ah, Mr. Martin, how goes it? Everyone at home, no stones left unturned?" She turned away from him, hastily gathering her clippers and yard tools together. "I have to go, so please excuse me." From contented work to fast escape. Martin wondered why.

Martin came down the wooden porch steps, and touched her lightly on the shoulder as she rose to leave. "Ms. Hauk, can we talk a moment?" He held her so lightly that he felt he had not stopped her, and stop her he hadn't. She moved away from him as if he had the plague. "Mrs. Hauk."

She stopped moving away from the place she'd been weeding, then looked keenly at him. Her lips moved over words she never meant to escape her, for her thoughts were for a different time, a different moment. She only remembered Dwayne slouched in the doorway, watching the rain, wondering if his father would bring Martin home. Why this Martin? Why this moment?

"Leave him alone," she hissed, her anger finding space in each word. Her sleek black hair was pulled into a ponytail, and she looked like a girl of about thirteen. The words coming from her seemed foreign, completely unlike the way she had greeted him before. He took a step back.

Once she started, she dared not retreat. "My son, Dwayne, likes you, Martin, likes you too much, do you understand that about him? Under that Big Man Athlete is a very shy man, a man who doesn't date women his own age, doesn't date women of any age, for that matter. Leave him alone," her voice took on a pleading note. "Please, let him find himself without your interference. It's very important." She tugged at the fingers of her work gloves, looking past him at the perfectly manicured back lawn, the edging of bricks around her flower beds, the white rose trellis holding pink buds of promise.

Not waiting for him to answer, she hurried up the back stairs just as Luther was coming out, holding a bag of potting soil. She rushed past him and left him standing with the bag, staring at Martin.

He slid it to the porch boards, let it rest against the railing. Feeling for his pouch and pipe, he packed it neatly with his little finger and struck a match on the railing. Puffing slowly, he sat down and patted the place next to him. "Come here, son." Martin moved on rubbery legs and sat next to Luther. Luther puffed and shut his eyes.

"Mm, that's good, nothin' like a pipe. Smells good, don't it?"

Martin watched him a moment, then said, "Your wife's upset with me, and I need you to know that she has no right to be. She got in my face a minute ago, over Dwayne liking me, and I really find it hard to understand . . ." Martin stopped as Luther touched his arm.

Dwayne came around the side of the house, and stopped short when he saw the two of them on the porch. Seeing his father next to Martin curdled his blood, made his stomach twist in pain. He never thought he would see two direct opposites: the tanned, well-toned white boy with the dark hair and green eyes, the graceful hands, the perfect set of his jaw, the perfect man. And beside him, his dad, the man he loved over and above life itself, the forgiving man, the man who didn't know he was black, the spokesperson for the downtrodden, safe with his pipe and unwilling to sacrifice one iota of well-kept grass for the lot of the wealth of the world.

Yeah, his father, the well meaning, misdirected stumbling fool who'd helped bring his sorry ass into this confusing world, a world that had hurt him deeply, held him back until he proved he was twice as good. This world that fucked with his body for its joys, left him weak and crying when he didn't have the love he needed. The same world now shared with the young man on the porch, sitting with his father. What did Martin Schoenfield know of his pain, his pressure from Johnny for the deep pleasures, the resoundingly wonderful ripples that filled his body and made his fingertips tingle? What did Martin know of that? Probably zip. He probably never had the memories Dwayne carried daily. He wasn't black.

Secret men, quiet men, men with eyes for Dwayne, sidling up to him and cupping his jeans admiringly, stroking his arms and hands, wanting to slip away. Just for a few moments, and Dwayne had let himself slip away, quietly into the dark, sometimes taking money from them when they thought he was extra good, sometimes just a smile, a jerk, and a release of being alone, alone again. And alone he was, facing his two attackers, and this wasn't even on the field, this was in his own backyard. Why these two? Why the inquisitive eyes? Did his past show?

"Hey, and I found 'cha. Hiding out among the hollyhocks, are ya?" He played bravado and slumped down on the bottom step. "So, how goes it, Martin? You up for some checkers tonight?" Why he said that he did not know, but to speak was enough effort, to make sense of it, he'd have to sift through and find better words.

"I've got dinner on hold for my folks, so it will have to wait until later, but, yeah, take me on. I've improved with my basic training. But I think you might have the advantage, being you're Luther's son." Luther gave him an eyebrow-raised look, wondering if his ability might be better than even he thought. He tapped out the pipe, letting the ashes fall to the ground, and Dwayne carefully smudged them out with his tennis shoe.

He pulled himself upright, and moved toward the back door. "I'm going to see if I can help your mother with supper, and then you guys can play to your heart's content." He touched Martin briefly on the shoulder as he turned, and he smiled down at Dwayne. "Don't forget to watch his backside. If he's a quick learner, like his daddy, he'll cream you." The slap of the screen door was all they heard as they looked at each other. Dwayne's brown eyes seemed misty. Martin found himself sliding down a step and putting his hand on Dwayne's arm.

"Dwayne, I'm really sorry if something I said or did caused this problem. Your mom's upset with me, she says you like me, and I know I like you, but this isn't anything to tear the globe apart, like, can't two people like each other?"

"It isn't anything you did, Martin, it's me. I have a problem I hate to talk about. I hate getting too close to people. You get messed over, you follow? I been messed with." He furtively glanced over his shoulder. "Like, I was a little kid, and ever since then, I have problems dealing straight on with women, and now I'm at a point where they don't even interest me. I'm not into girls at all, I'm scared is what I am." His voice faded as he leaned back on the steps and let the late afternoon browse over him. His athlete's legs and strong chest sucked in the sunshine, letting it calm him, but Martin, alert and on guard, felt a creeping feeling, a slow rising feeling run up his spine and over his head, a tingling sensation that maybe what he had heard on the phone may have truth in it.

"You know a guy named Johnny?" he asked

Dwayne swiveled on the step and glared at Martin. "You've been snoopin' where you shouldn't have been." He pulled himself to his feet. He towered over Martin, sitting on the step, cowering for some reason as though he expected a blow, but no blow came. Dwayne continued to stare at him, more in disbelief than real anger. "How do you know about Johnny?"

"I know nothing about Johnny, but last night, after your folks and I had dinner, and I was doing the dishes," Dwayne's obvious look of dismissal at him doing dishes for his folks sunk in. "I was by the phone and I caught it, and a highly emotional man named Johnny was on the line, and he seemed to be asking for you, but I knew it couldn't be you he was asking for. He wanted you to come down to his place, and he said, am I crazy, it's the same place you've been to for the last six months, and he mentioned guys from Detroit and he said they wanted . . ." Dwayne clapped his hand on Martin's knee.

"You can stop right there. Don't go any further. I know this

Johnny, and I'll handle him. It stops here, okay? Be cool. I know what I have to do." He slipped past Martin and went toward the back door.

"Dwayne, if I can help," he started, but another voice could be heard now, the voice of his mother, hanging over the balcony above, calling out that she smelled something in the kitchen, was he watching the dinner?

# Chapter Eleven

*All is fair in love and war*
*The tender draws the shortest straw.*
*Like Autumn leaves they vanish in the air.*
*Is this the time we say good bye?*
*I call his(sic) room, there's no reply.*
*Tonight we end this fleeting love affair*

*E-L-P "Affairs of the Heart"*

Shit, yes, he'd watched the dinner, watched it growing into a nice little potato and meat festival, watched it simmer to perfection, only to be set aside on the broiler of life when something more important was cooking. Your nap was more important, he wanted to shout up to her, but her blindness made him pause. Yes, I wanted you to have dinner, but not on the first anniversary of the barbecuing of Dwayne Hauk.

Sullenly then, he raised himself to his feet, and laid one hand on the bag of vermiculite set there by Luther. Set there in good faith by Luther. Set there for the use of his beloved wife, the thirteen-year-old ponytailed woman who had almost accused him to his face of running off with their son, the immaculate and pure Dwayne. The student, the athlete, giving up the chance of the scholarship for going it without football, no football, just brains, Claire's real hope for him.

He moved up the stairs, two at a time, and met his mother in the kitchen. "You're up!" he exclaimed, hoping this little offside comment might sway her from further discussion of what took place below. "Is Dad up?"

"Almost up. He's washing and changing his shirt for the grandest meal we've ever had. Is Amy coming?" His mother's voice seemed sincere, almost asking for the expected. Should he respond now with the truth? Why would she believe Amy was coming here for dinner, not even asked over, not even discussed? Why would his mother think Amy would be here?

"We're both up, and you promised Dad dinner, and where is it?" She looked about the kitchen, not knowing that all she asked for was waiting in the fridge, and in the broiler, and in the pan that may have been meant for dairy, but was now re-christened meat; all this he knew, but why did she stand and gaze at him with the eyes of a filleted fish? Why now should he have to answer? Mama. Amy's not here tonight, but don't worry, she'll be here when she can. She's an artist, Mama. She'll come when she can. But worry more about our friends downstairs. There's the real problem brewing. Dwayne's not with us, not with us; he was taken away a long time ago. Why should she care? Why should she even remember the handsome young man from downstairs? Didn't she have enough problems of her own? Didn't he have enough problems of his own, and what about Amy? In that stupid apartment with her friend fucking to pay the rent. Where were Amy's loyalties at that moment? Where, for that matter, was Amy? She knew the address, why wasn't she here? Why was he destined to be here? He should have been moved on by now, looking into his microscope, learning all the things he needed to know. Why was he stuck here with his family and the Hauks and the ever enfolding dream that wasn't even his?

"It's meat and 'taters time, Mom, get Dad in here. I'll set the table. Get ready for a feast." He tried to seem bright and happy. He washed his hands again, and set out the places for three, pulled paper towels out when he found no napkins; there had to be napkins, but his mind was distracted by all that had happened. Claire's abrasive suggestion that he was going to corrode dear Dwayne, dear Dwayne, so sweetly, so secretly corroded already, and then Amy thrown up as if he were supposed to be her keeper, too.

Micah entered the kitchen, spruced up in a fresh shirt, his tails tucked in with a last minute flourish. He looked happy and at peace. He was ready to sit down on a Saturday night when he'd missed prayers, but he would be sitting down with his wife and son. God had been good to him. He unfolded the paper towel, and spread it on his lap as if it were the finest linen.

Martin flipped the gas on under the cooling meat, and headed for the fridge for the salad. He carefully gave a portion to each plate, and his mother, seating herself, murmured over the nice way it looked on the plate. Could she even see it? He pulled the cookie sheet of fried potatoes out and slid a serving onto each plate, and last, he turned off the heat and sliced the sirloin into narrow strips, using the spatula to serve each plate the lovely lightly pink slabs of warm meat. The aromas were pleasant, the only thing missing was a candle and a bottle of good California Chardonnay. But water would do, and Martin filled three tumblers and popped open the fridge for some ice cubes. All ready. And now, as all was prepared, Micah decided it was time to pray.

A minute of prayer would be sufficient, thought Martin, anxiously shredding his towel in his lap, only a minute. But Micah was into blessings tonight, blessings he had and wanted God to know he had received, but Martin, cringing with his concerns for Amy and Dwayne, each in separate compartments in his logical mind, wanted the blessings to end and the real life action to begin, as in eating, and talking, and trying to sort out this mess he had inherited. Tomorrow, he vowed, reaching for a fresh paper towel, tomorrow I have to find an eye doctor to examine Mother. That shouldn't be hard. On Sunday he'd look through the yellow pages, find a responsible doctor, and then he'd have to get Dwayne aside, find out the troubling cause of his relationship with this man Johnny, whoever he was. It was going to be so simple, he figured, finally eating the salad. It was going to be something he could handle for two people he cared about.

The meal was eaten in pleasant conversation. Was it time to move the plants inside yet, could the weather change so quickly that they would be endangered another night out, and Amelia sucked a piece of meat out of a tooth and chewed it again, plodding, plodding through the meal. Martin wanted to shake them, shake the very cloth they ate over, send the whole mess into the sink, but he bided his time, waiting in the dying sunlight for the answer.

The crickets started up, and the TV was turned off. The lace curtains in the front room billowed out gently in the breeze as Martin stood in his briefs and listened for the sounds of the night on the street. A dog barked somewhere up a few doors, and the night seemed to slide over the whole city. Could everyone be going to sleep now? Could everyone just curl up for eight hours and be at peace? What about the taxi drivers he'd run into today? Were they all curled up asleep? Or were they sharing beds? Yours now for six hours, mine for the next eight? Who washed the sheets?

He moved back to the kitchen, shrouded now in darkness, and flipped on the light. The dishes were rinsed and set by the drain board, waiting for a saint or a pixie. He dashed some liquid soap over them and slid them into the sink, starting the water. I'm going to be a doctor, he said to himself, I'm going to be a doctor. He methodically washed each plate and rinsed it in hot water, sprayed the water over the water tumblers, rinsed each fork and knife two times, setting them in the drainer. I'm going to be a doctor.

He felt drunk without wine. It was only nine o'clock, and Micah and Amelia had felt tired after their day, and retired early. The movement in the bedroom, the sound of springs waxing slowly, made him aware anew that his parents still held fire between them. He smiled to know this. He kept up his rinsing and wiping, and grabbed the tablecloth in one wide sweep and held it a moment against his face, the smell of it, the crispness of the cloth, and only let it fall away from him as the scream entered his mind.

A scream, unlike any earthly sound he had ever heard. Nothing like what he imagined a scream to be. This voice, above all voices, came to him in the quiet of the kitchen, and he thought for a moment: an animal attacked. A cat being hurled. An unreal sound that stopped as soon as it started, then it started again. Now it was a wail, a loud wrenching wail that came from below, from down the stairs, from the Hauks' rooms. It came and it stopped and then it came again.

He flew down the backstairs like he had wings, and arrived on the lower landing, out of breath and on edge. He must have gone down those stairs in his underwear with the speed of light. He touched their kitchen door. Searched for the handle, and it opened to him. Martin entered their kitchen in the dark and fumbled for a light switch at the side. The room blossomed into light, a kitchen just like the one above in its layout, but the colors were different here, the edges softened by the ferns and violets sprouting on the sills. The windows shed no light: downstairs was darker, and the darkness of the hall next to the kitchen was suddenly filled with the careening body and face of Claire Hauk.

It was enough to see her standing there, gripping the corner of the wall, enough to see her pain, and he watched her body sag, sag from wounds he couldn't share. Her eyes stared at him, not wanting him to join her pain, only wanting him to know her pain as she stretched out on the floor of the kitchen. He saw no blood, knew the attack on her had come from somewhere else. Where was Luther? God, protect Luther! He didn't deserve this. Martin moved forward, unable to know that he would find no comfort tonight in Luther's grasp, unable to know that the night was not his friend, that his parents, rolling in love above, knew nothing of this, knew only that God provides. What was God providing here, he thought, slipping down the darkened hall. What had God surprised them all with? He stopped by Dwayne's door, ajar and the light coming from the doorway dim, and he pushed the door completely open, and taking a deep breath, he slipped into the room.

It was the same room he had gazed into in a dreamy mood the night before. The room of the athlete and the scholar, the neighborhood hero, the skateboard champ of the neighborhood, the man the kids all looked up to: the same room. Only tonight, it wasn't the same room. It was a room flattened. The only bulk in the room was the broad back of Luther, bent over the bed, pulling a sheet over his son's face.

"No!" screamed Martin, leaping toward the back of Luther, "don't do that! No, never do that. You'll cut off his breath!"

Luther turned on the bed, his huge arms dark and strong against the white of his V-necked tee shirt, his own face running with tears like a flood had come loose and wouldn't stop until God ordered it. He stood and faced the charging Martin and caught him easily in his arms.

"Son, son, quiet now, there ain't no breath to cut off. The breath is gone. He decided that." Luther held Martin strongly and stroked his back. "It's done and over. Martin, be still, now, it's done and over." The wails from the kitchen had turned to soul-searing sobs, the sounds of a mother who had lost her son, and at that moment didn't know if she could tear her own heart out and die with him. The shudders rippled down Martin's arms, and his fingers left his body. His hands had no feeling in them; it was as if the night had stolen his touch. He knew he was crying, he knew it because his shirt was spotted and damp and his nose was running like a little kid's, all over his lips his nose was running, and Luther held him and rolled his head against his shoulder. Letting all the wetness and crying rub against his smooth clean tee shirt.

For as long as it takes to wipe out a life, for as many sunups and sundowns the world asks of its spinning forbearers, for as long as it takes in minutes and hours and weeks and years, to pull one's self together. To move on unsure legs, to straighten a chair, to sit down only to stand again, to begin the pacing, the awkward unsure steps of mourning: these had all to be considered. Considered from a place far above, looking down at this scene, quietly working through the pain of not understanding anything. For what was there to understand? Dwayne was not alive anymore. His body, under the sheet, was motionless, and the arms of Luther after finally letting Martin go, moved to the kitchen to embrace Claire, leaving Martin feeling empty of a handle he could hold to, a grip of understanding, a solid place to lay his head and his real grief.

How alive he had felt that first day when he had seen Dwayne Hauk coming toward him, an aliveness he had never felt before. He had even felt like joking, like flirting. Why had he wanted to get to know Dwayne better? Were they soul mates? Had a destiny begun that now would never be realized? Was Dwayne the one he had been looking for, an unlikely combination, but who stirs the cocktails of love? He roamed the small bedroom, moving the pictures and mementos on the desk, shoving papers aside and then quickly tidying them again. His fingers were nervous and jumpy. He had to know if among those papers was an answer. If Dwayne killed himself, how? Did he intend to do it? Did he leave a written note to say where he was, in his mind, to go this terrible journey alone?

Luther was back in the doorway, his face a mirror of his wife's agony, and he spoke plainly. "Claire's needing a doctor, I think, she's not well. I need to call the police, I guess, get this thing rolling. Martin, what should I say when I call 'em? I don't know what to say."

The pages in his hands were neatly written, a long paragraph that caught Martin's eye. He held it gently and said, "I'll do that for you, Luther. Stay with Claire. She needs you now. I'll call the doctor and the police." He shoved the paper inside his waistband, and ushered Luther back down the hall to the second bedroom. "Does Claire have a regular doctor, or should I just get anyone?" Luther paused at the doorway, looking in on Claire on the bed, sprawled out in mute surrender, and tried to remember the name of her doctor. "Seems like it was Valerie something, Valerie . . . Mason, that's it, she's the one Claire goes to. On Vine, I think, for female complaints." He closed the door and Martin moved in a trance down the hall, touching the walls with his fingertips to guide his way. He passed Dwayne's room, quiet in the dim, so unearthly quiet, and went into the kitchen. The clock in the living room behind him chimed ten times, ten o'clock, early for a Saturday, early for death to reach out and grab a princely reward, untimely torn from this waking slumbering submerged crazy world.

Now that he had said he would do the calling, how did one go about doing it? What did a person say to the other person on the line, just turning from a chat with a co-worker, maybe eating a cookie with their coffee? What did one say that would keep the lid on and yet explode the news? Did he want sirens and police cars swarming over them? Would Dwayne want his parents to go through another hour or two or three of people roaming the apartment, turning the work table with Dwayne's neatly filed pages over onto the floor, seeing his body moved to a gurney, strapped down and rolled out? What if someone should laugh at that point? Laugh out of nervousness, out of fatigue, out of awkwardness. And here he stood, the great doctor-to-be in his underwear, dried tears pulling his puffed eyes into a crazy man's glare. Why was he here? The questions drummed through his head. This had to be handled well.

He moved to the phone and picked it up. The thoughts kept swarming. What to say? Who to call first? Should I go get dressed? Yes, the patient voice inside said, go get dressed. Yes, he replied to himself, a man in clothes thinks better, has his wits wrapped in cotton and linen, has a handle on it. He replaced the phone in its cradle. A feeling of calm came over him: what needs to be done, I will do. He started to head up the backstairs when he felt a draw toward Dwayne's room. He retraced his steps and stood in the doorway, fumbling for the overhead light switch and the room was brilliant with the lights from the three bulbs in the overhead. Now he would know. First, what killed Dwayne, and then, the note, if it was a note he had hastily secreted.

Martin, shaking as if he had a chill he couldn't get control of, moved to the bed and touched the sheet over Dwayne's head. He lifted the sheet slowly, expecting to see the hands still struggling against an unseen enemy wishing to drag him away, but the hands were calm on the chest, no gripping or tearing, and the face was placid, a gentle smile on the lips so carefully carved and molded in perfect symmetry over the set teeth. The face of his friend was relaxed, almost in repose. His forehead was smooth, a rich chocolate smoothness Martin could almost taste as he bent forward to look at the wrappings around his neck. A cleaner's bag. A simple cleaner's bag, stripped off a freshly returned garment. Twisted and torn now, but an hour before, billowing about his face as he sucked in the precious oxygen and let the bag get smaller and smaller, feeling it close over his nose and mouth, feeling the thin plastic come into his mouth, settling there and squeezing him, until the lungs kept looking for air, but there was no air, and Dwayne had to have been grimacing then in his determination, his final pinch of pain, the cry that said: Tear it off and live! But he said no, to be like I am, a sad misfit with a brain I didn't deserve, with all the crap I've dealt with, better to say goodbye now, let it go, Dwayne, let it go, and the brain registered, No oxygen up here, and the little flashlights came on, and they went roaming all over the body, looking for the trouble spot, and the spot said, I'm here, see, I need oxygen to keep going, and the troubleshooters said, We'll get you some, and they couldn't find any way to get the strong hands off the wrap of plastic at the throat.

So simple, to wipe out a life, Martin mused. So simple. The paper rubbed against his stomach, and he knew he had to read it, read it before anyone else did if he ever gave them the chance. He pulled it out and straightened it, sat on the edge of the bed. It was what he thought it was: a goodbye note.

The house was quiet. He heard the tick of the clock in the living room, then one chime for the half hour, 10:30 P.M. His eyes were not focusing properly. He rubbed them hard, then tried to read the handwritten message, but he faltered at this last chore of understanding. None of this did he understand. He hadn't done what he should have, that he understood. He never should have left Dwayne's side after he told him he knew about Johnny. Johnny. The key to this mystery, the Johnny who would fade out of this picture like he never existed: that conniving whimpering using voice on the phone.

The bastard! To use Dwayne like this!

How had he used Dwayne? What part did he play? Had Dwayne used himself in a way he couldn't live with? Martin rubbed at his eyes, cleared them for a moment, and bent intently over the note. The words were plain. There just were not enough of them:

*"Know that I love you, that your life must go on. I cannot tell you how sorry I am that I am not what you think I am. I got off the track a long time ago, and I can't seem to find my way back. Being black isn't easy. Pray for me and be kind to Martin. He understands. D."*

Yeah, I understand. I understand that this note will never get found by anyone. If you got off the track, it's gonna be because you were under scholastic pressure, yeah, scholastic pressure, and Johnny better watch out if he opens his mouth and comes sliding around. Because he's gonna be dead, man, dead as you are. And that's the diagnosis from this doctor to be.

He slid the note into a textbook on the table, and let it stay there.

# Chapter Twelve

*Got to get you into my life . . .*
*. . . another road, where maybe I could see*
*another kind of mind there. You didn't run.*
*You didn't lie. You knew I wanted just to hold you.*
*O-O-h you . . . you were meant to be near me . . .*

*The Beatles*
*"Got To Get You Into My Life"*

The calls finally got made. The answering service for Dr. Valerie Mason referred her calls to her stand-in that weekend. She was in the Catskills with friends, enjoying fellowship and cognac in a very expensive country inn named Cloisters. The young replacement did a passable job at sounding remotely interested in Claire Hauk's precarious hold on sanity, due to an accident her son was involved in. She phoned the pharmacy down the street, Walgreens, open 24 hours a day, and Martin found himself running the three blocks to pick it up. Some relaxant-depressant formula devised by Smith-Kline to take the edge off completely losing it. Luther mutely watched as Martin coaxed her to take the tablets, and let him move her clothes off and slip a nightgown over her nakedness. Three pills put Claire under. Martin washed her face as Luther shrank into the corner, watching Martin handle his wife as if she were thirteen and did indeed need a minister of love. He pulled the wrapper holding her hair into the ponytail out, and smoothed her dark tangles as he murmured to her that God was watching over them all, God knew best, did she love God?

The clock chimed once, and it had to be 11:30 P.M. Time for one more call. Luther watched Martin, nattily dressed in a crisp Navy blue uniform shirt and jeans, feet wedged into moccasins, lift the phone and called emergency for an ambulance. The dispatcher was responsive, quick to realize from the calm voice that the lady was under the care of her doctor, Valerie Mason, who was out of the area, and the doctor felt a rest in the hospital would be the best treatment. Yes, the dispatcher agreed, one was available and on its way. And no sirens, Martin emphasized. No need, agreed the dispatcher. What a sincere friend, the dispatcher noted, who called on behalf of the family, only asking that they follow the instructions of Dr. Valerie Mason, noted staff physician on Long Island and other parts, that no sirens be used, that the patient be handled in a quiet and responsible manner, due to the gravity of her loss. This Martin intimated with a voice so low and calm that he doubted he was really speaking; it was a shadow of a voice, a voice not to be heeded. But heed it they did. One quiet police car rolled up around midnight, and the officer, young and green, came in and surveyed the scene, noted Luther in his detached mood slumped in the easy lounger, noted Martin, the helpful neighbor, who just happened on the scene, fixing dinner for his aged parents above, now long since in bed and unaware of the tragedy below, only nodded and closed his notebook. "Sad, right?" he commented.

"Truly sad, officer. I can't tell you how this came out of the blue."

"Took it pretty hard, did she? Always tough to lose a child. How did it happen and where?" Martin pointed to the hallway and allowed the officer to look under the sheet. His manner changed abruptly. "Jesus H. Christ! He killed himself?"

"It appears that way. The mother is resting now. I got her some downers, from the doctor, but we need to move the son, and as quietly as possible, if you understand." The officer nodded dumbly, the follow up call on the sick woman needing an ambulance suddenly turning into something else all together.

"Those guys can't take him. He's dead. They can't move a body until the coroner says it's okay. I need to make a call." He went back down the hall, and gazed at the mute Luther sitting in the chair. Tough. Really tough. He went out to his squad car.

"Luther, Luther," Martin softly urged. "What do you want done with Dwayne? Did he want to be buried or what?" Biggest question, do you have money for a funeral? "Tell me what you want me to do."

Luther shook his head. "He never said. He didn't like the idea of dirt over him, I know that much, but I don't know what he would have wanted. Could we donate his body for doctors to learn from? Could we do that now, or is that too late? Claire would know."

"Claire isn't able to help us now, so you and I have to decide. Tell me, do you have extra money for a funeral?" Martin hated asking this, hated it more than any other part of the tragedy

"No, we don't have no extra money." He wrung his hands between his knees, and he felt angry at himself, angry that he had to admit he didn't have the money to bury his only son. Tears started coming again, tears he brushed roughly away.

"'We'll donate his body, that's all there is to it," Martin decided. "Can you write Dwayne's name more or less like he would?" Time was moving, Martin knew, precious time.

Luther nodded, stood up and followed Martin back into the

bedroom with Dwayne still on the bed, covered, mercifully, with the sheet. He caught his breath at being back in the room. He watched as Martin, standing up, rolled a sheet of paper into Dwayne's typewriter and started writing his last wishes:

*"To whom it may concern,*
*I've been upset with myself for some time. Afraid I will not pass all my courses this time. I decided to end my life without anyone else being responsible. My parents were the best, I love them and hope they will forgive me, but it's my life to end, and God understands. It is not my wish to be buried, I hate dirt and the thought of lying under six feet of it turns my stomach. Give my body to some doctors. Maybe they'll learn something.*
*Sincerely,"*

And Martin jerked the paper out.

"Sign here, Luther, sign it like Dwayne would have. As best you can." Luther picked up a pen and paused a moment, moved his hand in a larger flourish and wrote out a very believable facsimile. Good enough to be Dwayne's, considering the stress he was under when he wrote it, thought Martin, who had never seen Dwayne's handwriting. This will work. This is the suicide note.

The ambulance, minus the sirens and lights, slid into the spot usually reserved for Claire's grand car. She had left it at the shop that day, to have a taillight replaced and an oil change done, and Luther had whisked her home, giggling and joggled in the big bucket seat next to his tool box.

The cop stopped the men and explained something to them. They nodded and moved up the steps, carrying the gurney, its wheels folded up. The paramedics did their thing, dropped the wheels and moved the gurney down the hall and into Dwayne's bedroom, a tight fit, but they managed. They lifted the heavy young body with some effort on both their parts, gently straightened the limbs. Strapped everything tight. Moved Dwayne out onto the sidewalk where there were no roller-bladers to gaze on their departing hero. One more bites the dust, thought the white high school mentality, two-year graduate of paramedic school. One less black bastard to mess up this society. They left the doors open on the ambulance, and one man got in the driver's seat, and the bigot sat in back, to gaze down on the young man with the plastic around his neck. He said something to the driver, who turned to watch the other pull a sheet out of the rack and put it over his head, grabbing a piece of the plastic and holding it out, like a hang rope. He cackled at his prank, thought it very funny indeed until he pulled the sheet off his face and glanced at the driver to see his reaction. The man turned in the driver's seat was not watching him at all. His face was turned to the back door of the ambulance, and his eyes were round and staring, his face bleached white in surprise. Still smirking, the paramedic by Dwayne's side looked at the open doors, too, and what he saw made him jerk. He shoved the sheet behind him and pulled the cover over Dwayne's face. The smirk left his face as he stared down at his feet, not ever wanting to look back at the open doors.

To peer into the ambulance, to see his son one last time, that's all Luther had wanted to do. But what he saw take place curdled his blood, made him want to tear the paramedic apart, wrap him in plastic, shove his stupid grin down his throat. He wanted to kill that paramedic at that moment, for all the abuse of the slaves, and the lynchings, for all the browbeating his race had taken for three hundred years. He did nothing but look at the man, and his soul helped him then, the perfect soul that God had given him, and he let his hands loose from the clenched fists he had turned them into, let his breath come in slow and exhaled it slow, and the feeling passed. It passed.

"Good night," he mumbled. He turned and went back up to the door Martin was holding open for him. As they pulled the screen door closed against the night moths fighting to get in, they saw a dark sedan pull up by the side of the ambulance, and a stout man in a jogging suit and tennis shoes got out of his car, left it running, and went to the open doors of the ambulance. The paramedic handed him a clipboard, and the man pointed at something, and the paramedic lifted the cover off Dwayne's head, and the man nodded, wrote something down on the clipboard, and tossed it back to the paramedic. The man didn't look up at the house, at the two men standing watching in the screened doorway, just slid back into his dark car and pulled away. That simple. That quickly.

The young officer shut the doors on the ambulance and slapped the side. It moved off. He slowly mounted the steps and stood outside the screen. "I need to tell them where to take the body." He was uncomfortable at that moment, moving from foot to foot, swatting the moths away from his hair. He'd left his hat in the darkened car, laying on the seat in front of the dials, and blinkings, and muted voice of the dispatcher. The hat was the only listener.

"We just found a note, Officer. We think it was the last thing Dwayne wrote, but we can't be sure. You understand." The officer came in then, and Luther turned on the lamp by his lounger, and Martin handed him the page he'd written. The young man leaned over under the light, his holster and belt creaking in their leather richness, and he read quickly. He looked back up at the two men. "Where should they take him?"

"Where do most of the donations go?" That word sounded strange to Martin, even as he said it. We're not talking about canned goods or money in a collection plate. We're talking about a man's body, his earthly form, his God-given shape, the muscles and bones and blood that remain after the soul has gone.

"Columbia Presbyterian mostly, or the City Morgue, for now. We can keep him there until you decide. Cornell takes donors, too, mostly the homeless." And derelicts, addicts, alkies, but he didn't add that. "We'll go Columbia; it's closest. Good night, gentlemen. I'm sincerely sorry about this. My best to your wife, sir, and I mean that." He reached over and shook hands with Luther, who gave nothing back in the handshake. He had nothing left to give.

# Chapter Thirteen

*You don't tug on Superman's cape,*
*You don't spit into the wind,*
*You don't pull the mask off that old Lone Ranger*
*and You don't mess around with Jim*

*Jim Croce "You Don't Mess Around with Jim"*

Luther was in the backyard, gently spading the earth in the corner of the yard, mixing in some of the potting soil from the bag Claire had never touched. He stopped and wiped his face on his red bandanna, and dug the soil again. It felt good to be outside, in the sun and the lightness; it felt good to be alive. He wanted his son to know he would continue to live for them both; he would take care of Claire as Dwayne always said he was going to do for both of them after college. Then maybe another try at pro football. Maybe they had been wrong to want him to finish college; maybe they should have let him do what he did best, play football. But as he remembered it, the spotters for the League suddenly turned cool, seemed to think it might be better for Dwayne, after all, to go academic. They stopped pursuing him. It was then that Dwayne enrolled in college.

Why did that prick at him, that sudden reversal of wanting him so bad, and then not wanting him at all? And what difference did it make now? Dwayne was gone, never to finish college or play football again. He'd ask, anyway. One of these days he'd call up that old high school coach and put it to him plain. What had happened?

Amelia was moving around the kitchen, fixing lunch, her last time to feed Martin before he would spend his last day with Amy and then depart for Groton on the Mason-Dixon line or some such place. The Naval base wasn't that far away, so they would get to see him, she hoped, and Amy had finally given in and bought a second-hand Nissan, so she could chauffeur Martin and his gear up to the base. A good plan, and one Martin looked forward to. His time with Amy had been limited to their night at the gallery, and the afternoon toast at Jane's. He needed to see what she was going to do with her future.

He was standing on the little second floor balcony overlooking the backyard, and he watched Luther with his solemn turning of the soil, saw him pause to wipe his face, his dark skin glistening with the effort. He watched him pause as if thinking, and then toil more as the rich brown soil fell from his shovel. Was he thinking of Dwayne? Of what else could he be thinking? Claire was nowhere in sight. His glimpses of her were few and far between as she moved in a fog-like dream, went through the motions of walking and paying bills, sitting most often on the front porch under her billowing ferns, and letting the whispers of memories calm her mind. What use was there to fret and tear out her hair? What use to continue crying in her pillow, and letting Luther suffer alone?

She came to grips with it almost to the day when Martin was to leave with Amy. She needed to speak to him, to tell him she knew it wasn't his fault that Dwayne died; she knew that in her heart. Something told her that Martin loved Dwayne in a special way, but not an intimate way. Dwayne had simply felt a rush of feeling for the handsome white boy. They were all boys, she shrugged, pulling herself up to touch the fern in leaving. All such simple boys, not knowing what they were, never trusting to find their real value. What a waste, my son, you should never have given up. Our people don't give up.

Micah had been staunch in his feelings about the death of Dwayne. He had accepted it as God's taking back what was his. He never questioned the unfairness of it, never thought about the youth destined for something wonderful ending his own life, for his faith made him see that all choices are God's choices. This was meant to be. This was God's hand at work. Martin saw the futility of debating this point with his father, especially when his father reached for his yamulka every time the name Dwayne came into the conversation. The what ifs went unanswered, the yamulka went on, and if his father had been near the closet housing his prayer shawl, that would have been dragged over his stooped shoulders as well. Amelia, on the other hand, went to her friend's side each morning, brought her a small cake or doughnut wrapped in cellophane, set her teacup on the porch rail, and listened to Claire tell stories about when Dwayne started walking, when Dwayne got his first bike, when Dwayne went to school the first day; she still had his chalky hand-print somewhere stored in the boxes in the cellar. She'd have to get that out and show Amelia, who only nodded and smiled in her quiet reassuring way, knowing she couldn't really see it anymore, but she could hold it, and that was what was important.

On the day that Martin came down the steps, two at a time, to leave for New London Groton, he saw Claire standing by her front door. She was taking down her wreath of beautifully preserved flower blooms, each one dried and lacquered to last forever, and in her hand was the wreath Micah had given her when they first moved in. It was dusty and oddly bent, like the wires had been crushed together in their box in the cellar, but hang it she did, and she smiled at Martin as he stood and watched her, his duffle on his shoulder. She looked at the wreath and gestured upstairs.

"Your father gave me this a long time ago, and I never felt it was right to have it on our door. It's not very pretty, is it?" She tilted her beautiful black head, and the creases around her eyes seemed to soften. "But I think it's right now. Maybe I've grown a new pair of eyes."

He dropped his duffle and moved to her, and she turned to hold him, and the wonderful smell of gold and flowers and queens being fanned by servants filled his nostrils. Claire Hauk was going to be just fine. Martin wondered if he could borrow some of her life, bottle it, carry it with him, but the only memory he would never forget was the touch of Dwayne's fingers next to his on the lace curtain.

# Chapter Fourteen

*You take a look around the world*
*The future never waits*
*We're skating on the thin ice*
*And we're in the hands of fate*
*What we need's a little redirection*
*To find our blue lagoon*
*You know it won't come a moment too soon*
*Black Moon*

*E-L-P "Black Moon"*

The day with Amy was as good as she could make it, with her laughter and her hugs and quick kisses on his cheek. She knew he was hurting with a deep feeling of loss he couldn't explain, couldn't put his finger on, but the very few things he was able to tell her in a soft voice gave her the canvas to finish the picture. She murmured her understanding at his unexplainable confusion.

They were seated in her car, half way to Groton, parked on a bluff overlooking the Sound, eating sandwiches, deviled eggs, and vinegar chips. A small bag of chocolate chip cookies sat on the dash. A thermos of coffee was passed between them.

"Dwayne would have liked this view. He liked . . . what did he like? Amy, I never got to find out what he liked. He never talked about himself. Everything I know about Dwayne I heard from his parents. Isn't that odd that I feel so close to a man I never knew?" He chewed his mouthful of sandwich and waited for the thermos to pass to him again. Sipping the strong black coffee, the feeling of despair came over him again, the emptiness of his world, a world he had only begun to know. Amy only nodded, listening quietly as she nibbled a cookie.

"How much ignorance there is in the world! Outright ignorance in this day and age. The wars still going on in the world, the grasp for power is stronger than the joy of living. I hardly want to call myself human when I'm part of all this, and in a way, I am. Someone once said, if you're not working on the solution, then you're part of the problem, or something like that. Dwayne killed himself because he didn't respect himself, and how hard it must be to respect oneself when you face people every day who look down on you and your race because of your color. Your color, mind you, Amy, the one thing you have no power over! Anything else, almost, we can change, but this skin color is buried deep. We're Jews, but we're not treated like inferiors because we're Jewish; we're hated because we aren't Christian, we worship differently, and we've been ornery enough to make some money and hang onto it. And our people are blessed with good minds, most of them, with a few exceptions like Goldstein the landlord, but he's just ill, that's all there is to that, just ill.

"I saw him once, coming to collect the rent, and the man smelled of oily money, from his greasy collar to his dirty nails, and I watched him take Dad's check and bow and go back down the steps, and I followed him, and stood by the door when he went over to the Hauk's. He rang their bell, Amy, and stepped back to wait, and when Luther opened the door and invited him in, he looked frightened, just plain scared, and he shook his head, pointed to the doormat, and Luther laid the check there for Goldstein to pick up. He didn't want any possibility of Luther touching him, isn't that crazy? How does that make a man of Luther's intelligence feel, huh? Luther never made mention of it, he simply understood and let it pass. But for all these years this shit has happened, Amy, and it had to get to people not as strong as Luther. Maybe just the crushing stares from whites could cripple a black boy as he grew up, in spite of his family life. Or his church life, or all the Black preachers talking about there'll come a day, oh, glory, things will get better. Our time is coming, but when it doesn't come, what's a man now to do?" He had run on, and he stared down at his half-eaten sandwich. Amy nudged his arm with the thermos and he took a swallow.

"You don't know that Dwayne killed himself because he was tired of being looked on as inferior. You're only guessing that. Didn't someone tell me he was a great high school football star? Didn't his note say he felt he wouldn't pass his courses, didn't it say that? Being dumb is not a happy thought to carry, not that he was dumb, but what if he really felt he had to be twice as good as the whites just to get attention? What if he could only be as good as the whites, and that wasn't gonna be enough. It's like what women have had to do over the centuries: work twice as hard for half as much money, and still get to do all the housework. It stinks, I agree, and sensitive people get mowed over. Tough ones make it somehow, but Dwayne just wasn't tough enough, maybe, oh, I don't know, listen to me babble."

She glanced out the window at the rippling Sound a half mile below, the gray sweep of it moving ever onward toward the ocean, the clean, strong crashing waves of the ocean with no thought about its color. The ocean beaches ahead would be clear; the surf would roll its crashing waves over white sands and shoreline rocks, and the swirling chocolate of debris, sucked under by this sweep of rivulets joining rivulets, acting like a vacuum cleaner, pulling all the dirt out and down and away, into Mother Ocean to sift through and sort out, consume it by crashing it to pieces against the shore, drive it to the bottom and lay sand over it. The oceans cleaned up the rivers with their immense spaces to hide things and their vast hospitality. No wonder seven-tenths of the earth was water! The three-tenths left, crawling with mankind spewing its concrete, asphalt, and chemicals, needed all that resource for its daily sponge bath. The rivers were only carrying away mans' bath water.

Martin crumpled up his tuna fish sandwich wrapper and stuffed it back in the bag. He reached for a cookie and took a big bite. "I'm going to have to get tough, aren't I, Sis, if I'm going to get through the next six or seven years, to get to where I can do some good in this world? How the hell did you do it? You should give me some lessons, you little street fighter." He touched her hair and tucked it behind her ear. She gave him a gentle look.

"I did what I had to do and you will to, but the goals are probably different, yours and mine. Mine were for me, Martin, and for me only. Call it what you will, and you'll probably call it selfish, but I wanted to express my idea of art, and make people think I was the greatest thing since Goya, or Van Gogh, or Michelangelo, or whoever you think is the greatest artist of all time. A vain wish. But you, my friend, seem to be bent outward, toward all of mankind. You want to save souls, heal the sick, calm the rivers, stop bigotry, war, vermin, plague. Ah, big dreams, Mr. Microscope. You're gonna need power and knowledge to get that job done. You should go into politics, Martin, after you're through your training. Use your skills to heal the politics that guide this world. Now that would be something to work toward. Another Roosevelt or Churchill."

"You've got my number, Amy. I have some big ideas, but I have to slow down now, slow down while I catch up with where I want to be at forty. God, forty! Doesn't that sound old? But I will be almost forty, well, thirty-five, before I finish school and the Navy and any specialty I decide on. Somehow I don't see myself delivering babies in a small town in Missouri." He checked his watch and started gathering up the lunch papers. Amy offered him a last sip of coffee and he finished it off. "Cork it up, driver, we're on our way to the future!"

The last few miles before they came to New London Groton were spent in telling tales on each other, remembering holidays and gifts they gave each other, what books and songs they liked, what movies they enjoyed, what actors and actresses were sure fire, and the miles flew by and the time of parting drew near.

As it was close to dark, they decided to stop and get Amy a room near the base, so she wouldn't have to drive back in the dark to New York City and her bizarre living arrangement. Martin had skirted that issue the whole trip, but now as they neared the time of separating, he brought it up in an offhand way.

"Say, that friend of yours, Jane, is top drawer, Amy, really a fine person. How did you meet her?" Her hands tightened on the wheel but she answered casually enough.

"Oh, through friends at the gallery. She was trying to paint at the time, and not getting on with it. She really just liked the tubes of color, would buy them, or her family would, she has some money behind her, and just admire them, but she never liked to get dirty with them, you know, squidge out a line and swirl it around, then try another color and mix the two to get a shade. Jane just doesn't understand shade. She wants all the colors pure. Did you notice that striped chair in her front hall? That's her design. She laid out the white and black and yellow, but if you look real close, there's a tiny red line, like pinstriping, between each color to keep them apart. Now if that had been me, doing that print, that black would have crossed over into the yellow, smudged the red, sent a tornado-like funnel into the white, but that's me. And no print shop would have moved that design over onto the fabric floor for a sixty dollar a yard item. Much too chancy. Too pricey to fool with fabric that way, fabric design for the most fastidious people has to conform, you know, has to be what they expect. Jane found her niche, found it purely by luck when she did that piece of fabric. The buyers gobbled it up, asked for more, and she kept all her tubes by her palette, and went to solid colors already woven, cut them into the precise divisive patterns she liked, keeping all the colors separate and somehow it sold. Her checkered ideas are really quite original, but she likes strong hues, no mixing. Strange, though, she never wears strong colors herself, and her apartment . . . did you notice? All done in blue, with off-white touches, nothing bright or snappy. Rather subdued." She reflected a moment and Martin stared at her without realizing it. One question about Jane had opened up this whole Pandora's box of information on Jane's feelings about design.

"She seemed to care a lot about you," he ventured tentatively. Her eyes never left the road, but her answer came hesitantly.

"We tried to . . . be more than just friends. I'm afraid I failed her in that. But she tried, and I tried, and we ended up being just friends, not the real friend she really deserves, and I don't want you to get the strange idea that she hurt me in any way. Everything we tried, we tried together . . . " she stopped, bit her lip. "Anyway, she'll find the right person. She needs a special person in her life. She's not a loner, like me." Her harsh little laugh sounded like a cut off cry, but she handled it well, as well as she was handling the wheel on the two lane into Groton.

Three miles to the base, he noted, three more miles, and then she'll be gone. He hated goodbyes, made Amelia and Micah say their farewells in the kitchen and not on the porch in broad daylight. What would the neighbors think of all this hugging on the front porch? Instead he had taken his leave only to fully expose the neighbors to his tearful parting with Dwayne's mother. Sad mixed up world. What was he afraid of?

❧

Tall light standards every thirty feet along a chain length ten-foot-high security fence were the first sign of the approaching base. Squat buildings could be seen flicking by; from the distance they looked half buried in the earth. Some taller platforms held watch guards, patrolling slowly in their fourteen feet square well above the ground. Martin rolled down the window and breathed in the air coming up from the ocean he knew had to be over the rise, and down the tree lined shrubbed bank to the beach. He wondered how they kept the base private. Couldn't anyone just bring a boat in? He'd find out, he knew, that and a lot of other questions about how things worked on a Naval base.

The first thing he found out was that security was tight. The fence broke into a wide barrier of double meshed metal poles and then into concrete blocks, tall and formidable, where the gate started. They turned into a lane that narrowed in about fifteen feet to a concrete blockhouse where the guard stepped out behind the long bar blocking the entrance. The end was sunk in concrete with an eight-inch lens moving slowly back and forth, scanning the drive in, taping the newcomers. Amy rolled her window down and smiled at the guard. He didn't smile back.

"Hi," she said cordially. He ducked under the bar blocking their entry and asked, "What business?" Now that was welcoming. Martin fumbled in his side bag, pulling out the envelope holding his commission and assignment papers. He reached over past Amy and offered them to the guard. He crisply took them, turned sharply, and made a neat duck under the bar.

"I bet he's fantastic at limbo," Amy whispered, giggling, and trying to remain serious when she really wanted to laugh out loud. All this mystery, this secretiveness. Did they think they were really fooling her? Martin shook his head in warning, trying to be serious now that he was here. He didn't need any trouble just getting in the gate.

The guard returned and handed the papers to Martin, avoiding Amy's hand as she reached to make the transfer. "Please, ma'am, these are the Lieutenant's. You may step out now, sir." He walked around the car and opened the door. "You have gear I can help you with?"

"Here?" Martin asked, surprised that they wouldn't let Amy drive him in.

"Here, sir. That's the order, no visitors after six P.M. Sorry you weren't told." His voice emitted not a tone of sorrow. Duty, that was what he was into, just following orders.

"My bag, Sis." Martin nodded to her, and she released the trunk and it popped open. The guard opened his holster, and moved to the back of the car with the pistol extended.

"Oh, my God, Martin, what am I leaving you to?" She nervously laughed.

"It's the military way, that's what I've learned to love about this way of life. Want to be a career man, Amy, just so I can have this happen over and over." He got out and the guard put his pistol back in his holster, watching carefully while Martin pulled out the duffle from the trunk. He shouldered the pack and held it with one hand, his small hand bag held in the other.

"Got it, sir?" His former offer to help now appeared not to be needed. Headlights beyond the bar came straight toward them, an open military Jeep with two riders, the driver and a passenger. Amy started to get out of the car, but the guard politely said, "Stay in the vehicle, ma'am."

Martin said, "May I kiss my sister goodbye, if you watch real close, and I don't try anything funny?" The guard blinked once, nodded, and Martin took that as okay, so he walked around to Amy's open window and put his face close to hers. She held his face in her hands and kissed his nose. His hands were occupied with his gear, but he kissed her back on the cheek.

"Love you, Amy, give my love to Mom and Pop. Go see 'em for me, will ya?" She nodded, yes, she would, and he moved toward the bar, which now raised slowly. He stood in the headlights from both cars. Like a condemned man, he faced the base. Why the shots didn't ring out right then always mystified him.

The uniformed man in the passenger seat swung his body over the Jeep door, and saluted the guard, who returned it smartly. He walked to Martin and relieved him of the heavy duffle, easily swinging it over his shoulder, and reached for the side bag in Martin's other hand.

"I'm okay, I got it," but the man held his hand out more firmly, and Martin handed it to him. The young crewcut man took both the side bag and the duffle into the guard house, and Martin was waved to wait while they made a cursory inspection of the contents, unzipped the side compartments, peered and felt around, pulled out his electric razor and really gave that a once over, acting as if they had never seen one before. Martin moved from one foot to the other, feeling awkward with the Jeep lights on him and Amy sitting behind the now lowered bar, watching with the motor running.

Apparently satisfied that he was who he said he was, and his gear didn't carry any contraband, the young crewcut man carried the gear to the back of the Jeep and placed it firmly on the left side of the rear seat. He nodded to the guard, who saluted again, and the guard called out to Martin.

"Safe to board, sir." He saluted Martin. "You may leave now, Miss. Good night." He reentered the block house and wrote some notes on his clipboard. Martin got in the right rear seat and sat down. Amy backed out of the drive and paused at the main road. She put the car in park, and jumped out, running in front of the headlights and jumping up and down in her jeans and sweatshirt. "I love you, Martin, know that I love you!" she yelled. The guard came out immediately and watched her as she ran back around the fender and crawled into the car. The man driving the Jeep turned around and looked intently at Martin.

"My sister, guys, what can I say?" The men looked at each other, and overwhelmed with the seriousness of their mission, they didn't even crack a smile.

The building they stopped in front of had absolutely no character; no shrubs in front, no trees close to the low placed windows. Its three stories stood as a block of concrete with no life in it at all. His plans to have a neat apartment off base vaporized in front of his eyes. This was going to be, he realized, where they put him. For now, anyway, this was home.

Men in fatigues, smoking on the side of the building, casually eyed Martin, and several men walked by talking and stopped while he got out. He nodded to the men as one, and followed the driver and the crewcut young man into the building and down the long corridor to a set of metal stairs, which they quickly clanked up, moving faster than Martin was used to, and he followed them as gamely as he could. Two weeks off had softened him, he admitted. Time to get back into it.

At least he had a room to himself, he gratefully realized when they turned on the lights in a room about the size of a large bathroom. A bed with a neatly folded blue blanket, a desk, a small stand of drawers, a metal cupboard, and a cubbyhole of a closet. No door. They chucked his duffle into the closet space, set his side bag on the one lone straight back chair, saluted in unison, and pulled the door shut behind them as they left. Well, he thought, touching his temple in a soft salute: *same to you, boys.*

How he became used to the stiffness of the base, the phony salutes, the silly orders he couldn't understand the use of, gave him a surge of pride. He was going to adapt, he wasn't going to let his dream falter now when he had come this far. If only Dwayne could still be alive, to see his own dreams come true. A rip-off was how he felt about Dwayne every time he thought about the young athlete who never got his chance. Well, that would take time to settle, but in his heart Martin knew he would settle the score.

The military classes he attended perfunctorily, his real classes in the medical sciences were what he looked forward to. The four-year Bachelor of Science degree was behind him now, he had passed the MCAT in his junior year with top marks. The medical school associated with the base hospital was an above average training center. They had all the modern technology, the scanners and scopes, the finely tuned electron microscope Martin itched to be near. Lectures and labs took up most of his first year and he moved with quick sure steps through his second year. The third year he began his clinical studies, reveled in medicine and surgery, even liked OB-GYNE ("Oh-BeGin, stated his proctor, it's called Oh-Begin"). He became closer than he meant to with the women who came to the clinic, doing pap smears and birth control conferences, moved with ease through Psych and Neurology. Even Pediatrics gave him a boost. He found he liked dealing with kids, maybe because they were mostly well, but he did spend one week in an off-base hospital, working with head wounded children, and that was hard on him. Mostly the result of parental negligence, these kids had been hurt while riding in trucks or cars with their dads, who vowed they loved them, letting the two-year-old sit on his lap and help Dad steer, right up until the time the truck hit the concrete divider, or a semi, or the ditch. Why weren't the dads having the tops of their heads sutured in place? Either they were dead or just lucky. Martin wrote off Peds in his mind as a future specialty. He would have too much anger at the cause of these tragic accidents to be effective. And, God, he promised, I'm going to be effective.

In his second year, he sat for the USMLE, the licensing exam, and he knew when he left that crowded, silent, guarded room that day, he knew in his mind that he had passed it. He wasn't looking back. He never reread any of the questions, just punched the right number code at the computer, and moved on. He left a full thirty minutes before the test was officially over. The proctor escorted him out, and he ran back to the wards he was covering  for another student. He was back in a similar room, only not as many crowded in that day, for his fourth year final, he like to call it, the USMLE crawling over him again, the second exam, the big one. When he passed that one, and he did, very handily, he was now an older Martin, a four-years-older Martin, but now he was an M.D., a medical doctor. He wrote a long letter home that night, typed it in his room after a party off-base, a small celebration at the home of one of the medical officers, a congratulatory party that bored Martin after the men started firing questions about the exam: how'd you do on that one, why didn't you say such and such to that one, why a suture instead of a staple. He frankly got bored and left early, tearing back to the silent room that kept watch over him, to pound out the letter he knew would bring happiness to Amelia as Micah read it to her. Micah had finally, at Martin's insistence, taken Amelia to the eye doctor, but he had only shaken his head, rolled the light up off his forehead, touched their hands, and smiled as they left. Martin had sent the eighty dollars for the exam to his father, but the check was never cashed. It was too late. Amelia was now totally blind, but content to have Micah read to her and thread her needles.

Martin entered the base hospital on the First of July, rated as a PGY-l: post- graduate, first year. They called him an intern, the patients called him Doctor, and he called himself proud. He'd almost gotten to it, The Golden End. So many sleepless nights poring over Gray's, memorizing the pharmaceuticals, calling into memory the Greek and Latin, tying it all back to the whole thing: being a doctor. The hours on shift turned into weeks when he barely left the sleeping lounge, on call twenty-four hours a day, getting two, maybe three hours of rest, but he kept at it. Sometimes, in the dimmest hours, when he alone would be walking the halls and talking to nurses and looking at charts, Dwayne's face would float before him, silently smiling at him, happy for him. Why be happy, you fool? You're gone. Damn you, you're gone.

He had opened a box one day, completely unaware of the contents, and inside, wrapped in tissue paper, was Micah's wreath, only Claire had woven in some of her own delicate pressed and lacquered blooms, a dried sunflower, a red dianthus, frozen in its bloom; ivy curly and sharp to his fingers, and the wreath looked beautiful now after she'd brought it back to life and added her touch. A small card simply printed: In memory of your friendship, to me and to my son. That's all. No letter, no postcard. Just that one time, that one wreath. He put it on the wall over his bed, and when someone mentioned it, he said, "A keepsake. A friend who moved on." That's all he ever told anyone about Dwayne Hauk and his mother.

In his second year at the hospital, he found himself relieved of most of the rounds, left to find the arena he would fight in, and his hands slipped back comfortably to the microscope; it was here he found his greatest discoveries. If man was not meant to die of disease, maybe here he could be of the most help. Fight the damn bugs. He needed to decide, needed to go before the licensing board. He needed that license to get on with his work, whatever it was to be.

The third-level United States Medical Licensing Examination was held in a still smaller auditorium. The candidates sitting that day numbered one hundred and thirteen, by his exacting count. Of the subjects covered, reading, comprehension, physics, chemistry, biology, organic chemistry, and an original essay on medicine and what it meant to him, there were forty-five possible points. Martin got thirty-nine. He was licensed. The Navy wanted him back now, and for the next two years, he went for submarine duty, hardship time they called it, cut his time in half they called it, but he suffered like hell when he went through the basics of a dive. Struggled against his mind and lungs whenever 'Dive' was heard, held himself together and thought about the damn plastic over Dwayne's mouth and nose, and somehow only that image kept him breathing slowly, in and out, in the recycled air. Kept him calm when he knew he was breathing for both of them. So cool was he that midshipmen, standing on the brink of freaking out, turned to him and found strength in his handshake and smile, found solace when he felt he was giving them nothing but a pill, gave them the courage to say, "Man, if the Doc ain't scared, I ain't scared." But the doc was scared. He was almost through with the Navy, and they with him. He hadn't fallen apart, he'd kept his shirt tucked in, and soon, very soon, he would start his journey of redemption.

# Chapter Fifteen

*Good men through the ages*
*trying to find the sun.*
*We wonder*
*Who will stop the rain?*

*Creedence Clearwater Revival*
*"Who Will Stop The Rain?"*

It was cool that morning, so cool that his usually warm hands felt like they needed gloves, and he pulled the warming wool over his fingers and stretched the cuffs up his wrists. A good morning. A damn good morning to be leaving. He and the Navy had pulled together; he had done his time, he was out, they were still in. Still in time, still marching, still drilling. Still swabbing. He had some swabbing to do. But where?

The base commander had asked him to stop by before he left, had offered him coffee and a cigarette, which he had long since set aside. "The Navy would like to keep you on board, Lieutenant Schoenfield. You demonstrated a lot of service-useful implementations in your dedication to duty. Don't take us lightly. We will be happy to have you stay on. Free medical, free dental, free housing; let us be your future, Lieutenant, you have a golden future with the United States Navy." He said it proudly, stuffed out his smoke, and rounded the desk. "Can I take your silence as a yes?"

Martin paused a moment, observed the outstretched hand accepting him, but knew in his heart he was not cut out for the Navy, even though the Navy had served him well. He just knew he had to see another horizon, another application of his skill; he knew without thinking further that he and the Navy were separating today.

"Sir, with all due respect, I have to leave the Navy. I love the Navy, don't get me wrong, but I feel I am a scientist at heart, an explorer, a researcher if you will, and that I think is my final destiny, Sir. Thank you for asking me to stay on, I appreciate your offer, I am flattered by your offer, but I have to move on. Thank you, thank you," he murmured to the commandant, oh, wait, the commander, how had that confused him? The titles. Yes, the mystifying titles.

He knew in that instant that he had not mistaken the words, that commandant and commander had fused together in his mind, and he knew he was not of a military mindset. He knew it as fully as he remembered Amy jumping into the headlights and screaming, "Martin. I love you!"

It was all behind him now, and at the same time it was before him. The grueling hours of labs and classes, clinics and exams, prodding patients and listening for bowel sounds: all behind him unless he chose to use those skills in private practice. He needed some time off, some time to collect his thoughts. The chance of finding a position would come soon enough, he felt, but for now he just longed to drift awhile. A trip home was of primary importance; Micah's hastily short notes were not telling him what he needed to know about the state of their health. Amy had kept in touch, with him and with them as she had promised, but she never looked too deeply, never told him about eyesight and blood pressure, how the apartment looked, if they had enough to live on. Nothing but how good the food was, and the Hauks were certainly wonderful. She had done a portrait of Claire. Did he know she had marvelous bone structure?

Yes, he thought, gazing out the cab window, I remember that bone structure. I saw it in her son's face and in his hands. I will always remember the structure. And what brought it down. What brought it down was the same thing he had seen underlying attitudes in the Navy. The Black officers seemed to be always on edge, always slightly afraid they might come off as uppity, assertive, even equal. The ones that got on best played second fiddle, seemed to crave only the seconds, never reaching for the limelight and stating, "I deserve this, same as you." Was it that inbred, if not inborn, so blatantly imprinted that the Black men and women in the Navy couldn't get away from it?

He caught a train in Groton, and sped through the dying trees of autumn in the east. The days had been cool and the leaves were turning into brilliant gold, auburn and crisp before the snows tore at them and sent them spinning to the bonfires. The arrival time had been left open; he only told Micah sometime on the twenty-eighth and probably by train. A phone call from the station in Co-op City would have to do. The thought of an Ethiopian cab driver made him smile. It would be nice to see the same man again, the one who'd touched Amelia with gentleness, concerned for the bugs in her eyes. How or when he arrived home seemed not to matter. The seat in front leaned back on him and he leaned back as well, curled up on his side and slept most of the way into Co-op City's station.

"Co-op City! Co-op City!" The porter's voice awakened him, pulled him out of his dream, a dream of pleasant achievements, where he replaced an eye in its socket, and it worked so well that he turned in the dream to the next table in the operating room's amphitheater, and carefully reattached a finger to a small hand, and the eyes above the glass shone in wonder and the sound "O-o-o-h" filled the air. Passengers began to move around him, picking up articles strewn on the journey, wrapping mufflers around the heads of children, stuffing empty wrappers and soda cans into paper bags to be left on the seat for the porter.

"Need any help, ma'am?" he asked the lady across from him, bundling her sprout into mittens and scarf.

"No, I'm fine, but thanks for asking. You coming home to visit or on leave or what?" she asked, noticing the uniform.

"Just finished my tour, ma'am, and anxious to get home, see my folks, you know, enjoy the break."

She smiled at him and touched his arm. "We need more men like you," she sighed, resting her hand on her boy's head.

"Thank you, ma'am, I'll keep that in mind."

The last stragglers were moving down the aisle as Martin stood and stretched. He buttoned his uniform jacket and stepped into the aisle, reached back under the seat for his side bag and swung it easily out and up. Ready if you are, he said to himself.

Wind caught his breath as he stepped down from the train, cold wind, colder than he had expected for late fall in New York. Snow must be coming in, he felt, looking back and forth up the platform for a familiar face. Why would anyone be there? No one knew when he'd be coming. It would have been nice, though, he admitted, if someone had been there. He stood in line with the other shivering passengers, waiting for the porter on the platform to hand out the luggage from the outside compartment. He was almost to the head of the line when he felt a hand on his shoulder. He swung around jerkily, startled by the feel of the unexpected hand. His face was five inches from Luther's.

"It's you!" he exclaimed, and his happiness at seeing a face from home, a face that cared about him, a face he would never forget as long as he lived, made him throw his arms around Luther and kiss him soundly on both cheeks. The lady in front of him in the line, the same one he had offered to help in the crowded aisle inside the train, turned to stare at him, and he couldn't resist it, he just had to say it now, or pay hell for it in the next life.

"My dad, ma'am, can you believe it? My dad, come to get me. Only three weeks after hip surgery, that's the miracle. Aren't we lucky?" She continued to look from the Naval officer's face back to the sturdy Black man in work clothes. She lifted her shoulders in a shrug, tugged her little boy swathed in woolen closer to her, and turned back for her bags. A short man rushed forward to greet them and they walked away together, but the woman took one last little peek over her shoulder at the strange father and son pair.

Luther chuckled to himself as he lifted the duffle and carried it under his arm like it was a beach blanket. Martin felt pride that Luther could be that strong, and he enjoyed mightily the strange looks they got as they walked down the crowded platform toward the street entrance.

"You've gained some weight, Leftenant, that you have. You look almost as big as Dwayne was. 'Course you've got some to go, and you'll need some shoe polish on 'ya, but you're gonna pull, all right." He kept on laughing to himself, went ahead of Martin up the stairs in the terminal and pushed open the heavy brass-plated doors. The wind pushed them along the street and talk was hard to do when the air struck their lips and made their uncovered heads sting.

Luther crossed two streets and cut behind a van parked in an alley. In front of the van was his work truck. Real close to the terminal. No fuss, no problem. He tapped on the door of a warehouse, and a man opened the door, saw it was Luther, and reached out his hand to welcome him in. Luther shook his head. "Not tonight, Frank, got to get my son home. Thanks for lettin' me use your spot." The white man nodded, glanced at Martin up by the work truck, and smiled. "Nice lookin' boy you got. Bet you're glad he's home." In the dark, maybe he actually thought I was Luther's son, he wondered, and if I was his son, I'd be proud of my old man. Mighty proud. Solid, protective old bear of a Luther. What would his life have been like had he been born black to Claire and Luther Hauk? Martin Hauk. He even liked the name. Dr. Martin Hauk. Man, what a thought. Not the Jewish doctor, son of Micah and Amelia Schoenfield, but Martin Hauk, son of Claire and Luther Hauk, Dwayne's little brother. Older brother.

"Messy night coming, boy, we're in for an early sleetin', I can feel it. The old folks will be tampering with their thermostats tonight, imaginin' all sorts of mysterious illness down below. I'll be up all night if I'm right." He unlocked both doors and placed the duffle carefully behind his seat before settling in and starting the engine. He looked at Martin in quiet appraisal. "Hear anything different?" Martin listened to the engine, unaware of the sounds that emitted from it. "Listen closely," Luther urged, touching his foot harder on the gas pedal. "Now you hear it?" Martin tried to grasp the sounds of the engine, how it might be different, and he landed on an answer. "Smoother, I'd say, like it got oiled real good, or you changed the trannie." The motor pool boys had used that term. He still couldn't change oil.

"You're on it, mister, you got it. How'd you know? That wheeze is gone, ain't it? Got it out. Put in a rebuilt transmission, forked up four hundred dollars and rebored the lower half, three valves replaced, but she's as good as new. I knew you'd notice!" He beamed with pleasure as he pulled the vehicle out of the alley and picked up speed on the one way out of the terminal mess that left most of the traffic behind. Should have been a cab driver, thought Martin, the way he nipped in and out and shot that old truck with its sparkling new guts out of the city and onto the interstate for ten miles, then turned on the Bruckner exit and crept up Hill Road and through the old neighborhood.

"How'd you know what train I'd be on?" asked Martin, climbing out of the truck in front of the house. The full dark had slipped in, and the lights from the building were on, downstairs and up. No one was at the window upstairs tonight. Luther locked the truck and carried the duffle under his arm.

"Didn't. Claire called the base, they said you'd checked out at four, knew you had to get to a train. Micah said you was coming in at Co-op, so I just checked the schedule, saw three trains come in and just waited. Didn't want you pulling in and no family there to see you." Hours he'd been there, had to be hours, thought Martin, following Luther up the damp steps. The wind was gentler here, but they must have had some rain, the grass smelled of it.

Their footsteps alerted Claire. She was at the door in her jogging suit, Claire, who never did more than stroll, holding the door open for them, and it seemed so natural to go into their home first, as natural as the spring lamb turning to its mother. She held him close, touched his face, beamed like she was ready to burst with pride, then said, "Well, Doctor, this calls for a celebration. Wait till I go up and get your mom and dad." She hurried through the kitchen and up the back stairs, calling out ahead of her, "He's here! Luther's got him! He's here!" Moments passed as Martin stood in the living room, touching the lamp and the back of the lounger; nothing had changed. The same clock ticking. The same hassock with an ashtray and pipe perched in the middle. The Hauks were intact.

Micah came through the doorway and into the kitchen first, in his bathrobe and slippers, and behind him Amelia followed, smiling with a radiance he couldn't explain. Claire's face behind, beaming over the pair, looked like a mother angel shepherding her flock, guiding her people toward their goal. Micah's face lit up on seeing his son, moved his feet in a fast shuffle toward grasping him at last, and he kissed him soundly on his forehead and put his arm around his shoulders. He turned to Amelia, and brought her hand toward Martin. "He's here, Mother, he's home." Amelia started to cry then. She fumbled for

Martin's face, and pulled him down toward her smallness. When had his mother gotten this small, he reflected, she was more like a house wren, not the sturdy fast-moving woman he remembered being raised by. His arms went around her and he couldn't help himself: he picked her up. She squealed with surprise and delight, and he held her in his arms like a groom bringing his bride over the threshold.

"Put me down, you fool!" she laughed, feeling the center of attention and not sure if she really liked it. He restored her to her feet and she straightened a lock of hair. "Och, what can I do with you, and you a doctor now. You're too old to spank." Micah kissed her cheek and Claire called from the kitchen.

"Time to celebrate! I've got wine and cheese, and some rye crackers, you always ask for them and all I usually have are soda crackers, so come, everyone, come on! Martin's home!" Her voice filled the room with a warm excitement. The glasses were poured, a very nice Liebfraumilch, and Martin caught a glimpse of three more bottles set to cool in the fridge when Claire was bringing out a bunch of purple grapes, frosted with sugar and chilled. "The sugar's to kill the sourness, they're not very sweet I found out after I'd bought them. But the sugar helps, and they're so pretty frosted." She bubbled on, hovering over each of them, refilling glasses, getting napkins, moving around the kitchen and the living room, lighting candles, turning on a radio to a soft blues station. It was joy for Martin to see her this way, to know that she was alive and enjoying her life. His thoughts did not want to turn dark, no, not tonight. He didn't want to remember the last time he'd been here, the night of Dwayne's death. His promises to come home for a weekend, get away from the base and his duties and see them had never found a way to happen. His stay at Groton had been a sustained effort to finish as fast as possible.

"It's great to be home, to see you all. Still playing checkers, you two?" He sat back and sipped his wine while the two older men began their detailed explanations of their last game, which Micah won, and Luther proudly proclaimed that at last Micah was as good as he was, or almost, and the two went at it again, over the almost, and finally a piece of paper was brought out and the diagrams were started: first play, next play, mistake play.

"Martin, I want to show you something," said Claire, picking up her glass and urging him to follow her. "We'll be right back, Amelia, just want to show him our workroom." Amelia smiled and nodded, touching Claire's hand on her shoulder. Claire moved down the hall, flicked on the light and entered Dwayne's old room. Martin followed her, his glass in hand, but he wished he had refilled it for this visit. He'd need a good gulp to get him through this.

Claire pushed the half-opened door wide, and flipped the switch. The room was not a bedroom anymore: it was a fairy land of dried flowers and wreaths. Ribbons and bows in all colors covered the walls, silver chains and golden stars were lined up on shelves, little bird houses peeked at him, small porcelain angels were woven in angel hair and sat lined up on a work table where Dwayne's bed had been. The floor was covered in tinsel and crepe paper and tissue wrappings. They crunched softly as he walked in, and he looked up at Claire.

"Did I break something?"

She only laughed. "Heavens, no, that's the wrappings off the angels. They just came today, aren't they adorable?" And they were: little four-inch triangles of robes, softly sculpted hair, of all hues: red, black, yellow; each one lined up and carefully prepared for some event like a choir to come. "Well, what do you think?" she asked, waving her hand over the room.

"What is it?" Martin asked, confused for a moment what the room meant.

"It's our workshop, Amelia's and mine. It's what we do: we make decorations, wreaths, centerpieces. We work together. Your mom designs all the work, tells me what to do, holds my hands and goes through the motions, and man, have I gotten good!" She set her wine down by the angels, and reached under the table for a file box. It was stuffed with index cards. "All orders, Martin, from every craft shop and boutique in New York! We are selling this stuff like you wouldn't believe. We made more last week than I ever made at Goldstein's in a month! That's my surprise. What do you think?" She glowed in front of him, the Queen was shining, she was making money and doing what she loved to do. And she had made Amelia a big part of it. He whistled in appreciation.

"Lady, hats off to you. I'm impressed. Does this mean I won't have to go out and doctor now?" Martin watched her smile and then her nod. Then her no-no shake of the head.

Luther poked his head in. "Neat, ain't it, how they got this going? Got to hand it to the ladies, they can turn garbage into glory."

"Garbage? How dare you call this garbage. I'll garbage you," she laughed, chasing him down the hall. Martin picked up both their glasses, and went back to the kitchen for a refill. He kissed Amelia on the head.

"Mama, your workroom looks wonderful. You and Claire have got to be delighted at your success. You like it, too, don't you, running your own business?"

Amelia turned and touched his face. "I love it, Martin, I do so love it, and I can hardly wait until we start each morning. We put in long days, today we stopped early because you were coming, but tomorrow we'll be at it again. All the angels will be on a round board, you see, and Luther augers out a little spot where Claire inserts a tiny music box, oh, it plays the most delightful little Christmas songs, then we have some trees we add, and a small ornament, red or green." Micah got up then, and said something about the goyim and Christmas, and wasn't it time for checkers, and he and Luther moved toward the back stairs. Luther only shrugged his shoulders and followed. "Scrooge, we call him," he whispered to them and winked.

They laughed together as they drank more wine, cleaned up the last of the cheese and tossed the remaining rye crackers out into the yard for the birds. The frosted grapes had gone over about like Claire thought they would. "Maybe we could use them in a centerpiece," she suggested, and Amelia doubled over in laughter. So simple. Not even funny, but his mother, happy with her life, loving her Claire and her work, maybe slightly lightheaded with the wine, thought everything was funny now. It wasn't much later that Martin guided his mother up the back stairs, waving good night to Claire, who stood at the bottom of the back stairs watching them ascend.

"Martin, send that old coot down after the next game. He'll be getting calls early if this cold keeps up. Tell him he's not as young as he used to be. He hates to hear that."

"Will do, and, Claire, thanks for a wonderful homecoming."

"My pleasure, son, my pleasure." She waved and turned to finish her cleanup. He had forgotten to tell her how great her violet plant was doing on the window sill. It had grown to twice its size, and the blooms were as deep purple as the frosted grapes.

# Chapter Sixteen

*Is this our life on earth*
*Another dawn we face*
*Is this the moment of truth*
*For the whole human race*
*Is that the last man down?*
*Is that the last life laid to waste?*

*E-L-P "Farewell to Arms"*

The checker game went on another hour. The radio played Mozart, at least he thought it was Mozart, and his mother moved easily through the rooms she knew by touch. He stood at the bathroom door, talking to his mother as she washed her face and arms for bed, sipping the rest of his wine, and wondering if he might slip down for another glass. The lightheaded feeling he'd hoped for hadn't come yet. In all the excitement, he'd used up all the alcohol held in that little thrice-filled glass.

Luther met his gaze down the hall and pointed with his finger a down motion. Martin nodded. Luther rose and touched Micah on the shoulder.

"You whip me one more time and we ain't playing no more." Micah beamed with the compliment, slowly rose and started to put the game away for the night. Amelia came out of the bathroom and said good night to all, blowing a kiss to Martin. Micah moved toward the bathroom and his lavender soap, and Martin followed Luther down the quiet back steps. They stopped to look at the back yard in the flood lights, and Martin was again amazed at how beautiful it looked, gleaming under the misty droplets that polished it like a perfect jewel.

"You got a way with the living things, that's for sure, Luther." Luther smiled in pleasure.

"Wait'll you see the tree I planted for Dwayne. Show it to you tomorrow." He flicked off the light, tested the door. Shot the dead bolt, moved into the kitchen quietly, and went to check the front door, leaving the porch light on. He came back with a grin as wide as Kansas.

"Ready for something a little stronger? That wine is like grape juice if you ask me. How about something with some kick?" He rummaged under the kitchen sink, brought out a fifth of Jack Daniels, and poured two shot glasses to the brim. "Now you watch. As soon as I put this to my lips, that darn phone'll ring." They clicked the shots together, and just as Luther had predicted, the phone began to ring. "See? What'd I tell you? I couldn't be an alcoholic if I wanted to." He set the glass down, reached for a pad of paper and a pen, and picked up the phone. Yes, he realized as he listened, yes, it was cold tonight, but couldn't they wait until tomorrow? It was almost one A.M., he'd have to double charge, and he hated doing that, but the dog . . . you say the dog has puppies? How many? Seven, you say, shivering, you say? I'll be there.

He went down the hall, said something to Claire, who murmured in return, something about his heavy coat being in the kitchen closet, she'd sewn that button on, and he came back and found the coat. Pulling it on, he reached for the shot glass and handed it to Martin. "Do mine for me and sleep tight on it." He gripped Martin's shoulder in a farewell and went out the front door, warning Martin to lock it tight but don't slide the dead bolt. He'd be back in three hours, he figured, and he went down the slippery steps on sure feet, guided by the porch light. The truck leaped to life, the lights turned on, and the four light little taps on the horn were for the ones he left behind, cozily snuggling in for the night.

Quiet was what met him when he came up the stairs balancing the two little shot glasses, stopping half way to take a sip off each so none would spill. He turned off the kitchen light with his elbow and moved into the darkened living room toward the window. Now he wished he had that illicit cigarette he'd so nonchalantly turned down earlier in the day. Now it would taste good with the whiskey and the slow heat coming into him from the radiator. Heat worked good here, after all the years of puttering and adjusting and replacing the worn parts, never getting so much as a nickel taken off the rent by Goldstein. Ah, the Goldsteins of the world. How to handle them, Martin mused, settling down with the glasses still balanced neatly in each hand.

He tucked his feet under him and kept sipping, once from Luther's shot, then from his. The whiskey went down easily. It must have been his night to get tight, and he knew he could do it on two shots, scarce as liquor had been to him in the last four years. Yes, he'd get snooty on these two shots. He knew it. He giggled. He wished Amy was here tonight. She'd love to see him sitting with his two shots.

It was affecting him, he realized dreamily. The curtains were softer as he looked at them. Same old curtains, but clean, like someone had taken them down and washed them in good suds and hung them over the balcony to dry. Probably Claire. He set the glasses down on the window sill and went to the bedroom to peel out of his clothes. May as well wash up now, while I can still see straight, he mumbled to himself happily. Soap, water, washcloth, towel, face the same in the mirror, need a shave. Tomorrow the shave. Tonight, the decadence of two shot glasses of Jack Daniels.

Returning to his father's chair by the window over the radiator, he sipped from his glasses, finally pouring the last of one into the other, and swallowed the last dregs. Feeling mighty pleased with himself, he used the toilet and remembered to turn to the right into his old room where he found the bed in the dark and dived under the covers. His last thoughts in his spinning head were, I wonder how many brain cells I killed tonight? He passed out.

The dream started almost as soon as sleep overtook him. There was a large man, very large, with a crooked staff and a white robe, a long flowing beard, and he had a huge vat before him, and Martin knew it was chocolate, deep rich simmering chocolate, giving off vapors of warmth as he stirred. Around him and behind him were drones, sexless creatures in robes of yellow wool, moving on gossamer feet (he thought they looked webbed, but he couldn't be sure) and in the arms of each drone was a bundle, small and wrapped in blue for some, in pink for others, and each bundle was unwrapped and its albino skin and closed eyes in a newly formed human face seemed incomplete, not ready, an embryo form of a new life coming. The huge man, towering over the others, had pale yellow skin, and deep-set black eyes, his white hair was wavy and drifted over his face as he reached for the small embryo held out to him. He held it gently, lovingly, and lowered it into the vat and no cry of pain was heard, only a sound of awe coming from the drones. For when the dripping embryo was lifted up, he was no longer an albino, with no color on his frail body, but a beautiful deep rich chocolate, more filled out now, more content and relaxed, bigger and more lively; it moved its arms and stretched as if he had been without a real form until now.

The moving waving leg-kicking little child (for that was what it was, Martin knew) was re-wrapped in its colored blanket and the drone moved off, only to be replaced by another who repeated the same act of unwrapping and handing the albinos to the dipper. He repeated the dipping, stopped once to stir the chocolate, and continued dipping and watching the re-wrapping of the children as if they were bonbons. There were more drones now, and the level of the chocolate was becoming alarmingly low. The dipper noticed it, and called out to the drones to get more, but one turned to the one behind who turned to the one behind until there was no drone to turn to. There was no more chocolate. None. The dipper stroked the bottom of the kettle, smoothed the last of the chocolate over one last child to be, and sighed.

What to do. This work of completion had been assigned to him. What would The Man Upstairs think when he found out how badly he had let things come to this? No more chocolate. There had to be. He turned in anger then, shouted words Martin didn't understand, but his face grew red with rage as he shouted for something he wanted to fill the vat. He needed something to fill the vat.

The bundles were laid in a neat line, stretching way off beyond the line of Martin's vision, but he knew that line would be endless. The bundles would keep coming. The drones ran under the wrath of the dipper, turning over haystacks, looking behind closed doors, rushing to find color to fill the vat. That was what they needed: color, before they were finished.

An old drone finally went to the kitchen, and thinking she had found a barrel of chocolate, so excited was she that she failed to read the label. She rolled it proudly toward the dipper. Her toothless mouth smiled so cleanly, so proud was she or he, what was she? The dipper touched her forehead with a spoon. (Where did the spoon come from? Watch, Martin, just watch.) He pulled the cork from the barrel, and let the contents fill the vat. It bubbled and gurgled, and everyone moved to gather their wrapped embryos and stand in line again. But the color in the vat was different; the dipper noticed it at once. The color was a deep raspberry red, like a cherry, and he moved to stir the bubbling mixture, and some of the chocolate left in the bottom seeped into the raspberry jelly, and a new color came up: a soft burnished bronzed red not unpleasant to the dipper, who at that point had no way to turn, had only orders to obey, to finish the embryos with color. So he wiped the sweat from his brow, leaned on his staff, and began again with the dipping, and the new babies came out strong and lusty, with black hair growing almost immediately, long limbs muscled before birth, quick hands that opened and closed as if grasping for bows and arrows, well built sinewy limbed youngsters destined for tents and long walks.

Well, he had done the best he could with this color. The dipper took a moment to survey the drones still coming. The vat was almost empty again. Now a new problem. The jelly was gone; such a fluke that it was found at all. And the bundles! Still arriving, some filling the very last place as far as his eye could see. He hated it, hated it more than he could imagine hating at all, but he was done. Finished. No more color. A small drone, not carrying a bundle, pulled his robe, and he looked down at her/him. Martin strained to get close, but he couldn't see the words coming from her mouth, couldn't translate what she or he was saying, but the great dipper only nodded, yes, it might work. And a great cask was brought in, much larger than the barrel of raspberry jelly, and this was hoisted on the shoulders of many drones, and set to rest on the lip of the vat, and the dipper pulled out a huge stopper, and out poured a creamy sugary substance. (Molasses, Martin guessed, it has to be molasses, only thicker and lighter, like whipped molasses).

"It won't do," cried the dipper, and Martin heard him this time. The drones, liking the color, touched his robe in respect, nodded their approval. He thought for a moment of asking The Man Upstairs what he thought, but he was way behind schedule, way late, and the lines of drones with blue and pink bundles stretched way out past his vision as he raised his white head to scan the horizon. No choice. Have to go with it. But the sugar, so bad for newborns. They'll be rubbing their eyes to get it away from them. But he had no choice.

He bent to his work and it was endless. The vat kept refilling from the huge vessel, and the newly dipped embryos, coming out crying because of the sugar, did pull at their eyes. They stretched their eyes so hard they stayed pulled back at the sides; that's how the sugar affected them. What am I dealing with, the dipper groaned? He lifted the spoon and touched it to his lips. Butterscotch. Only butterscotch. But the embryos were covered in it, came up with their eyes slanted and the coating stayed on them. They were a glowing yellow, fine textured, trim, neat, compact. He suggested washing them immediately, but while the color faded slightly, and the water shrank them in size, the eyes stayed pulled up slightly at the outer lids. Well, a mistake, he admitted, but one has to work with what one has, and there are so many done this way, maybe they can band together and make something of themselves.

He was tired. His shoulders ached for a good massage and a light cup of ambrosia, but his work was not complete. The end of the line had been reached. He knew it in his heart that the vat was dry again. He ordered it washed and returned, and the drones did his bidding. He washed his face and prepared to leave, to go to his rest. The Man Upstairs had put his feet up hours ago, set his timepiece for a fairly normal work day, but the clean vat only eyed the Dipper with contempt. Why contempt? He had done his best. "I've done my best!" he shouted over the remaining drones with their pink and blue bundles held out to him. "I've done what I could! Go home with what you have. Let it be what it must be. If it has no color, don't come crying to me. I don't get overtime!" He stalked off then, pushing his way through the drones with their uplifted bundles, wondering how they were going to explain this to the parents waiting below. What a mess, and no one to complain to. It will have to go down in history as the saddest day in Heaven when the color ran out. That day white men were born, and the story weaves on from there.

The dream ended there for Martin, but he remembered it again the next day and for many days after. He liked the big dipper fellow, wanted him to have a happy ending, too.

Martin came up with an ending he liked for the dipper dream. He sat by the window over the radiator, watching the snow coming down in the Bronx, and came up with a nice finish to the dream. White men were an accident, that he plainly saw. Things were going along fine until the white men, struggling for power, disrupted things. Not the poor dipper's fault. He had surely tried. Now what can we do for him? His ending. How's this, Martin plotted: It had all happened by accident, by running out of the substances of color that filled the vats, and when it came to the attention of The Man Upstairs, he had sat back amused at the mistake, but like any good card shark, he wanted to see how the new players dealt their cards. He wrote the dipper's job out of existence, and let the bundles already dipped or not dipped continue their journey without intervention. HIS work was done. Let the ones below decide. Let them carry on their color on earth through progenation.

The dipper took another position in Heaven, gave up an early retirement, but was greatly relieved two hundred years later that his work days were over. He took two of the faithful drones with him, and settled with his wife in a small retirement community in Florida. No one there ever suspected his prior work. He tentatively applied for Social Security benefits under the name Big Dipper, and he and his wife of five hundred years were surprised and delighted when they got their first check. He dearly loved the orange juice, freshly squeezed, almost as good as ambrosia. (And that was for you, old man, Martin saluted the snow.)

# Chapter Seventeen

The continent of Europe got some of the first no color, then the Asian continent; Antarctica, the isle of Greenland, all were sprinkled. The move to America by the no color, shoving the red men back, back, crowding their country and sending them onto reservations. The red man and the white man fought for this country, but the white man prevailed. And in his prevalence, he needed strong backs and slave mentality to run the fields, till the soil, tend the animals, do the hard work. Where to get those muscles? Where else but in Africa, a rich teeming populace, simply living their lives as they knew them to be, until the whip came down. The dark passages of the ships bearing their subjected load of humanity steered toward the shore of the great new America. The Southern states must have gotten the first of the children of color. They held them as possessions, not as part of the humanity they had forgotten to recognize. Their own children were held up to each other, and they remarked on the superiority of the clean fresh no color skin, and they accepted their mantle of governing the Black man.

They liked themselves so well that they kept close to home, made their children think they were better than the coloreds, yes, they started to call them coloreds, and for some reason yet unexplained, when they found no one to marry outside their family, they started marrying cousins and brothers and sisters, and what an evolutionary brood came out of that sequestered decision. Eyes meant to be spaced far apart soon became closer together, brain cells that would have expanded on new genes and influx of fresh chromosomes withered and stayed small, and each new flock came out smaller minded and narrower eyed than the one before. What had happened? Where was the good stock?

The men in rural America kept to their farming, shepherding their flocks, often mistaking them for their offspring. The years rolled by, and the big cities came closer, crowding out the trees and open fields, kept coming until Pond Ridge, Missouri, had to become a city or it would be crushed in the urban spread toward its guarded borders. But the naming of the city didn't dampen the vigor with which the creeping world came to its doors. Television came in, and a newspaper was actually started, the first printing sharing the news that children would read about in print, many could read, only at a third grade level. And those were the adults. Small town America was alive and kicking, and fighting any encroachment into its ways.

The no-color heartland communities read about the colored

communities and they shuddered in fear. Why now, they reasoned, when we have gotten this far without color? Why should we change now, accept the colored ones, they must be from a different land, a different time. They must be held back. And held back they were, some coming to work on their land and live in small shacks without decent water, for that was their lot, to be less than the no color. The colored ones accepted their position, felt the whites must have the knowledge of a greater truth, and their submissive ways, their unassuming ways, led them further down the path of being dominated.

There were those in Pond Ridge, Missouri, who had grown up, side by side, with the no colored, and Beech and Gloria Cheevers felt they had a good life. Beech worked for the railroad, laying ties, and Gloria worked too, taking care of the children born of their Baptist-blessed marriage, and she took in laundry and did sewing and visited the sick among the poorer Blacks she knew along the river. The Mississippi was their boundary, the river they never crossed over, the edge of their world was the far bank of Illinois. To go further meant the unknown, and the big cities, and the problems they didn't want to deal with. For them, the comfort of their small log home, their own land, their neighbors, and church fellows were enough. Their oldest son, John, was in high school, and to them, that was enough. John was a bright and engaging young man, good in sports, able at the numbers, adept at English, writing a prize-winning essay in junior high, much praised by his teachers, all white, and that had to count for much more.

"Land, if he doan beat all," sang his mother, reading his poems and essays to herself in the kitchen. "That boy is sure smart. Guess we got to thank all mighty Jesus for this 'un." She hummed to herself as she pounded out the biscuits, set the beans to soak, felt the good earth under her feet, knew that God was promising something special for this boy. And if he did well? The rest would follow: Arlon and Cloteria. Why not all of them doing well? Bright they was, she knowed they was bright.

Beech hung up his coat and entered the living room they used for really living in. He skimmed over the bent heads doing their lessons on the square top table they ate at and slept near. His short clipped hair showed a few strands of gray, but the still dark eyebrows were curved over gentle brown eyes that misted up over sad stuff. The body under his work clothes was firm with muscles from his work, and his stomach was flat as a washboard, in spite of all the good food Gloria put in front of him. He entered the kitchen off the living room, and it was merely a nook in the house, barely six hundred square feet in size. He wanted so much more for his woman, his Gloria, and how the sound of her name made him tremble: Gloria! The Glory! And he saw her, bent at the stove, her soft roundness beckoning to him, and he yearned to hold her just then, at that very moment, and lay her bare, and hold her still in his arms, naked they would be, naked to love and to the high almighty hereafter. He thundered for her in his loins; he wanted her sweetness even at that moment, the dinner hour, the hour with the children, the hour of prayer, and thank you, Jesus, for all we have, but he wanted more. He wanted more for her sake, not for his sake; being with her was enough for him. Being a daddy to John and Cloteria and Arlon.

John Cheevers was well liked at school, fairly held in esteem by the white administration, and his strong good looks, his dark brow over hazel eyes, his square shoulders and cleanliness won him the attention of many of the girls in the school. But he was a chaste young man, not giving to flirting or patting the girls' behinds like so many of his classmates. He kept his hands to himself, did his schoolwork, helped the teachers when they needed a hand, ran eagerly after classes down to the football field in autumn and to the diamonds in the spring. A natural, that was what he was, and the coaches kept hoping for him that he'd win a big scholarship and be set for life. John didn't see himself as especially gifted; he just worked hard and listened well and helped the teams he was on get to the finals in both sports. They didn't win, they were really too small to get past the bigger schools with more talent to draw from, so he and his teammates hung up their dreams and prayed for a scout to come sniffing around this tiny school. They were at least big enough to have cheerleaders, and some of the girls, looking so cute and smart in their tee shirts and short skirts, stirred up a longing in John that he had not encountered before. Girls. So slim, and smooth, and fresh smelling. Maybe he should start dating, he thought to himself on his long walk home, carrying his spikes and gear in a blue bag he had gotten for Christmas. Maybe have a real girl friend. But what would he do with her? He didn't drive like so many of the other students. The whites, and some Black families, did have cars, but money was the biggest worry to him. He had no money, except for the pocket change his dad would give him each week for snacks, or sodas, or a magazine. No money for a show, or a dinner. No real money.

One of the cheerleaders, Marilyn Stewart, was always real friendly to him, stopped to share a story, or ask a question about homework, showing John an algebra problem she was having trouble with, and she beamed at him as he explained it slowly, drawing the required figures for her, showing her how 'A' related to 'B' and the answer had to be 'C'.

"I must be stupid," she said to John, "you make it seem so easy.

I wish you were the teacher instead of Miss Whipple." She smiled at him in a way that was friendly and even, not making him feel strange to be chatting with her. She really was a nice girl, John knew, and other guys thought the same thing, but in a slightly different way. Bobby White, for all his good looks, blond hair, rakish blue eyes, nice tan, expensive clothes, position on the team as the quarterback, had a different idea in mind when he started stopping Marilyn after practice and complimented her on her turns, and cheers, and great legs. She blushed under the attention: he was a senior, she was just a sophomore, but her heart raced with excitement over the attention. She had to tell somebody. After Algebra class the next day, she pulled John aside and told him she was doing a story for the school paper, about the football team, did he have any favorite stories about the players he'd like to share? He said he didn't do much sports writing, but that all the guys were great, real good guys, some better'n others, but that was kind of personal, just stuff he'd noticed and that didn't make very good copy.

"Like Bobby White. He's a good quarterback, don't you think?" She eyed John closely, waiting for his answer, hoping for a resounding accolade of the boy she was determined to snare.

"I don't know Bobby all that well," he started, and his mind ran back to the few times he and White had stood face to face. It was usually after a poor play, poor by Bobby's false idea of this being a one-man show. Or someone not understanding who was going to do what, and the team had been wandering about in confusion until the coach blew the whistle and shagged his lard ass out onto the field.

"What happened here, boys? Looks like nobody's doing their job. White! What the hell happened on that play?" What happened on that play, that simple handout and pass out to Rogers, was that Bobby forgot his play. He ran the ball instead, confusing the players ready for the pass, and the whole thing looked like school yard capers. No mess-up on the part of the players, only the quarterback decided to have himself a thrill by running the ball himself, discarding his earlier called pattern. John was disgusted at this, secretly raging that the guy was a hot dog, out to make himself look good, forgetting the other men on the field.

"Coach," Bobby jumped in, unstraping his helmet, and laying it on his bent thigh, "Cheevers just jumped the wrong way, threw me off balance for my pass, so I tried to make the best of it, run it as far as it would go. Sorry," and he strapped the helmet back on and moved off to other players guardedly watching the scene.

"Cheevers, what the hell? Can't you understand English? He's calling the plays, boy, don't second guess him. Now let's run that one

again, and this time, Fuller, come on in, Cheevers, you sit this set out."
The coach waddled back to the sidelines, and blew his whistle, and the
Marauders of Pond Ridge hit the practice team, trying to shake off the
absence of their best and strongest player, John Cheevers. They didn't
like it, not one bit, but they shrugged it off, and only wallowed more
deeply in their fantasy of being the guy Bobby asked to go with him on
Saturday night. Bobby had a neat little Mustang, a gift from his daddy
when he reached sixteen, and that candy apple red machine set him
apart from every other boy in that school. The girls fairly hung over
Bobby White, and Mr. Cool he was, easily getting to the goal line with
more than six of them. He was a scorer. They liked to hear his stories
of the conquests. God, to be so lucky.

His eye of late had turned to the flaxen-haired sophomore, that
Marilyn Stewart with the cute butt and nice chest. Nice chest for a
sophomore, he noticed. Bet she'd feel firm and ripe and ready to be a
good one nighter. Yeah, he'd play her just right. Get her down and
dirty. Wipe that cute preciousness off her little snout. He laughed to
himself as he brushed past his adoring fans, heading for class where
he'd have to really knuckle down and get some notes from someone.
He'd slept through most of the year. But although his grades were
passing, he wondered if the old boys rule was in play here.

Help the boy along, gives so much to the school colors. The
Marauders would be down the tube without him. Brilliant, that boy is,
positively brilliant when he's got a pigskin in his hands. Go pro, you
watch. That boy'll go pro, right out of high school. Which wouldn't be
a bad idea, his father mused, watching him. Doesn't have the good
sense to pick up his room. Never a kind word to his sister, won't even
help me wash his own car. Oh, well, the bemused father mumbled to
himself, he'll be out of here in a year. Play the game. Live for Friday
nights when the other men would clap him on the back and damn! That
did feel good, to be the father of a great football player. What else
could a man want of his son?

But to answer Marilyn honestly, to tell her that Bobby White
was a shit load of trouble, that he had hurt a lot of girls younger than
she was, had told stories about them behind their backs while they were
still swimming in a make believe world of first love; well, to tell Marilyn
that would look like sour grapes, but John half-way guessed her interest
in Bobby and he wanted to protect her.

"Bobby's okay, like you know he's a great player, but to tell you
the truth, he's kind of a ladies man if you get my drift." She looked at
him with incredible blue eyes, soft lashes curling around the lids, no
make-up except for a little rouge and light gloss on her full lips.

"So why should I care about that? This is about sports, Cheevers, not about me dating him!" She bit her lip and hurried off in the milling students between class. He hadn't really answered her, or maybe he had.

The fall senior prom was the big to-do of the year, and the gym was decked out in pink balloons and silver crepe paper. The tables were lined up by Miss Whipple for her biggest organizational feat of the year, and the janitors only dragged a little slower as if to infuriate her attempts at creating a Garden of Eden in Pond Ridge, Missouri. The Queen and King were voted on, and to no one's surprise, Bobby White was the King, and Jennifer Sprock, the valedictorian and science award winner (her mobile of the planets took third at State) was chosen fairest of them all. Except she wasn't really fair. Fate had played some cruel trick on Jennifer Sprock. Her face had been pitted by early acne, then sand papered off to almost good as new, but a faint blotchy look always made you stop, stare, and then forget her face, she was so darn nice.

She and Michael Blink were dates for the big prom, and everyone wondered who Bobby would ask, and the seniors were hushed, watching him walk down the hall: eeney, meeney, minie mo, which one of us will he ask to go? They'd all dated him, felt his hands up their skirts, let him do . . . It, just so for this one special moment, this one star-filled night under pink balloons and silver crepe paper, just this once they could ride the Magic Carpet and be with Bobby when he was King. But their hopes were dashed to smithereens when the word got out: he wasn't taking a senior, something they all thought he should do. It was tradition, no senior girl should sit home on prom night, no senior should have to give up her place for an underclassman, who would have her own turn, that was only fair. But fair is not for the likes of teenagers on high hopes of grabbing a plum, at least that's how Bobby felt about it as he casually stopped at Marilyn's locker and waited for her to finish up her secretarial duties for Bookends, the after hours' bookworm club. He had come up from the gym, freshly showered and nicely damp, only to find she wasn't there yet. He hated to wait for broads, hated it with a passion. He had almost started to leave when he saw her speeding down the hall toward him, only to stop in surprise when she saw who it was lounging by her locker.

"Hey, you gonna keep me waiting all day?" he called, and she walked tentatively toward him.

"Had to get my club notes in order before I left, can't leave them in a muddle. So what's the big deal, Bobby? Have a bad practice?" She toyed with him, feeling her chest pounding and her face hot as she opened the locker and slid her books in.

"Had a great practice. Have to get a few boys settled down. That Cheevers is ready to have me blow him apart, telling me how to run the backfield. Like I don't know the backfield. With my eyes closed. Let him try to do what I do, that stupid nigger" He laughed and ran his long white fingers through his still damp curls. He watched her face and she didn't smile at him.

"John Cheevers is a friend of mine, Bobby, and I don't appreciate that kind of term being used about him. It's mean and small and I really think . . . " but he cut her off.

"So you're in love with the dude, makes me no never mind. Want to go to the prom with me?" The words came out effortlessly, the words were just coming off his lips, and she wanted to scream yes, yes. But she didn't scream. She only said, "I'd be honored, Bobby White, to be your date for the prom. I've never been to one, so it's a big deal, right? Long dress, my first, really. Wow! That is neat. Yes, I'd love to go, thanks for asking me." He nodded and moved off the lockers. "See ya in class," he called back, moving down the hall with a saunter she could never begin to imitate. His date! For the prom! Would her mom let her go? She had to. She just had to.

# Chapter Eighteen

*It's good to be king of your own little town,*
*Have your own way*
*Get a feeling of peace*
*At the end of the day.*

*Tom Petty "Good To Be King"*

Joan Stewart was tall and spare. She had slender hips and a flat chest. Her unmade up face graced the chapel at First United Church almost every morning, cleaning and tidying the building her husband, Macy, stood in on Sunday mornings, delivering the sermons that so stirred her soul. He gave her very little else to be stirred up about, feeling that sex was a very private matter, much too private to share with his wife. The birth of Marilyn had been practically an accident, and he had fervently promised God that no more fornication was to take place between them. That they had been married over a year, and living in very cramped quarters were the only saving graces he allowed to be entered as evidence that he had tried his best to remain chaste, but the pursuit of the woman had been relentless. How she howled after him until he finally succumbed, and it had been bang up, he had to admit, but in his prayers the very next day, he vowed never to enjoy those fruits again. If he so denied himself, ever more sure was his pathway to Eternal Heaven, and God would rejoice for his sacrifice. And it had been a sacrifice, he admitted to himself sitting on the toilet, reading *Oui* or *Playboy*. It had been an extreme effort, he realized, holding himself tenderly until the erection came; it had been only with great effort, and he pumped himself, and felt the wonderful rush of release, God! How merciful to me. A-a-h, thank you, God, you've kept me safe again from using a woman for an unseemly act.

The news of the prom request left Joan stunned for a moment. "The Senior Prom? Why, Mari, you're only a sophomore. How can you go to the senior dance?" She watched her excited daughter tearing off her sweater, reaching for the milk bottle, grabbing a glass, and settling comfortably on the stool by the kitchen's island. "How can you do that?" she asked, watching the toss of the head and the blue eyes over the curling lashes. How, indeed, could she not do that?

"Seniors can ask whomever they please. They can't tell you who to bring. If I was a senior, I could bring Dad if I wanted." That picture faded before Joan's eyes as soon as the image began to appear. Better a dead mackerel.

"Well, we'll have to ask Daddy and pray over it," she fleetingly summarized, ending the conversation. Always the same, Marilyn thought, finishing the milk, and rinsing the glass as if she were a wonder woman. "I'm off, Mom, got to do that Chaucer paper." How like your father, Joan mused, set the pleasure aside for the work. "The date? Who asked you? Not John, I hope, your dad would never approve. We know you're friends, but, you know, there'd be talk . . . "

Marilyn turned in the kitchen doorway, and faced her mother. "Mom, I hardly think John would go to the prom, much less ask me. We're friends, not social equals." She flounced out and up the stairs, giddy in her happiness. Joan still did not know who the prom date was. Well, let Macy handle it. He always handled these matters better than she. Hers was the silent path winding behind his, and she suffered in silence, only letting her small voice cry out at times, when she tried to hold him or caress him. She even had the nerve to come into the bathroom one time while he was shaving, and put her arms around his bare chest, and he had shivered at her touch, and said, "Please, Joan, the Lord is watching." She had crept away that day, feeling like a harlot, even worse: like a leper with no hands. Never again, she vowed, never again will I place myself before him, wanting him as a woman wants a man. This, too, I will set aside, and for the love of God, I offer it to you.

ॐ

The dance was a smashing success, everyone said so, and Miss Whipple blushed under the compliments in her grape-colored organza with the sweeping train. She even had a beau that night, Mr. Stockton from the Walgreens' store, all primed and lively from the snootful he had lifted off a senior trying to slip in with it. "Not so fast, young man, let me feel your pockets," and the doleful youth 'fessed up that he'd taken the liberty of lifting a fifth out of his father's car. "In his car, you say? Then you may have done him a good turn while you're lamenting your loss. Drunk people don't make for a safe road for our young people." He clapped the boy on the shoulder and sent him off; lightening his load was how Elmer Stockton saw it. But the image of Miss Whipple, coming giddily down the hall, greeting students and remarking on corsages, caused him to slip into the little boy's room and take a good hard hit on the neck of that fifth. Much better, he thought, twisting the cap, solidly placing his feet one before the other and ready to meet the dragon at the pond.

For there was a pond, or at best, a wishing well, crudely constructed of rocks and pâpier-maché. Hopefully it would last the evening, and she checked it frequently for leaks, but thankfully, none had seemed to develop. Most thankfully due to Pastor Macy Stewart, the sweetest dearest man ever to grace a pulpit, and she should know, bearing his messages before her as she remembered him giving them. A true man. Why there weren't more out there was the sole reason she had never married. No more Macy Stewart's to light up your evening. And read the Bible like he just relished every sanctified word. A blessing, that was what they had, a rare blessing in their fold. Worked that wishing well like it was the pond the angels would dip in. Lined it with plastic, sealed the edges with a lighter, made it water tight and ship shape, so pleased was he to give her a hand. How had he come by the lighter? Oh, no matter, she fretted, touching her hair and watching for Elmer.

It had been a harrowing moment when Macy faced Marilyn across the linen dinner table, saw her pleading eyes, and sweet, sweet face, imploring him to let her go.

"Bobby is the nicest boy in school," she wheedled. "Everyone looks up to him. Why, you said yourself if you ever had a son, let him be the spittin' image of Bob White. There, you did say it, Dad. Just last Sunday, from the pulpit." She looked to her mother for affirmation and Joan touched her napkin to her lips.

"I believe that was in a separate context, Mari, one your father is more familiar with." He glared at her and turned smiling again to Marilyn.

"My point, in sermon, was to show that athletes are playing their hearts out, giving their all for the game, but the message of Christ is to give HIM all our efforts, forget the play, and only enter into it as a way to strengthen ourselves for the Lord's work. That's how I feel about the matter; as for you going to the prom, that is something you and your mother need to discuss."

"Oh, Daddy, how can I thank you?" she cried, rushing to him and hugging him about his neck and shoulders.

"I think we understand how you feel, and as you enter that special night, remember you're my daughter and carry yourself as such. You can do a lot of good, Mari, by sharing the message of Christ's next coming to all your classmates. Life doesn't begin or end on prom nights. They are only a passing." He bowed to his food, and began eating quickly and with some zeal. Joan, for all her shortcomings, did prepare a bountiful table and he loved to eat and eat, until he felt a long walk was way overdue.

"My constitution," he stated, leaving her to the dishes and clean up, slipping out the back door and winding his way up through the woods to a place he liked to sit, an old tree fallen in the path, no one around except the creepers and chirpers saying goodnight in the dark. He filled his lungs with the good tobacco of a Camel and fell back to dreaming. Good life, this one. Good family. What harm can the mite have on a special day in her life? Let her have a little dance. No matter to me. My perch is safe. He gazed at the stars and lit another cigarette. Time passes so quickly, he had only seen his daughter as a spindly wobbly leggy little girl, and now she was blossoming, becoming a woman. Let her try her wings. He would not stand in her way. But should she fall, should she become less than what he wanted from her, then she was God's to care for, not his. He had made his sacrifice.

The dinner at the prom was the best they'd eaten in that school for years. Someone must have come up with an original idea: don't feed them cafeteria food, let's have it catered, and catered it was. The nicest restaurant in Ste. Genevieve had sent over dinners for sixty-five, at half their normal price due to the solicitation of Pastor Macy Stewart, the soul of the community. The dinners were all nicely domed in metal heater hoods, small missiles of heated lamb chop or a rib eye (they had a choice) twice baked potato, with real bacon bits and curling melted Cheddar cheese, green beans with slivered almonds, and a sprig of parsley to add a festive touch. Not that they needed it. The DJ played romantic ballads during supper, and when the tables were cleared away by the underpaid gloomy janitors, the partners assembled on the floor and waited for the King and Queen (she really did look nice that night, pancake make-up can do wonders) and Bobby and Jennifer led their court though the first slow dance and then partners became real partners and dancing to an up-tempo beat took over. The music was loud, the boys fast and funny, ties were loosened and long skirts held up, and the whole silliness of it came crashing down on them. We're seniors! We're almost out of this trap!

The chaperones tried gamely to do a step or two, but for the most part they languished against the wall. Elmer Stockton had developed some colon problem; he had to apologize frequently as he ran off to the little boy's room, to take some medicine he knew would calm his troubling colitis. Miss Whipple bravely faced the dancers, set a smile on her face, and prayed that this night with Elmer wouldn't prove her downfall, since she preferred men like Macy Stewart: tall, straight, nondrinker, nonsmoker. The very shades of Hell would pale before the virtue of such a man. She only wished he and Joan had come as chaperones, but the business of the parish had to come first, she realized. Sermons to write, the sick to visit, chores at home to accomplish for his wife: such were the trials of a truly dedicated man of Christ. And so like him to want his sweet child to have this special evening on the arm of a great man among the student body, their own strong young warrior, the ever-charming Bobby White. And didn't he look gleaming in his tight fitting tuxedo, came all the way from St. Louis it did, in a box with tissue paper they said, and the other lads did look slightly dowdy before the King, only being able to come up with blue serge suits or gray slacks and a blazer.

Lights flickered on and off, on and off, in the hand of the dead tired janitor, hoping the crowd would clear out and let him at those floors. Mess of food crushed on the gym floor. With any luck, they'd be out by two A. M., but no hope to salvage the floor by morning. Damn stupid waste of time. All these hop heads, feeling their oats. Be a kid in nine months, he'd bet his eye teeth on it. At least one always got its kick start on fall prom night.

Borrowed cars, rented cars, grudgingly offered family sedans left the parking lot by the high school at quarter past eleven. A decent hour, much too decent for the likes of Bobby White, sitting primed in his cherry red mustang, wearing the tuxedo to end all tuxedos, and beside him, the prettiest girl at the bash. "My, my, and don't you look sweet?" He smiled at her and she had to admit she did look pretty nice that night. Her mother had gotten the lady up the street, who was good with a needle and thread, to come over afternoons and help her pull together a frock; they called it a frock, Marilyn grimaced. But it was a lovely dress. Turquoise and shimmering, it met her leg halfway down, and the top was sleeved in a perky little cap over each of her tanned and glowing shoulders. Modest and becoming, her mother had said; not too suggestive, now, her father had volunteered from his perch.

"Well, now, and what to do? You want to zip up to St. Louis, see the big city? Or shall we take you home right now, right when the evening's young, huh? What do you say, Madam? What is your choice? I am your slave, to do your bidding." He gallantly mocked her with a sweep of his broad shoulders, gently tapped the wheel as he turned through the streets around town. Familiar streets. Streets she'd grown up in. And she was grown. She was a woman now, wearing the turquoise dress, and feeling her mother's rhinestone earrings pressing into her ears. Yes, a woman, out with the man she adored, really adored. Just to feel his skin, just for a moment. She blushed at the thought. Hold it there, missy, hold it there. But she did so love the stares and whispers all night, the other girls fawning over her; what's he like, have you dated very long, did you just find out he liked you, god, I envy you, a night with Bobby White, I should only dream, and she lingered on those remembered faces.

"Say, I'm almost out of gas," he noticed. "Got to make a quick stop while you're deciding what to do with the rest of this night." He drove the car onto Shell's lot and kissed her quickly on the cheek. "Be right back, love." She touched her cheek in a quiet flush of happiness, watched his broad back in the wonderfully fitted tuxedo walk away from the car, same saunter, same jaunty aimless happiness with just being alive, and she watched him pay the attendant, and got him to come out and pump the gas, being a slow night and him in a tuxedo and all, the fumes, you understand. The young pimply faced attendant only stood in awe of the quarterback he saw on Friday nights, really got to see him up close now. Wait'll the guys hear who he'd pumped gas for.

Bobby slid back into the seat and started the engine. It roared into life, gave her an exciting tingle just to be sitting in his car, the envy of every other girl in Pond Ridge that night. She didn't want it to end, didn't want this glistening dress to hang on its hanger, and didn't want Bobby to leave her side. She wanted him to be by her side. But how to keep him, when so many wanted him. They wanted him, but he had asked her. That was the final thing. He chose her, above all the rest.

She turned to him in the seat and asked, "Where are all the others going? Surely not home this early."

He scratched his chin, barely able to say what he had wanted to say. "Jim Murdoch's dad gave him the keys to his cabin, up on the ridge behind town. But that's just what I heard, don't know if it's for real or not."

"Well, slowpoke, let's go see!" Her eyes stared out the windshield as the blocks of town flew by, and they were out on the county road and the faithful car did very well up the slope to the ridge. Lights were on at the cabin, and sure enough, there were parked cars, and girls in ball gowns standing against fenders, and guys walking up and down the steps of the one story neat looking log home. Someone had built a bonfire. Bottles were handed around. Some of the girls had changed to jeans and tight fitting tops.

"Yo! We're here! Party time!" he shouted out the window, and the group gathered around the car and handed Bobby a glass of pink liquid. "Oh, my God, not this crap!" He got out and circled the car, opening the door for the woman in turquoise, who moved onto the sandy ground timidly, even shaking a little. Might be time to go home, a little voice said. Might be time to realize that this is not a good idea.

But the others pulled her along, murmured over her dress, weren't the songs they played just great, how's about a bit to drink, you look like you need it, and she did need something right then while Bobby was off flexing his muscles and shoving some guy who made some crack. He came back all in a huff, and she asked, "Something wrong?"

"Squirt thinks he's a smart ass, made a joke about you, didn't like his tone, smacked him a good one, making a slam on you. So you're a sophomore, so what? You're a lady in my mind, and no senior's gonna run you down to my face and not meet my fist. So there!" And he smacked his hand hard on the wall of the cabin and he winced. She cried out for him, and held his hand and he said, "Hey, it's okay. Just don't mess with my woman." His woman! How defiant he sounded. How proud was she that she held his hand, and they moved together against the wall behind the cabin, and he kissed her, softly, roundly, putting his tongue into her mouth. "I'm sorry, I shouldn't ought have done that, but I get wild when I'm near you, raging wild, I can't help myself." He seemed genuinely sorry and she reached for him and he turned toward her in that dim light and she kissed him back, pushing her tongue into his mouth.

"Oh, Marilyn, when you do that, I know it's for keeps. I know you are the one meant for me. Here, here, come on, we need to be alone for a minute. I have to treasure this." He held her hand as they walked up the steep path behind the cabin, and he found a spot where the grass was soft and he pulled her down next to him. The night was warm and windless. A pleasant fall night after a week of sun over the drying leaves. She sat in her turquoise dress while he fumbled with her zipper, and she realized her dress was coming undone. He touched her shoulder and his hand was so warm and caressing that she let him do it. He stopped at her bra and she unhooked it. He sat back in awe of her. "Why, baby, you are the most. I love you, you know that, I love you." He reached behind his back and pulled out a flask. "Just a nip, mind you, to ward off evil. Just take a sip, sweetheart, while I just enjoy gazing on your perfect body." She sat on the grass, her bodice shifted to her waist, her newly developed breasts proud and upright in the moonlight, and Bobby White had to take a moment to reflect on his good fortune. God almighty had to have a hand in this, he chortled. Perfect night. Perfect setup. Perfect body.

And to top it off, she was sipping, slowly at first, then a little hungrily. "Hey! Watch that. It creeps up on you like I'm about to." He rolled over on her, moved the flask from her hand, and set it by a rock. No spills. Good move. He touched her breasts and god, they were great breasts. She moved under him, saying something about her dress, but God damn it, he'd already noticed her dress, what more did she want?

She held him close, kissed him, and then he knew he wanted to have her, right here on the hill over the cabin, on their big night. He wanted to have someone, and she was there, so why not her? He'd even paid five dollars for her stupid corsage, a white carnation and little babies breath, all wrapped up in tissue paper when he picked her up. And that tall stupid preacher, wishing them good evening, have a wonderful dance, well, he'd friggin' tell that pastor what he could do with his good evening and have a happy dance. He could stuff it, that's what he could do with it.

He was mad, that was all he could make of it: he was mad. Why, he wasn't sure, but as he ripped the turquoise dress right down the seams so carefully sewn by the good neighbor, when he tore into Marilyn, he felt not a shred of remorse. She asked for it. She got it. She got it good. Got it hard and fast. Got it like she dreamed it would be.

❧

John had thought about going to the prom. He really thought he should ask Maralou Harper if she wanted to go, just as friends, but just at the moment of asking her, Jeb Nichols had beat him to it. And Jeb really liked Maralou. So it was only fitting that he should take her to the dance, only they went in his Uncle Fred's liveried car, the one he used to make his living during the week. A cabbie he was, and a nice old man if John was any judge.

He had no money for a corsage anyway, and his Sunday suit was almost outgrown, and he hated like anything to talk to his dad about money for clothes. And for a prom, that seemed indecent. So he sat on the back porch the night of his senior prom, and he dreamed of lights and flowers and hoped everyone had a good time. His mother joined him, shutting the screen door against the mosquitos, and she said, "Prom night an' my boy's home."

"Well, at least I'm hoping that someday I'll have a bigger prom to go to."

"An' why wouldn't you be thinkin' that? Proms come an' go, but you steadfast, your prom'll come, I promise you." She looked work-worn to him, sitting in the rocker by his side, a still-young woman with a hard life.

"Mama, why are we so dang gone poor?"

She sat stiffer then, turned to him, and said, "Why, John Cheevers, whoever said we was poor? What tripe you been lissen to? We ain' poor, we's rich. Rich! I gots a savin' count. We got a roof ovah our heads, we got chickens to feed, we got eggs. I got more ironing coming in then a body has a right to claim, an' your dad works his butt off to keep us all healthy an' fine. What you talkin' this poor? We ain' white trash, sonny, always know, we ain' white trash. We's the kings, that's what we are, the kings! Only the rest doan know." She looked over her shoulder at the screen door. "We is God's chosen ones, 'cuz we ain' forgotten how to love. An' that's the big difference, John. Always keep the will to love, an' God will sure 'nuff take care 'a the rest."

# Chapter Nineteen

*So stand on me. I'll catch you falling.*
*You can stand on me, and I'll help you find a way.*
*Stand on me, I can see our ship is turnin'*
*Stand on me,*
*We're sailin' on the wind of a better day.*

*E-L-P "Better Days"*

The senior prom didn't end the school year, only kicked it, but the seniors acted like it had. Some, like Bobby White, were lucky enough to be going off to college, he with a half scholarship to the University of Missouri at Columbia. Others were going into the family business, and some were getting married and settling down, with dime store and warehouse jobs. A few would be put on at the railroad, but after that there wasn't much except trying to scratch a living out of raising hogs or growing corn and wheat.

John Cheevers had decided on law enforcement after all, with his friend prodding him to go for it. The exams were set up and he did very well. He would need to take classes at the junior college in the next town; there'd have to be a ride to that, he figured, but he and his dad would come up with something. Then the twenty-four weeks of police academy. There was still high school to finish and the last games of football and then spring baseball.

He had seen Marilyn in the halls almost every day, and she acted like she didn't see him or didn't have time to chat, so he waited for her to come to him. She seemed more solemn to him as he watched her face staring straight ahead as she went in and out of classes. They had a few together, but for the most part, she was separate from him. He never got to ask her about the prom night, and he hoped she had looked beautiful and more fervently, he prayed Bobby White had been a gentleman. He never thought twice about Marilyn when the locker room jocks got quiet around the vivaciously talking White, never guessed the reason for the sudden hush.

It was well into February, a sunny fair day, breaking up the Missouri winter as it was wont to do. He saw Marilyn walking down the bank by the dugout. He was alone, relaxing and enjoying the quiet after doing some laps on the cinder track, still spotted with ice and snow.

"Well, hello, stranger, I been missing you. Everything going okay? Liked your story about the cat in the paper. You are really a good writer, you know that? After this year's over, I'm going to try my . . ." and he stopped to look at her face streaming in tears.

"Why, Marilyn, for Pete's sake, I didn't mean to make you cry. Come here, sit down, sit down, what's made you cry?" He patted the bench beside him, moved his old running shoes onto the ground, and finished tying his tennis shoes.

"John, have you ever felt like life just isn't worth living? Just wish it would dig a big hole and stuff you in? John, oh, John," she cried, turning to him and letting him put his arm around her, patting her other hand on her knee. The hand held a crumpled wet Kleenex.

"We've all had those times, Marilyn, they just pass, that's all. My mom says. . ." and she jerked her head up and glared at him with red rimmed eyes.

"Oh, John, don't give me your mama's sacred words. I just couldn't bear them right now, right now, when my life is hell, when I don't have a place to live even, when I have to get out of my own house, find a life, my dad said, find the life I have chosen for myself. He said that to me, John, and I'm only sixteen, I can't find work, I sure can't find it now, with this" and she pointed to her small rounded belly, "this thing growing in me. John, do you understand what's happened to me? What I let happen to me?" The tears started gushing then, and John watched her helplessly, holding her thin wracking shoulders against the sobs, and he did now understand.

"The bastard," he whispered. None of this could be her fault, his flawed reasoning told him, the man has to be the one responsible. Marilyn could not have asked for such a thing to happen to her, but happen it had, if her distraught face told him nothing else.

"And your parents? Surely they understand, people make mistakes, this isn't the first time a child has been born outside of marriage, it's not like you killed someone or something. What do they say?"

She stood before him and leaned on the wall of the dugout. "I'll tell you what they said. My mother said she can't have a daughter who's not married live in her house and get big with a child conceived without the blessing of the church. The fucking blessing of the church, something she's had for the last sixteen years, the holy blessing, and nothing in it for her, believe me, I know what my parents don't do, and love each other is one of them. And my pontifical father, the patron of all saints, called me a whore flat out, and started packing my things, while Mother went to the garage and emptied boxes of their worthless junk, and brought them meekly to him to use. All my pictures, my clothes, even the sheets off my bed, my teddy bear . . . " and the tears started again. John stood and touched her shoulder.

"Where you goin'?" he asked quietly.

"I haven't the foggiest notion," she responded through her wet lips. Her nose was running now, and the Kleenex had become a soggy blob.

"Wait here," he said, and he jumped out of the dugout and went around in back where he unbuttoned his cotton flannel shirt and stripped off his white tee shirt, slipping the flannel back on and buttoning it up. He came back and crawled in, handing the tee shirt to Marilyn.

"Wipe your face, and let's get out of here," he suggested. She buried her face in the whiteness and blew her nose. He glanced at the shirt and knew he wasn't asking his mother to wash that. He'd be washing that one, he knew.

And what to do with her? He couldn't just leave her sitting in the dugout, crying her eyes out. Her own people had turned her out. He'd have to consult ma, he knew, she knew how to take care of such matters. He felt better just thinking of his mom and dad back at the log cabin, even Arlon and Cloteria seemed dear to him. Mom would know what to do for Marilyn Stewart and her unwelcome baby.

They walked the mile in the dusky twilight, John trying to think how to explain this to his mother in the most polite way, phrasing it this way and then trying a different tone, and then pausing in their walk and gesturing to make his point in silent preparation. Marilyn solemnly walked beside him, watching his lips move over his tenuous words. He had it right, he agreed with himself at last, that sounded real good. He held Marilyn's hand the last path and smiled encouragingly at her.

"It will be fine, you watch, my mom can do anything."

Who else among her friends had offered to help? Her best girl friends had only looked wide eyed and used the first excuse to dart away and start the rumor mill spinning. Heartless, all of them, heartless and faithless. One friend had helped her move her boxes into her garage, but she told Marilyn not to tell her mom. She wouldn't like it. Like it? Had she liked it, sleeping in their garage last night, using the back bushes for a toilet, washing her face in their bird bath? Hell, no, she hadn't liked it, she hated it, and the growing burden within her dragged her down further as the nausea made her throw up all over the woman's azalea bush. "Serves you right," Marilyn had spunkily said, wiping her mouth. It could have been your daughter, only she got her period after going out with Bobby White.

Mrs. Cheevers was out on the front porch, shaking the flour out of her biscuit rolling cloth, when she saw John coming down the road with a girl. She didn't know the girl, only saw she was white, and that face looking up at her boy was a beautiful face, a Madonna's face. Oh, my, Gloria worried, not fall for a white girl. So much trouble, son, so much problem. Stay with Sallie Buck or Maya Taylor or any of the girls from church, but not this one, she prayed, please, God, not a white girl. She went down the steps to meet them, and John said, "Mama, this is Marilyn Stewart, the cheerleader I been helping with her algebra," and Gloria looked at the girl's red rimmed eyes, took her whole body in with one practiced glance, and said, "John, this girl needs some water."

Gloria put her arm around Marilyn, and Marilyn couldn't help it. She let her head rest on Gloria's shoulder, and let herself be led up the stairs to the porch swing. John hadn't even had the chance to get his nicely practiced speech in when his mother said, rather sharply for her, "The water, John, an' be sure to get a good glass, not the dipper." He went in through the screen door, nodded to his brother and sister bent over coloring at the table, and they watched him get a good glass and sprint out the back door and down to the spring. The water was cool on his hands, and he splashed his face and drank of its coldness, filled the glass full and ran back to the front porch around the house.

"Well, finally," his mother said, taking the glass from him. "You got chores to do, like in the barn." He nodded and sprinted off again, and the next hour he spent sweeping straw and loading some manure out of Clara's stall, stopping now and again in his efforts to gaze up at the two women rocking and talking in the old porch swing. Damn! All that practicing and finding just the right words to win his mom over to helping Marilyn, and there she was, that little fox, smiling and drinking her water and listening to his mother with her solemn eyes and nodding like she knew exactly what Mama was advising her to do. Got her to smile. That was a start.

# Chapter Twenty

*I don't mind you comin' here*
*Wastin' all my time . . .*
*I guess you're just what I needed*
*I needed someone to please*

*The Cars "Just What I Needed"*

Beech Cheevers had to hand it to Gloria. She sure could make fluffy biscuits, and he sopped up the good red eye gravy made with buttermilk, and would have licked his fingers except the dinner guest, laughing with the kids, and showing them funny animals with her fingers, might have spotted him. Sweet girl, he thought, nice of her to come home with John for dinner.

Gloria gave him the high sign and motioned for him to grab some plates and help her clear. He moved to follow her, balancing the gravy boat on one palm, and carrying the bread basket in the other.

"We've got it," she called out when the girl moved to help clear. "You youngin's go out an' watch for fireflies." The children moved onto the porch, giggling and showing off for Marilyn, and Gloria started pumping the old handle, sending spurts of well-aired well water into the sink. "Get me some hot to mix with this," she ordered, and he obeyed. Not like her to be so curt; he figured he must've forgotten their anniversary or her birthday, but nope, he had those written down. He poured the hot water into the sink, and she raised her hand when it was hot enough. He poured the rest of it into the tin pan she used for rinsing. The steam rose around her face and she wiped her brow with her sudsy arm. A bubble got caught in her hair.

"Beech Cheevers," she complained, "when we gonna get us a hot water heater? You could get a hot water heater from Tubbs, a used one maybe, an' we could just turn on the faucet an' have real baths instead of that tub. John's been taking cold showers at the spring so long he's gonna shrink up from the cold."

"Whoa, Glory, you never said you wanted no heater put in. Lands, if'n you wanted one, I'd a put one in long ago. Thought you dint want to pay no higher bills, you said. No gas man comin' out here to hound us. 'Course they got 'lectric, but those clickers run real fast in circles, running up the tab, but if'n you want one, I'll go see Tubbs tomorrow, right after work." He picked up the drying towel and started wiping the warm wet plates as she went back to her washing and rinsing.

"If the child is going to live with us, she's got to have a proper bath. Alright for us to scrimp along an' make merry of it, but she's usta city houses, with plumbin', Beech. Now you wouldn't want her to think we was cheap or backwards, now would ya?"

Beech laid down the towel, and reached for his pipe and pouch on the sill over the window. "Now I wouldn't be askin' too much, in my own house, what you mean by that, her livin' with us? Why she be livin' with us? Where's her people?" He packed the pipe and lit it with a kitchen match. He dragged slowly, letting the fine tobacco melt into a soothing smoke.

"She doan have no folks that wants her, Beech. She got a baby comin'."

"Son of a bitch," he got out, wondering what hell his son had started here. The quiet ones always surprised you, he thought, still water runs deep. Didn't think the boy had it in him. Not as smart as he had hoped. Long road ahead. Sorrowful long road for that little guy coming.

"Not what you thinkin', so stop that. John's not the daddy, the daddy is the big white quarterback, that White boy everyone holds so high an' mighty. Well, he ain't talked to Marilyn since he took her agains' her will, didn't have the decency to be a man an' come callin' after he hurt her, an' now she got a chile comin', an' her folks has turned her out. Clothes an' all. Where she to go, Beech, if she can't stay with us?"

He puffed his pipe slowly, glowing in the friendly wave of pleasure he felt rippling through him. His son warn't the daddy. His son warn't the daddy. Thank Jesus for that. The rest seemed a small price to pay for that good piece of news.

"Can you finish up alone, Glory? I want to check Clara an' put some ointment on her, she looks red around the udders. Doan you try to milk her for a day. You got enough milk for now? Give her a rest." He moved toward the porch, puffing on his pipe, standing a little straighter than he usually did at night, a little cocky tonight, she thought, turning to watch him go through the living room.

"Beech, you dint answer my question."

He smiled back at her over his shoulder. "I'll call on Tubbs tomorrow, Glory. Just tell me where you wan' it." The screen door slapped shut behind him as she peered around the corner and saw him sit down on the top step between Marilyn and John to watch the kids chasing the fireflies in the grass.

She smiled to herself in contentment as she turned back to the dishes. I be so lucky. Always bin so lucky. God sure do put some blessins on me. An' now this chile come to us. We got oursells a lamb to care for. You send her, dint you, God, send her 'cuz you know we tough, we can do fer her. We gots all this to share.

Bless dishes, dear God. That means we eat, and Lord, I do thank you for that.

# Chapter Twenty-One

*Levon, Levon likes his money.*
*He makes a lot, they say.*
*Spends his days countin'*
*In a garrett by the motorway.*

*Elton John "Levon"*

Pond Ridge, Missouri, was settled in the rolling hills and dipping two lane road close to seventy miles south of St. Louis, down Highway 55. Most folks just breezed past it after hitting Ste. Genevieve, batted their eyes, and swept past it before they came up on St. Mary's. Hunting for out of the way antique shops with old cow bells and straw baskets, they didn't notice it was a tidy little town with a solid white First United Church, and a freewill mission in an old house almost certain to become a church if they could just get past a membership of six families. They had a Black Church, A.M.E. affiliated with more than two hundred members. Most of the families living in the town itself were white, but there were some two hundred notable exceptions. The town had a Knights of Columbus meeting room. There weren't enough Catholics to have a hall, and that worried them sorely. Most Catholics drove into Ste. Gen. or further to Farmington to hear the Mass on Sunday, and these few held themselves up as the only truly deserving ones to enter the Kingdom of Heaven. But others disagreed, quietly thinking the Pope was plain foolish, always believing he was right. Didn't Jesus accept some error along the way? That was what forgiveness was all about, trying again, being newborn to Christ, giving themselves a new chance. And some surely asked for the new chance weekly.

The farmhouses were set out north and south of town, two to five miles space between them, hanging onto life in a dry rocky terrain, providence daring the men to plant crops in the shale soil. Some tried, most failed, but Beech Cheevers had an extraordinarily nice piece of ground, laying to the northeast of Pond Ridge, formerly a commercial chicken farm, and the ground, well fertilized by the long departed flocks, left him with a nice cash crop of corn, beans, and wheat each year. He had no heavy equipment to work his fields, but other hands from the two to five mile farms came to help when they saw the harvest ready. Beech kept four sows and a boar, selling their pigs at a modest gain, kept Clara fresh each year by buying stud from Tubbs, the plumber, and for all eyes to behold, he was successful in bringing home the bacon from the railroad, and raising it, too.

The well-tended spread behind the Cheevers' farm, on the western edge of the Mississippi River, belonged to a trusteeship in the name of Sylvia Corothers, a long ago name from the past. She settled the land in the forties before anyone else had, and lived there with her husband and growing family, nine live births, but only three made it to their teens before they died in a smallpox epidemic that started in a slave shack, or so the rumor went. Why none of the Black children died didn't seem to change the story: the disease had started with the colored. A traveling Black midwife took care of the Corothers' children, did the best she could in that time of no running water, no indoor plumbing, no inoculations to ward off the smallpox. The children withered and gasped their last breath in the arms of Sylvia, and her husband quietly dug the graves he had grown accustomed to seeing.

Days turned into weeks. The seasons changed on the massive holding, kept up by the hard working husband of Sylvia Corothers and the strong black backs of the tenants, until one day in the deep of winter when he went out to the barn, he gave it all up, threw a rope over the running beam high over the lintel, moved up the nailed steps to the hayloft, and jumped as far as his neck and the rope would let him. The Black men helping him work the farm found him that morning at six, swinging gently and at peace. They cut him down, and some said later that one man rocked Sylvia's husband in his great arms, and cried while the rest sang a spiritual to help his departing soul. Oh, it had departed, there was no hearing that hymn, but the thought of doing it at all was a good one, and no one ever knew, except maybe Sylvia. She took to her bed often after her husband died; she was close to forty by then, and thin and dry as a piece of parchment, but the Blacks didn't leave her. They came and did their work, helped out in the house as well, had their womenfolk air her rugs and change her bedding, saw to it that Miss Sylvia got her meals, and she began to pick up a little. Maybe it was the collards after a life of too much gravy; maybe it was the fresh radishes and the ears of corn sliced off and fed to her, spoonful by spoonful, but the love that poured from the five shacks down at the foot of the farm near the river gave her a new handle on life. She gained some weight and found new vigor. All they got for their effort was the same thin envelope once a month. And, of course, all the gleanings from the farm. The blackfolk did okay, by all standards. Even the ones living off her place, the day people, she called them, even they prospered.

She had no one, she realized, pulling her shawl around her

shoulders on the great white porch, no one in the world except the helpers. No church men came to see her, and she would have spat in their eye had they dared. Her husband didn't put up with all that tom foolery. Damnation if it must be, but he wasn't holding no sissy preacher's hand to get into the pearly gates.

One small boy always caught her eye, and she saw him first when he was two. His great round eyes and perfect baby teeth, set in his smooth brown face, made her call him My Chocolate Soldier. Whenever the women would trudge up the hill with cleaning to do or pails of hot, aroma filled victuals, she always asked, "Now where's my little soldier, my little chocolate man?" When she'd see him, she insisted he be put on her lap, and she'd kiss his short tight curls and press him to her breast. She read to him a lot, and became kind of the baby sitter, the women agreed, moving off on their chores through the two story farmhouse. Blessing she is, they agreed giggling; hope he don't wet her. The books he liked to touch, and she showed him how to carefully turn the pages, so as not to rip them, and he was ever so gentle, watching her face purse the words. When he was close to three, she had read through almost all of the books she had saved from her children, and he went on his own feet now, dragged out new ones, and sat on a stool by her slippered feet and listened to her read. At four, he pulled the book out of her hand, shut it, and told her a story, awkwardly and slowly, but making a very good point about dogs and cats and chickens on a big farm, and nothing to eat but rocks until the rain came, and then the carrots shot up and everyone was happy. The end. Sylvia clapped her veined hands in delight, called all the women down that day, and asked him to recite the story for them. He shook his small head firmly.

"Nope. Just for you, nanny S." And the old woman's heart completely melted over him, her health improved immensely in this oneness with the child after that day. She spent all her time in his company, moving around on his arm as he grew straighter and taller, insisted he get the very best education, although she had sponsored clothing and expense money for the shack children as she fondly called them. But none favored her like he did, none sought her out, read to her, kissed her hand goodnight, like they do in France, he explained; none winked at her, and no one, no one could say a word against her favorite.

It was never determined for certain how she died, if she had a stroke or a heart attack, but the bells in First United Church tolled one wet morning in the early eighties, and no one knew who they were for. The small local grocer had heard from the milkman delivering that one of the shack blacks had gone up and found her on the porch steps, all slipped down in a bundle of wet mud. Not a way for a lady to die, and the grocer had asked the pastor to ring the bells anyway, in case anyone cared. Something to mark the passing of a nice lady who couldn't help it if she was rich.

How rich was she, the Blacks wondered, sitting down that night in their shacks? Who was going to pay them, now that she left? Would they have to leave? No one knew, and hearts were troubled that night as they tucked the young ones in. They gazed up the path from their shacks, through the cherry and apple and plum trees, saw the lights were not on in the big house. The stand of trees separating their homesteads from the lawns and spaciousness of the big house seemed to be a solitary boundary, between what was theirs and what would never be theirs.

Life began again the next day, and the men went off to the fields and the barns, and the women, not knowing what else to do, they had for so long done the same thing, went up the path to the big house, and began cleaning and scrubbing and waxing. When they left that day and returned home to stir their own suppers and take in their dry laundry off the stretched lines, their menfolk had heard nothing new. Surely someone would come and tell them what to do: a lawyer or a doctor or the pastor from the ringing church. Even the grocer might have news.

When a week went by and still no word, a representative was sent into town to inquire about the families on the Corothers' place. They never hesitated on who should go: Stone Franklin was always cleaned up and ready for movement, his shoes polished, his mare handsome and brushed in her mahogany sheen, the saddle a last minute afterthought on his seventeenth birthday by his best girl, that Sylvie, they liked to tease him.

It was with a heavy heart that he went into town that day, not to store, school, or church (they didn't come to this church anyway, had one down in the hollows they prayed at with Rev. Walters), to find someone who would know. The grocer directed him to the new pastor, Dr. Stewart, and the pastor said he didn't have the faintest idea what to do. "Best, my son, just to go back to your home and wait until someone comes to you."

And that's just what Stone did. He went back to his people and said, "She left the place to us. It was her will that we have it." Such joyous celebration that night. The five shacks glowed with light and music, and several furtive trips to an old still, pumping up in the hills, brought back some kick for the fellows that night, something they rarely imbibed, but tonight was special. They was landowners, by Lord. They had met the truth and waited for it and they were landowners.

Each month Stone found something strange, something he did not expect to happen: the mailbox had five thin white envelopes in them, just as if nothing had happened. He ripped each open, the first time and every month thereafter, signed the backs of the checks, marking "X" on Theopolis' because he couldn't write, only mark, but his mark was good at the bank, and the money was all placed in an account by Stone, now turned eighteen and fully able to handle the affairs of what he liked to call "the Settlement." Out of this pooled fund, he invested some, saved some, bought items in bulk, purchased a sulky and small pony to aid in the transport of goods and lumber to improve the shacks. He made sure electric was brought in, at some cost to the county because of a shared cost plan, but he held his own, and got the power down to the shacks. Looking better than they ever had; those shacks now had neat porches and flowers growing round, and small gardens became bigger gardens as the women had more time now. The children were growing and no little ones underfoot. Still not enough homes for everyone. Half of the new owners moved off Settlement and rented homes in Pond Ridge. They drew their rent and pocket money from Stone. Theopolis called them the "tweeners": not on, not off, just in-between.

Sylvia's big house, standing spotless and painted and trim, looked very much lived in, and the care they all took to keep it beautiful made it into a shrine. No one played in that house, but the older children were allowed to read in the library, taking care to be careful with the books, and they were allowed, if Stone was near and approved, to use the indoor bathroom toilet and get icecubes from the refrigerator. That was all. No one was allowed to go upstairs except to dust or wax and no item was to be moved from the house, for that was stealing, and they all knew the heavy penalty stealing carried, at home and at large.

This, then, was the life enjoyed by the Black men and women living one mile from the town of Pond Ridge, Missouri, on the north, one half mile on the southern section. No one ever questioned their right to be there. No one ever said a word. The situation would have stayed much as it was except that Pond Ridge was growing, and the inevitable newspaper came in with a reporter named Tom Sweet, who was not sweet at all. He was young, and rough, and smoked cigarettes and was given to nosing around. He nosed around real close when he happened on the Corothers' walnut posted metal swing gate, and he was one surprised white man when he was stopped inside the gate by a Black man holding a shotgun on him.

"You got business here?" the man asked, holding the gun level with one hand. Tom dropped his smoke and ground it out.

"This the old Corothers place?" he asked. The man eyed him coldly with slitted yellow eyes. A nigger, Tom reflected, a damn hired hand, acting uppity.

"We call it 'the Settlement,' but it ust to be the Corothers place, till she died an' lef it to us."

"Oh, she did, did she? I must've missed that part of the story. When was that, you say, when she left it to you?"

"That ain' none of your business, mister, now pick up that stub an' high tail it. You on private prop'ty." He raised the shotgun again, and Tom Sweet never hesitated to pick up the stub and turn quickly to walk briskly down the lane. He looked back once and saw the tall man doff his hat to him.

Back in town, he started asking questions, and the dates and times of events fell into place, ten years it had been. Ten years and no one even asked. A great story. How much land was back there? He went to the survey office, asked to see the Corothers' plot, and the pages unfolded before him, sixteen pages of neatly laid out lots, all marked with stakes and ribbons, totaling an amazing 1,080 acres of wilderness, and crop fields on the Mississippi flood lands: a beautiful home, five tenant houses, a brook, three spring fed ponds, two horse barns, a field of hog styes, a fowl house. The surveyor said, "Last time I saw it they had a heated hen house, too, up on the ridge. Yes, that's how I remember seeing it. Beautiful place. Every one of them Corothers dead. Sad. No heirs."

No heirs, thought Tom. Well, the tenants seemed to think they were heirs. He'd find out real quick about those blacks up there pulling guns on him. The press has some power, and he was gonna use it against that nigger who had the nerve to stop him.

He got the publisher's permission to run an intro story, asking the community to come forward with any old stories about the mysterious sequestered Corothers clan, said he was doing a period piece about the growth of Ste. Genevieve County, wanted everyone to join in before the centennial celebration scheduled for September. Any other stories will be gratefully reviewed, he lied, then dropped into the wastebasket. It was the Corothers place that caught his fancy, and the unseemly crowd running it.

The story caused a rush to attic and basement for pictures and souvenirs of times past, and the press room in the paper's office brimmed with clipped photos and dry-edged papers about their families, but nothing about the Corothers came up as he pawed the pile. A blank. A mystery. Tom sat back, lit a cigarette, and pondered his next move. What move, he blithered to himself. That was it, my big move.

Nothing. When did niggers get the right to take over white men's homes?

"Tom, got a minute?" called out Mr. Blake, the paper's publisher and chairman of the newly founded Chamber of Commerce. Four members. Dues paid.

"You bet, sir," responded Tom, on his feet and cigarette stubbed out. He went into Mr. Blake's sparse office and sat down. Mr. Blake was handling a letter very gently by its edges, reading it over and over as he gazed to the window and then back to the paper. He rubbed his glasses on his sleeve and put them on again.

"Tom, I got a letter about your Corothers story, and I think you need to know about it. We better back up a little and listen to what this man says." Tom reached for the letter, and Mr. Blake gave it to him gratefully.

Impressive stationery, had to hand it to them. Nice embossing. Good credentials. GREAT credentials. Filbourn, Mackey, and Spitz, St. Louis, Missouri. No firm to fool with. Tom twisted in his seat and loosened his tie. The usual legal heading, the street address, the post number, the opening, crisp in its tone:

*To: The Bugle, Editor, Publisher*

*Not knowing to whom I address this message, I only request that a knowledgeable member of your writing staff, perhaps someone more grounded in finding fact rather than digging in graves, present themselves to my office in St. Louis on September One, 9:00 A.M. sharp, to be informed of the matter of the Corothers Estate, held in Trust by this Office, and that person shall be informed as to the delicacy of the matter before him and not before. The instructions of this office as to the secrecy of this matter shall be forewarned.*

*Respectfully,*
*J. Clinton Albright*

"What's he saying?" asked Tom. The gibberish was lost on him.

"He's saying get your butt to Sain Louie on the first, and get your story. He apparently has it, and he'll fill you in. I'm not going. That's for sure. I don't like lawyers, never have. You started this, Tom, with your intro in the paper. You go see him."

❧

So it was on the first that Tom roused himself early, and drove to St. Louis to meet a Mr. J. Clinton Albright. The office was easy to find, in a good solid brick re-hab on a fashionable stretch of buildings, went up in the elevator and met one woman at the outer office who let him wait to see another woman who led him to J. Clinton Albright who, as it happened, was just coming into the office.

"Sweet, right? Good morning, come with me, please, let me check a matter, and I'll be right with you." He moved away in his dark suit and returned, beaming, in a moment.

"Mr. Mackey is ready for you. Please follow me." The man moved briskly away, and Tom sauntered after him. Big deal. Big firm. So what? They weren't going to shake him that easily. He was on a story. He felt it; they wouldn't shut him up.

He was whisked into an office, and then through a door into a bigger office, and the damn room was huge. All windows on one wall, a shimmering stream of morning light falling on a long oval desk in front of a small silver-haired man in a pinstriped grey suit, sipping coffee and standing over some notes he was reading. The man smiled up at the two as they entered.

"Sweet, is it?" he offered, holding out his hand in a genuinely friendly manner. "Nice to meet you. Mel Mackey here. Just call me Mel. Thanks, J.C., for bringing him in. I appreciate it." Mr. Albright smiled his adieus and left them, closing the door softly.

"Well, and isn't it a grand day we have? Look at that sunshine!" He waved his short arms around the windowed wall and basked in the warmth. "Love the weather. We have had some good days. And the crops, son, how are the crops doing in Ste. Genevieve County?" The eyes that pierced Tom's were icy cold for all that warmth.

"The crops? I really don't know, just haven't checked the locals for that." Spiteful question. Pointedly spiteful. Tom would have to be on his guard, he knew.

"In a growing county and you don't know crops? Son, let me tell you, I was an old farm boy, and if you don't know crops, you won't make it on a paper. People want to hear about those crops: how they're doing, when the rains will come, does it look like an early frost, why, you got to be practically an Almanac to make it in the country."

"I'll give that some thought, Mr. Mackey."

"Mel. I really think Mel will work, okay, Tom?"

"Yes, Mel, that will work."

"Good. Now to the matter at hand. Sylvia Corothers is a long past friend of mine, a delightful lady, who, incidentally, chose to marry Hubert when I wanted to marry her, but that's another story." He actually looked paternal as he smiled at Tom, who didn't ask for the story.

"So, as the story goes, she went her way, and I went mine, but she kept in touch with me, let me handle her little affairs when I was starting out, just to give me a boost, and then, at the end of her life, she came to me and she wrote out her will. This was after Hubert had hanged himself and left her alone. Sad that he should die that way, but maybe burying nine of his children turned his mind. Who's to say? Not me to judge. But my Sylvia, a-a-h, Sylvia Corothers, as you know her, or don't know her, a-a-h, that's right, you don't know her. She was a spunky girl. Came from North Carolina, as pretty as a picture she was, and was up until the day she died. She died on the porch steps, they told me, and my people came, and got her body, and she is now resting in a cemetery in North Carolina along with her people. She never wanted to be buried at the same place where they put Hubert and the children, said if she did, it would damn the ground forever. 'I must have bad seed,' she confessed to me. I think she had a good heart and bad luck."

Tom listened carefully as the man poured out the story. It was a good story. He probably couldn't use it, but he was listening all the same.

"Do you want coffee? Sorry to be so rude, I completely got lost there a minute." He pressed the button and asked, "Rachel, when you get a minute, would you bring coffee to our guest. Cream? Yes, surely we have a cream user here. And sugar. What say, Tom? Sugar?"

Tom meekly agreed to cream, no sugar, and Mr. Mackey piped, "Just as I thought. Coffee, cream, no sugar." He moved his papers, sat down and was eye level with Tom.

"While we're waiting, I just want you to know that everything that has happened at the Corothers place, at 'the Settlement' as it's now called, is entirely in keeping with the wishes of Sylvia. I'll explain shortly," and he stood and accepted the tray from Rachel and placed it near Tom's reach. "Thank you, Rachel, that was nice of you." She smiled in leaving.

He sat down again, picked up his papers, then tossed them back on the desk. "I don't need those anymore. I've reread them a hundred times, and they are tight, Mr. Sweet, legally tight. I truly looked for loop holes, looked for ways that Sylvia had miscalculated her last requests, but they were all sound. All her wishes, backed up by her family money, which she came into some time back, and then the value of the land in Pond Ridge plus the improvements. Well, I would say, over two million, all told, a nice hunk of money, wouldn't you say?"

Tom only nodded, reached for the coffee, spilled in some cream, and sat back with it.

"The place has been running just as she hoped, due to a very smart young man who took over, just a kid then, moving the money we sent down, but he managed to make some good decisions, and we've been watching him, that's what we get our fee for, to make sure it went the way she wanted it to, but it will all come to an end soon. Her heir will be taking over when he's thirty if he's still single; that was her stipulation, that he be single, and at last check, he was twenty-eight and not married, not by any legal record. Then it's up to him to decide what will happen to those acres and that house. It will all be his, and what he does with it, only time can tell. Now that's all I'm allowed to pass on at this point, and mind you, I wouldn't have said a word except for the story in the paper that brought you to my attention. For now, let the blacks run the place. The true heir will come into his own when he's thirty. Then it will be time enough for you to dig into any further facts. Can we say that's fair?"

Tom said, "Do you mean, sir, that she may have an illegitimate child, one waiting in the wings even now to pounce, to take back what's his?" The idea had just crossed his mind.

Mr. Mackey stiffened slightly, pushed back his chair and rose. "I think you may have missed the whole point here, Tom. My Sylvia didn't ever betray Hubert. Of all people, I knew her best, and to think she would step outside her marriage vows, well, you don't know North Carolina, or maybe you know it about the same as Pond Ridge. Better look, look close, you may miss the big ending." He winked at Tom, offered his hand, and ushered him to the door. He was out before he had a chance to fully digest this piece of news. Maybe old Mrs. Corothers had strayed; maybe old Mel Mackey with the crush on her had gotten her with child, maybe that kid was hidden away, joyously awaiting his thirtieth birthday. God, with two million coming, who wouldn't wait, and watch their blood pressure? Old Mel Mackey had a hand in this, Tom felt sure about that, had more than a hand in it if his guess was correct. Someone would be mighty happy when the heir reached thirty, and that someone had, undoubtedly, sprung from the Mackey gene pool.

He drove back to Pond Ridge, tasting the richly creamed coffee on his tongue and lips, feeling he had touched a really good story: about the coming of the heir, the final solution for the 1,080 richly rolling acres, the laments of the blacks as they were driven off, especially the slit eyed nigger who had shown him out with a shotgun as his guide. Pay back time is coming, he gloated. You folks don't have much longer here. How you made it this far was sheer luck. Everybody knows niggers are too lazy to farm.

Mr. Blake refused to run any further story that was based on hearsay and speculation.

# Chapter Twenty-Two

Beech and Gloria Cheevers went about their business, running their farm, and finally getting the hot water heater put in. It took some doing, seeing there was no space left inside the log house, so Beech and Tubbs hired one of the Blacks from the Corothers spread, with time on his hands and everything ship shape up above, to design a room around the hot water heater. He looked from one to the other, said this was plain foolishness, designing a room around a hot water heater when the place had no bathroom. Why not make it bigger, at little more cost, and make a bathroom?

Gloria worried over this, looked over her expense books, checked the growing savings account, and finally agreed to a bathroom. "More for Marilyn than anything," she intoned, sealing the deal, and Tubbs and Beech leaped to the project as if they were going to enjoy a bath together. Four weeks later, and not more than one thousand out of the account, the room off the kitchen was bright and clean: a linoleum floor, a claw-foot tub Tubbs had been saving, a sink with old porcelain handles, and the water ran, it ran and ran, the kids found out until they were soundly scolded. The toilet, with a wooden water box up five feet, had a pull chain, and everyone had to try it just once, then they ran frightened back to the outhouse until the newness wore off. School was different. The water closets didn't startle them so, but often they went without flushing, afraid they'd be sucked into the white bowl.

Since Marilyn had come to live with them, John had been living in a small bunk house room off the barn. Arlon had joined him, feeling like a sissy if he shared a room with a girl, and he weren't no sissy. A slender, smart eleven year old, he loved John and felt so close to him that he called him, "Dah," when no one was near. Not that he didn't love Beech; he just had been close to John so long that he looked up to him with envy and admiration.

Beech had been the one to collect Marilyn's things, had gone to the all white neighborhood in Pond Ridge, found her friend's address, and rapped lightly on the back porch door. A small golden-haired woman had answered, opened the door, and said, "No, I don't have any work for you." She almost got the door shut before Beech slipped his hand in and stopped its closure.

"Ma'am, I ain' here about work. I'm here to collect the things in your garage, the boxes belongin' to Marilyn Stewart. Your daughter let Marilyn store her things there until she found a place to live. I'm here to get those boxes, thas all, ma'am."

"I have no idea what you're talking about. I don't know you and my husband would be very upset if I let anyone . . . " and she paused, "anyone, mind you, go into his garage and take things. You need to come back when my husband is home." She got the door shut and pulled the lock firmly into place.

Beech wasn't a man to be set aside so easily. He started again, speaking louder through the storm door. "Ma'am, my information is correct. If you'll just come take a look, see that some of those boxes hold the things belongin' to Marilyn, your daughter's friend, we can wind this thin' up an' I won't have to take off from my job to come over agin. I'll be outta your hair today, ma'am, I promise." She hesitated then, he did seem to be a straight shooter, but then you could never be too careful these days, opening your doors to strangers, letting them lead you into a dark garage. She shivered.

"I'm sorry," she repeated, not sorry at all, grimly happy that she had the power to keep this man from intruding on her. Sure, she had heard of Macy Stewart's act, wiping his hands clean of his daughter's sin, had heard it from the pulpit just last week, and the week before, how shamed he felt for his daughter, living in sin, but he had provided all of the love and charity he could afford. His daughter was lost to him, but the flock before him . . . that was his real concern, that they all be saved, that they live virtuous lives, untainted by drink or tobacco or fornication. His mission was in the world and the sacrifice of his daughter to the Devil was not of his doing.

"Ma'am, do you know who I am? I'm John Cheever's daddy, the baseball player an' on the football team, too, John Cheevers. He's a friend of your daughter's, too, an' he speaks mos' highly of her. Surely it wouldn' take but a minute of your time, to let the door on the garage up an' let me get Marilyn's things."

So it was true. Marilyn Stewart had gone to live with a darkie family, probably the family of the father of her unborn one; it made her sick to think of it. "Please go, Mr. Cheevers, please. I'm not a strong woman. I feel a headache coming on."

Beech stepped down from the porch and eyed the woman. She didn't look sickly to him. She was afraid of him, scared he was gonna rant and rage and rape. A sad state of affairs. He noticed the woman in the next yard, unpinning laundry, most of it diapers, and he changed his tact. He moved across the hedge separating their yards and called to her.

"Yo, Missy, hi. I'm John Cheever's daddy, come to pick up some boxes stored in Miz Bronson's garage, things belongin' to Marilyn Stewart, an' I think Miz Bronson would 'preciate if you would come on ovah a minute an' be with her while I get those boxes."

She smiled agreeably, set down her basket, and moved easily with him over the hedge. Mrs. Bronson fairly sprang out of the back door, calling, "Margie, don't have to trouble. Everything's okay." Bolstered by Marjorie standing and chatting with the man, she opened the doors to the rarely used garage, and spotted boxes she had not known were there.

"Those must be the ones," she started, moving to open the back bay door.

Beech set about moving the boxes into his truck bed, and Marjorie gave him a hand, cutting the work time in half. She paused when they were finished, said, "Wait a minute." She ran back to her house, up the steps and inside and back out in two minutes, carrying a big plastic bag.

"These are for Marilyn, tell her it's for the baby, all clean, and not really used. They grow so fast." Beech opened the cab and laid the bundle on the seat.

"That's mighty nice of you, Miss Marjorie, she sure will be needin' baby things soon. I'll give her your regard." He tipped his cap to her, nodded to Mrs. Bronson, and darted into the driver's seat. The engine roared to life and he backed out, shifted gears, and waved one last time at the two women standing by the open garage.

"Nice, nice guy," murmured Marjorie, turning to head back to her yard and laundry.

"Marjorie," intoned Judith Bronson, "that wasn't really necessary, giving away things to the likes of that family. The Church could have used those things. The rummage sale is coming up."

"But they may not get to the sale, Judith, and besides, I'd like to think that they'll be put to better use on that little one's back. He'll have a long row to hoe. Multiracial always do. It's a shame, really, just a shame, that people hold so much stock in the color of a person's skin." A loud cry filled the air.

"That's my cue, Ethan's up, and Bart will be home for supper soon. The plant's closing early today, isn't that nice? He'll be able to help me with dinner. You and your daughter want to come over for barbecue?" The often asked question, the quiet response of no, they had other plans, but thanks, take a rain check.

"See ya," she called back, legging it up the yard in her nicely fitting jeans, grabbing the basket and running up the back steps to her baby.

The bathroom remained the focal point of the log home. No meal could start without the washing and the splashing, and Gloria found her pleasures were doubled while she sopped up the new floor, grumbling with a smile on her face as she wiped up the spills and set out a new bath mat. We is so lucky, she crooned, so lucky. And the baby's coming soon. Do remember that, Missy, she reminded herself, time to call Luretha Tubbs and have her come by to check on Marilyn. Her size hadn't changed much, Gloria noticed, but some hid it well. She sewed her some tops that hung loose, and Marilyn insisted that as long as she was able, and no one asked any questions, she would continue to go to school. That gal's got pluck, Gloria admitted, watching John and Marilyn head out for the county road to catch the school bus at daybreak, tagged by Arlon, catching Marilyn's school bag and heaving it over his shoulder. Which one likes her more, Arlon or John, pondered Gloria, or is it me that loves her?

Beech had a way to go at the shops, the men standing around, mostly black friends, some white, young men with earnest faces and unskilled hands, chawing about the work ahead, planning the way the hand cars would run to the new lay. He was a friend to every man on the job, and seemed unusually calm the morning one slim young Black closeted him with his glare, and said, "I gots to know. Are you sleeping with a white girl, that Marilyn who run away from her folks?" The others turned away, ashamed, but mildly interested that such a thing could be said. Beech looked back at him and simply shrugged his shoulders. The younger man persisted, moving close to Beech, getting in his space.

"Ain't right and you know it, Cheevers. Ain't right, you with a wife and kids. What you have to say for yourself?" The kid stood then, and didn't move a muscle. Strong kid. Cheevers had liked him before but he admired him now, bringing the words to light that had been on everybody's mind.

"Where you from, son, I doan know as you said."

"I live in town, but The Settlement is my land, that and my family, and we don't like what we hear went down, we don't like it one bit. One thing to marry for love, another thing to carry off a preacher's daughter and get her with child. Yes, I'll say. The Settlement don't like it."

Beech drew in his breath then, let it out slow and easy, rested his hand on the boy's shoulder, and said, "Amen to that. I'm not for carryin' anyone's daughter off, an' if I did, my Glory would beat the tar outta me. That child that lives wit us, she's not wit my child, not wit my son's. She be wit the child of Bobby White, an' he's lon' gone, to play on another field. Anybody who tell you differen' is lyin', an' that's all of it." He headed to the hand car, and the men looked dirty at the young black kid from Settlement, and they clamored for the chance to ride with Beech that morning. A good clear morning. The air's all clear.

# Chapter Twenty-Three

*It'll come at you so fast, my friend,*
*It's thank you and good bye.*
*Caught in the river.*
*You can't stop the flood.*
*That's the power of money.*

*E-L-P "Paper Blood"*

Marjorie's very best friend, Becky Forest, loved it when she heard the story retold with certain embellishments she allowed Marjorie to get away with: the neighbor, the straight laced Judith Bronson, a divorcee, a pillar of Macy Stewart's United flock, cringing before the harmless knock on her door, carried into shitsville over her frantic concerns that she might be vamped, the very morning of the Women's Wednesday Organizational meeting.

She retold the story that night to her husband, Donn, area manager for Cyclone Water Purifying Systems, and man, did he have a good laugh. She loved to make him laugh, but there wasn't much funny here, they realized. How sad. The whole town closeted up with this black/white issue. They had made friends wherever they went, knew many of the two to five mile farmers, dredging up their water from impure cisterns. It was a worry to Donn, all that water out there, much of it tainted with shit floaters. He showed the samples, explained the problem, and most times, he got a door shut in his face. He asked Mr. Blake at the paper to just run a few articles about the dangers of running impure water through the human body, but Blake turned him over to his assistant, a sour chubby guy, who smelled of Kools, with an unfitting name like Sweet to boot.

"Say, we really do have a problem here, this is a big problem, we don't have a city water plant to watch over things, we got to do it house by house. These folks don't know it, but they are no better off than people in the Third World countries, pissing upstream, and letting all the shit come down into their wells. We got ground water here, it carries in a channel under this land, and it comes up in everyone's water. You bet, Mr. Sweet, we got a major problem coming. You won't notice it at first, but it" . . . the practiced speech, the selling spiel that went over so well in other counties. Sweet seemed bored with his dissertation on water, seemed not interested in anything except sorting through his mail, left Donn Forest with the idea that the man didn't really care what happened here, didn't care that his whole landscape and its people were in for a shock, a huge sick medically uncontrollable epidemic.

No one knew who started it, but the rumor started going round that the acres above the town, the Settlement acres, were being considered for a development, a project that would put Pond Ridge on the map, restore its fiscal hold on the tourists, expand the town into an oasis of living beyond one's means. For that was what it was all about, the town knew: to get new people to invest their money and buy goods in their stores, and let them build up their church with the offerings, that was their dream, but underneath it was the small town hostility to anyone doing anything to change what they all believed in: a pure white, no color community, with some darkies doing odd jobs, but kept in their place, not recognizing that a new time was coming. That time would never come to Pond Ridge, Missouri, they vowed; no more Black women was going to teach their children, no darkie man was going to join the Rotarians, no way that was gonna happen. Not in this lifetime.

It may have been this intrinsic knowledge that led Sylvia Corothers to set her estate aside for the year her heir would turn thirty, and she did not mistake her intended heir. He was worthy, she felt, she knew him as she knew herself; she was waiting, her hand outstretched from the grave in North Carolina, for Mel Mackey to do her bidding. That she knew would be her triumph over the bigotry and separatism she had seen visited on the shack people, her people, her sisters and brothers who tended to her and came with their food and good wishes, never expecting more than their thin white envelopes, never asking for more. She wanted more for them, she wanted them to have equality and fairness, good homes and quiet evenings, prayers over decent food, lights over their children's heads, lights to study by and learn under, not be held down by their color, their wonderful chocolate soldier color. By that year, things should have changed.

It was the year that Stone Franklin turned thirty, and there was no over-the-hill party for Stone; he had mentally separated himself long before. He was in St. Louis at the time the letter arrived at the Settlement, busily involved in an environmental program to engage more committees in developing inner city youth programs for the disadvantaged, for even now as a lawyer, he dabbled in current events, lent his name to community enrichment programs while he plodded away in front of juries and judges, ever developing his skills as a prosecutor. He had joined the Prosecuting Attorney's office in St. Louis after passing the bar, and he lived very simply in his one hundred and eighty-dollar a month apartment on Lemp Street, had saved his nights for studying and writing brochures for his numerous charities, hoping one would lead him to something better. He had almost forgotten his cousins down at The Settlement, and he would have, except for his once a month trip to get the envelopes, deposit the checks, pay the bills. But this time, the week after his unheralded thirtieth birthday, the envelopes were not there. In their place was a solemn looking envelope from a man he did not know.

The letter was harmless enough, a normal legal-looking envelope, fat in his hand. He brought it back to his car, a nice little late-model Nissan, and slit the envelope in the privacy of his leather seat. It began simply enough, addressed its contents to the members of the Settlement, thanking them for their virtuous care of the grounds of Sylvia Corothers, for which they had been agreeably compensated, but that a time had passed, the time of the waiting and now the heir of the estate would be named and forthwith, that person, herein to be named, would resume` the stewardship of the lands belonging solely to him, and only to him as decreed in the last will and testament of Mrs. Sylvia Corothers. The page ended.

Before he moved to the second page, he paused, settled down in his soft leather, glanced at himself in the rear view mirror, her old chocolate soldier. He realized that now it would all end. No more checks each month, no more plotting and scrimping on the tenants to get his money for the car and the apartment in St. Louis, no more of that. The real heir would now step forward after all these years of silence, and get his just dessert.

How unfair, mused Stone, to let all my works go unnoticed. Without me, they all would have fallen by the wayside, been in shelters by now, their little pickinnies struggling to get food or education. I've been dealt a mean blow, to be set aside so easily. How can this be explained? To what end? Ah, a sad day for my friends on the lower end of the land, my dear sweet friends, Theopolis and his wife, the Johnsons with their hopes of opening a chicken restaurant, the Milbornes with the three growing sons, the Newberns with the slightly disadvantaged deaf girl, and she was so nice, that little girl, very bright and charming, tapping out her rhythms on a washboard. And now, to be dismissed like this, being set off the land they'd always known . . . injustice, that was what it was, Stone firmly calculated, injustice. The white man against the black, again and again. How could he stop it? It seemed so unfair to him, after all the years he held Sylvia Corothers in so high an esteem. How could she let him down now, after all the years he had spent keeping her memory alive; just how could he explain it to the tenants soon to be shut out? There's a white man coming, he practiced his speech, a white man, who legally owns this place, we got no choice, we got to move on, you got no choice, now, folks, I done my best, yes, those were the words he would use to settle the anger and helplessness he knew he would hear.

The second page. He turned to the second page and resigned himself to read it all, not being a quitter, and the words stumbled one over the other, the words blurred before him. There was no other heir to reap the benefits, there was no other name imprinted before him, there was no other heir named but . . . Stone Franklin.

It can't be, he gasped, rolling forward over the steering wheel. It can't be. They must be wrong. She couldn't have done this. She couldn't have plotted so far ahead, to a time when blacks might have a chance. Oh, surely, he must be dreaming, must be wishing it was true, but he read the letter over and over, savoring the crisp paper, reveling in its message, and he suddenly looked through the windshield and, God, he knew it was true. She had surely remembered him, had honored him, and all her saved wealth would now be his, his alone, because the paper said it was so.

His heart bounded with joy. No need to return to the city unless he wanted to, no need to stand in front of those white snooty judges who minced his words, corrected his understanding of the law, interpreted things just as they chose, and used the legalese to confuse and confound him. No more groveling, the very thought of it stoked his hatred. He didn't really hate those white judges; he just wished that more of the field would be taken over by black judges, fair black judges. Maybe he saw himself in a flash in a black robe (even the robes were black, why not the wearers?). With this windfall, maybe he should consider running for a judgeship, but not here, not in Ste. Genevieve "White Boy" County, no, but maybe back in St. Louis. Maybe try for the alderman's job, or run for prosecuting attorney, and succeeding, jump in on the next judicial election.

The future looked very bright for him, he knew in his racing pulse and beaming face, he had them by the balls. No one was going to run his affairs any longer. For now, he had to check the account at the Pond Ridge Bank, make sure the accounts looked accurate, in spite of his sloughing off amounts to cover his personal expenses, all part of the job, he reassured himself, and much less than a white proprietor would have charged. And hadn't he acted in fine good faith for his fellow tenants, protecting them these last twelve years, holding them on the land they believed was all theirs? He had no reason to tell them that the truth was different, except to tell them he was surprised as they were, that he alone held the deed, but that wouldn't change things, he reasoned out as he drove along back around the ridge and down the graveled road to the cottages. They would all live just as they had, only now the thin white envelopes would come from his hand directly into the account, and for their purposes ( he reluctantly agreed to offer), one of them could now be the steward of their own money. Couldn't be fairer. His mind swelled with the graciousness of his own act of generosity. They would not object. He was sure, pulling in and parking the Nissan behind the sulky. How could they object? And if they did, what legal recourse did they have against him, and what would put them in the mood to attempt it?

A meeting was called, and the men coming in from the fields washed up and changed shirts, so as not to look like swine before their illustrious lawyer brother who had helped them so much. The women slipped in and washed their underarms and powdered themselves, to smell sweet before his city ways, and the children, gangly in their teens, only stayed as they were, belligerent and hungry for dinner that looked like it was going to be late with bigshot Franklin dropping by. The teenagers were the only questioning ones, wondering what the big fuss was all about. Surely he was bringing good news. They expected that after all the protected years on the Settlement, even their books and lunches and spending money had rolled freely into their hands, and they needed more money, these youngsters, for tapes and clothes with good labels, and a nice night out now and then, even if they did have to take the horses.

Everyone assembled on Theopolis' porch, mainly because it was the biggest, and they had long ago given up arguing with the man who couldn't write his own name, only mark, but his shrewd estimates of the weather and the political scene had given him a place of honor, something he wasn't about to give up in his sixty-seventh year of life. He chaired the meeting, telling people where to sit, offered soft drinks from his own refrigerator, and settled back in his rocker to hear what Stone Franklin had assembled them to hear. Stone stood on the bottom step, looked up at all the waiting faces, and began.

"Ten years ago, maybe twelve, I haven't checked the exact time, Sylvia Corothers left this place to us, and we've been here ever since, nobody questioning our right to be here, but now, it seems some question has arisen, and they found a will, and in it, it states that a community can't inherit property, that's the law, only a person can, and Ms. Sylvia must have known that, so she set her sights on today, the time when I would be thirty, and she left the whole place to me, and that means, folks, that she left it to us, for you are one with me, we all know that. So it's in my name, and I expect to move into the big house, but nothing's going to change, trust me, nothing's going to change, only we need to increase your salaries, what with the extra expenses you've got with education and growing kids, and I think, due to the legal climate, that a member of you should administer the Settlement account from now on. That only seems logical." He paused, waiting. The hue and cry never came, only the smiles of his friends, and the moving feet coming down to say hello and good for you, and good for us. It's all legal then, we can get back to work? No running us off? No, he repeated, no leaving. Weren't the crops coming in, weren't the pigs farrowing and the hens laying? Wasn't Pond Ridge richly rewarded with their produce being trucked and sold at two cents a pound more than market?

Everyone seemed pleased that nothing would change, for the tenants had heard of changes going on outside in the whole country. They weren't stupid people; they only stayed close to home. That didn't mean that they didn't know there was a world outside that still didn't want Black folk to have anything. But they were protected here, under the hand of a Black man just like them, even better, one of them; his folks had died within a week of each other and not so long ago that they didn't remember he was out west then, couldn't get back for the funeral, but didn't he come one time in April and put flowers on their graves? Yes, he wouldn't forget them. He was one of them.

There were sixty-seven young adults and parents living on or near the Settlement that night of the announcement. No one left until six months later, and she left to get married to a St. Louis boy she had met at trade school. And she wasn't pregnant, they all assured each other. God is watching out for us.

❧

Stone Franklin kept his apartment in Saint Louis, kept his charge cards paid up each month, kept his job at the prosecuting attorney's office, and gave his proprietary rights over to Theopolis, the man who could only mark. The bank accepted the transfer, barely disguising their disgust when old Theopolis made his "X" on the transfer papers, only smiled benignly at Stone who gave them a curt response.

"It is the wish of the heir," he stated and they couldn't argue with him over that. They knew nothing about his inheritance, knew nothing about who ran what out on those 1,080 acres; the account was their business, and nothing else.

One last matter had to be attended to and that was the visit to the lawyer's offices, to tidy everything up, sign the papers of acceptance, move any fiscally mobile assets into his own name, and thank the firm for their efficient observance of Ms. Sylvia's wishes. He met Mel Mackey on a Thursday, met him at his desk in the same light filled room where Tom Sweet had drunk his coffee, met him and disliked him immediately. A toady, he concluded, a man who had hoped to get something out of this more than he had, a typical lawyer, a small-minded Jew with no other qualities Stone admired than that he chaired an excellent law firm. So what, he said to himself, crossing his well-pressed slacks. I can do the same if I choose, only I don't choose for now. Better to wait and see what money there is here before I go jumping ship and dodging bullets.

"So what we have, Mr. Franklin, is a very cohesive plan for the property, laid out in great detail by Mrs. Corothers, and she asks that her wishes be followed. That, of course, is up to you, you have the strings on the money purse from this day forward, but she did want all the children on the Settlement to feel it was their home as well, and I'm sure you're in agreement here, no one should have to leave. Are we clear so far?" Mackey's flint blue eyes stared into Stone's.

"Yes, quite, I understand that was her intention."

"Well, then, it's just a matter of a few forms, the bank releases, the new name on her account, and then we're about finished. I hope I haven't kept you longer than you anticipated."

"No, Mr. Mackey, you haven't kept me at all. I had set aside some time for this, knowing it was important, for me and my people, so, no, you haven't detained me. I do have a court appearance at eleven, but I should be able to make that easily."

Mackey shuffled some papers together, pulled out an asset list, and Stone bent forward eagerly, barely hiding his interest in the bottom line.

"Well, as you must know, Mrs. Corothers had several holdings, and we have had the fairly good fortune to have been her investment advisor over the years, and, if I say so myself, we have done a good job for her." He paused over his notes, let the matter rest while he shuffled and regrouped and avoided the final accounting.

Come out with it, Stone fairly screamed to himself. How rich am I? Instead, he leaned back and adjusted his crease, letting Mackey know that the money was of no real consequence, that the people back home were his main concern.

"So we've tallied and adjusted for taxes and our legal expenses, and the end figure may seem small, considering her holdings. But you'll have control of the stocks and bonds from hereon out. You may want to have some legal advice on how to handle those, I'm not sure of your experience in those areas . . ." he paused, giving Stone a look of readiness to serve should Stone be willing to carry on the relationship.

"I appreciate your concern, but at this time I have my own counsel." And the counsel was his own. His very own. He didn't need anyone dithering over his numbers. That matter he could handle by himself, maybe get a CPA to help him avoid taxes, but beyond that he planned to manage the booty by himself.

Now get to the point, the reason we're assembled here today. Tell me the bottom line, sign the draft or whatever you legal fools need to sign, and let me be rid of you, fumed Stone in the back of his mind. The front was occupied by looking cool, relaxed even, and he avoided adjusting his slacks one more time. One more time might make him appear nervous, unworthy of this bequest he was about to receive, and above all, he didn't want to appear anxious or greedy, only consumed with concern for the Settlement.

"Then the matter is final. I only hope you won't find fault with some of our decisions as they affect you now. For example, say you may think we should have gone gold when the market went up so drastically, seven hundred dollars the ounce, but we followed the silver trade, less of a profit, you understand, but more solid, more in keeping with our conservative investment approach. Yes, we may have made more, but we held onto our silver futures longer and came out with a nice profit. J.C. did that for us, a great little helper and knows his market."

Mackey held a paper out to Stone who accepted it and read it. It absolved Mackey and his cronies from any wrongdoing in their investment choices, using the best advice they had at the time, using their skills at making money out of money, and Stone saw no purpose in not giving the man his signature.

"If Sylvia trusted you, can I do less?" and he signed his name in bold scrawling script, dotting the eye and squaring the tee in Stone.

Mackey accepted the paper back, relieved at the waiver of any future grudges against the firm. He handed Stone a green folder, presenting to him the final accounting, and he said, "If there's ever anything we can do to help you, Mr. Franklin, know that we're here for you. That completes our work, and I bid you good day." Stone was ushered out the door before he knew that it had closed, moved down the hall with his green portfolio, not knowing what it held, but knew it held more than he had dreamed of in his years as an attorney.

Once back in his car, he thought about flipping the pages and seeing for himself what it told him, but it was after ten and he knew he had to be court at eleven, so he set the bound papers aside and wished himself into a later time, after the day, when he could sit and pour some Chivas and truly luxuriate over this morning's gift to him.

The trial he was to orchestrate went as he had planned; the judge, for once, held his opinions up to the light and agreed with him. Bond was set, the young woman was out on the street, peddling her wares at fifteen dollars a throw, and a new date was set, to see if they couldn't help this damsel in distress, as Stone worded it. The judge had been fair that morning. Maybe he wasn't really against black financially deprived young whores at all. Maybe there was hope.

The girl should be put away as far as Stone was concerned. He wanted her prosecuted, but he didn't want to appear mean spirited against the youthful offender, wanted her to come to court next time with a better explanation of her financial affairs. Maybe she could get on at Church's Fried Chicken, why, that's an idea. Help her and help himself, appear the concerned Black patron of the community at large. Being a prosecutor had its downs with what he knew about life on the streets, and the main man's squeeze on this young flesh.

All in a day's work, he reasoned, all part of the game. The key fit neatly into his lock and he entered his simple pad, turned on the lamp by the end table, rummaged in the fridge for a snack of cheese and two fingers of scotch. He kicked off his expensive loafers and sat back with the green portfolio. The first page listed the Firm's name, in big letters, and the name of Sylvia Corothers, almost as large. Wishes, bequests, remembrances floated before his eyes, money sent elsewhere was how he looked at it. Fourteen thousand in legal fees! He gasped, feeling his pulse rising, the bastards. Fourteen thousand, leaving him with what? He flipped the page and page two settled him down. There was the meat of the deal, the sweet, sweet real life tail-end final computation of where the money was, who was holding it for him, waiting for him to come announce himself, the stocks, neatly labeled, the bonds, the savings account, the residuals from the portfolio so nicely put together by Mackey. I'll take anything, he knew in his heart, anything, now, I need this now. And the end number, the one jiggling before his eyes as he sipped the last soft curled warmth of the Chivas was one million, two hundred, thirty-seven dollars and sixteen cents. It seemed fair, a fair enough amount, he figured. A good kick start on what he wanted to accumulate. Not bad, not bad, he smiled. And more to come, oh, yes, lots more when he invested this and watched it pile up. All in all, a good day's work. The land value of the Settlement was fixed at one million, three hundred fifty thousand and some change. Set it aside. So safe.

Whether or not to stay on at the prosecutor's office was the big question. Time to decide that later. For now, he would enjoy long lunches and turn down some of those pesky cases they kept dumping on him. There wouldn't be any more dumping, that was certain. Blacks were tired of being pushed around, and the system had acknowledged a certain unfairness in hiring practice had existed. The white folks were hurrying up in their attempt to even things out. Token blacks, that's what we are, tokens. Well, he'd been a token long enough. Now they'd see how he could push back and not be afraid of getting fired. They wouldn't dare, not in the new legal climate.

Sylvia Corothers' spotlessly kept home would do nicely as his second home, for he meant to keep his apartment, maybe trade up a year or two on the Nissan, maybe invest in some smarter clothes. Tomorrow, while at work and on their time, Stone planned to call his tax accountant and see if he could handle the investing of his estate. If he couldn't handle it, he might have a recommendation of a competent and above board firm. Let the bean counters get their fee, it would be worth it, to free up his time and plan the future, look into investments on his own, maybe open a nice little office in Pond Ridge. Yes, that's the ticket, he realized. Close to the Settlement, so he could keep an eye on it, yet just ninety minutes from St. Louis, so he could come in, say, every other day. Life was getting sweeter all the time.

This was what he had waited for, this figure, this movable money, this money that had nothing to do with the real estate of the Settlement. That was an entirely different matter, the land of his people. That was set apart, that could just sit and be as it was, he figured. He could do wonders with this amount, he didn't need the land right now, his people needed the land, to keep on growing and earning, they needed the land. He didn't. At this wonderful juncture, he didn't need the Settlement at all.

# Chapter Twenty-Four

*Send me somebody to love.*
*Somebody to love.*

*Queen*
*"Somebody( to Love)"*

Paulette Pardine had lived in Pond Ridge her whole life, never made it outside the city limits except one time, when she had to have an impacted tooth extracted and she had been taken to Farmington. A little bigger, a little better. She wanted bigger, that was for sure, wanted better than still living at home with her widowed mother, grandmother, and brat of a brother.

Her mother, Clarice Pardine, was a school teacher, and one of the few Blacks teaching in Pond Ridge. She only was accepted because she was exceptional in her skills and patience, a very exemplary woman by all standards, and widowed due to injuries her husband suffered in the Korean War. He died in a Veterans Hospital and his ribbons were still a source of pride to his son, Grady. Paulette never gave them much thought. She had been very young when her dad died, and Grady had been in diapers; the teaching job that kept them all going over the years was the least the community could do for her mother. Besides, the Governor had sent her a letter about her husband, and she hadn't been too shy to take it with her when she interviewed with the school board.

Still home in her thirties! God, it disgusted Paulette as she trudged off to the bank each morning to smile at the customers, make change, sell money orders, cash checks, make deposits. All stupid meaningless little tasks and her boredom fought against it. Lately, however, she grew more interested when the Settlement people came in, for she knew something that very few people in town knew. Settlement didn't own Settlement, it belonged to Stone Franklin, the attorney who had opened a new office on Main Street in one of the charming old Victorian homes. She was tempted to stop him in the street one day, ask him if he might be needing a secretary, surely he would have to hire someone to file and catch the phone. Pay would have to be about the same, she wasn't about to take a pay cut, and she actually began to plot how to get him to notice her. It wasn't difficult. Besides being tall, well-built, and well dressed, she had a quick mind and the ability to make small talk. She didn't surprise herself at all when one lunch hour she went up the street and entered his office. What did surprise her was the young white woman, a customer of the bank, Becky Forest, sitting behind a desk in the small vestibule.

"Becky, is that you?" asked Paulette, slightly off guard. He had needed someone, and she had stood around too long thinking about it. Now it was too late.

"Paulette, hi. I just started yesterday. Donn's gone so much with his 'save the world with better water' that I just got bored sitting at home. No kids, nothing to do except clean the stove and that gets old. So I answered Mr. Franklin's ad, and he hired me on the spot. How can I help you, though, that's more important."

"Oh, I just wanted to see if Mr. Franklin could help me set up a will for my mother. Seems she never has gotten around to it, and better to have that detail taken care of, wouldn't you say?"

"Oh, my, yes, keeps things so much nicer at the end. He's in St. Louis today, in trial, but he may have some time on Friday. Would that work for you?"

"No, not Friday, I have a big day on Friday. Let me just call later, make an appointment. That way Mother can pick the time." She picked up a business card off the desk and moved to leave.

"Sorry you missed him. I'll tell him you stopped in," Becky called cheerfully as Paulette let herself out. Damn! My luck. Beat out by a white girl at that, wouldn't you just know.

The afternoon went about the same as it always did. She counted her money at four thirty and left the bank promptly at five. The walk home was pleasant: kids were out playing, both black and white and she actually remembered roller skating on this same block as a child. But I'm still here, she murmured, still here. I need to break out, get a real life, maybe move to a bigger town, meet some nice man, and get married. She'd met plenty of men from the area around Pond Ridge, met them at the gas station or at church, met them in stores or right on the street. She knew lots of men. It was a rare weekend night when she didn't have a date, and, often as not, her date was white. Her mother said nothing, Grady rolled his eyes, but Grandmother Stevens got bent out of shape, more bent than she already was at eighty.

"Daisy, Daisy," she'd croon to her granddaughter. "Doan be crossin' over that line, now. Bad thins happn if you give up who you is. Doan go white on us, girl, doan be givin' up your birthright." The old lady would rock and preach whenever Paulette got within earshot.

"Ain't likely to happen, Granny, I tried washing it off, and it's stuck there, so there's no way I'm giving up this birthright." Or birthmark, or cross to bear, whatever else she could call her color. She knew she would have gone further at the bank if she hadn't been black, knew that as surely as she breathed. They let Sally Koon handle loans, and she just got the job after getting her GED. She should've yelled at that, asked her mother for advice, but her mother only said, "Oh, Paulette, the bank's been good to you. You get sick days. You get a yearly bonus. Don't be too hasty, we need you to have that job, we're counting on you. I'm counting on you." The matter was set to rest.

The only time she kicked up her heels and had fun was on the weekends, and she did look good, all dressed up in high heels that usually made her taller than her dates, but so what? She wasn't ashamed of her height. Not her fault if the guy was short. Not her fault at all. Now that Stone Franklin, he was tall, and good looking, too. Granny would like the dashingly dressed Mr. Franklin. He'd fit her picture of what a man should be. Time to talk to her mother about writing a will, what with Granny still able bodied and Grady still underfoot. God, how he rode her about the white men! Didn't like them one bit, with their new cars and trucks, their shiny scrubbed faces, their stupid little voices, trying to sound like men. Even Grady's voice was deeper and he liked to remind Paulette that if she needed a real man, he could get her a real date with a friend of a friend.

It's not that simple, she reminded herself, just finding a man. Maybe she didn't want a man at all. Maybe she just needed to get out of Pond Ridge and see something besides the bank, the beauty shop, and the endless fields of crops. Wasn't anything ever going to change in this stupid town? Come on. Change, she prayed. Wake me up to something new.

# Chapter Twenty-Five

*How long has this been goin' on?*
*I ain't quite as dumb as I seem.*
*Ain't any use in pretendin'*
*How long has this been goin' on?*

*ACE   "How Long?"*

Martin Schoenfield had used his time wisely. He'd done a lot of swimming and boating with Amy, had spent picnic hours with Claire and Luther and his folks. The laughter and good times had to come to an end for him, for he was, as he checked his savings book, down to his last money. Time to get a job, do research if it suited him, find a niche he could grow in, find a field he liked. He had a resumé put together, sent it around to hospitals, clinics and pharmaceutical companies. The response was heartening. His credentials and med exam scores stood shining, and several interviews were past him before his bright spot opened. The firm, Pearson Pharmaceuticals, had long been a leader in research for a cure for AIDS, and among their staff were some very important researchers, one even a Nobel Prize winner. The salary seemed more than he could have hoped for, so hands were shaken, papers drawn up, and the move to New Jersey was imminent. Newark, New Jersey. Not where he'd hoped to land, but he may not stay long. Besides, it wasn't that far to New York, and he wanted to keep tabs on the Hauks and his parents. Amy had finally gotten herself together, and for the time being was residing with Jane, not as they thought it would have been at one time. No, just very fast friends, each supporting the other. Amy was actually dating a man Martin had met one evening: tall, blond, English-born, here working for a computer company. Nice fellow, that Ned Baker.

The thought of doing something for Dwayne still crept into Martin's mind, more often during his sleep, and the restless feeling he woke up with made him positive that there was something he needed to find out: about why Dwayne ended his life, and who could have played a part in his giving him so low an opinion of himself. The note had given him no help; he tried to recall their last conversation, on the back steps the day before he died. Could the phone call from Johnny have been the nudge over the edge? Who was this Johnny and how to find out? Maybe Luther would know. Luther knew as much as anyone about who Dwayne went around with.

The question seemed to surprise Luther. "Johnny? A Johnny, you say, called the day before Dwayne died? Only Johnny I remember was a snot nosed white boy who played football with Dwayne in high school. Never did like him. Played second string and Dwayne didn't bring him over to house, like he did some other guys. Naw, must be some other Johnny."

But Martin had his lead, and like a good detective, he went to the high school and went through the old yearbooks in the library and found the grinning face with little effort. Johnny Melton, second string quarterback, Glee Club, Biology Club. That was it. The last name would help; he ran his finger down the pages of the phone book, found seven Meltons listed, and spent the next half-hour on a pay phone, dialing up Meltons before he got the very one, the very one, he wanted.

"Hello," came the voice over the phone.

"Hi. I'm wondering if you can help me. I'm trying to locate a Johnny Melton who played football with Dwayne Hauk, say about five years ago. You know anybody like that?"

The phone went dead. Not the response he'd been getting, folks trying to be of help. No, this guy hung up, just like that. Martin wrote down the address and took a cab over to the street, letting himself out at the corner. He walked toward the number and went up the steps. An apartment building, probably an eight-family, and he checked the names under the mail slots, and there it was: Johnny Melton. 4B. He clipped up the stairs and found the door marked 4B and tapped lightly.

"Who's there?" The same voice he had heard on the phone.

"Just me," he called out. No sound came from the inside. Suddenly the door was jerked open. A slender sickly looking man stared back at him with deep bluish green eyes set in hollowed cheekbones. The man definitely was thin, too thin, Martin observed, preciously hanging-on-to-life thin. He gripped the door and stared at Martin.

"Who the hell are you? Are you the guy who called about Dwayne?" Speaking made him cough, and he turned and let himself bend over to ease the coughing. Martin slipped in and guided the man to a dirty couch covered with an equally dirty sheet. He sat him down, went into the kitchen and got some water in a halfway clean glass, and brought it back. Johnny reached for it and drank gratefully.

"Thanks, I can't get over the cold I've got. Can't shake even a damn cold." He pushed his blond hair off his forehead, and Martin noticed the signs of aged skin and blotchy red spots along his hairline. Definitely HIV, Martin observed, approaching, if not already in full blown AIDS, and not too much time left.

"Johnny, I wouldn't bother you at all except I need to know something, something about Dwayne. Do you remember calling his home late at night, about five years ago, to tell him to come over? There was a party going on, and from the sounds of it, the party was all men. Do you remember speaking with Dwayne that night?"

Johnny eyed him closely, took in the clean hair and smooth skin, the tapered hands held between his knees as he seemed ready to listen. Listen to what, Johnny thought. What the hell does he want from me? Why now, after the dude's been dead five years? Why bug me about it, I didn't kill him. Why now, when I'm almost dead myself? What good?

"How'd you know the party was all men, 'less you was the one who answered the phone that night? Never told him, did 'cha, never gave him my message. Hung up on me, if I recall. Yeah, that was you, Jew boy, fancy Jew boy. What were you doing there, beating my time? Huh, is that what this is all about? You was getting it on with Dwayne, and you were jealous. I have the last laugh." He began coughing again, turning his face into the sheet, and drops of blood spattered his lips. "Look, I don't feel like trading stories about who got it better, you or me, but just so's you know, I didn't have anything against him, not then, not now." He wiped his mouth and drank more of the water from the glass on the filthy floor.

"One more question, then I'll leave. Why did the scouts drop Dwayne, one minute wanting him, the next minute forgetting he was alive? Why'd that happen, Johnny?"

Johnny laughed then, a harsh mean laugh. "You mean you don't know? Them scouts! They pounded hard to get him to sign, almost got him, but they didn't pick me!" He jabbed his thumb into his bony chest. "Me! They never took me seriously, and I was every damn bit as good as he was, at my position. They never wanted me to try out, and boy, that did soak into me. He was no better'n I was, but he was Black, and that's supposed to make a better athlete? Bull shit, I say." He drank more water and his face was now blotched all over from the exertion. Martin feared a heart attack or lung collapse, right there, right in front of him. No amount of mouth to mouth was going to save this guy. No amount was ever going to be attempted, if the truth be known. Martin continued to wait for his answer.

"The scouts," he quietly urged.

"You want the truth? Here's the truth. I 'fessed to the coach that Dwayne had buggered me in the shower, tore me a new asshole, left me broken for a week, blood in my stool. Yeah, I told the coach after what I knew about them scouts after Hauk' s ass. His precious ass! Let him go fuck himself!" He started coughing again, and Martin got up from the stinking couch and touched the man on the knee.

"Take care of yourself." He let himself out, ran down the stairs and gulped the New York air as if it would cleanse him after breathing the foul air of the man's breath. So it was as it was. So Dwayne had come on to Johnny, but rape him? Not likely. Much more likely that Dwayne had been seduced, led to believe he had a friend to care about, in a way only he could understand. Some friend. Spoiled it for him, got him feeling down, not to have the scouts hammering to have him.

He ran to the corner, and then, out of anger and sorrow and regret, he ran another block full pace before he leaned against a light pole and caught his breath. A cab was coming up the street. Martin raised his hand, and the woman driving it stopped. No way, he thought to himself as he entered it, slammed the door, and shrunk back in the seat. No way the Hauks will ever hear this story.

"There had to be other guys he hung out with, maybe before high school," continued Martin, stopping the checker game and holding the piece up in the air. "There had to be, Luther, you just haven't looked back far enough." He plunked down the checker, and Luther casually moved over it and two others and scooped up the three.

"You want to play checkers or go over Boy Scout camp? C'mon, I almost got 'cha. Let the old man win one for a change. I'm way ahead, anyway. You just not paying any 'tention."

Martin clicked on something. "What'd you just say? About camp? What camp? When was that?" He leaned forward eagerly, and Luther took the moment to relight his drafty pipe. Never could stay lit. Change tobacco, must do that. Alls this old pipe need is a change. The clock chimed out ten bells and he sat back in ease, almost the winner here, almost got two puffs.

"Not a real Boy Scout Camp, just a weekend for Cub Scouts, I guess they call 'em. He was about eight, I think, Claire'd remember." He pushed back his chair and called around the corner to the workroom. "Claire, how old was Dwayne when he went to that Cub Scout weekend?" There was silence, and then Claire peered around the corner, a ribbon tying back her hair, and a ball of vines held in her hand.

"How old? Why? I don't know, maybe seven, maybe eight. We didn't want him to go at all, if I remember, he was so little, but he was so excited and anyway, Petey's parents were letting him go, and the counselors that came and got him seemed like nice young college kids, one was black, the other white, and I don't know, maybe we were right, Luther, maybe he was too young, because they brought him back early, stomach problems, throwing up, and not feeling good. Guess he just missed home." She sighed then, and went back to the workroom.

"How do I get in touch with Petey?" Martin asked. A lead. May not be anything, but the detective in him, so like the researcher, was digging in.

"Shoot, I don't know. He'd be about twenty-eight now, and as nice a young man as I ever seen. Came to see us after Dwayne died, turned out real nice, had a gal he was living with, and she came too, and she was a nice gal. Said he was in real estate, over somewhere, some company." He watched Martin's face, and pushed back in his chair.

"Oh, I know this part, got this part. Claire?" he hollered. She came around the corner again, this time with two angels in her hand.

"Yes, sir, what? You keep bugging me, and I'm never gonna get these done by tomorrow."

"Petey, Petey Renstrom. What's the name of the company he sells real estate for?"

"All-American Homes. Why?"

"Why? Well, I think Martin's gonna buy us a home, that's what I think."

Claire raised her eyebrows, tapped him on the head with the angels, and left them again. Martin rubbed his hands together, moved a checker, and Luther pondered the move. He ducked his pipe into the ashtray, looked at Martin to see if he really meant to do that, and Martin nodded.

"Darn you, boy, you got me in a corner now. Now Old Luther's gonna have to do some fast steps to get aroun' that move."

They hit the beds about the same time, Claire coming in shortly after Luther had begun to snore. She rolled him on his side, and lifted her weary legs in to try to fall asleep before he rolled over on his back again and started the in-and-out-snuffle-thing he did with his nose. One of these days, she rose on her elbow and glared at his blissful, unaware sleep, one of these days I'm gonna, I'm gonna, but his noise didn't start up again as she watched. Maybe if I'm lucky I can fall asleep before he starts up again. She waited and listened but no snoring, none at all. She peered at him again, his face captured in the light coming in through the window. Silence. Why now, she sat up in bed, why now does he play games with me, when I need that snoring to put me under real good. She nudged him and he groaned and started a little snuffle going and in peace at last, she snuggled under his arm and next to his rib cage. The last thing she remembered was the soft throbbing of his huge heart as it relaxed and pumped, relaxed and pumped.

Martin felt the softness of the sheets around his face, and he thrust them back and stared at the window, moonlight and streetlight streaming in on him. He had the job to start next Monday, only three more days here, and he still had to find out what was troubling him. The last day. The last day on the porch. The day Claire had been cross with him. The sack of potting soil. The same sack Luther had used to put the tulip tree in the ground, the same one blooming in the back of the yard even tonight, Martin felt sure. Even tonight it would be beautiful in the back of the yard. Luther was proud of that tree, Dwayne's tree, he liked to call it. His fingers trembled over the huge buds, his arms reached around the tree and he circled his own reach. The tree was still slender and young, but smudge pots could be seen glowing in cold weather all around the base of the tulip tree. Really too far north for these, Martin had known, but the tree survived under the watchful eyes of one Luther Hauk. Nothing was meant to die with Luther Hauk around. Nothing.

But the words, what were the words Dwayne used that day, sprawled in the sunshine, letting the warmth soak into his chest and thighs? What had he said? Got off the track, no, something like that, but not those words. What words then? Try to remember, Mr. Thinks He's So Smart, Micah's title for him when he got too big to spank. Started long ago, but those weren't the words either. What difference does it make? Something had happened and maybe Dwayne's friend, who had cared enough about him to come and visit his parents after he died, maybe Petey Renstrom, only now it was probably Peter or just Pete, maybe he could shed some light.

All-American Homes had three offices in the Bronx, the first lady told him. Mr. Renstrom was affiliated with the one on Orchard Street, but perhaps she could help him instead. No thanks, no commission for you, young lady. He called the Orchard Street number, and the answering machine said no one was there right then, all busy with customers and open houses, but just before he hung up, he realized the taped message was giving him home phone numbers for all their agents. He picked up a pencil, and waited patiently through seven names until he heard the name he wanted: Petey Renstrom, 454-9087. He hung up and called and the woman who answered, she sounded neat and happy, he liked her voice, said Petey was in the shower, could she take a message?

"He could call you right back. Could be five, ten more minutes, how that guy loves to use up all the hot water," she said good naturedly. Got himself a good one, Martin noted, real peach. He gave her Luther's number, and sat back down to finish a piece of the apple coffee cake Claire had stirred up to tempt Amelia's fading appetite.

"She needs to eat more, she only picks at her food, Micah tells me. She does much better if I pamper her a bit, spoon it into her, and my! doesn't she like ice cream! All that fat, though, I got to stay away from it, but she needs the nutrition, Martin. See if you can't get her to eat a bit with you." So he had, and only managed to eat part of his cake before she was picking up the crumbs from her finished portion.

The phone interrupted his hovering over Amelia's plate, and he reached for it. "Martin here," he said, "oops. Hauk's residence. Sorry, just a guest. Forgot myself."

"Petey Renstrom here, returning your call. Important, huh? Well, everything's important when you're selecting that new home, finding just the right agent. Have you picked one out, one you'd like me to show you?" Ever the agent, the salesman. Must have missed the name Hauk.

"Petey, I'm a family friend of Dwayne Hauk's. Do you remember Dwayne?"

"Hell, yes, I remember Dwayne. How come you're asking?"

"I need to get with you, and have you tell me everything you can remember about a camping trip you and Dwayne went on, back when you guys were kids, say maybe seven, eight years old. Can I stop by and see you, take a little of your time?"

"Man, you just caught me going out the door to work, my night to man the phones at All American, but if you want to stop in there, I'll have plenty of time to kill. Believe me, sales are way down this month. Too close to school startin' up, I guess."

Martin cabbed it to the office, found All-American in a neat little string of mall shops, and was mildly surprised at the pleasant and efficient little office. Four desks, four file cabinets, a wall plastered neatly with pictures of homes for sale, grouped by neighborhood and then by price range: nicely done, thought Martin, if I wanted to buy a home in New York, which I don't.

Petey Renstrom was a slender black man with wavy hair and a row of teeth Martin would have pictured in a toothpaste ad. About five ten, he wore a gray suit and pink shirt, set off with a purple and green tie, smelling of soap and Design cologne, he looked like a model.

Martin had to tell him, had to let him know, without sounding stupid, that the man looked great.

"You look great," stumbled Martin.

"How am I supposed to look? You pictured something else? Hey, man, this is me, and I am me, and I like lookin' sharp, and if the brothers don't like it, they can kiss my old patootie goodbye. I been selling more homes than the home boys ever thought could be sold. Mostly to blacks, and don't that just stir up the ginger? Black folks with money to buy homes. So what about it, I say, black, white, the only color's green, if you get my meaning."

"I get your meaning," Martin said, sitting down by the desk in the customer's chair.

"You called about Dwayne, and honest to God, I can't believe he's gone, 'bout five years now, honest to God, I thought he'd outlive us all. What do you think cranked that boy out?"

"I don't know, but I'm a family friend, my folks live over the Hauks, and to this day, I can't believe Dwayne killed himself over grades. Did you know he was carrying a GPA of 3.8 when he died? Does that sound like someone despondent over grades?"

"Shit, man, old Dwayne never worried about grades. He used to tell me, 'Petey, just do your dog gondest, the grades will come out just fine.' He got me through some tough spells, we knew each other ever since we was five or so, kindergarten, and my word! He was the best friend I had. Took me for a loop when he cashed in his chips so early. Sad. Sad, and his dad about the nicest guy in the world. And look at sweet mama! Ain't she a pretty thing, even in her forties, that lady is all class. Love those folks. Love 'em."

"Well, I think Dwayne met someone, someone way back when he was a kid, who may have hurt him, maybe molested him, and I think you might he able to help me with this."

Petey ran back in his mind to the days in the woods behind the play ground, out of the eyes and ears of the mothers and sitters of the little ones; the days when all the boys fondled each other, and had their first erections, played with each other, and felt each other's bottoms and balls, but this was no place he was going to bring it up, not here, in front of a total stranger. The topic better move, Petey Renstrom thought, better move quick or this conversation is over, finis, caput. This dude wasn't going to buy a house in the Bronx anyway.

"Can't recall anything special, you know, kids will play games during the time they learn about their bodies, but nothing happened to Dwayne that didn't happen to all of us." There! He'd said it, and that would be his final speech on it.

"I know all about doctor games, but something may have happened to Dwayne, say, on the Cub Scout outing. What do you remember about that?"

"Man, that's a long reach, years back. Let me see. I don't think Dwayne even stayed the whole weekend. He got sick, if I remember, puked all over. Man, he looked scared to death, puking on the floor of the tent. I remember I was the one that found him, ran and got Kirk, he was one of the counselors, a big black guy I was scared of, he was so big. But a nice guy. He wasn't our counselor even, but he came and helped clean Dwayne up and got him some popsicles and then Dwayne went home. That's it. I stayed one more day and we had a good time, I remember, a real good weinie roast, and marshmallows all curly brown on the edges. Burned my lip." He pulled his lip down. "Still have the scar."

Martin noted something, caught something like a whiff, and he asked Petey, "If Kirk wasn't your counselor, then why'd he come in and take over? Where was your counselor?"

"Oh, that was something they were trying, to get the races closer, to better their understanding. The white boys got Kirk. We got Mick. He was white, and a pretty nice guy, kind of fond of patting, but a nice guy, least ways to me."

"What's that mean, fond of patting? That doesn't sound like something you liked."

"No, it don't mean nothing, it just means he seemed over helpful at times, like when we was zipping up after a whiz, he'd come by and shake us off. Like touch us and say stuff like, 'Keep yourself clean, boys,' stuff like that. And straightening our jams at night, he'd like to make sure we weren't all cramped up. 'Let those balls breathe, boys,' he'd say, stuff like that. Kinda dumb stuff, kinda stuff you probably should 'a known how to do anyway, without his help. But he was okay. Like, he didn't bother me at all."

"Then why didn't he come and see to Dwayne if he was the counselor for your tent?'

"Don't know, can't recall all of that. Oh, I do remember now. 'Not Mick', that was what Dwayne said. Yeah, I remember now, just like he said it. 'Not Mick', so's when I saw Kirk, I grabbed Kirk. Dwayne was flopping all over, spewing that puke, and Kirk was real nice to him. Kirk's not in trouble, is he?" Petey seemed genuinely concerned, afraid he had remembered too much.

"How would I find out about this Mick you mentioned?"

"Lordy, I don't know. Gawd, man, that was twenty years ago. That guy's probably far from here. Guess the only thing you could try if you think it's worth looking into is the Boy Scout records. Them or the YMCA. They sponsored that weekend for the black kids, most of us had free tuition, we didn't have much back then." And we won't have much more if that phone don't start ringing, Petey thought to himself. Martin stood and shook his hand.

"Thanks, you've been a big help."

"I have? Tell me what did I do? Tell me anything, maybe I can sell a house tomorrow."

Martin had one more day before he had to pack up and say goodbye and head for Newark. One more day. He put it to good use. Had breakfast with Micah at the corner deli. Played checkers with Luther and let him win. Carried boxes of centerpieces for Claire out to the now older model black car she still owned and loved to drive on her deliveries. A few more days won't matter, he told himself, but in his mind he had to get to the root of this gnawing problem. The problem: was it a problem, or something he only imagined. Was Dwayne just a homosexual who couldn't feel comfortable with it? Or had something damning happened to him, something that made him fear his own sexuality?

The YMCA records didn't go back twenty years, the crisp woman told him. No records beyond ten years. So if this guy, Mick, was twenty then, then he'd be forty now, and may still be active, hurting others, may even have boys under his care and tutelage, may be a priest or a real sick-o doctor, a teacher with grade school boys, lots of potential little kids to correct and shake their wheeezers. Sick, Martin thought, I've got to answer this, once and for all.

He called the local Boy Scouts, and these people made him thankful for nothing else to do but keep records of their achievements. "Oh, yes, we did do a lot of community good at that time, sponsored many an outing, got businesses to foot the expense. Are you doing an article about this, and if you are, you need to speak to John Shelby. He's our memory bank here, knows everyone who ever helped us out, great old guy, an earliest, earliest Eagle Scout and Order of the Arrow. You want me to connect you to John?" The connection took just a moment, but the moment was lost as was the connection. Martin re-dialed and asked for John Shelby.

"Shelby speaking," came the slow drawling voice.

"Mr. Shelby? Glad I caught you. Doing an article for the *Times*, mainly focusing on the early efforts of the Boy Scouts to involve black youths from the New York area. Give 'em a leg up on being out of the big cities and out in the woods, you remember those times?" Martin shifted easily into his lie. Not such a big one.

"Who you say you're with?"

Martin scrambled. Was it the *Times* or had they been bought out? He really didn't know, so he ran a bigger yarn.

"Where they print it, I don't know. I run these stories for so many papers, one *Times* runs into another man's *Journal*. To be up front with you, I'm working for United Press. You've heard of United Press?" He'd have to be dead not to have heard of United Press.

"Hell, yes, I'm an old newspaper man myself. What can I help you with?"

"Time frame here now, sir. I want to know what happened during the summer of '78, what Cub Scout deal you had going on, where it was, the names of the helpful counselors who sure should get some praise, even this late in the game. What'd ya say, sir? Memory bank, the lady said you were. What can you remember of that summer and an outstanding counselor named Mick?" Really press him. Find his button if it still worked.

"You must mean Reverend Mick Townsend, nicest guy who ever volunteered. Wouldn't take nothing for his time, gave it all up to help others. Sure, I remember him. He's a parson now, over in Glen Haven, nice little church, been there once to see his daughter baptized. You say hello to him when you see him. And you write some darn nice words about him. There ain't many like him!"

Martin clicked the phone down. So Mr. Mick had a last name. He had a flock. Oh, my, wouldn't that be fun, to sit down chin to chin and relive old times. Petey had told him just enough to whet his appetite. If only he didn't have to leave for Newark. If only. He could look forward to this meeting. Yes, it might prove more interesting than Reverend Mick Townsend ever dreamed.

# Chapter Twenty-Six

*Watch me ask the bartender*
*For a drink he can't make.*

*Christine Lavin "Mysterious Woman"*

It wasn't that long a train ride, but Martin felt tense and stiff in his neck when he arrived in Newark. The send off had been a quiet one, the good wishes and hugs, the basket of food from Claire, and the lone Luther bringing him to the train.

"Do you think Dad will ever drive a car?" puzzled Martin.

"Soon as hell freezes over," responded Luther, weaving the still peppy truck through the traffic. "Why should he, when he's got me to do it for him? That man's getting lazy, I tell 'ya, have to do his pickin' up more and more." Luther, the protector saint, the patrician of all the family, the weight of the world juggled easily on his broad back.

Pearson Pharmaceuticals commanded a full block in Newark with their labs and offices, their meeting rooms and social areas, the huge vestibule with the gleaming chrome and the glass-topped desks. A nice ship. A port he would need to fit into. He was graciously maneuvered to the fourth floor, met a lady who guided him back to the labs. He nodded and shook hands, and only really saw what he wanted: the microscope and the clean desk. He smiled at all about him, but his mind was already on the work ahead. Some of it he planned to do for Pearson, but some of it he planned to do for mankind. The same thing, he compromised, all the same thing.

The work plan, as he saw it, got him in on the middle of a bunch of nothing. They all had theories, the supervisor explained to him, all had theories, but none of it was proven, and if what they had come up with was any revelation, well, he'd died and gone on to heaven.

"It's a mess, that's what we've got here with this AIDS thing, a big mess, and a galloping fast mess it brings with it. Can't stop the stuff, only bleach and light and time does that, but you know what, Schoenfield? Those poor buggers out there infected with this shit: they don't have no bleach, light or time. They are goners, but maybe, just maybe, if we put the old noses to the scopes, maybe we can spot something that will stop this cursed thing from taking over. That's our hope, our only hope. Rubbers just aren't working, and we've pushed that angle until it squeaks." Dr. Willmore ran his section, ran it like a fine tuned violin, ran it, and ran it, and nothing ever happened.

Martin did his share of microbe exploration, ran his lines and split his genes, found several promising leads that only ended up, by closer observation and repeat procedures, to be dead ends. Nothing so far, but soon, they kept telling each other, soon the breakthrough will come. Most of their tests they ran through fruit flies, the fastest medium for reproduction and result, their large chromosomes easily identified, their rapid movement from egg to adult gave a fast forward on any gene changes. For if they could only alter the gene, insert one that had a built in resistance to AIDS, a hyped up body screen that would not allow HIV to enter, a steel screen, a force to keep out infection, a new immune system . . . Yes, that's what they were looking to do. A grand plan.

Martin had been attentive and alert, came in early, stayed late, for what else did he have to do in Newark, New Jersey? The town itself, while solid, had no special meaning for him. The closest and oldest synagogue had moved to a new location. He knew no one, and the people he met seemed flat and without hope. They should meet Luther, he thought, or maybe Luther should move here and shake them up. Schools in bad shape, politicians wavering over really basic choices, real estate down, the city slogging downward.

The work kept him going, work he saw as a blessing. He often thought back to Dwayne and the Hauks and his folks tinkering around in the flat, but his attention was more often fixed on the fruit flies. So fast, they were. Little dots of wings and body juices so important for the scientists. They held the key to why things were placed where they were, why wings ended up on thoraxes, why the antennae were on the head, why they were always the same color. The same color. Interesting, he noted. They were always the same color. He bent over his microscope and slipped in a slide of the fruit fly chromosomes, enlarged ten thousand times. Very simple, really. Ventral points, lateral suffusion, lipid pools, all neatly wrapped around the gene string, the DNA of the model. What if he tampered with that gene string, broke it apart, moved number three into the number six spot? What then would happen?

Martin's attention increased as he plotted the division and supplementation of the new gene string. All neatly laid out, to be infused into the embryo fruit flies. Of all things imaginable, antennae were now on the back end of the newly hatched, and they had no wings. The newborns feebly felt around with their butts, died early, and Martin went back to the gene string. The color. Which gene controlled color? He isolated the tag end of the string, set it apart, and injected it with chlordane hydrate, and the resulting fruit flies came out a dazzling red, burnt almost to a crisp they looked. Other colors. He needed to mix in other colors. And the next group of color genes he hit with nitrous cobalt, and they came out blue, one hundred blue fruit flies came to life. Beautiful they were, and they lived almost three days before they dropped to the floor of their air-conditioned glassed cells. So I can do it, he breathed. I can change colors in fruit flies. But how would it be if I could adjust the color of men, leave them in the middle, not black, not white, just coffee mocha, cappuccino with rich cream, a very dark tan, nothing changed in the features. We'd still have a flattened large-nostriled black nose showing up, we'd still have the pinched, hawk nose, snub nose, round nose of the whites: that he couldn't change. But the color, he realized, the color, the pigmentation, that was the easy part. And how would it be done, this test? It would have to be in a small populace, maybe a good percentage black, maybe not. Maybe a population of less than 2,000, large enough to gauge the results, small enough not to cause a public outcry. A rural setting, maybe in the Midwest. Not too close to a big town and the reporters.

A quiet happening, he visualized. A quiet place where he could see if the color of a man's skin controlled his destiny. The samples he would make would have to be enough to last for a one-time chance, enough to do the job, on say, a community of 2,000. Life span? He knew he could create a lifetime for these splitters, these darling little changers of color, but the results would be permanent. He had to think clearly about those changes. Did he have the right to try this? If we're all born equal, with no prejudice against skin color or religion or sexual orientation, what crime had he committed?

The last of his experiments proved to him that a soluble gene-splitting agent could act on active, fixed gene strings, could change the chromosome picture for the whole being in a matter of weeks, could alter the cell pattern, one by one, each one nudging the one next to it, by osmosis, saying, "This is the new code. Get with it."

The most efficient way, he knew, was through inoculation, but on what premise could he induce a whole community to accept his injection? Smallpox, diphtheria, tetanus: they all knew about those. DPTs had been around for fifty years. Could he disguise it as a way to ward off AIDS? Highly immoral, he reasoned. No, the people he planned to have assimilate his mock serum/ color changing/ gene-reformatting dose would not be able to know about it until it was over. Then they'd have to deal with it, just as Luther and Claire had to deal with it, like Dwayne had failed to deal with it, if that was the problem. Maybe it wasn't just color that had confused people. Maybe color had been a guidepost. Then let's knock down the guidepost, exalted Martin, slapping his leg. Knock it down and see what happens. Let's split the difference. Half and half. Let the white's get fifty per cent darker, let the blacks get fifty per cent lighter. Fair is fair, he reasoned, feeling like a magician at the simplicity of it all.

# Chapter Twenty-Seven

*The mountain is high, The valley is low*
*And you're confused on which way to go*
*Come on and take a free ride*
*Come on until you're by my side.*

*The Edgar Winter Group* *"Free Ride"*

"So, Dr. Schoenfield, you are settled in? Just how is the work going?" asked Frederick Pearson, hefty, nicely fifty, neatly shaven, expensively suited, president of the company, doing his duty and calling in his lieutenants, as he referred to them, for monthly briefings.

"I'd say we're close, sir, real close. The real breakthrough should be within a year, if my estimate is right."

"You say a year? That's bang-up good news, Doctor, bang-up good news. And you find everything you need, all the right equipment? We try to stay up to date," he added modestly, waiting for the praise he knew would come.

"Oh, nothing else we could have, sir, nothing at all. All the best, I assure you, and I've seen some laboratories in my time." Pearson seemed pleased, sat back and eyed Martin. He leaned forward and lowered his voice.

"Just between you and me, you know it may take longer, right, but you hate to admit it." He waved off Martin's denial with an impatient hand. "We have to do other things, to keep moving, and I often have to lend a hand to fellow explorers in order to keep our larder full, you understand?"

Martin nodded that he did indeed realize that other matters besides AIDS research presented problems.

"From time to time I've loaned out our team, to help with special problems, and just such a problem has reared itself. I have a close associate, in St. Louis, who is interested in buying a large tract of land for the purpose of developing a luxury community, right on the Mississippi River, a beautiful spot, so he tells me, but there is no local water control there. The county has never convinced the city to buy into their shared filtered fluoride storage tanks, and the site itself would be wonderful if it weren't for the doubts about the purity of the water source. You know as well as I that a contaminated source, or source of unspecified purity, could condemn a project of this magnitude, several million dollars at stake. The land belongs to one person, and he is most anxious to sell, as you or I might be if we weren't going to use it. The seller has submitted water samples, samples that are so pure and clean that the buyers can't believe in them. The water seems too good to be true. The buyers want a sample drawn by an independent, qualified analyst. So what I'd like you to do, on company time, is do a thorough analysis of the water in that area. Find its source, determine its purity, identify any life forms or bacteria we have free floating, and give me a written report, let's say, by the sixteenth. That should give you plenty of time. By the way, the project is in Missouri, a town called Pond Ridge, and for now, your reasons to be there should remain private. Don't discuss this with anyone here or there. Only I should find out what may be lurking. Clean bill of health is what I see. But when there's developers involved and millions at stake, a man must be cautious."

Martin accepted the project, left the room with a winging heart. Just the community he'd hoped for! Offered to him on a silver platter. Or at least silver plate. The perfect chance. Surely those communities were mixed, both black and white. Surely he could get his gene splicers into the main water source; there had to be a place that everyone shared some sort of common water, like the main drag, the city hall, the police station, the library. Oh, whatever. Towns had to be alike in some ways. He would find out and the sooner the better. His excitement rose as he packed for his vacation; for him this was a vacation, out of the lab and back into life again. Life as he wanted it to be. Three vacu-tainers of splicers were nestled in rubber and wrapped in cotton batting, stuffed in his overnight hand bag. The rest of his gear he folded neatly in a two suiter. No need to bring a suit, he surmised, just jeans and cotton pullovers, and two pairs of hiking boots, in case one pair got wet.

He made up his story on the plane, and put his finishing touches on it as he drove the hired car from St. Louis to Pond Ridge. The interstate wove him onto the two lane and into town. Yes, he smiled to himself, noticing a tall black woman leaving the bank, and another up the street: it was a good spot. Here in the Heartland. No better place.

The real estate office caught his eye and his plan began. A prospective homeowner, looking for three acres, a nice fix-her-up home, and plenty of quiet. The recipe for success. The woman in the office showed him some recent homes, newly up for sale, and he pondered and examined and said he'd walk around and give them some thought.

"The schools? How are the schools rated?"

"We're in the 'C' rating for size, but your little ones won't take a back seat for learning. Our teachers are 'A' in my book." She beamed at him, touching the pictures lovingly.

"And water? How does a town this size get its water? I didn't see a water tower on my way in. Are you on county?"

Her face looked puzzled. She answered slowly. "Now about water, I'm not too sure. We all have our own wells, and those are kept up by the homeowners. The pump people here are real good. Can't beat the Williams Brothers. They fix 'em in a hurry. You're never gonna be down more 'n a day."

"So who do you know that knows the most about the water? You know, if it's good, fresh, clean? Who might I ask?"

"Donn Forest is the water man in town," she blurted out without thinking. She bit her lip. "Leastways, he works for better water, which is what you want to know about. He sells conditioners, so he might be biased, but it wouldn't do you no harm to check with him."

"Thanks, I'll do that, Miss. Where might I find him?"

"His wife works for Mr. Franklin, the attorney. She most likely can tell you where to find Donn. He travels door to door. Hard to catch old Donn." She smiled as Martin waved good bye.

So this Donn Forest sells water conditioners. Knows his water. Just the ticket. He'll know where to point my nose. Tomorrow will have to do. Need to find a place to sleep, have a bite to eat, and get some rest. The flight and drive had tired Martin, and he needed a good long shower.

Days End read the sign over the two story Victorian home, and that just about summarized his choices. He parked on the wooded lot, barely big enough for three cars, and entered the front door. The hostess was pleased to see him, since he was the only guest, and he offered money up front, but she demurred, saying that was quite unnecessary, would he like dinner? He enjoyed a glass of port in front of the cheery parlor fire, and ate an immense meal of broiled catfish, hush puppies, collard greens and slivered almonds mixed in with the tenderest pieces of meat he dared not identify as pork. For dessert she gave him a slice of peach pie with a dollop of homemade ice cream, and right then Martin wanted to marry the woman.

"Mighty fine meal, ma'am. Mighty fine. I'm in town, looking to buy a house, and I hear a Mr. Donn Forest knows his way around the countryside. You wouldn't by any chance know Mr. Forest, now would you?"

"Donn? Shucks, we all know Donn. Him and Becky's like kin folk. I'll give him a call and tell him you want to meet him. He'd love it. He can talk your arm off!" She left with his dishes and came back in a few minutes with a small snifter of brandy and a message.

"Donn will be here in the morning, about eight sharp to meet 'cha. Now wouldn't I make one heck of a secreeterry?" She laughed as she brushed up the crumbs and left him with his brandy by the glowing embers of the fire. Nice lady. Nice place. I wonder how she'll like being a mulatto, he reflected.

Donn Forest's voice filled the lobby the next morning, hastening Martin's steps as he went to meet him. A florid young man, slightly balding, with a wide grin and ears that stood out just a little. He offered his hand to Martin, shook it warmly. "Dr. Schoenfield, is it? Well, pleased to meet 'cha. Ms. Tandy here says you're interested in the country life. Too young to retire, ain't 'cha? Bet you're scouting out a place to start a practice, and boy, we could use 'ya. We got a self-taught midwife and a licensed chiropractor, and that about sums up the local medical staff. You get hurt, you better hitch to Farmington or St. Louis. Well, grab a cup of coffee for the road, and let's show you our town." He kept up the talk, light banter, howdy-dos to the people he passed, and Martin came after him with the styrofoam cup and a bagel wrapped in brown paper.

"There's the grocery store, good people. There's the bank. Good people. There's the city hall, nice, ain't it? All good people here. We get along."

"Water?" asked Martin politely, biting into his bagel. "How do you get your water?"

"Oh, it's water you want to know about. That's my field, water. This is a backward town when it comes to water, and so help me, I'll be the first to admit it. All water comes from wells, and this street, the main drag if you will, feeds off a central well, pump hangs at about six hundred feet, got plenty of pressure, but I for one, and about the only one, see some problems coming for Pond Ridge if we don't get some central purification program going. Or join the county system. Seems like the folks just don't mind dirty water." He lowered his voice. "They don't like to hear that, but I've got some samples in my car that will blow the top off your test tube, believe me. Nasty stuff. Never touch it myself. I buy my drinking water," he added proudly.

"So where's the big well?" asked Martin, sipping his coffee and acting mildly interested.

"Behind the city hall. Got a little well house to keep out the kids and the weather. Tamper proof, they say, but any fool could loosen those lugs on top and drop whatever down the shaft. Kind of a close town, though. Who'd think to mess with the water?"

"I've never seen a working well," Martin admitted, and Donn showed him around the back of city hall, stepped over some bushes, and pulled open the door on the concrete bunker.

"That's it, the whole kit'n caboodle. Sad, ain't it? Still on an old pump, and not two conditioners in town. My work must be elsewhere, that's for sure. No one here's buying my idea. But mark my words: this town needs to spring into the twentieth century or this water will be the death of them." He rambled on about greener pastures and the ways of the world and folks not listening to good sound reason. They walked back up the street, past the grocer's and the drugstore, stopping by Donn's new station wagon.

"Here, Doc, here's just a sample for you. Now you take a look at what lurks in there, and you tell me what you find. I'll expect a report, and don't be surprised if I print up some flyers with your name on them: Doctor Schoenfield, new practitioner in town, states the water will kill you unless you buy a Cyclone Water Purifying System, call Donn Forest, 654-6789. You like the sound of that? I sure do." He grinned and slammed his tailgate. "Nice to meet you, Doc, good luck to you and your family. And remember: buy stock in distilled water. Always a sure seller." He drove off in a hurry and Martin finished his coffee and the bagel as he watched him leave.

No need to press further. He had all he needed to satisfy Pearson back in Newark. Had it all without even opening a tap. Tonight would work out just fine. A wrench was all he needed, and a flashlight. Town should go to sleep at nine if last night was any indicator. No movie house in Pond Ridge. What did people do here, he mused, for entertainment? Television must be it, he figured.

# Chapter Twenty-Eight

*Sweet home, Alabama,*
*Lord, I'm comin' home to you . . .*
*Watergate don't bother me.*
*Does your conscience bother you?*

*Lynard Skynard*
*"Sweet Home, Alabama"*

Stone Franklin did an unusual thing when the tax bill from Ste. Genevieve County was laid squarely on his desk by Becky. He opened it and swore out loud. Becky raised an eyebrow, and discreetly left him at his place. So whopping big! This crummy county wanted that much for one year. This was just the real estate bill, he realized, the personal property taxes would be coming in next, maybe already mailed, being it was November, and man, there was no way he was going to fork out that kind of money for 1,080 acres he didn't even like. He hated it there, he had to admit, had always hated it with its folksy ways and damn collard greens, his tenant friends ever shuffling by and treating him like he was goddamn royalty. Screw it. He didn't need the likes of them clouding up his future. The CPA would give him some advice, how to duck under this and walk away from it. The guy was good, even knew old Mel Mackey at the firm. Old coot.

"Duck under it? Hell, that's what I warned you about, you keeping all of it. Turn corporate, Franklin, just as soon as you can. Escape those taxes. Let the tenants pay a share. You'll still have controlling interest, but those guys down there are living under your protection, and your dollars are paying their freight. Go corporate, Franklin. Set it up. You know how. Stop by when you're done and I'll work up the new tax figures for you."

A corporation. Now where were those forms? Yes, here, he fumbled for them. Here they are. Set it up, nice and tidy, keep fifty-one percent, so I can bail out if I ever need to, and let them have the forty-nine per cent. That should be easy. A gift to them, really, a nice gift with a kicker at the end, but he knew old Theopolis was watching the Settlement's money, and he knew that old boy could count better than he could write. They didn't even know what a corporation was, much less that they were going to become part of one, but he would need their approval. Or at least Theopolis would have to approve. Stone's old typewriter, the same one he had taken to college, served him well as he typed in the names, the legal description, the name "Stone Settlement, Inc." in the appropriate blank. All legal. All ready for the signature, or in this case, the mark. What was Theopolis' last name, he wondered, pausing over the keys. Leave it blank. He'll have to tell me.

With the office quiet, as it had been since he opened (Pauline Palmetto, or whatever her name was, never did appear for her mother's will), Stone left the office and turned his pager on, just in case St. Louis needed him, not that he thought for a minute the signal would come this far. Need to get a stronger signal, he planned, need to be where the real action is. The brand new Nissan purred nicely over the bumpy road out to the Settlement, and he let himself in the big gate and left it open to annoy Hodges, who felt like that gate was his. Stupid, slack-jawed, squinty-eyed nigger, thought Stone to himself. Never did like that man and his stupid tough man shotgun. Going about pretending to be Mr. Land Owner. Hell, he knew better, but just got uppity with the news. News affected people in lots of ways, Stone mused as he turned down the path to the tenant homes, for they were no longer shacks, but neat bungalows of white-washed siding, with holly hocks and daisies growing around them, nestled neatly in deep piles of manure, like they all should be, thought Stone, nestled in manure. He did admire their vantage point, though. From where their homes were, he could see the spring-fed pond, which had been the center of their building, each home spaced neatly around the acre of water, fresh and clean, bubbling and cold, even on the warmest summer day. A boat was tied up at the community dock, and to Stone's pleasure, he saw it was Theopolis, not out in the fields, but here where he wanted him.

"Theopolis, my man, how goes it?" called Stone, rising up to the occasion and going down in his spiffy suit and high polished loafers to shake the old man's hand.

"Can't complain. Crops brought good money this year, wife not belly achin'. Sun is shinin'." He squinted at Stone in his finery, felt a twinge of regret that he'd never had the same chances. Couldn't even write one word. Nor spell his name, same problem lots of folks had, trying to spell his name. The 'X' worked just fine for him. No fuss.

"I've brought down some papers for you to sign, and I think you should be happy about this. My accountant tells me it's the best for all of us, to make us legal, no white boys coming after us, trying to snatch away what we've all earned. My accountant, and he's a lot smarter than I am, says we got to do this, to protect ourselves from being taxed to death. Corporations get a lot lower tax rate, and that's what I'm shooting for, to save us all a whole lot of money." He stopped to take a breath and watched the old man's face.

"Whose money gonna get saved? Yours or ours?" He stood up on the dock, a full six footer, bent a little in the shoulders, but still strong and able. "You fine a loophole for yoself, Stone, or is this gonna hep us all?"

"Theopolis, do you think I'd turn my back on the Settlement? Do you think for one minute that the welfare of all my people down here don't mean diddly to me? I'm out there every day, bustin' my buns to get things better for all of us, and you make me sad when you talk money among brothers."

"Sorry, Stone, forgive an old man. I'm just cautious, you know, bin that way all my life. You be gone so much, you act mo' white than black. You seem, sometimes, to be a 'wanna be', an' thas the truf of it. But youse a whole lot smarter than I is; if'n you an' your man say this be it, then I woan' stan' in the way." He scrawled his 'X' where Stone pointed, his last name still waiting to be typed in.

"Last name, Theopolis, last name. I need to put that in, back at my office. What is it?"

Theopolis gave him a puzzled look, sat back down, and picked up his rod. "Same as yours, son. Your daddy an' I was brothers. Shame you forget."

But shame wasn't at all what Stone felt as he wheeled the car around and headed back through the gate, a gate he almost missed by a hair as he honked at gun-toting Hodges, starting to pull it closed. He honked again in irritation, and the man stood back as the dust from the speeding tires fell over him like dirt on a log.

The papers were duly completed and posted that night to the county of Ste. Genevieve, and the county revised its tax bill, sent a letter of explanation, and the part that was due, fifty-one per cent to Stone, the forty-nine per cent to the Settlement, was greatly reduced by the move to being a corporation. But the amount still stung to Theopolis, who had it read to him, and he asked that he be driven to town, and pointedly waited for Paulette, the nice black lady who handled his affairs, and she sure smelled good that morning, and it made his work lighter when he showed her the paper and said to draw up a cashier's check from their account and he would sign, mark it, make it okay, whatever would work. No damn place for him. He paused to look around. The post office across the street caught his eye. He didn't write letters, so he didn't get letters, but he noticed a little black boy park his bicycle and run up to get a drink from the fountain. Theopolis leaned to the window, wanted to shout a warning, but the boy only drank his fill, wiped his mouth, and jumped back on his yellow Schwinn. Close, mighty close, he breathed. Could'a been trouble. Lots a trouble.

His business finished, he had no more use for this town than a one-legged man at a dance. The sulky served him just fine, with Milborne's youngest riding the breech, and Theopolis sat back and enjoyed the ride, enjoyed the stares of the people walking along Main Street, savored the fact that though he hadn't wanted to, he had spent big bucks back there, big bucks, money that was partly his, partly his family's and mostly the Settlement's. For it was those people who looked to him for guidance, and it was to them that he had an undying commitment. Stone Franklin was no kin of his. No, he reasoned, nor should he be. He didn't deserve to be Black.

The scene repeated itself one week later. Theopolis pulled into Pond Ridge to draw off more money for the personal property taxes, and they counted everything that mooed or cackled: every chicken, every hog, every head of cattle, double for Bruno the bull, valued at $2,000 dollars, not including his stud fees, which Theopolis craftily handled himself, never reporting the cash deals. He was no fool, no. He was catching on to this white man's world. Keep your trap shut, your wife's lid on, your kids at home, and pray for rain for the crops. Mottos to live by.

❧

Hallelujah and God be praised! Stone couldn't help himself when he got the letter, and Becky only shut his door and left him to his happiness. The city folks do know a good thing, he gloated. The old ties with Mackey had not been broken. His work at the prosecuting attorney's office had bored him silly, made him anxious and hopeful for his ventures on the weekends to the casinos and ballrooms he swaggered into. Good looking, he knew he was. Single, the ladies all noticed, fawning over him with their low cut gowns and drink orders, but the booze was cheap, he was on a roll, most times, and he did, in fact, recoup his money and then some. They all knew his name by now, asked him to surely come back. The room's free next time, Mr. Franklin, and back he came, and the coffers kept filling, but for some unknown reason, he was never satisfied. He liked the games, that was it. The games were what he liked.

This new one might present some problems, he recognized. He might have to dig deep and come up with some very fancy reasoning to get Theopolis over on his side of things. The St. Louis conglomerate, comprised of Mel Mackey, two other lawyers, a developer named

Raymond Pearson, and a contractor with a good reputation for pulling it all off with top quality houses, mint houses, with sunken tubs and skylights, GenAir kitchens, built in bars with wet sinks throughout the house, wet rooms, and greenery rooms, Florida rooms for year-round living, suspended over limpid rock-lined pools that glistened at night under the path lights. Nice affordable living at $175,000 for the starter homes, more if you had it to invest. The view was the big deal, and the good clean spring fed water spilling over the sluices and into ponds with fresh fish and turtles and giant fronds and cattails. Samples of the water he had collected himself. Abundant, this land, the promos would claim, and not be lying.

Too bad, he reflected, stroking his jaw, too bad I jumped into changing to corporate to save on the taxes. Had he left it sole owner, this deal would be put away tonight, and the price, always negotiable, would have been paid into his pocket only, and the beginning price was in the two million, eight hundred thousand range. And a buy at that, he figured. Two thousand an acre was a bargain, what with the St. Louis' good neighborhoods going for two hundred thousand an acre. Try Chesterfield or Ladue and the price would be higher than that, he mused. But behind is behind, he settled in his thinking; what's done is done. Theopolis would have to be presented with the facts, and if push came to shove, he still had the fifty-one percent to make it go over, and Theopolis could count that far. Where they would move was their problem; his pork chop would still taste the same. The date wasn't important, he noted, anytime was a nice time to start out with a new bundle. He could double it in the casinos, if he put his mind to it, double it in one year.

A trip out to Settlement was in the offing, and this time he opened up the big house and built fires in the fireplaces. He had the grocer bring in ham spread and crackers, fresh grapes, four cases of mixed soda, Pepsi, Coke, and Sprite, fourteen bottles of imported beer, which he never touched, and several decanters of white and red wine. The tenants would not be expecting this little party, and the group as a whole, not used to fancy living, would knuckle under when they saw how much it would benefit them. Sure, they wouldn't be on Settlement any more, but there were lots of places up and down the Mississippi from this spot that they could rebuild and restart their lives on one million dollars of their own. Maybe they'd split it up, set out on their own, leave Missouri behind, find that life didn't stop at Settlement. It was just a jumping off place.

He sent a boy down with a handwritten note of invitation, to a small party he was hosting for his friends, and the hour of eight was designated, that very night. He walked through the spotless house, mounted the stairs and took a long shower under the reassuring spray. This will come off, he smiled. I know they will go along with this sale. They never would be so rich again in their whole lives, and their children would benefit if they decided to move, benefit by seeing how the other half lived. He slipped into fresh underclothes and a silk shirt, a soft pink, and pulled on dusky gray slacks, adding a maroon smoking jacket for just the right touch of grandeur and being the host.

Everyone from the littlest to the biggest kid came up the path in the snow, and little flakes came floating down as he welcomed all at the door, bid them welcome, and they dutifully filed in, pulling off coats and boots and heaping them in a big pile in the front hall. The hall overflowed with steamy leather and red and black wool, wet slick rubber boots, snow melting on the tile, but the woman who did the main cleaning saw to it that the newspapers were spread, and the boots were lined up neatly due to her urging.

Theopolis, rosy with the weather and glad to have been proven wrong about Stone's affections, shook his hand and set about finding spots for everyone to sit.

"Not so fast, my friend, let the young ones and all of you, grab a plate and have a tasty before we sing a few songs or talk about just folks, like old times. I have a bit of business," he sided to Theopolis, but in a louder voice, "come on, you all, grab a plate. Sodas for the kids, something a mite stronger for the adults." He winked at Theopolis and guided him to the cooler, handing him a freshly-opened beer, a Dutch brand, and Theopolis sucked on it with relish.

"That's mighty nice beer, Stone, never tasted such a nice round brown beer." He carried his bottle and plate back into the living room and sat in a large chair by the fire, reserved for him, he noticed with a certain amount of gratitude.

Stone moved through the crowded room, shaking hands and touching the heads of the smaller ones, now almost as tall as he, how time had flown. He nestled in between Theopolis' wife and her neighbor, whose name escaped him, but he remembered she had been one of the older women who tended to Ms. Sylvia. Willie or Nillie or Tillie. All back safe. All's well.

Someone had dragged up the washboard, and the deaf girl, Crissy, now married to Daniel Milborne, drummed her fingers down the board and hummed a few songs to everyone's pleasure before she modestly put the board behind her and enjoyed her husband's kiss on the cheek. She was good, Stone noticed, never let her loss affect her talent. Which is what it's all about. The children ran back and forth for more ham spread and crackers, more sodas. The men tipped the decanter and bravely carried the unfamiliar cut glass as they moved back to their crouched places or folding chairs.

So it was time, Stone determined, time to confront them with the wonderful opportunity offered to them. He rose and lifted his untouched glass of Chardonnay and said, "This is fine, us all together, but I need to have your attention so's I can discuss an offer that's been made to all of us." The room quieted when the master spoke; the teenagers were shushed into quiet, and all the round eyes in the black faces turned to their host.

"A grand opportunity has been presented to us to sell the Settlement." The faces turned to each other, and a soft round swell of 'nos' swept the room. No voice was singled out, it was one voice he heard. He ran on. "Don't be in such a hurry to say no. This is the biggest chance you folks will ever have to own a piece of land that doesn't have Settlement stamped on it. It'll have your name," and he pointed at Milborne, "and your name," and he pointed at another man whose name he didn't remember. "You folks own forty-nine percent of this, and I've been offered two million six hundred for the whole sha-bang. That's a lot of tuition money, and new land money, and nicer home money for each of you. Don't say no until you think it over."

The pleasant firelit room, with the swags at the windows and the plush carpeting, fell hushed when he stopped speaking. He looked from one face to the other, but all the faces were turned to Theopolis. The man rose from his designated chair of honor, stood by the fire, and said one word.

"No." Plain, flat out, no discussion. Just a firm no.

"Now, Uncle Theo, you might take a minute to think about this. The offer's a sound one, the planners tell me they're going to make a grand community here, a mixed community (he struggled), so it's not like you wouldn't be making a small sacrifice for the greater good of all black folks. We'd all get a chance to live here (if they could afford it, he secreted) if that was your choice. Now think about it: how's livin' on the Settlement much different than livin' on an old plantation? You want to bring back that kind of thing? You want to hold back your land so's no poor young Black family can't come and enjoy these hills, and this view, say, I think that's selfish thinkin', yes, I do, and I'm one proud Black man who don't want to see that kind of thinkin' direct your decision."

Theopolis was standing, but he bent and slid his plate under his chair, set his half-finished bottle of Dutch beer on the mantle. He moved to the center of the room, and said in a fine even tone, "Much obliged for your evenin', Stone, much obliged. We plan to have you down, when you have the time, but the answer, since I'm asked to speak for all a us, an' I think I do," and all the adult heads nodded, the teenagers shaking their heads back and forth vehemently, but they weren't taken into account, not a bit. "The answer is still no." He passed Stone in his maroon smoking jacket, and the heart that beat under that jacket was, indeed, smoking. How old-fashioned this old coon was, how out of touch with growth and capitalism. How like him to turn a perfectly good dollar away. You old fool, Stone started to say out loud, but he uttered something else aloud.

"You'll be sorry, my friend, sorry that you didn't follow along here, for I am the one who gets to have the final decision. I hold the controlling interest in Settlement, and it will be sold, and being a fair man, you and the others will get half, half of what I get, and no quibbling there. I deal as I see, but we won't be friends after this, with my having to force my way to get what's best for the people coming up, the ones who haven't had your advantage, living here like kings and queens. You'll see. A day is coming when black folk help black folk, you'll see . . ." he sputtered. He kept talking as the empty soda bottles were neatly lined up on the table, the galoshes pulled on, the scarves pulled tight around wide-eyed faces looking back at him as they went out onto the porch. They all left, so quickly, so finally, the only thing left was the puddle of soggy newspapers, which Stone grabbed up and shoved together in a huge ball of dripping mush, fairly fled to the kitchen to hunt for a plastic bag. Shoving it all in, he turned to face the empty rooms, the dining room, and the warm and cozy empty living room. He locked the front door, peering through the glass as he noticed a real storm coming in. The snow had started while they had been talking, and now it swirled and came down heavier, great wafts of flakes striking the house and landing on the bushes.

They should all be in bushes, back in Africa, he grumbled, throwing off his jacket, slinging it toward the couch. They'll get their money, whether they like it or not. Spring Pond Acres was a dream of people bigger than they were, and no one was going to stop progress.

# Chapter Twenty-Nine

*Keep your eyes on the passerbys*
*When the eagle flies*
*And your brother cries*
*When the going gets rough*
*Are you big and bad enough?*

*The Four Tops*
*"Are You Man Enough?"*


Martin Schoenfield hadn't meant to be sloppy about his report on the water, but on his return to Newark, he had been sidetracked with some personal business, a family matter, requiring him to take a short leave of absence, fully understood by the firm after his valiant sortie into Missouri, and the test tube of tainted water got set aside for the time being, along with his dirty laundry and unpaid bills. He flew into New York, met, as usual, by Luther, who brought him up to date.

"Claire's been after her, mind you know that, to take her vitamins and eat lots of leafy stuff, but, Martin, she just sink lower and lower. She don't tie no bows or help in the workshop, she just failin', and that's the whole of it."

Failing? How could she be failing, what with the extra money he sent and the Hauks shadowing her every move? How could she be failing? He had to see her, strip off her shyness and check her chest and lungs, feel her feet and legs, have her checked over, if not by him, her son, the doctor, then by someone else. She'd be back up to running speed before he left, he vowed.

The vows didn't get clocked in on the right hour, that was all there was to that. He hadn't made his vows soon enough, he had been concerned over the new job, his time spent looking into Dwayne's past life. How had he missed the signs that crept and stole her breath? How did he feel, looking down on her stilled body, laying in the big bed, how did he know that she would die on his very visit to hold her once more? She slipped away, maybe while Claire was downstairs, maybe while Micah had been sifting through the cellophane-wrapped packages in the refrigerator, looking for something to tempt her appetite. Maybe while she felt alone and spent, not caring anymore. Or maybe, he reflected, touching her still face, maybe she just went on to the Promised Land. Whose promised land? Did God care about Amelia Schoenfield? Surely he had to have noticed her.

The burial was swift and slightly noticed. Micah had hung his shawl over his shoulders and put on his yamulka, trudging slowly behind Martin into the truck Luther had swept out and wiped down. Why they went in the truck to the service, only Claire could guess. She followed in the black sedan, driving herself, alone in her grief. Her very best friend. Her little gray top knot was gone.

Amy came to the service, dressed in a slenderizing black dress she must have borrowed from Jane, who stood by her right side and held her hand. Ned Baker, her Englishman, stood on the left, holding Amy's purse.

They spent the next few days shoving clothes into bags for the poor, held up pictures of Amelia at ten, at twenty, at thirty-five, and after that, there were no more pictures. Had she just stopped wanting her picture taken, or were they all too busy to turn the lens on her? Micah suffered the most, quietly sliding into each morning, moving through the days on dead feet, lighting the candles, and saying his prayers, clutching his shawl ever tighter around his shoulders, letting himself be led, for the first time, to his bed at night. He failed, so simply and fully before their eyes, failed: to keep breathing seemed an effort. He only roused one day to howl at the news that Hymie Goldstein had passed away. For this event, he poured a stout glass of port and said his own prayer of Thanksgiving, that God had taken a good soul and had made things even by taking a bad one at the same time. All's even in Heaven, he purred over his cups. Tonight God runs things.

Martin called the office in Newark, explained that his mother had died, his father was failing, and could they only give him the time he needed to settle things appropriately before his return. Mr. Pearson's secretary said, very confidentially, that he was needed back, as soon as his family matters were well situated, that Mr. Pearson, only this morning, had received calls from St. Louis about a report Martin was working on, could it be someone else could handle it for him, someone here and "on the job"? Her tone irritated Martin immensely, so cold and professional; she must have seen some stupid tape on being a customer service rep, but she had forgotten the part about being sincere. He hung up the phone, and at that moment could have cared less about Pearson Pharmaceuticals in Newark, New Jersey. Let them all hang for all he cared. He went down the backstairs and into the yard, embraced the tulip tree in the snow, and only went in because he had to remind Luther it might be time to light up the old smudge pots.

It was on the third, Martin noted the date, when the representative from Hymie Goldstein came to call, for the express purpose of getting the rent. It had long been done that way, Josh Laurent knew, and it would take the tenants some time to begin using the mail and join the efficiency of the postal service. He, for one, did not plan to make these calls more than once, informing the tenants of the eight or so rentals managed and owned by Hymie, that in the future they should avail themselves of money orders and postage stamps.

When the loud knock sounded at the Hauk's front door, Martin was helping Claire finish an order for a boutique. Luther was in the bathroom, cleaning up after an early morning call that had meant moving a spent furnace (should have bought the Temp Star, he had warned them five years earlier), about three hundred pounds, down a flight of seventeen stairs, out on the concrete stoop and with the help of a young boy, who just happened to be coming by, get it up and into his truck. He gave the boy five dollars and the kid winced at taking it. "No trouble, man, you'd have done it for me," but Luther grabbed the boy's jacket, and put a ten-dollar bill in the pocket.

"Be good to your mother," he offered as advice, and drove off to the dump, then back from the supply house with the new unit and a helper from the dealer to lend him a hand. He had needed that shower and change of clothes, for if the weather kept up as cold as it was for the season, he'd be back out in an hour.

Martin answered the door and held the storm door wide open for Mr. Laurent, who quickly introduced himself, and mentioned the rent.

"Ah, the rent," murmured Martin, gesturing for the man to come in out of the cold and take a seat. Josh Laurent set his briefcase down, and put his white hands on his knees, waiting like a perched cat for its dinner. Luther came in at that moment, freshly scrubbed and hair still damp, moved to the back room to call Claire to come draw up the check. She did so, quickly going to the kitchen and getting her pen and checkbook, and made out the check on the kitchen table before coming back to hand it to him.

"Much obliged and thank you. You're up to date, always have been. Good tenants you've been, what, six, seven years, and my, you have a nice place to live, if I'm any judge." He stooped to get his briefcase, slid the check in the outer pocket, and said, "Now the Schoenfields, I believe, they're upstairs? Is that right? Do I have that right?" His question was directed at Luther, who sat down in his chair and beckoned at Martin. Martin felt he had to speak up, had to inform the man of the fact that the Schoenfields, hearing of Mr. Goldstein's death, had purchased the proscribed money order and postage stamp and had mailed it already.

"Then my business here is finished! Glad to have you folks, stay on until things get settled, but don't be too surprised if Miss Goldstein won't be wanting to come back to New York, may even take a liking to this place. But that's all speculation at this point, only . . . a guess," he changed his words, afraid the young man and the old Black man might not know what speculations were. He takes us for fools, thought Martin, standing by the well-dressed attorney, thinks we don't know guesses, much less beans. Luther said nothing, sat in his chair and examined his hands, and Claire went back to the workroom to finish her order.

Martin started to let the lawyer out, but an idea pricked at him, made him shut the door, and set his hand on the lawyer's arm.

"Do you have a minute, sir, for me to show you some things?" The lawyer checked his watch, said he had a moment to spare, and Martin said, "Won't be a minute, sir, I'll be right back."

He raced up the stairs, found Micah slurping his tea, waved in passing, and ran back to the stack of boxes holding the pictures. There they were: Amelia in front of the building, Amelia behind the building, Amelia smiling broadly in the kitchen, and one great shot of her in the bathroom, rolling her hair. He grabbed them all, and ran back past the half-nodding Micah to the Hauk's living room.

"I haven't even told you who I am, Mr. Laurent, correct? I'm the Schoenfields' son, here about my mother's funeral, we lost her just last week." Mr. Laurent mumbled a condolence. "Well, thank you. I appreciate that." He asked Mr. Laurent if he wouldn't mind stepping into the kitchen where they could go over some things, and Josh Laurent looked quizzically at the silent Luther, who only waved them away.

Martin spread the snapshots, in order, and started talking in a quiet conversant tone. "Now I wasn't born in this house, almost twenty-nine years ago, but this is where I grew up, and see this? This is a picture of my mother, holding my sister on the front steps. Yes, she was pretty, that she was, but I'd like you, for just a moment, to set aside the subject of the picture, and look at the background. Do you recognize it? You don't? See the numbers over the door, well, one's missing, but we can imagine there was supposed to be a three there, can you allow me that much?" The lawyer nodded, squirming slightly, not sure of what he was being convinced.

"Now, here's my mother in the backyard, do you see the backyard? Do you see anything growing, any grass or trees or bushes or flowers? None, I see nothing growing. Come here, Mr. Laurent, take a look out this back window." What Josh Laurent saw startled even him, used to nice yards and fine flowers, startled him into an "O-o-oh" of appreciation. Even under the snow, Josh saw trees, shrubs, and brick walkways.

"You don't see that in the picture, do you, Mr. Laurent? Nothing like what it is now." He pulled the man behind him and showed him the radiators in the flat, all painted a gleaming silver, no flaky bumps under the final coat, immaculate radiators, looking brand new but close to seventy years old. "Notice the injection fonts, Mr. Lament, all new and sealed and turn on a dime. Air in, some water out. The jets perform perfectly. This place was kept up, you notice. Now Hymie Goldstein wasn't much for doing this stuff, so he had a good team helping keep this place up, right, have to admit that."

Yes, Mr. Laurent, noted, a fine team. Martin gestured at the woodwork. "Fine woodwork, wouldn't you say, all in prime and first coat, no peeling layers here, the Pope would bless that paint job." Martin moved to the bathroom, held the door open, and what Josh's eyes beheld, as he gazed around the modern room, with new Kohler fittings and a deluxe lipped shower stall, the slate floor and handmade cabinet with a beveled mirror, made him gasp. How had Hymie done all this without telling him, he thought? And why this place for, well, black folks, the ones he feared . . . how and why had he put so much effort into pleasing them? Hymie should have raised their rent, he calculated, six, six-fifty a month and no less.

"Show you one more thing, Mr. Laurent, and then I'll let you loose." Martin wound down the cellar stairs, brightly carpeted, and the walls done in fresh white paint. He led him back into the boiler room and even Josh had to step back. This was no boiler room. It was the best looking room in the whole place. The huge boiler, serving both floors, was neatly wrapped in silver foil, the ends tucked in with strong duct tape. The gauges gleamed, the pressure was excellent, the dials all glowed and ticked in efficiency; the whole room looked clean enough to eat in. No white caking of water deposits on the pipes, all black and clean. The red-doored furnace, converted to gas (this had been coal, Josh remembered, had to have been coal, some still are), gleamed with its edging of polished brass. A perfect unit, he praised, God bless Hymie for leaving me with this. If the daughter does come back, as she was rumored to be thinking about, now that the old man was out of the picture and her Latino lover had taken a mistress, well, he would be awfully proud to have her take this over, remove one less rental property for him to supervise.

"Nice, isn't it, to see a property kept up? Much different, I'll wager, from what you've been seeing on your rounds. And don't get me wrong, Mr. Laurent, I know it's difficult for you, too, to lose an old friend, to have to pick up his endless yoke of responsibility, but I imagine, I'm just going to hunch, that you get paid for your work, am I right?"

Mr. Laurent looked at Martin and smiled, yes, he got paid, his smile said. The young man flipped off the furnace room light, and guided them both back up to the kitchen.

He turned then and showed Josh one last picture: a picture of his mother in their kitchen, very much the same kitchen they now stood in. The background, which Josh by now knew he was supposed to be looking at, showed no cupboards, only planks laid on metal holders, an icebox that still used ice from the heavily ragged delivery truck, the big chunks chipped off and carried by the housewives into the kitchen and put in the bin in the bottom. Josh smiled at the remembrance. Brought him back to the cool chips he'd sucked on as a youth. Hymie had done right here, he concluded, at least he'd done right one place. Two apartments still had ice boxes in this day and age.

"So that ends our tour, Mr. Laurent, the tour of the house that Hymie owned. But before you leave, I want you to know, and I am a witness to it, that every improvement you see in this property, every spiffy radiator, every wrapped piece of duct tape, every new gauge and new appliance, supposed to be furnished, was put here by one man, and it wasn't your Mr. Goldstein. It's the man sitting in that living room, one Luther Hauk."

Josh did a mental turn, held onto the back of the kitchen chair, and collected his thoughts. Which direction does this go now? What was this young man up to, anyway, was he to make a claim against the estate? Was that what this was all about? He looked at Martin.

"Now I'm going to be straight with you, Schoenfield. Anything the Hauks did to improve this property was their own doing; no one ever asked them to do it, they only bettered their own life, keeping things up. The rent hasn't changed, has it, in the seven years they've been here? No, Mr. Goldstein was kind to let them stay on, against his own personal . . . a-a-h, persuasions, let them stay on, so I hardly think it is appropriate for you to suggest . . ."

"Oh, I'm not suggesting anything, Mr. Laurent, not suggesting anything at all. Property appreciates, we know that. This flat, in 1950 went for twenty-eight, maybe thirty thousand, safe bet? Today, you'd be tickled pink if you got it for one twenty-five, even if it had some flaws. But there are no flaws here, Mr. Laurent, even the tuck pointing is in perfect shape; the chimneys have all been relined, did I mention that to you?" Martin started to move to the living room, but Josh stopped him.

"This is all predestined, Mr. Schoenfield, all laid out. I'm sorry that the Hauks gave so much of their personal income and free time to keep up the home they were only renting, but the law's the law. Things are laid out, so to speak, and the only heir is the daughter, if she claims her estate (which he knew she would, had practically begged him on the phone to wire money, money to get her back to New York).

"My informant," lied Martin, "only this morning, told me that Mr. Goldstein left no will, but even if he had, the will would have to be probated, and without one, it will most certainly be, and any claims against the estate will be heard in a proper estate court, by a probate judge, and to that end, we will prosecute our claim. I will act as Mr. Hauk's counsel in this matter. He is too beset with the loss of my mother and Mr. Goldstein to function properly at this time, but I am functioning just fine, Mr. Laurent, just fine, and we will probably see you in court."

The nicely tanned young man, in jeans and a blue pullover, his feet stuck in moccasins, held open the storm door, and gestured for Mr. Laurent to leave. Josh turned on the raised metal threshold, neatly placed to keep out drafts, how thoughtful and efficient, mused Josh Laurent, how entirely unlike Hymie at all. And the whole picture flitted in front of him: he saw old Bishop on the bench, grouchy and stooped, slipping into his papers and Black's law, flipping through the pictures presented to him, of the yard and house and the missing number; he saw as if someone had painted a picture for him, what the young man in the dune soccer shoes and jeans would do if he spiffed up and came to court in a suit and a black tie, which he knew this man owned, only secreted it away, playing him for a stooge, was what he had hoped for. Not in front of the bench, he vowed.

"You have made your case very nicely, Mr. Schoenfield, and I will take it under advisement. Let me get back to you, say, in four days. Let me toss some figures around, and see what I can do, before this gets to be a problem: for the Hauks, for you, for all of us involved at this very sad time." Sounded good, he praised himself, set his hat on his head, and wished Martin good day.

Martin put his head out the door. "Dr. Schoenfield, sir, just for the record. And the figure's sixty thousand, settling all accounts, and after Probate, the figure is going to move to seventy-five." He waved then, and stepped back. Shutting the door against the nice tight-fitting lip.

Josh Laurent was no fool. He knew he was up against a fighter, a man with facts and pictures and a neat story that would sway a judge with any compassion, in these times at least, to bend toward the claimants. He sighed as he entered his Volvo, started the engine, and gazed up at the house. "Settle it," he spoke to himself. What's sixty thousand when the man left more than three million for his dribbling foolish daughter?

# Chapter Thirty

*Take my love into your breast*
*Commit my spirit to the test*
*You will see him, like a knight*
*His armor gleams.*
*We'll fly above his angel's wings*
*Above the clouds in rainbow rings*
*We can sail a ship of dreams.*

*E-L-P "Footprints in the Snow"*

Gloria looked forward to Easter, a time of fullness and richness in her home with a fancy bathroom, the home she had opened wholeheartedly to the Madonna with child. That was how she looked at Marilyn, a poor lost sheep, who did her chores and never complained, who helped with dishes and kept the young ones busy with cutting and pasting and what all she had going. The porch table held a banner being painted for the church wall, and Gloria did enjoy watching Marilyn and John parade around the front yard, each holding a lighted candle to ward off evil spirits. The evil spirits. Did they crowd her thought that night? Bein' a big baby tonight, when they all was having fun and throwing wrapped candy in the air for the dogs to chase. Spoil their fun, wouldn't I? She shut the door and wiped up the kitchen.

But Easter is comin', sure as I can smell the spring blossoms in the morning air, see the glistening wetness on the dry grass that will surely be green before long. How is it, she stopped and wondered, how is it that a body can give up their girl, not come asking about her, not wonder one lick if she be warm or fed or with good people?

She took the pastor aside, next Sunday after service, and held his arm and asked him that very question.

"Sam Walters, you a man of the cloth. How can a brother pastor turn his own out, an' never come to see if she be well, or if she be sick? How does God work in such a man?"

"Ah, Sister Glory, we all ain't cut the same. Maybe the man is sick hisself, maybe he don't know he's welcome. You ever asked him to come see you an' have tea and sit with you? You may have failed him, Sister, in not being open and loving, as God wants us to be." He smiled down at her, his girth wrapped in flowing red robes, and he smiled so nicely that Gloria felt ashamed.

"I ain' never ast him, 'cuz I know, in the spirit, that he wouldn' come to our place. But you, Reverend, you maybe could go call on him when there's time, say we like to have him come by, say he is wanted and needed. If he ain' got no bigger family than hisself an' his wife, why, they could come join us for Easter, an' let him know I'm a good cook an' the place is clean. We even got an indoor toilet now."

Sam Walters laughed heartily over that, touched her shoulder, and agreed to stop by and extend their invitation for Easter. All in his circuit, all men the same.

What with all he had going, working a regular job at the bottling plant in Farmington, keeping his old car running, visiting the sick and trying to please his wife by throwing a coat of paint on the house, Sam Walters put in his time. He suffered over the fools he met, suffered more over the agony he felt for their souls, never gave up his last breath at night before he prayed, "Let it all pass, Jesus, let us all be at peace. Let us fight the big fights together as Christians."

It wasn't until the last sleeting snow had started to melt in early April, three days before Easter, that Sam Walters found himself with a few minutes to spare before he had to stop and see Widow Brown. He turned his old car onto the street where Joan and Macy Stewart lived. The temperature had fallen into the teens, and there was a strong wind blowing a cold drizzle, catching his great coat as he stepped out of the car and moved his big legs up their front steps. He knocked two times when he didn't see the bell, but once spotting it, he pressed it. Evening had started in and the porch light flicked on. A woman peered through the door glass, and then her head went away. A man opened the inner door, inside the glassed storm door, and Pastor Walters recognized Macy Stewart. They had been at the same meetings in town, had been at the League of Women Voters' lecture, and were both part of the Chamber of Commerce. No need to snub the folks that is trying, felt Sam, ever hopeful that all would turn out, according to God's plan.

He smiled broadly at the familiar face, cold and silent before the glass, and the storm door didn't open in welcome.

"Sam Walters, Reverend, Pastor Walters, coming to call," he said loudly, getting his voice over the wind. He pulled off his stocking cap, wanting the man to see who he was, but the Rev. Dr. Macy Stewart only stayed quietly behind the glass.

Then he spoke, and his voice fitted around the seams on the door; it came out to Sam as a wind swept echo, surrounded by aluminum. "Bad timing, Walters, we're just sitting down to supper. Another time, maybe."

He started to close the inner door, but something moved Sam

to strike the glass with his knuckles.

"The time seems to be right now, Dr. Stewart, for you and me to visit about your girl, the girl with the Cheevers' family. They'd powerful like you and your wife to join them at Easter time, spend the supper hour, have some of Mrs. Cheevers fine cooking, and man, she is a good cook." The wind tore at his scalp as he stood on the stoop in the cold, tore at his soul if'n he had let it in, but a fierce determination gripped him. The man had to listen and if'n he was nice, the Lord might help him along.

The good God Almighty had to have been turned away that moment, had to have been tending to a greater need, for the face of Macy Stewart went flat against the glass. It looked squashed there, pressed so hard.

"Get off my porch, Sam Walters, get off my porch! This is my home, not the Chamber of Commerce, and I say, get off my porch!" He stepped back then, shut the door firmly, and peered at Sam through the little glass window. Dark was settling in, and Sam, shuffling back down the walk, tugged his stocking cap over his woolly head, covering the myriad of snowflakes that melted and ran down his face as he sat back in the car and started the engine. The snowflakes kept melting, and they ran down his forehead and over his cheeks, but the real drops, the warm ones, were coming from his own eyes.

❧

Easter was indeed a special day, and Gloria rejoiced in her family and friends, stopping by with goodies to trade, her secret recipe ginger cookies for their warmly-cinnamoned sweet tater pies, the food all lined up on the counters and flowing over onto the cool porch. Beech had slaughtered the boar that had gone lame in the back leg. Wouldn't last out there, he figured, when the touchy sows knew he was lame, so he felt better that old Stock, as he called the stud boar, had done his best to keep going, and gave all their bellies a lift at his passing. His meat was sweet and tender, like the turkey Glory basted and cooed over, running the butter over the breast and down the legs. My, my, didn't that woman have a way with butter and legs. And he wanted again, at this unseemly time, to lead her to the back bedroom, and lift her skirt and just stand with his body next to hers. Nothing more for then. Just her skin against his.

How Stone Franklin spent his Easter Sunday was no one's

concern, and no one invited him to sit and eat, not even Theopolis extended his usual invitation. It wouldn't have mattered: Stone was on a plane to Las Vegas the day of the big feast, thinking ahead to making a big roll off his investment, thinking if he could just hit the big one, he wouldn't have to settle for just being a lawyer and a millionaire. He could be set for life. The gaming tables should have known it was him, Sylvia Corothers' chocolate soldier, but they didn't seem to dip and dive the way he wanted. The truth was, when he packed up his wrinkled laundry-done shirts and limp slacks, his dirty socks and underwear, when he boarded the plane on the twenty-sixth, he was shy about sixty thousand dollars, but Caesars Palace loved him. Man, how they loved him. How to get it back, he worried. How to not slip back and have little or nothing. This he knew was his plan: to win at gambling and never lose again. Or the thought hit him: to not gamble and play his money close to the chest. A-a-h, but he loved that wheel, those dice, the chances he had the money to take. It fed on him, enriched him most times, this weekend was just a timeout. He'd be back, and he'd get every dime he had lost this weekend.

The holiday came in and went out and little else changed. Majorie bundled the baby up and brought him with her when she kept barbecuing in the snow, her little pit sending heat to melt the snow on her back porch, and Bart went on over and shoveled the neighbors' walk when  he saw that no one moved inside the house. John and Marilyn rolled balls into snowmen in the yard, and the kids, especially Arlon, loved to catch Marilyn with a snowball. Gloria watched them through the window, wondered if maybe she wasn't too old to do it, but slipped on Beech's big overshoes, tied a rag around her head, pulled into her coat, and lambasted them all with the first really good snowball fight they'd ever been in. Snow at Easter but the last they'd see of it for this year.

The Settlement folks stayed on their place, not having much to do with the town, only letting the grumbling teenagers get to class and then back, to tend the animals and the fields,  plowing the cold frost under to enrich the spring soil. Afraid Theopolis might see them, they never drank from the now public water fountain outside the post office, the kids  snubbed the water, bringing spring water in Hi-five nippled plastic bottles to school, the men carried their familiar and worn canteens on their hips, their trademark of being from Settlement, and the women, proud and disdainful of anything but wanting to stay true to Settlement and its separateness, held off their thirst until they came back home from shopping or working in homes, came back and drank from the cool springs on their own land.

Mr. Blake at the *Bugle* pondered whether he could afford to keep Tom Sweet on. Times were poorly, he figured; Tom would have some trouble getting on at another paper. And Paulette Pardine, after spending an atrocious Friday night with Will Lomax, a husky white lad who thought he was God's gift to women, fought him off and stripped off her ruined stockings before she went to bed at three, crying like a baby without its bottle.

The Days End hostess, Tess Tandy, poured water on the ashes at midnight, tucked a bottle of rum under her housecoat, and went whistling up to bed. No comers today, she fussed, but the day of the bed and breakfast is fast approaching. Hang on, girl. Daddy had said that many days have to pass before you find your end, but she'd found hers, had painted the sign herself, Days End, and so it would be. Next Easter would be different, she vowed.

# Chapter Thirty-One

*This ain't my first rodeo,*
*This ain't the first time this old cowboy's been throwed.*
*This ain't the first I've seen this dog and pony show,*
*This ain't my first rodeo.*

*Vern Gosdin  "This Ain't My First Rodeo"*


The swirling clouds of spring, almost ready to burst in their fullness, hung over the town and the acres surrounding it. Beech smelled spring coming, heading out to milk Clara before he went to work. Kids stayed well all the winter, Marilyn getting plump now, and Beech looked forward to the moment of her child's birth, when his son's name would be cleared, once and for all, by the doom sayers. John getting out of high school in just two months, and then to be an officer, a lawman. He couldn't have been happier that morning, leaning against Clara's warm side, working that spurting filled udder of milk.

Tom Sweet was asked to look around for another job, and he agreed it might be best; the town just didn't suit him. Too many Blacks for his taste. Far too many. May as well give them the town was how he looked at it. Everywhere, they were, eating and drinking and acting like they had right to do it. It irritated Tom sorely.

Becky was told by Stone Franklin that the property he owned, the Settlement, the old Corothers place, was going to be sold, he would be moving on, but he had surely appreciated her efforts for him, and he would write her a good letter of recommendation should she require one.

Rev. Dr. Macy Stewart continued to stand in the pulpit, Sunday after Sunday, urging his people to stay true to Christ, live a God-fearing life, keep the commandments, and more of the same old sauce they had heard so long it didn't even enter one ear and go out the other. They'd done their Sunday church going, rushed back home to eat fried chicken and french fries, watch football or help the kids with projects, do laundry, and pay bills. A typical Sunday.

The only excitement the town sensed was when an entourage of big equipment crept down their streets from the highway, huge caterpillars with treads, on floats pulled behind semi tractors. Flat beds of dozers, and ditch witches, followed by three of the biggest dump trucks the townsfolk had ever seen. The lead man drove a Jeep, and the whole procession went through town and out Settlement Road without looking back. No one except Stone Franklin could have told them what was arriving at Settlement that day, and he was in St. Louis, signing the papers for the sale.

Hodges seen 'em comin', and he locked the gate and ran with his shotgun held in front of him, across his chest, to get Theopolis. "Lordy, lordy, my land," Hodges cried, "they dun come to get my lan. How this be? How they do this? It's ours, ain't right," he sobbed.

"Stop your tears, Hodges, I'll handle this," said Theopolis, laying down his saw by the woodpile and walking back up the fields to meet the construction men. A tall man, dressed like a cowboy, came forward to meet him at the gate. Theopolis nodded in greeting.

"We might be a little early, but the weather seems to be breaking, and we thought we may as well get the equipment down here and in place as soon as we could. Free us up for later." The man stood respectfully before Theopolis, meeting his gaze, and Theopolis only shrugged his shoulders.

"Ain' heard it was a dun deal, kind of caught me off guard, Mister. For now, let me ask if you could just bring your gear in an' park it on the side there, ovah that shelf of rock. Don't try to pull that big stuff out in the field. You'll get stuck, sure as hell fire." Theopolis opened the gate and Hodges only watched him in anger.

"You gonna let them come in? Just like that? No fight, no nothin'?"

"Fightin's for fools, Hodges, plain fools fight wit their fists an' guns. Let 'em rest. You ain' seen no diggin' or bladin' yet, has you?"

The man dressed like a cowboy swung into action, waved the big tractors towing their floats of cats and dozers, and they backed them into place and unhitched them. The ground was scarred up a bit, but Theopolis said nothing, just watched the powerful machines being set down, their day of chomping and churning, belching blasts of oil and smoke into the clear air, was yet to happen.

# Chapter Thirty-Two

*Strange magic . . .*
*Oh what a strange magic*
*Got a . . .strange magic . . .*
*Got a . . .strange magic*
*Oh, I never gonna be the same again . . .*
*Sweet dream, sweet dream . . .*

*Electric Light Orchestra "Strange Magic"*

Martin flew out of New York on a Wednesday, light traveling before his eyes, light he wanted to follow, to find his mother and tell her he was sorry, so very sorry he had not been there for her. He stumbled into his room late at night, tumbled into bed in his clothes, and slept like the dead he would soon become if he didn't get some real rest. The phone woke him early the next morning, and damned if it wasn't the CSR from Pearson.

"Dr. Schoenfield, you're back with us! When will you be coming in? Mr. Pearson is on pins and needles now, waiting for your water report."

"Will be there by ten, and no sooner." He rolled over and slept two more delicious hours before he showered and shaved and put on a blue suit, paisley tie, and soft brown loafers. Pointed shoes he hated, loafers were his style. Change that, he muttered, if you can.

He took a cab to the company offices, went through the halls and up the elevator to his lab, peeled out of his suit jacket, loosened his tie, and slipped into a lab coat. The test tube of water, so nicely provided by Donn Forest, needed to be examined. He had to look at it finally, make his notes, and get this thing over with. He never felt less like working that morning, wished he had eaten; his stomach grumbled and arched little screeches back to him, but he stayed at his scope, making his slides, finding all the things he knew were going to be there: big clunky things, things that spoiled the taste, long slimy things, things he didn't really expect, round wonderful things, and the thing he knew he would find if Donn Forest was any judge: fecal coliform. E-coli. Huge masses of it, crowding out the less noticeable floaters. Fecal coli. The death knoll.

He rang for a steno clerk, and a young man bustled in as if he had been waiting by the door. He set up his little lap top and waited for Dr. Schoenfield to begin his assessment. The words came out easily, quickly; the words flowed from Martin, as if he were the clearest thinker in the world. What he said about the water went well beyond scientific terminology; he stated simply that it stunk, literally and figuratively.

The man went off with his little machine, ran the text through WordPerfect Spell Check, made three copies, and came back to Martin for his signature. Martin signed. The man left and that was that.

Frederick Pearson reached greedily for the papers, held them a moment before he put on his reading glasses, gasped once, and then became all business again. A conference call was set up by the insincere CSR, the voices entering into the exchange sounded doubtful at first, then angry, then satisfied. Calls would have to be made. The equipment was already down there. Who was going to pay for that, the contractor fumed. Does anybody know where Stone Franklin is? Raymond Pearson spoke last. "Well, what did we expect with a nigger owning it?" He was the first to click off his line.

Mel Mackey looked over the contract, checked the signatures, even the lazily drawn 'X' Stone had offered as the partner's signature, but Mel knew all he needed was Stone's anyway. The 'X' meant nothing, the secretary had simply notarized the papers, and put her seal away. The wording Mel read over fast, looking for the escape clause, the magic words he knew he had put in, and there they were: "subject to local inspection of site, land amount, transient value of encumbrances, water purity." There! The precise word he had been looking for: water. All was safe. All was according to Hoyle. No money had exchanged hands, only the agreement, and he went to his wall safe and lifted the cashier's check for three million, four hundred, seventeen thousand and thirty-four cents and ripped it neatly in half. That's one for our side, he gloated. Try to put one over on the white folk, did you, Stone? You had to know it was bad all along. Smooth that guy, smooth, but not richer.

❧

Settlement stayed up late that night, and for the nights that followed, stayed up together and prayed. They even asked Sam Walters to come by when he could, and he made his time easy with them, came by every night, held their hands and sang with them. The teenagers drew back against the walls, wondering what all this fuss was about: weren't they about to be rich? Who wanted to stay here anyway, with fields and crops and animals that mooed and cackled? Better they take the money and run, they all agreed. Modern men and women, they felt, didn't turn down good money for manure. Spring was warming up the fields, and the kids all knew they'd have to put away their tapes and radios, tie their hair back, and go out to work after school. A drag. A dead drag. Only two cars on the place, and that stupid sulky old Theopolis drove in, looking like he was king. Well, he was about to be King in a different place, a place he'd have to go and find. He weren't, no, wasn't, they corrected their grammar, he wasn't no king to them.

Stone Franklin picked up the message, an urgent one, on his pager when he got back in range. He had spent the last week in Vegas, and had not done what he had hoped to, not realized the profit he had estimated would soon be his. He had lost mightily at the green tables, in spite of the courtesy suite and the free meals, had lost over five hundred thousand dollars, an astonishing amount, an amount his ego could not grasp at that moment. He knew he had to replenish his folding money, get back out there, he figured as the plane took off for St. Louis, get back out there with the two mill from the deal with Mackey, get his five hundred thou back, and then they couldn't stop him. From there, it would be all cream and butter.

The message said to contact Mackey, and he did so, after a nice dinner at Giovanna's Little Place in Maplewood: a splendid wedge of meaty lasagna baked to perfection, topped with melted provolone cheese, crisp romaine lettuce with black olives and artichoke hearts dripping with parmesan fragranted oil, warm italian bread, crusty, smothered in real melted butter. Let them wait. He picked his teeth and glanced about him. The only black man eating here. He tossed his toothpick on the plate, shoved back his chair, and went out to flash his American Express Gold at Arthur. He added two dollars for the meager tip and sauntered out the door, waving for a cab to take him back to his car at the office. Never brought his Nissan out and about. Never know. He'd get back to Mackey, pick up his check, but no one was rushing him tonight. He was doing his thing and that's what counted.

The answering machine in his skimpy apartment on Lemp flashed with a blinking light. He paused for a moment, wondering if he shouldn't just let it wait for morning, no messages he really needed tonight, but he slipped off his handmade shoes, draped his expensive jacket over a chair, poured out a slipper of Chivas, and pushed the message button. The voice he heard, would never have expected to hear, and in such a tone, a shriek really, not a voice: "Franklin, you low life, you tried to pull one on us, and this is Mackey talking, don't be coming around here anymore, you hear? The deal's off, finished. Bad water, we're told. You got shit floating in your water, you and the folks in on this con game. Don't call, don't get in touch with me. Tonight ends it."

Stone flipped the device to replay and listened one more time. The scotch stuck in his throat, made him gag slightly as he turned to go to the bathroom. Flipped on the light, used the toilet, looked at himself in the mirror. How had he tricked them? What was going on? That water was pure, pure as God could have made it. Settlement water had always been pure, the springs coming up with freshness and life and coldness, the coldest water he had ever tasted.

Only need to straighten them out, he reasoned, make them see that some mistake had been made. Call someone besides Mackey on the committee. Find out what happened here. The gentle approach, the concerned approach, the approach that was going to put him in a higher income bracket than he had ever dreamed. Who knew about this? Surely the word hadn't gotten back to the Settlement; they had no phones, didn't believe in them. His ace in the hole, he sighed. The old man might be able to save some of this loss if Stone only played his cards right. Damn, he needed some cards now, down to four hundred thousand in his account, and damn! He didn't need this piece of shit news, not now when he was so close. Tomorrow, he told himself, shutting off the lights and slipping out of his clothes, leaving them in a pile by the bed. Tomorrow, he postured, I'll take control of this ship of fools and get things right again.

He arrived at the office of the prosecuting attorney, only to find a letter on his desk, a slender letter of one page, folded neatly in thirds: *See me today before you leave. Zachary Miller.* Short and sweet. Well, he'd do Mr. Miller the favor of responding before the end of the day, and in his neat pinstriped suit, his Bellini tie, his crisp white shirt, he sauntered right down to Mr. Miller's office and let himself in. Miller was at his desk, his secretary seated by his side taking dictation, but he looked up smoothly, told her to take a break, and eyed Stone straight on.

"Your note, Zack, had a tone of urgency, so I thought I'd pop on in before I get swamped and give you my attention."

Zachary Miller stood and moved around his desk.

"Stone, we hoped things would work out for you here, shorthanded as we are, but to tell you the truth, you don't seem to really want to work at this job. You just kind of drift in and drift out." He turned to some papers on his desk and held them out to Stone. "These are the cases you were working on for the past six months, and in every instance, except one, you never came to court, never had your brief ready. Why, Stone? I know you could have done it. Why didn't you show for these cases? We had to throw someone else in at the last, and in almost every case, because of this sloppiness, we lost. Lost big. The county loses when we don't put away felons and rapists and muggers. Why didn't you show?"

Stone held the paper, looked down at the case log, and shrugged his shoulders. "I don't know about these. They were supposed to be handled by someone else, I think, and now that things aren't going well, it looks like you're going to punch the old race button. Is that it, Miller, the old race button? Have I got you there?"

Miller shook his head. "Stone, no one was rooting for you more than me. Your race has taken a beating for too long, but let's just be square with each other. Do you think it's fair to take off every other day when the rest of us have to be here? Do you think it's fair not to do your work, the work you've been trained for, the work you're very capable of doing? Do you think it's fair that you shuffle off work to white paralegals when you're the man in charge? No, I don't think so. I think you have to rethink your approach here, Stone. Leave us and try something else. You're let go as of Friday." He turned away and Stone held the paper only a moment before he threw it down.

"Friday, you say? Bull shit, I say! Is that how you think I'm going to take this, just sashay out of here, bobbing and nodding and backing out the door? You sure are a fool, Miller, if you think I'll take this lying down. You are one big fool if you don't think I'll fight this shit trap of a firing, firing a black man in an all-white office. You don't think I have friends? Connections? I will not rest one minute until this is resolved, and believe me, you are in for a fight here, believe me, this is a fight. Firing a black attorney, a good black attorney, letting his place go to a white man! You will wish to hell you'd never met up with me, let me tell you!"

Miller paused at the corner of his desk, surveyed the angry face of Stone Franklin, felt in his rhythms and his tone the pain he was feeling. The pain of believing his firing had to do with his color. A shame, really, when it came down to that. A shame the man had failed himself and now blamed it on his color. A scapegoat. Would a white man do that, use his ancestry to cover up his own failing? A white man wouldn't have that option.

"You do what you think is right, Stone, I can't advise you on the outcome. But the truth is: you didn't do the work, and if you don't do the work, you can't stay on. And about being the only black here, that's ludicrous. This office has many blacks working for us: the number I'm not sure of. I never did count those things, don't believe in it. Black or white, that's not the problem here. Do yourself a favor: hire an attorney. Don't go at this alone, get some counsel to help your case, for our case is all tied up . . ." and he gestured at his papers, "all tied up. It's as plain as day: you just didn't want to work, and that ends our discussion."

Stone blathered some more, lifting his voice to echo down the halls, called Miller a bigot and a racist, stormed and railed against the white man, and against Miller himself, railed against the Ku Klux Klan and the powers that be, but he was gently led by his tailored arm out the door and he found himself staring at the faces peering out of offices and watching him as he moved down the hallway.

"This is only the first round!" he shouted as heads pulled back and doors quietly shut. "None of you bastards has seen the last of me!"

# Chapter Thirty-Three

*Tearing me apart, each and every day*
*It won't be long until you're alone.*

*Journey "City of the Angels"*


Martin Schoenfield slipped back into his job at Pearson Pharmaceuticals, slipped back in and started running tests over and over on the viruses they had isolated. He scanned the scope and divided and split the virus into a million fragmented parts and held his breath when each isolated fragment bloomed back at him larger than before. (He even shot a dart of radioactive phosphorus 32 on it.) The damn thing didn't know when to stop growing. Kept warm and wet, it rolled and luxuriated in itself, waiting to spring its deadliness on the next unsuspecting lover. For it was the lovers that got struck down, men and women, homosexual and heterosexual, children coming into the picture, confusing the boundaries of how intense the fight should be. If left in the homosexual population, no one, not even the broadest minded atheist would have lifted a hand, but this new spread, the encroaching population destroyer of passersby and children, this posed a problem that everyone had to deal with, if they ever kept company at all.

Maybe, with any luck, they could slow it down, keep it separate by care and education, shut it down to the point that it would die out on its own. Using prophylactics had helped for a while, but just when things were slacking off, the abuses began: AIDS-infected people deliberately infecting another person, who unwittingly and unknowingly infected their next partner. One of the magazines held out to him at a seminar told the story of Brazilian street people, with no money and no hope, actually exposing themselves to the virus, shooting it into their arms, to get better care and housing and food, so they wouldn't have to beg. The government had care providers set up in fine buildings, fine by their street standards, where they ate and laughed and watched TV, took their vitamins, and enjoyed some of the best years of their lives, before they succumbed to their eventual end.

It was in his third week back in Newark when the message was handed to him at his desk that a call was to be returned as soon as practical. Why had practical become the substitute for possible? When did that change, he mused. The number was Luther's, and Martin quickly set his work aside and called. Claire answered the phone.

"Hello," came the voice, softer than usual.

"Claire? It's me, Martin. Got your message. What's up?"

"Oh, Martin," she cried, and her voice broke as she continued. "Oh, my sweet friend, it's not good news. It's never good news from us, is it? Why is it . . ." she tried to speak. "Why is it we can never just have good news for you?"

"The news. What's happening?" asked Martin, gripping the receiver tighter.

"He left us last night, after dinner, just said he was tired and would Luther tuck him in? But Luther had a call, so I went up with him, and we sat together and had a glass of port and he seemed fine, weak, but fine. He kissed me good night, Martin, just kissed me so sweet on the hand, said good night, and he went up the hall to the bathroom, so I left him. Damn! I never should have left him!" Her sobs began again over the phone.

"Claire, Claire, wait, now. You can hardly hold his hand when he's washing up for sleep, you know how Dad was, so proud. He never liked being slower than everyone around him, hated being the one that dragged. He just saw that he was dragging, and he got out. That's all, got out." Stop the world for a minute, Martin wanted to cry out at the passing scientists and lab workers. Stop for just a goddamned minute! A great man has died: a loyal man, a true friend and teacher. Gone. Gone. But to be missed.

"What arrangements did you make?"

"Luther called the synagogue and one of his friends came over, took care of the bathing and dressing, made all the calls. The service is set for Thursday, oh, that doesn't give you much time, does it, will they let you leave again? Oh, Martin, and you with this wonderful job! Tell us what to do. Do you have to come? Oh, of course, you have to come . . . I'm a mess, aren't I, Ms. Business Woman, a mess, a mess . . ." Her voice broke and cracked. "Amy's been wonderful, been over to the synagogue with her young man, ordered the flowers and selected some prayers for him. The rabbi says that Micah was ready. God, when is anyone ready? Shit, I'm never gonna be ready." Her fresh sobs and broken gasps made Martin want to hold her and fight off the pain she was feeling.

"I'll be home as soon as I can pack. Tell Amy I'll be there. And, Claire, tell Luther, I . . . Tell Luther, I . . ." but his own voice cracked then. He only said, "Goodbye."

It was no trouble at all to leave Pearson Pharmaceuticals again, no trouble for him to explain that his father had died. The CSR only raised her eyebrows over this request for additional bereavement time, a request she sincerely doubted and her voice didn't lie.

"Another death, Dr. Schoenfield? How sad for you. And your father this time? I'll pass your request onto Mr. Pearson, and I'm sure he joins with me in expressing our sincerest sorrow." There was no sorrow on her face as she punched in the E-mail, let it float into the sanctuary to be read and nodded over, and a deep sigh would follow, Martin could almost hear it. Paid leave. How did that ever get started?

To come back like this so soon after Amelia left him, to come back to stare down at his father's closed casket. Martin could almost see him wearing his yamulka and snuggled down in the polished lined coffin, rented for a few hours, shrouded in his prayer shawl: not fair, he wanted to shout. Not fair at all. Where did God need these people more than here? Why take them out when they had so much love to keep giving?

Amy wept beside him, clutching his arm in the dark blue suit he had pulled out of a dry-cleaning bag for Amelia not so long ago, had shunted it back in, never had it cleaned, and here it was again: the dark blue suit he hated to wear. As God is my witness, he prayed, I'll never wear a blue suit again. And I'll never come to another funeral service.

Micah was buried upright, wrapped in ceremonial sheets, far straighter than he had stood in the last stooped years of his life. Many of his friends came, held Martin against their chests, prayed over him, kissed his face and Amy's, stood over the casket and mourned with them. Micah's old cronies. Praying for his soul. The soul that had gone on before them, they reminded themselves. Say a prayer for Micah. He went on ahead.

Amy let Josh Laurent know that the apartment would not be needed after the first; let the contents be removed and the premises left in good condition, interjected Mr. Laurent. Martin packed up his own things, personal clothing and outgrown books, old papers and pictures, packed up his father's few clothes and sent them over to the synagogue's used clothing shop. Called the utility companies: gas, electric, water. Did it all with a numbness that kept him from crying out. There had been enough tears, he realized, seeing Claire's swollen eyes, and Luther's closed ones. For whenever he would approach Luther, the man would close his eyes and hold up his beefy hand.

"Not now, son, not just yet," and he'd move away.

He spoke with Amy about the furniture. She shook her head.

"I don't want any of it, none of it. Do with it what you like."

Martin went through the rooms, and put a piece of white masking tape on each item with a price, but stopped in front of the roll-top desk that Micah and Amelia had hoped one day would grace the parqueted floor of their own home in White Plains. "This can't go," he whispered. "This will go downstairs to the Hauks." And to the Hauks it went, after the newspaper ad brought in lookers and seekers for fine antiques. They were dismally disappointed that day, but some young people, starting out with nothing except their love glowing between them, bought the chairs and end tables and lamps, bought everything except the checkerboard and checkers, which Luther confiscated without a sound, took under his arm, and no one said a word.

Claire and Luther made a bed up for Martin on their couch, clean fresh sheets and a soft argyle mohair shawl spread over it. He wondered how they knew he couldn't sleep upstairs with the quiet and the taped-on furniture facing him. He loved them the more for knowing. They ate a simple dinner, and they drank blood red port wine that night, shuffling pictures back and forth, smiling at some, holding others up to the light for the date. Claire showed Martin her savings book, one entry causing him to smile. Sixty thousand dollars was a lot of money to the Hauks. They all knew how they had gotten it.

"Your plans, now, let's hear of your plans," asked Martin, pouring more port and enjoying the peace of remembering.

"We're thinking of moving, Martin, away from here, into a small apartment for a while, just until we get ourselves back to even. What do you think?" Claire stared hard at him, knowing she would change her mine and Luther's if he didn't agree.

"Wise move, I think. Just for now. Who knows? Maybe we'll all get a place together soon. Maybe we'll hit the jackpot, and be so rich we can do whatever we damn well please." He laughed over that, feeling the wine now, and knowing it was time for him to say good night before he got maudlin. Maudlin. Not now. No time for maudlin. Not ever again.

# Chapter Thirty-Four

*You're as cold as ice.*
*You're willin' to sacrifce our love . . .*
*You never take advice, someday you'll pay*
*the price, I know . . .*
*You want paradise,*
*but someday you'll pay the price . . .*
*You digging for gold . . .*
*fortune in feelin' but*
*someday you'll pay . . .*

*Foreigner "Cold as Ice"*


Theopolis was up early that morning, earlier than he usually pulled on his trousers and washed up for the day. He didn't know why, but he needed some time today, before his work started, time to walk the place and feel that it had been his for a while, but the good Lord knew something better was coming, else he wouldn't have sent those big dozers and tractors to hound his sleep. They stood like sentinels on the edge of Settlement, stood there and didn't move; no fire in them, only waiting for the turn of a key to spring to life and tear his land apart. The trees would go, they always went, beautiful big oaks and spreading elms, fruit trees ready to bear the buds for spring, like little bonnets of hope. The sweeping spread of soft dark earth would be bladed off, only to be missed when the new homeowners started to plant flowers and trees, little sprigs held up by rubber wrapped wires. Why knock down the grown ones and start over? What sense there? Theopolis only shook his head as he rounded the spring, dipped up a handful of water, and drank the cool clearness of it. Good water. Best water in the world. Thank you, God, for bringing us here. Thank you, God, for letting us stay on here. And, hell to damnation, thank Stone for letting us be here this long. Nothing is promised forever, he remembered, keeping his peace.

Stone Franklin was also up early that morning, showering and spraying Dune all over his chest. Smell good today. Smell like a winner. Wear something simple, something humble, and he flipped through the clothes on the hangers, finally settling on a dun-colored shirt with khaki slacks. Lizard belt. Slap that out. No belt. Simple, Stone, keep it simple. Denim jacket, kind of folksy. Perfect. He surveyed himself in the tall mirror, and sat down to slip on a pair of worn-looking boots he had forgotten to throw away. I'm perfect, he smiled at himself, perfect right down to my perfect smile. I'm a chocolate soldier, that's what I am. Today I lead my troops out of the valley and onto better things. Today . . . I try to save my ass.

Screw that contractor who kept hissing about the cost of moving that stuff out. Screw that stupid investor, who sighed and nibbled his pen, and said he had an appointment, could this wait until later? Screw 'em all for not listening to him: that the water was good, that some mistake had been made, why not check again? No one would listen. Mackey refused his calls, turned him away, let him speak with J. Clinto Alstupid for five useless minutes, what now?

He had no choices, he fumed, gunning the Nissan into life, and headed out on the highway toward Pond Ridge. He had lost big at the tables, knew he had played badly, taken some chances he shouldn't have, lost too big to ever get it all back, but if he had a small stake, maybe a couple hundred thou, he could swing into that casino again, hear them shout his name in welcome, get a free room and an eyeful of chesty broads, always hanging on him, crushing his press, but nice to smell. He'd be back with a stash, with some folding.

And he wasn't through with Zachary Miller, the bigot, either. That was set aside for now, until he got some chips back in his corner. That can wait. For now, he figured, I got to get Theopolis and the gang to buy out my share, which they gonna do, I know they gonna do, he smirked. They want that place so bad they can taste it as well as those collards. Get old Hodges bent out of shape again. Get him going on the side of buying me out. Yeah, old stupid squinty-eyed high yeller nigger: he be my piece of play. He wants to own it. They can taste owning it all, but it's going to cost them, going to have to explain an old mortgage to Uncle Theo, show him the way it goin' to be.

Theopolis was coming up the trail by the spring when Stone drove the Nissan onto the Settlement, letting himself in, and nodding with pleasure when he saw the big dozers sitting idly by. Great! They haven't moved them yet. Still bickering over the cost and who was going to pay. Stupid white folks. Arguing over pennies when there were millions to gain. Where should he start? Was a million five too high? Knowing they were going to give him over three, and he had told the Settlement folks they'd be getting one million plus, left him with a tidy profit. All's fair. All's fair in the business world. Much more than they ever needed, much less deserved. Without their chocolate soldier, they'd all be dung by now.

Settlement had saved their dusky asses, he gloated. I saved them for the past twelve years. It was my skill and learning that brought them this far. They should be mighty grateful. Mighty grateful. And now I'm going to let them have it, with a mortgage, but damn! Everybody white's got a mortgage and a foam pillow. Let them come on up and be counted. You want to be counted? Get a mortgage!

Stone stopped the car and slid out onto the damp grass. He moved with an easy loping gate toward Theopolis, who only stopped and watched him come toward him.

"Morning, Uncle. Great day to be alive, wouldn't you say?" He stopped and knocked a clump of dirt off his boot. He raised his eyes to Theopolis, who only stayed and stared. Stupid old coon. This will be easy. "Noticed the machinery is still waiting to get started, just panting up there, waiting for our say so. And I said to myself, just this morning, coming up from a sleep-tossed night, something's not fitting right here, something's not giving the way it should, and darned if I didn't say to myself, 'Why, Stone, have you searched your soul? Have you asked the Almighty if this sale is right? Can you honestly look at your face in the mirror and not wonder where all the good Settlement folks have moved to?'"

Theopolis took this all in, and started to walk again toward his house. Coffee would be brewing by now, and his little sweet wife would be thumping out fresh biscuits and stirring chicken gravy, poaching eggs, and slicing melon, flipping toast onto a blue platter. He was hungry right then, and a talk with Stone about his dreams and hopes and squirmings were not on his mind. But a feeling of control centered him, a feeling that breakfast first and a pipe and some talk might be in order. In that order.

Stone suffered through the meal, hardly raising his eyes to look at Theo's wife, a trim little wisp of a woman, entirely devoted to Theopolis and his wants. A good woman, Stone had to admit, kept her place. Let the men eat and hung back for the crumbs. Ate alone when company was about, and Theopolis had his share of company. Always bringing gossip, always keeping him updated on things of interest, like Stone closing the Pond Ridge office. Now why that, he wondered? The man's moving on, Theopolis surmised, moving on. Selling Settlement and moving on. An' why that be? Maybe that call he'd made had been smart. Beware the dog that brings the bone.

"Now that was tasty, Aunty, mighty tasty," Stone said, wiping his mouth and settling back. Theopolis reached for his pipe, and Aunty slipped forward and struck a match for him. Too much, Stone thought, these folks are too much with the old ways. Brighten up, folks, a new day has dawned.

"Now that bad sleep you had, Stone. Where that come from,

that bad sleep?" Theopolis leaned back and puffed his pipe.

"The light just came to me, Uncle, that I may be acting too hastily here, selling this land to the white folks, thinking they'll make it open to every color. Seems I may have been mistaken. Seems the plan might be to have a closed community here, not let colored in at all, and that didn't set right with me, shook me up when I realized I had almost been duped. But the Good Lord must be watching over his flock, must be keeping tabs on what Sylvia wanted for me and you, sent me a messenger, she did, said, Stop! Stone! Stop! Go to Uncle Theo, ask him to forgive you for your false dream, ask him to run the whole shabang." Stone watched the passive face, puffing steadily on his pipe. Theopolis politely asked for more coffee, which Aunty immediately ran to fetch.

This can't last much longer, fumed Stone, stretching his legs and smelling the scent of Dune wafting in his nose. We should be done by now. Me outta here. Him gloating over putting one over on me.

Theopolis sipped his coffee, added some cream, and stirred it slowly with a spoon. He licked the spoon and set it down. The cup went up for another sip, and Stone was sweating. Why sweating? Why now, when he never sweated?

Theopolis began speaking. "The whole shebang? You mean you wan' us to have the whole shebang?"

Stone nodded. Now it comes. The tricky part, the mortgage part, the part the old coon wouldn't understand, X's and all. "It only seems fair, that you get to buy Settlement ahead of those white cockroaches, for that's all they are, bugs, trying to take from the Black man what's his by right of domain. I mean, you been here the longest, sweated those furrows, brought in the grain, helped birth the animals, kept this place up to be the nicest lookin' place for miles, why else do you think they want it so bad? I can't do it, Uncle, can't let them have it. You buy me out, take a bank loan, and I'll be outta here, and you will have Settlement to yourself, once and for all."

"That musta bin a powerful dream you had, to turn this all back to us. Powerful dream. Nothin' else change yo mine? Nothin' you migh' wan' to tell me?"

Stone shook his head, took a swallow of coffee, and bore down again. "What's right is right, Uncle, you know me as I am. Straight-talking son of my daddy. Wouldn't he look down at this offer and say, 'Right on, son, get right with God and your people.'" Stone wiped his forehead with the napkin and laid it back on the table. "What's a fair price, Uncle? What would you think is a fair price for what I'm giving you?"

"Now we're talkin' about two differen thins here, Stone, a price an' givin' doan seem to jive. You be givin' us a whole lot of debt, an' we is poor people, we works the lan, an' we milk an' we grow, but we ain' rich, not by a lon' shot. If you be givin', I 'spect you wan outta this place with a mite less than what the white boys offered to us, am I right there, you would sell your percent for a mite less?"

The conversation had turned, and now Stone seemed at the mercy of the fates. Yes, he wanted out, but for as much as he could get.

"One million eight would suit me, and that's far less than I would receive if I let the wolves in at the door. The wolves, Uncle, that'll shred this land and knock down the pig styes, sell off the chickens and cows, take down the barns, brick and board, and sell 'em at auction to the highest bidder. Can't bear to see that happen, can't even begin to tell you my sorrow over that happening. Poor Ms. Corothers. Why should it come to this, bickering over a little old mortgage? You could handle it, Uncle, you and all the good fellows here. You could pull together, make Settlement yours, meet that note and sweet Jesus! One day it's all over. You own her, fair and square. That's the American way!"

Theopolis tapped out his pipe and turned to check the wall clock. The hour was eight and he moved from his chair. "Wood to cut, geese to feed." He plodded to the door, took his cap and kiss from Aunty, and went out onto the porch. Stone scurried after him, let the screen shut behind him, and stopped behind the broad back descending the stairs.

"Uncle, we weren't quite through. This is important to me, to us, to settle this now, before another day goes by. I need my sleep, and until this is settled . . ."

Theopolis turned on the bottom step, his hand resting on the freshly painted rail, stood for a moment, taking in Stone Franklin and his anxious face.

"We could go one-five, Stone, an' thas a hard bottom. One five an' thas it."

Stone stumbled down the steps, embraced the older man, and fairly wept for joy. "I'll take it, you got it, hand shake good enough?" One million five hundred. Perfect. Perfect, he figured. Back to where he was. Back up and running. The hand shakes were firm. "I'll draw up the papers," began Stone, but Theopolis stopped him.

"I'll draw up the papers, have 'em sent to you. You look 'em over, see there what you need, sign 'em, notarize 'em (Paulette had tole him about that), an' get 'em back down to me. Take two, three days, to know you mind, aftah what you seen in that dream. Take your time now, Stone. This be a big un for you."

Theopolis turned then, and waved at several other men starting up the path between the fruit trees, past the big house, and out into the fields. The whole crew, loving every minute of it, sucking up to mother earth, loving the mortgage, too, beamed Stone, flooring the Nissan and speeding past them to the gate. Let them eat my dust. I'm history.

The papers came in due time, four days it took, kind of long, but in a neat long legal envelope, all proper and the correct postage stamped on, no delivery charge. He greedily ripped open the envelope and surveyed the writing, line by line, sitting in his cheap apartment on Lemp, sipping Chivas at eleven in the morning for this occasion, wondering if he could get a flight out tonight to Vegas, his markers were still good until the real money floated in. His eyes ran over the lines, ran over the figures until they stopped, dead stopped at the offer line: "One hundred thousand, five hundred dollars." Could the old man be that stupid? How could he believe it was thousand and not million? He read it again, turned the page over, sipped his scotch and then set it aside, reached for the phone to call the lawyer. In his earnest reading, his ready mind had not taken a second look at the stationery, so finely embossed in his hand. The richness of it, the texture, the feel. Damn! The old monkey had used Mackey! The spunk of the turd! Had used Mackey and his filthy connections! To bilk him! They were all in cahoots, and by God, he knew his daddy was churning in his grave.

If Theopolis used Mackey, then Theopolis knew: knew that there was no buyer, knew that the money was never going to come to Stone, knew that the deal was off. He knew, damn him, knew that as sure as a bear shits in the woods. Knew he had him, and let him strangle on his praise Jesus and my poor dear friends at Settlement. Fuck Settlement! Let them all rot in their crummy water. Serves them right. One hundred thousand and five hundred more would get him up to speed. He'd be out of that mess. Let them all sink in it.

He zipped off to the bank, had his signature notarized by a white woman, sped in the Nissan to the post office, and sent off the papers that would separate him from the Settlement forever. He caught the last plane to Vegas, enjoyed a cocktail served by a white stewardess, and ran into town in a rented car to stay up all night, and he did all right that night. Made over twenty thousand on the crap tables, turned in early, he had some sleep to catch up with, but he was back in the casino at seven, smiling and shuffling the coins in his pocket, setting his marker on the big one.

# Chapter Thirty-Five

*I could say day, you could say night.*
*. . . saying its black, when it's white . . .*
*You lookin' at me, me lookin' at you*
*It's always the same, a shame, thas all . . .*
*I could leave . . .*
*but I don't go, it would be easier I know,*
*I can't feel a thing from my*
*head down to my toes.*

*Genesis (Phil Collins) "That's All"*

"It's been almost three months since we saw her. Maybe we should just go on over and see her," stated Joan Stewart over the breakfast table. "Macy, she is our daughter, and what she did, well, we know it was wrong, but God wants us to understand, take into consideration certain forces. Maybe we should just stop and take stock and let some of our words go into practice. Can we do that?"

He glared at his wife, gave her such a look that she brought her eyes down and dared not raise them. He rose from his chair, threw down his napkin, and stormed out of the house.

"Macy!" she called after him, but he didn't turn back. She watched his car drive away and slunk back to the kitchen in her chenille robe, her hair still in curlers, cried over the sink as she splashed in the liquid detergent. God help me, she cried, and the tears came pouring out of her, came from her dry sockets and made them whole once more. She was not going to stay with a preacher who only preached, never believed, never thought that redemption was for him. She cried while she wiped up the counter, she cried while she packed her bags, she cried great swollen tears over the wasted years, the wasted body she had left, and found she still had a voice. She used it to call the only cab company in town, an older black man, who ran his old Checker for little or nothing. She sat in that cab with her reddened eyes and said, "Take me away from here. Anywhere but here." Freddie took her to Days End (what else to do with her?) where she was met by the sweetest kindest lady who helped her upstairs, kissed her forehead, made her tea, and her new life began.

She slept for most of the day, came awake just as the sun was slipping down for the night. She dressed in a simple house dress when she heard voices below in the dining room. The upstairs was warmly carpeted, with doors leading into guest rooms with adjoining baths. So pretty, she thought, moving through the rooms. Like a Victorian house.

Supper was being served, and Tess Tandy was bustling between the kitchen and dining room, setting up an extra table for unexpected guests who had seen her inviting sign and stopped in. Not one to shirk duty, Joan went into the kitchen, and surveyed the clean warm room, with its six burner range and bubbling pots. "Let me help," she suggested, and Tess handed her the cloth and napkins and pointed back to the dining room, while she eyed the simmering food. Joan entered the room, and set up the table, asked the diners if they would like a glass of wine or tea, went to get the drinks, and came back with them as easily as if she were serving her family. Her smile broadened with pleasure when she recognized one of the men from her church, bringing in out-of-town guests. She went for bread, crackers, and butter, filled water glasses, stopped to check on the other occupied table, now being served bowls of salad by Tess, and the two women went about their stirring and serving as if they had always worked as a team.

The fare was richly simmered beef stew with carrots from the Settlement, left whole in the bubbly, onion-filled broth. The bread was homemade, crusty and crunchy, the butter churned from a Settlement urn. So much of Settlement here, thought Tess, wiping her hands and bringing on the peach cobbler with ice cream for dessert. Joan was moving through the room, serving coffee and inquiring if anyone would enjoy port or a liquor, and the fire in the grate needed a log, so she slipped out and grabbed three, and fed the fire while the diners relaxed and enjoyed the blessings of a pleasantly satiated belly. The tips were generous, compliments abounded over the food and the service, all promised to come back soon.

"Come Friday, turkey and stuffing, and stay the night! The rooms are lovely, each with their own bath, all antiques upstairs. Do come back!" Tess closed and locked the door at ten thirty and sank down on the sofa by the fire. How had she pulled off twelve guests with so little trouble? How had she ever done this alone? She watched as Joan swept up crumbs in a little pan, carried the dirty dishes to the kitchen. Her ears heard the water tap start and she rested back at the luxury of it all. Help. She had help. If only she could convince her to stay.

Leaving was not part of Joan's plan. She had left her own home behind, the pleasant bungalow not a mile from where she happily wiped the plates and glasses, set them on the high shelves over the work table, dead center in the big room. She scoured the pots, putting the leftovers in tightly fitting dishes in the huge old fridge, swept the floor, and forgot for a moment that she was not head of the house. Forgot it as simply as if Tess Tandy didn't exist, wasn't standing in the doorway with her hands on her broad hips, smiling at her.

"Done all my work, have you? Now I guess you'll be asking for a raise." She moved to the center counter, pulled up a stool, and plumped herself down on it.

"Joan, you and I need to talk about me keeping you on here. With you here, we could do some great things. You have a gift with people. They like you, like to have a glass of wine if you suggest it. Now that's a gift and good money in liquor, too. Food is cheap here, but the drinks cost, and you ran that stable through two bottles of port and some cognac. Girl, I need you."

Not as much as I needed to hear that, Joan dreamingly thought, the praise sounded so clean and fresh. She had not heard a word of praise in twenty years, had not been as happy as she was now, watching Tess on the stool. She set the broom back in its little closet and pulled up a stool next to Tess.

"The truth is, Tess, I need you more than I ever dreamed I would need another soul. I've left my husband, you see, and I don't plan on being summoned back, nor if I were, and I don't think he will, I don't plan on going back to him. I felt more caring and true love in this house tonight than I've ever felt in my entire adult life. I can only see that dining room at Christmas, with candles and greens on the mantle, with a tree as big as we can get it, oh! Tess, I see myself being very happy here, if you'll only let me stay, work off my room and board. I don't need that big room, that's too nice for me. Let me take the little one, with the single bed. Let that be mine, and I'll work so hard, you'll never want me to go."

"Baby, now don't go getting mushy on me. You don't need to whimper to get a place with me. Tess Tandy knows a fine woman when she sees one, and you are darn good in the kitchen. Can you cook, by any chance?" And the next two hours, before they pulled the curtains and poured water on the embers, were spent poring over cookbooks and trading secret recipes, nodding with pleasure as they realized their joint knowledge of homemaking was going to enlarge their menu, increase their business, even do some advertising in Blake's *Bugle* about their specials. They were giddy and happy as they followed each other up to bed, Tess with her brandy snifter filled for her good night sipping; Joan with a glass of white wine with a lemon slice, her first in a long time, and they shook hands in the hall over their new partnership.

A friend, Joan murmured, pulling the quilt under her chin. Now I find a true friend. The wine made her pleasantly sleepy, but she was eagerly planning ahead to the next day. How about starting a breakfast club, getting the folks to stop in for muffins and croissants, fresh from the oven? And cappuccino! Could this town be ready for the silky smoothness of strong black coffee and whipped cream? We'll find out, she smiled, snuggling deeper into the quilt. Oh, Lord, thank you for this blessing.

ذ&

Macy Stewart came back at twilight, noticed the porch light was not on, and grumbled as he let himself in. Sloppy housework, with all he had on his mind. Sloppy housework he didn't need to suffer, and she would hear of it. He called her name as he flicked on the living room light, went to the darkening kitchen and observed no dinner on the stove, no smells of food, and he turned ugly then. One thing to bring up that damned whore of a daughter; another thing entirely to leave him without his supper. Where could she be? Too late for calls to the sick, which she dutifully did for him. Too late to be marketing; the fridge had plenty as he peered in and grabbed a piece of leftover meat loaf. Stuffing it into his mouth, he headed upstairs, and noticed the drawers open, the closet door open, the bed unmade. Not like her at all, he mused, sitting on the edge of the bed and pulling off his shoes, still chewing the tasty meat loaf. He licked his fingers and rose to go back downstairs. Looking out through the glass in the front door, he saw the neighbor going by with his kid on a training bike, and the neighbor noticed him and raised his hand in friendship, but Macy only stared back.

The night pressed in on him, and he began to perspire. Where was she? Why had she left him with no word? The ever chatty Joan. What was he to say to people, people who looked up to him as their pastor? Pastor's wives don't run off; he knew there was no man lurking over the flat-chested Joan, so where was she? Had she gone to the darkies to see Marilyn? Had she defied him in that nasty matter? He'd be damned before he welcomed that whore back home, snuggling her little mulatto and blessing him with holy water. He'd be damned before he saw that great infraction of God's law. Smug and secure in his faith, he rummaged for more food, stuffed it into his chewing mouth, and turned off the kitchen light to go upstairs.

My faith alone will see me through, he promised himself. My own shining countenance will be a blessing when I overcome these small boulders set by the common people. His clothes were shifted onto hangers, and he straightened the bed. Donning pajamas, he entered the bathroom, and washed his face and hands, drying them on the guest towels as a way of letting her know when she returned, for he knew she would return, where else would she go? Letting her know that God's words, not hers, rang in this home. He shuffled behind the towels in the linen closet and brought out a copy of *Playboy,* and he smugly settled himself on the toilet seat with his jammies around his ankles, and performed his ritual of uplifting and stroking, pausing to cry, "Great Jesus!" at just the precise moment. The magazine slipped to the floor and he hardly noticed. Beads of sweat ran across his forehead; his hand felt slippery and unclean as he rose and washed it quickly. That's over, he said to the face in the mirror. That's over for now. What a relief he felt as he retied his pajama bottoms. What a relief to go to my rest unsullied and with no cause to ask God's forgiveness for defiling a woman. The hungry lips of the woman, sucking him in once so many years ago, sucked him in, but he'd held fast against their draw, their steamy whispering sucking. He had been on God's side, and God, surely, must know it. Her lot is tossed, he resigned himself: lost she is, to God and his word.

&a.

Becky Forest, now unemployed and with time on her hands since Stone Franklin had closed his meager practice without giving it a chance, worked on her tan more earnestly than ever. She trotted along with Donn on his fruitless calls, rang up her folks in St. Louis for loans sporadically, but loved the sweet guy so much she never dared tell him he was on a lost mission. Her stops at salons with tanning beds were her only vice.

"See, sweety, see that pink along my thigh? That will be tan tomorrow, you watch, I'm going to be your bronzed goddess." He'd chuckle and touch her golden hair, liking the little straight cut ends brushing his fingers. He had a girl, all right, a real pretty girl. A wife. A partner, even if she didn't know a darn thing about water and what it takes to make a sale.

Becky's friend, Marjorie did her barbecue thing for Bart and Ethan that night, settled the little one with a rib he chewed on happily. She watched the lights come on all over the neighborhood and touched Bart's arm.

"Haven't seen the neighbor or the daughter today. Do you think we should shoot over and see if all's well?" Bart glanced through the darkness at the quiet house next door, no lights on, and he shrugged his shoulders.

"They don't want us bothering with them, Jorie, that's her way. No husband, no way she would want me to come trotting up like a puppy dog to say, 'How're you doin?' That woman wants us to leave her alone. Remember how she treated that Cheevers guy? Well, white or black, I don't think she wants no men at all knocking on her door."

"Sad, though, she seemed to be such a nice woman, and I like her girl. But what you say is true. Don't run over. I'll check on her tomorrow." She picked up the gooey sauce-stained Ethan, planted a big kiss on his face, and carried him to the kitchen sink for an impromptu bath. Bart cleaned up the dishes and shut the pit down, stretched his flannel-shirted arms over his head and kissed the night.

❧

Gloria Cheevers fussed over her bathroom, keeping it so squeaky clean that Marilyn felt like an intruder when she ran her bath. Loosen up, she wanted to chide Gloria, let it be. But she let herself be coddled, let herself be loved, and Gloria's soft exploration of Marilyn's now expanding stomach gave Marilyn peace and comfort with the child she carried. How I wish, she thought, slipping down into the warm tub, watching her belly riding the crest. How I wish this baby was John's and not Bobby White's. She sat up in the tub and giggled. John's wife. How unlike John to give her more than a touch of his hand on her shoulder when they went to school, but so like him to carry the garbage out and bury it without a grunt of disdain. John's mother was her focus, she reminded herself, letting herself slip back down in the bubbles Gloria insisted she have. Let Momma be there for me, oh, Lord, I do love that woman. But Luretha Tubbs, now that was a different story. Old Luretha, with her plodding step and her bird-wise stare, probing the most intimate parts of her body, rubbing her hands over her swelling girth, now that woman must know black magic or witchcraft. She worked slow, but she steadied in on Marilyn, twisted her big lip in her fist, and paused to tell Gloria, when she didn't think Marilyn was listening, "That girl's so small. We got some tough pullin' comin', Glory, tough pullin'."

That time's not here yet, sang out Marilyn, not yet. And I love these folks. Love them all. Screw Dad and Mom. Left me for being a loser. I'm not a loser, she reminded herself, running the water over her hair. I'm not a loser if this family loves me. God loves me. And the little squirt. Well, I'll learn to love him, too, that's the way I was raised, even if my folks don't quite see it that way. That diploma will get me a job, and I can raise my own, and do my own thing, and no one can tell me what I can and cannot do. So there.

The timid knock at the door was met with a joyous, "I'll be out in a minute, Clo, and you can have my bubbles if your mom will say so." For this had long been a ritual in the house: Cloteria would love to snuggle against Marilyn, feel her baby, love to slip into the still warm bubbly water and pretend she was a grown up woman, too. Cloteria loved Marilyn, loved her white sister who sang with her and braided her hair. Loved her kisses and holding. She dearly loved Marilyn and wished, oh, so hard, that Marilyn would stay forever and ever.

Arlon had his own thoughts, and he loved Marilyn, too, loved her so much he cried when Miz Tubbs was all that rough on her. He asked John one night, asked him like you'd ask a Dad, whyn't he be the father?

"Me the father? Well, it didn't go that way, that's all, Arlon. We're friends, that's all. Marilyn's my friend, and a guy jimmied her, hiked her skirt, and left her wounded. That's not me, brother. I don't hike no skirts on women, and I don't run for cover. You got that? You understand? Cheevers men don't run out on women."

Arlon only nodded in his thirteen-year-old world, nodded himself to sleep beside his brother in the bunkhouse. Man, a cop, he dreamed. John's going to be a cop. Like I'll get a break if I step over that line, like he'll be there to shoulder past all those white boys, say, "Leave that boy alone, that's my bro." Man, that would be neat, if he could only work up the courage to do something wrong. Gloria would have him for good, and his pa would kick the shit out of him. Maybe the cops would go easier if'n he ever crossed over to bad ways.

The town and the Settlement fell asleep that night, each in the arms of someone they loved or almost nearly loved: Gloria rolled over and nudged Beech into a frenzy she wished to hell she hadn't started, being as tired as she was, but the man was good, oh, so hard and sweet. Sam Walters and his tiny wife made love in a great swelling roll of their worn out mattress, but the lust and the fun he felt beside his wife were all offered up to Jesus, and in his Name. Tess and Joan had a Cappucino with their new machine, and Tess, naughtily, slipped in some Kahlua, which really set Joan into a tizzy of laughter. Marjorie and Bart put Ethan down together and fell asleep, curled around a teddy bear they'd shared since high school, and the house next door, with no one in it, the house of the stored boxes for Marilyn Stewart, stood empty and hollow. They had moved out, the woman and her daughter, left everything the morning that the woman with a headache realized her skin was getting darker.

It didn't happen all at once, it didn't do more than sneak in, cell by cell, but the folks began to change in Pond Ridge, in ways they didn't see at first, then by the time they saw it, they only gasped. The first soundings should have warned them that a change was coming.

Construction types, in jeans and pullover sweatshirts, came back into town, ran on to the Settlement, and barreled back through with their floats of trucks, dozers, and caterpillars. They drove the huge dump trucks out, the monstrous vehicles grumbling and shaking and sending diesel smoke up over the town. They left their dust behind and nothing more. They were gone.

The Settlement folk came into town more now, sat at the lunch counters, and jingled change and made little trips to the bank that they hadn't made before. The shanty folks really owned Settlement, the word got around; the blacks owned the choicest property bordering the river. Mr. Franklin had given it to them, so went the gossip. They owned Sylvia Corothers' place, and how had that happened, they wondered. The sleepy-eyed guys by the pumps, the early rising truck drivers heading out to Oklahoma for the over-the-road owners. How did this happen, and for real?

Paulette Pardine only kept her nose down and did her work at the bank. She loved old Theopolis, gave a cheer when he came in to do his business, and she among all the employees at the bank reckoned his accounts. She was the only one that he would see, and the president, noting the significant growth of that account, asked her if she would be so kind as to tend to old X marker and help him get along, as he put it.

Oh, I'll help him, you bet I'll help him, fumed Paulette over his accounts. This is one account that's going to get its interest paid and on time; this is one account that won't get set aside. These folks earned that place. Dipped, dived, and scrounged for it. Their account will get top priority. She resisted the president when he wanted to invest some money on behalf of the bank, resisted it when she pointed out that the investment would not be a wise one, held her guns low and said no, not with the Settlement money, and the president bowed to her, and the investment in a shaky deal fell through, and she looked good. That Mama looked good to that old president of the one lousy bank in town.

Stone Franklin had left the Midwest by this time, taken his token share of Settlement and run off to Las Vegas, living his dream of being a multi-multi billionaire, never stooping and scraping for nobody no longer. He had filed his pointless suit against the Miller faction, had fought it heartily and mightily, hired the best white legal mind in St. Louis, who pulled every race card, but the stupid bigoted white judge, always that white judge, had seen fit to uphold the old boys' club one more time, had seen fit to say that Stone hadn't fulfilled his contract, hadn't served up his time, hadn't done his penance. A fucked up mess, this white against black. When law and order should have prevailed. He would file again, he promised himself, file again and get a better answer to his prayers. But for now, his money luck was steaming strong; he was winning at Keno and blackjack. He had a good portion of his money intact. He would strike again and come back, get that Settlement yokel, that 'white boy' Theopolis, back in his stable. That man needed a good caning.

# Chapter Thirty-Six

*She took me to her doctor . . .*
*Any love is good lovin'. . .*
*She looked at me with those*
*big brown eyes and said,*
*You ain't seen nuthin yet . . .*
*Na,na na . . .*
*You ain't seen nuthin yet . . .*
*Thas what she tol me,*
*I ain't seen nuthin yet . . .*

*Bachman-Turner-Overdrive*
*"You Ain't Seen Nuthin' Yet"*


Pain is something you live with as you get older. It comes, you take an aspirin and it goes. How it goes away you never quite figure out. How does the body know that's it's a tooth and not a toe? It just goes away.

But these pains didn't go away, sighed Marilyn, shifting in her bed and watching the clock. They kept coming, and then they'd stop, then they'd start again. She ran back in her calendar, and watched the pages flipping over and over, and she sat up in bed and called out.

"Glory!"

The bedside lamp was switched on, and the beautiful face she loved stood in the light and leaned toward her. "Chile, what is it?" But before she asked, she knew. She knew as strong as her heart beat in her chest. She knew when she saw the scared white face, beseeching her help, praying for her help. "Shoo, shoo," Gloria murmured, slipping in beside her. Holding her hand, she put the other on the girl's tight stomach, the strong muscles almost vibrating under her hand. "Young 'en wants out, huh? You think he be ready, you think I should get Ms. Tubbs?"

Marilyn shook her head, hated the thought of Ms. Tubbs again, hated to think she would be here, the plumber's wife, for god sakes! To help her bring this baby.

"Don't call her, not yet. It might be just false labor, you know. Let's you and I sit on it." Gloria nodded and held Marilyn close to her side.

"You time 'em, sweet one, an' I'll get you some tea." Gloria hurried to the kitchen, set a big pot of water on to boil, much more than she needed for a cup of tea. Why she didn't know, but they always boiled water, and she wanted to show old Luretha Tubbs she wasn't no dumb un. She went in and roused Beech, said maybe he'd be needed: Marilyn was in labor. He quickly pulled on his clothes and stood like a lamb to slaughter in the kitchen, waiting to be needed.

"Should we wake the kids?" he offered.

"What the hell for?" she responded, setting the tea bag in the cup and pouring some of the hot water over it. "Why you wake the kids? What they gonna do, but gawk at us? We can do this, Beech, she almos our chile. If'n Ms. Tubbs can't get here, well, we just manage by oursels, like we always do. Don't pull chicken on me. Marilyn might do better with just you an' me. She doan like Luretha much, you sense that? Doan like all that squeezin' an' pursed lips. That woman think John's the daddy, an' she gonna crow big-like if the little one is one shade darker'n albino. Crow big at us, that darkie fool. I doan like her much neither," she added, carrying the cup in her hands and going back to Marilyn in John's old room.

Land! She'd been away just a minute it seemed, but the bed was empty, and Marilyn was squatting on the floor, breathing in and out like a wasted balloon.

"Your tea, I brung you the tea," she mumbled, but she set it down on the bedside table, turned to Marilyn, and crouched beside her.

"Can I help you back in the bed?" she whispered, but Marilyn only shook her head, the beads of sweat lining her forehead like dew.

"It's coming," Marilyn groaned.

"Beech!" hollered Gloria, springing to her feet. "Beech, get in here!"

Beech heard the shout, sprang forward toward the front door, but her voice called out to him again. "In here, Beech, I need you in here."

In here meant Marilyn's room, a room he had never entered since he carried in the new mattress. A room he only knew was for her, their new boarder. He stared in on the two women crouched on the floor, clinging together to the mattress he had paid for, and he wondered why they needed him here. If the baby was coming, shouldn't he be running for the midwife? That's how it always was done; he'd seen it in the picture shows, saw it over and over, with the young one screaming her heart out, knew that hot water and midwives took care of these things. Why me in there, he thought?

Marilyn groaned and breathed heavily, then went into panting, quick breaths, in and out, and Gloria held her and rocked her.

"Ms. Tubbs? You want Ms. Tubbs?" he asked.

"We too late for Ms. Tubbs, Beech. We way too late. We be doin' this oursels, you and me." She stroked Marilyn's hair and motioned with her eyes for Beech to sit behind her.

"Rub her back real gentle, Beech, rub it gentle. Help her pains move that baby down." He did as he was told, sat behind Marilyn and touched her nightgown, found her flesh beneath and kneaded her spine gently and slowly.

"Firmer now, Beech, firmer. You helpin' here. We helpin' here, ain' we, love?" Marilyn nodded, yes, they were helping, and her hand found Gloria's, and she squeezed it.

"Shouldn't John go for Ms. Tubbs?" Beech ventured, and at that moment, his knee was soaked through, wet through, and he drew back at the wetness hitting him. Water. Water on the floor, lots of water. He looked at Gloria.

"There's watah on the floor," he observed, watching Gloria's face. She looked at the puddle.

"Thas good water, Beech, baby bringin' water. We got our baby comin'!" She kissed Marilyn and rocked her, and Marilyn rose up against the mattress and her face got very red. She was pushing now, bearing down, and the look on her face, of utter concentration, the look of centered determination as she hunkered back down and expelled a large gasp of air. She rose up again, straighter, took three breaths, and sat back down on her haunches, and pushed.

"You be there, Beech, you check if the baby's down."

"I be checkin' where?" he answered, feeling all queasy of a sudden. "Where this is I be checkin'?"

"Slide your hand under. I can't reach from here. See if you feel anything. Lord, man, you know the spot if anyone would!"

Beech Cheevers, for all his love making skill, felt strange letting his hand slide under Marilyn, felt weird and taboo and all sorts of racial nonsense flicking his brain, felt a surge of power and wonder he had never felt. His fingers touched a firm mass, like a globe, and he said he felt a head. He didn't know for sure it was a head, but what else could it be in that warm wet jungle of an opening?

"I got a head," he said, thinking that he had done his part. Let them take over. I found the head, let them find the rest. It should follow right along, he didn't need to be here no more. Got to be up at six, let the women finish this. I guided the way, found the head.

Marilyn rose up again on her knees, took a deep breath, and sat back down to bear out her destiny. The head came through, and Beech, still feeling the globe, let his hand stay there, saw Marilyn stopped and turned to him.

"Stay there," she gasped. "I need you."

Oh, Lord, he prayed, let this be over soon. Let this little one just fall out right now, let this be over, bless the women who do this, I ain't cut out for this end of the deal. The front end, I can do, but this back end, this final part, I doan do so good. Let it be calf that need turnin', I be there. Let a pig roll over on her little sucklin', I be there, but Lord! Doan give me this, he prayed. Doan make me be needed here.

The baby's head was in his hand, he felt its small round wetness, and he slipped a finger over the closed eyes and the tight lips. It was a baby's head, and he held it. But Marilyn fell against the mattress, slumped there in exhaustion, and he knew something was wrong. Too many miles he had traveled on this birthing path, too many miles, to see a mother keel now, when the last push was needed. How to get that last push?

"Hep me, Glory, hep me get her up on the bed. Hold her from behind, here, hold her against you, we got to move or we gonna lose 'im!" They struggled under her weight, but Gloria pulled Marilyn in front of her and straddled her, her brown legs wrapped around Marilyn's white ones. The nightgown was pulled up, and Beech Cheevers faced the most wonderful thing he had ever seen. A head, a perfect round head, glossy and wet, the closed eyes, the sealed lips, the wanting to be here, but not here, stuck on the cusp of life.

"You wanna be here, boy?" He came alive in that hope, that moment, and he reached to touch Marilyn. "One more push, Marilyn, an' we got our boy. You give me one more push, an' this be ovah. You hear me, little one? Hep me, Marilyn, hep me, an' I be here to hep you."

She wakened to him at that moment, opened her eyes and smiled, and for sure, he knew he didn't imagine it, a glow came around her head, a light he knew didn't come from the lamp. A nimbus, his preacher had told him, a nimbus surrounds the head of the blessed, and he needed a blessing.

"Push, Marilyn, give it a push! He need a send off!" Beech felt the head in his hands, and his long fingers slipped past the head and into the opening and he found what he needed: the shoulders. As carefully as a practiced hand, he turned those shoulders with a twist and felt the push gave him the rest and the baby slid into his hands. The wet wonderful slithery baby fell into his lap on the bed. He grabbed the sheet and pushed it into the baby's mouth, pulled it out, wet and stringy, picked the baby up and held it against him upside down, that was in the movies, and slapped him on the back. Two times he slapped and the baby moved and hiccoughed and he laid him back down, blew in his nose, wiped the mouth again, held him up and slapped him again, firmer, and the real crying began. He would have gone on all night, rocking in that wet bed, holding that baby and hearing him cry his strong lusty call, but the baby was here, he was breathing, and Beech slid off the bed and left the womenfolk to attend to the clean up. Man who had to get up at six dint need to bring in the diapers, too.

ૐ

Bory Cheevers Stewart breathed his first air and turned a smile on the world. He never stopped smiling. He smiled when he nursed at the breast Marilyn offered him tenuously, coached by Gloria. He thrived and got a tooth and banged at his mobiles, and later Marilyn let Cloteria run him around the yard in a box. He was one loved little man and he knew it. The toes were all there, the eyes, blue and wide, the hair, soft and blonde, the fat creeping into his skin, plumper 'n a gooseberry, he was one beautiful baby. And he was mocha. Not black, not white: just melted chocolate dipped in whipped cream. He was cappuccino.

Word gets around, and the word was just as they all had thought it would be. The Cheevers had brought Marilyn in because their all mighty pure John was the daddy. Oh, the hoots and tipped glasses over that one. The pious Cheevers, the righteous ones, had a mulatto child, and John had to be the daddy. Going for the Po-leese Force he was, and bringing his ragtag along with him. Taverns opened early and stayed open late. All the truck drivers had a laugh over this one, the wives settling down alone and wondering what the fuss was about. So he was mulatto. So what?

Gloria took her troubles over to Sam Walters, and he stopped by his car as he saw her coming. Lord, what do I say now? Your son just made a mistake, did like most boys, felt his oats. It ain't against God that people love each other. Love don't know no color, but the words stayed on his lips.

"We got a new one at our home, Reverend, an' he need to be baptized. I told you he warn't John's, but I think I musta bin wishin' somethin' that warn't there. Leastwise, he's here, an' we do love him, wherever he come from, an' would you bless him?"

Sam Walters paused in front of her, standing proud in his almost new green coveralls, said something he was mighty proud to say and let

~ 248 ~

the world be damned.

"Sunday it is, and you bring the boy and his mother, and we'll celebrate like we never have. This boy is God's first, then we'll sort out the parents." He scrunched himself behind the wheel and drove off to the plant. Lord, one day, please, Lord, need me full time, so I won't have to keep slapping those caps on sodie for the world to suck up.

Tess Tandy heard about the Cheevers baby before anyone in town did, and she suffered under knowing it. Suffered for Joan, who was not ready to face the news that Marilyn had, indeed, been with a black man, held his child in her womb, and gave birth in a darkie shack.

What shack? Tess fumed with herself. The Cheevers were good people, the Settlement was next door and they were good people. What's all this about, she mused, setting out the cups and biscuits. What the fuck is the uproar? You drop an "o" out of good, and you get God. What's the deal?

"I went to see my grandson today," Joan breezily said, when they were setting up for the morning trade. Tess did a turn, mouthed an "Oh?"

"He's beautiful, Tess, just beautiful, and Mrs. Cheevers is a fierce proud grandma, and she has a right to be. But damn it! I'm proud, too. That baby ... " She shook her head as she folded napkins. "We got to go out and see him together, Tess. Would you like that?"

Tess knew in her heart she would like anything Joan would like. They were two in their bodies, but so alike in their minds.

Becky Forest stopped in for breakfast, and Tess complimented her on her rosy glow.

"Been out tannin', I see. You gonna ruin your skin with those rays. Let it rest, Becky. You're fine as you are."

Becky did look closer at her legs as she slid back in the car. Her legs were darker and she hadn't been near a tanning booth in a month. Maybe it just takes time, she figured, snuggling against Donn. Maybe all it takes is time.

Many of the folks, long accustomed to each other, leaning over fences and sharing flowers, maybe they just didn't see that they were getting darker, and their neighbors were getting lighter. Maybe they just didn't look as close. Maybe they just let it slide, let it whirl, but one man noticed, noticed it big, and that man was Tom Sweet. Still hanging around the *Bugle*, half on, half off the payroll, looking for something else, far from there, he spoke to Mr. Blake one day and said, "You been golfing or fishing. You look tanned."

"Looks like you got a little color yourself," rejoined Mr. Blake.

Tom stood a long time in front of the mirror, and he was

darker, not at all the shade he had come in with. He was mulatto colored, and he cussed at the trickery of his reflection in the *Bugle's* bathroom mirror. He excused himself, pleading a fever, and went back to his rented rooms. Stripping out of his clothes, he switched on the bathroom light, and there he saw for the first time what he feared. His body was darker, much darker, not from tanning, he guessed. No, he never tanned, got freckles instead, but his whole body was the color of creamed cocoa.

The sweat poured off him in his dread, ran down his sides from his armpits. The hot shower and rough toweling did nothing but add an edge of pink to his sensitive skin. Somehow, somewhere, something had changed him, and it wouldn't wash off.

≈

Showers and baths were being drawn all over Pond Ridge that week; the water table must have dropped nine inches. No amount of scrubbing was bringing back the whiteness. The whole town, with the exception of five or six octogenarians, was getting darker. Changes were happening among the blacks, only their skin was starting to lighten. Several were afraid of the blotchy looking pink and white faces that sometimes came with a pigment condition, leaving the complexion mottled and unpleasant to see. But this didn't happen to them. They only got lighter.

≈

Paulette Pardine was skeptical at first, then concerned, then relieved. I am not all black, she said. I could pass for half-white. I may have a chance at a better job at the bank. Hallelujah! It must have been rubbing up against all those white dudes that did it. And those were the same words old granny spoke from her rocker as Paulette left for work.

"What I bin tellin' you, girl? You mess wit dose white boys an' you lose what God gif you."

"Then, gran mom, better tell Grady to quit messin' with those white girls, 'cuz he's getting as light as I am!" She jaunted off up the sidewalk in her high heels, and felt like kissing the postman, who stepped aside, and watched her sassy gait sashaying up the street to the bank. Granny kept up her rocking, only checking once or twice each minute at her hands, which remained as black and withered as she prayed they would. Her soul only did a quick flip flop when Clarice headed out to school, wearing a yellow blouse and brown skirt, looking very svelte and smart for an old gal, Granny had to admit. Her skin, too, was lighter, and Granny only let one admonishment fall from her lips.

"Leave off that night cream, sister. You bleachin' yoself out." Clarice only smiled and went on to school, not understanding anything about this change, but her insides still felt the same, and that's all that mattered to her or her students.

≈

Sam's wife spoke with him about it, spoke quietly and firmly that a change was coming, her hands were lighter, the legs she walked on had whiter skin, and she was afraid.

"Sam, what is happening to us that we're goin' white? How did we fail? We never wanted to be nothing but what God made us. Why is this happening?"

He held her close and spoke with a sureness he didn't feel. He told her about miracles and changes and following God's word. He spoke of all these things with his mouth against her hair, but he saw his own reflection in the glass and he knew he was lighter, too. Much lighter than the rich mahogany he had always been. How to explain what he couldn't understand.

It hadn't happened to the Settlement people. He had seen old Theopolis at the bank Friday, and he was as dark as the day he was born. Only the folks off the Settlement were changed. And only in Pond Ridge. The men and women at the plant looked at him funny, not knowing exactly what was different, but he knew they saw it, and had no words to explain it.

The white truck drivers left earlier than usual, bought their gas away from town, laughed a little slower than they usually did, what with this mess they saw coming, talked a powerful lot about how much hot weather they'd been driving through, Texas and the pan handle, but at night, at the truck stops, they scrubbed like hell.

Macy Stewart felt it so hard his breakfast came rumbling back out of his throat. He couldn't hold anything down, nothing. The mirrors were turned to the wall all through the bungalow. Calls on his answering machine went unanswered. A pressed button erased them all. The problem was not just his, he hastened to remind himself. The real problem was all over Pond Ridge: everybody had either lightened or darkened. His mood bordered on lunacy: he envisioned Marilyn and her son rising above the throngs, riding a wave of retribution, flailing them all with the same stick she had been struck with. Sweet words of praise, words of thankfulness and joy in being true to God resounded in his head, an echo of the words he had spouted from the pulpit just last Sunday. Powerful words, he reflected telling them all, healthy and tan and beaming up at him, that, yes, his daughter had done just what he'd feared. He admitted it openly as he had only intimated before: his daughter had left God and gone to the dark side.

"And my loving wife has suffered fearfully over this," he expounded, "fearfully. She has turned away from life, found herself drained of the strength to remain my wife and partner in Christ's name, and for her I also pray. I miss my wife," he added, touching his hem to his eyes. "A man needs his wife's comfort when he comes home, needs her welcoming smile, her hand on his brow. But there is no hand for me, brothers and sisters here today. No, the Lord has seen fit to set another boulder in my path, but like the Good Book tells us, carry your load. Don't shift the blame to others. Watch your own behavior, for Judgment Day is coming, and Oh, Lord! Won't we be ready? Those of us who held true to The Word, kept his commandments, honored each other, gave to the sick and the poor, never let the sun set on our anger. Oh, Glory be!" He raised his arms above the exultant crowd. "Let Judgment Day come. I am ready, Lord. And all of us here are ready as well, so safe we are in His loving embrace. Save today, this Sunday. Carry it with you all this week. Be here for gospel study Wednesday night. Mrs. Talbot is bringing carrot cake. And next Sunday, we will have more to celebrate. Amen."

But Sunday passed to Monday, and as everyone in town under eighty passed a mirror, the truth was out. They were all changed. Everyone with cells that were actively growing and multiplying, all save the very old, were changed. In a bat of an eye, by time's reckoning.

Donn Forrest rolled out of bed after kissing the sweet bronzed stomach of Becky. That tan looked good on her, he admitted. Like her dark as an Amazon maiden. Even her hair shone more brightly against the tan. He peered closer to her as she slept peacefully. She looks like she was dipped in cinnamon. Maybe those tanning booths were all right after all.

Those booths must be taking over, he mused as he drove through town. Everyone he saw looked like they'd been going, and he parked at Days End and went in to have a cup of that addictive cappuccino they'd gotten popular. Everyone hailed him, saw he was the same as he'd ever been, and wished they were. Some of the tanned faces greeted his still-white face with a degree of envy. Wish I could get tan like that, he admitted to himself. Even Joan Stewart and his old friend Tess Tandy sported the new color, proudly and naturally, as if this was just one more change they'd see.

Mr. Blake from the *Bugle* signaled him to join his table, and Donn sat with his steaming cup, with a peppermint stick for a stirrer, and saw Tom Sweet nervously glancing away from him.

"Why, Sweet, you're lookin' well," Donn started, but the man's frightened eyes made him stop. Things had changed Tom, too, and not to his liking.

"Stop right there, water man, you stop right there," he hissed. "This is the work of some devil or monster, making us all go round in this pasted-on color. You haven't changed. Why haven't you changed, Mr. Water Man?"

"Always drink distilled, or water from a home with a Cyclone Water Purifying system. Didn't I warn you, folks?" His gaze took in the quietly listening patrons. "The water done it to you, just like I said. Clean up your water. You'll all be back to normal."

A born salesman. A hunch played out. The orders he took that morning would make him the top salesman of the month in Cleveland, Ohio's headquarters. They'd be working overtime filling his orders if his hand could write fast enough to fill the orders. He went back home and sat by the phone, never left his kitchen table that day. Five hundred orders he got without putting one mile on the car or saying one word, at six hundred a crack. Twenty percent sales commission, plus a hefty bonus for topping fifty sales. Damn, he reflected. Some of this money's going into Dixie Bottled Water stock. Thank you, Lord, he chuckled, for whatever you did here.

Marjorie and Bart didn't have six hundred dollars to put in the purifying system that was going to bring them back to white. They rather liked the new color, and didn't mind at all the stares they got. They were all the same, she and Bart and Ethan, all cocoa on the outside, the same person inside. They laughed over their little barbecue pit that night while they saw the installers running themselves ragged putting in the six hundred dollar units that would make everything the same again.

ℰ

Mr. Blake, for all his time put in as a publisher of a weekly, prided himself on knowing a damn good story when he saw one. He urged Tom to forget his worries, let it slide, it might just dissolve and go away. Meanwhile, he had a story, and he actively pursued it like a cub reporter on his first city hall beat. He got out on his feet and rang doorbells, talked to everyone he could, white or black, but he couldn't tell any more unless he looked real close at the nose or hair. Couldn't tell much more when they held pictures up to him, photos taken just last summer, or winter, or last week, and then they stood on their porches or in the yard and let Tom take a new picture.

The *Bugle* ran a special edition that week, the presses spitting out the story he had written in his mind and only needed to get down in columns. He only needed to use one word: "Why?" and run the before and after snaps, but his chance to fling some poetic prose overtook him, and he wrote a long story that had no beginning and had no end.

ℰ

Macy Stewart scuttled out on the stoop and grabbed up his copy, hugging his robe around him, shiftily glancing up and down the street. No one was going to see him in this condition. He'd die in this house unobserved if that was God's will. No hovering bitch of a whoring daughter would run him in front of the jeerers, the nonbelievers. He'd stay put and wait for this to pass. The paper, spread on the cluttered dirty counter, only confirmed his worst nightmare: she'd done it to the whole town. He spotted a picture he knew from somewhere, and he blushed when he saw it was Joan, arm and arm with another woman. A lesbian, he breathed out, had to be a lesbian. Both of them having a good laugh for the camera in front of the Days End. So that's where the fool ran. Not to a man. To a woman. Oh, if only he had the courage to preach this Sunday, shout from the pulpit that sex with the same sex was a sickness, would be the final curtain God would pull down, next it would be with animals, and he shuddered at the filth of them.

The answering machine kept humming and clicking, his flock needing his guidance and wise words. He never answered them, but changed the message he was giving them, telling the callers to just wait until Sunday. His words would make everything clear. Sunday was going to be his sermon of the century.

But when Sunday morning came, warm and clear, he showered and scrubbed and looked closely in the mirror at his dark skin, gave it all up in one heave into the toilet, what little breakfast he'd eaten came back to taunt him in undigested hunks. He ran scared, then, all through the house, grabbing what he needed, packed three suitcases with clothes and degrees and framed diplomas. Crammed everything together in the back seat of the car. Locked the house. Ran to the car and drove out of Pond Ridge before the first toll of the church bell.

# Chapter Thirty-Seven

*If goodbye was a moment*
*If this moment was light*
*If your heart was an open window*
*And these teardrops had wings.*


*Vance Gilbert*
*"If These Teardrops had Wings"*


Sam Walters had done his sermon before his people at the little church of Evangelical Brotherhood. Had said what he had to say, and told them all to go on with their lives, let the rivers run awhile longer, feed their families, be kind to everyone, and let this Sunday be a time of joy. He baptized little Bory Stewart, did so before his followers, and they all looked on the child with the golden hair as if he were Christ come back to them. The Blacks from Settlement stood quietly together that morning, separating themselves from the town blacks, all gone mulatto. They eyed each other warily.

After service, his wife had coffee and sweet rolls for the ones who hung back to talk, but Sam had a mission today. It isn't every day you take a child in and baptize him, in the name of your church, without wondering why the child's grandfather, himself a man of the cloth, didn't step forward to object. Not that Sam would find anything but an objection if he confronted Macy Stewart with the news, but the news had to be brought and Sam knew he was the messenger.

He approached the same stoop he had been turned away from in the snow, but this morning, the flowers were peeking up and the lawn was lush, if not a little overgrown. Maybe the time for peacemaking had arrived. He girdled his hope around him and tapped on the door. No answer. No sounds from within. He checked his pocket watch, the old railroad timepiece his daddy had left him, and not much else. The church, he figured. Must be at the church and probably a better place to sit a minute, tell him what a fine grandson he had. Tell him that God forgets mistakes, forgives trespassers, only wants us to love each other.

The First United Church was filled to the brim that sultry morning: ladies in hats and men wearing suits over scrubbed faces. Too hard scrubbed faces. All a luscious brown, which made even the yellow teeth seem white. Sam looked for the parson's car in his spot, and not seeing it, pulled in to use the space in the overcrowded lot. He entered the back way, tapped on the vestry door, and heard nothing. The choir was lined up in the hall, waiting for the opening lines to bring them in, and Sam only nodded at the peering questioning faces so like his own.

"Pastor Walters, Rev. Stewart isn't here, he's always here. We're half past eleven, and we always start at eleven. Do you know if he's coming? He said he'd be here today, for a special sermon." Mrs. Talbot was devoted to Rev. Stewart, a prince of a man she liked to tell her hoped-for converts. Join our church, was her testimonial. Find your true self, was her promise. A regular drum beater for Dr. Rev. Macy Stewart. Plus she made great cakes.

A flash of light came across Sam Walters' eyes as he looked past the choir and into the church body. All the faces were the same: all mulatto. They had come today for an explanation from their pastor, but the pastor, not at home, not in church, not in sight, had left them hanging. No one hangs on Sunday when they turn out for The Word. He'd said his piece already, said it for his mulatto flock, now he figured he'd just have to say it again. The same words, to different ears. But all the same. All the same.

He touched Mrs.Talbot' s arm and urged her to lead the choir in. She hesitated, looking over his shoulder at the vestry door, but she resigned herself to what had happened. What else could happen to her after she'd led such a righteous life? Perhaps Dr. Stewart was too gravely ill to come this morning. Perhaps he had sent a replacement, to send his word. Thus appeased, she ushered her band of flowing robed members to their places and started a hymn they all knew.

The waiting crowd, grown tired of shushing wiggling children, found relief in the song, sang lustily and loudly. A second hymn began and the choir roused the group to stand and clap for joy, that a Sunday was here, and God was listening. They were not at all surprised when a man, much like themselves in color, only bigger and taller than Dr. Stewart, mounted the pulpit and placed his large hands in front of him.

"Good morning, good morning, and God be with you. I'm Sam Walters, from Evangelical Brotherhood Church, a branch of yours, and this morning I am here to tell you that God loves you. If you leave here today with no other message, know that God loves you."

The audience grew hushed, glancing to each other, prodding the neighbor in the pew in front. That's Rev. Walters, the black minister. From Salvation Army and the Settlement. He's going white, too, lost his color. The people whispered and held back, waiting to see what this man had to say, this man who, for all they knew, caused all this color changing to start. Someone had, and they sure knew it wasn't any white man. Who envied who, anyway? Ever see a white man envy a black?

Even a four-fifty an hour white parking attendant knew he was one up on the black businessman, parking his BMW. Sam settled his bulk against the speaker's stand, eyed the door for the missing Rev. Stewart and began.

"I baptized a child this morning, a beautiful boy child, and he was as golden-haired as his mother. The mother didn't come alone to my church, she came beside a woman you might know, might not know, but her name is Gloria Cheevers." Some heads nodded, they knew her, or of her. "Now Ms. Cheevers is a good woman, and if you know her, you know I speak the truth. The child I baptized is not her grandchild, and that I want you all to know. That child is from a white mama and a white daddy, who left her with the child in her womb, and you may not believe that, but I believe that." He stopped and drank from a glass of water set there by Mrs. Talbot. Bless her soul.

"Was your daddy black or white? Do you know for certain that you are not mixed up some way, some lost way? Do you know for certain, in God's heaven, that you ain't a touch of both, black and white? Do you like the color blue? We all like the color blue. Do you see the dark skies at night and are you afraid because it's black? No, you ain't afraid. God smiles behind that darkness, and in the morning, he brings the light. You smile at the light. We all love the light. But we need the dark sleep of night to restore us, to bring us rest and comfort, supper and sleep, letting it all come round to wake us refreshed." He drank more water, wiping his lips on his sleeve.

He continued, the parishioners leaning forward for his words, words that seemed to comfort them in the distress of losing their precarious hold on life as they knew it. Oh, there'd be some explaining to do, back at the job on Monday, back in Farmington or for some, St. Louis. Plenty of awkward glances to face down. What about Monday, a man wanted to shout. What about Monday, not preachers' day, not Disney World. How do I pick up and move on?

"We have today," Sam paused. "We have today, and that's all that's promised to us. We may do with it what we wish; He gave us that free choice. We can cry and batter our heads into our mirrors, we can slink off and hide, because what we were is gone, or we can say, 'Welcome, Jesus, to my heart and my head and my home. Welcome, Jesus, let me be thankful for my beating heart and my family and the ones I hold near.' You haven't changed, brothers. Nothing has changed. You have only enlarged your family. No man is left out now, no man, and no woman, and no child. That boy I baptized, he's just like you. He's between. God gave him between. His daddy didn't do that, whoever his daddy is, and it ain't a Cheevers. His mamma, little white Marilyn Stewart, didn't ask for the between, you ain't asked for the between. We are all the same, just as God promised it would be. Right now, we is between. Like life is between birth and heaven. Our real goal, if we believe. We only here a short time, folks, mighty short. We becoming what we gonna be for eternity. Eternity! An' that's a powerful long time. Get ready for eternity. This town, this town should be proud of what has happened, proud that God smiled on the kind of people we are. We were separate before. Now we are one. And no one can pry us apart."

Sam motioned for the choir to start up a hymn, and the congregation stood up with tears in their eyes, and they looked at each other and sang and sang that hymn. God had chosen them! How had they missed it? Had they been looking behind or forward? Where were their eyes not to see that if they truly believed, and for the first time, many began to believe God would bless them, now and forever. Amen. Service was over, and the Rev. Walters moved through the aisle to stand at the front door and shake hands.

The man who wanted to shout about Monday grasped Sam's big mitt in his. "Thank you for those words, Pastor. Best words I ever heard preached here. Sick to death of Stewart and his spiteful ways. Turning out his only kid. The gate to Heaven is narrow, but The Book don't say which color gets in first. I want to be saved, and I think I will be. Watch me on Monday, Pastor. Anyone says one word, and I'm going to tell him I'm part of a miracle. Watch me! Watch me!" He went out to his car with his arm around his wife, and his two children, darker than he was, smiled back at Sam. Sam twiddled his fingers at the kids and they giggled.

The choir encircled him, and many of the women hugged him, and told him he was a gift to them, a real joyous gift. Wouldn't he come share the pulpit again should Dr. Stewart need his help? Yes, he assured them, he was ever ready to step into Dr. Rev. Macy Stewart's boots, should he ever gain the knowledge, presence, and training to fill those gifted shoes.

Those gifted shoes were pressing on the accelerator at that moment, pulling into St. Louis, heading for his mother's house in Webster Groves. Won't she be surprised, he wickedly smiled to himself? Won't she and her lily-white friends freak out when I pull up and ask to stay for the time being? Take me to church, Mama. I do so love the church. Want to be your good boy. Oh, the color? Never you mind. God loves us all, remember that lesson? Right at your knee. Your baby's come back home, Mama. Right back home to Webster Groves.

Donn couldn't help it; he just couldn't restrain the laughter. He slapped his thighs and waltzed around the kitchen table. One thousand orders! Can you believe it? One thousand orders, but not one from Settlement. Why is that, he pondered, studying his sheet of orders, not one. But nothing changed there. If this water did turn those blacks to cream, and those whites to mulatto, why didn't those Settlement people get changed? He sat back then and wondered if maybe the Settlement didn't have the same water. If it was the water, and it damn well better be the water, else his balloon was going to pop. The water. The same water he had given to that doctor, what was his name? Scornfield? No, no. Schenfield? Close, but what was that guy's name? Ah! Schoenfield. Dr. Martin Schoenfield.

Wouldn't he be surprised to learn what has happened in Pond Ridge after he left? Need to send that guy the clippings from the *Bugle*. May not count for much, but the guy did seem to worry about the water. Maybe he could get that doctor to say the water was the problem. Could be the same problem all over the state. Over all the states. Tomorrow I'll find out who he is and where he is and send him those pages. He'd be interested, somehow Donn knew he'd be interested.

Martin Schoenfield opened the bulky letter from Pond Ridge, and was startled and mildly pleased when he saw the pictures and the broad smiles of Tess Tandy and Joan Stewart. He relaxed in his chair, pulled his coffee closer, and read the neatly outlined explanation by a Mr. Blake, the publisher, apparently, of this, he turned to look, the *Bugle*. Ah, yes, the *Bugle*. He settled deeper in his chair and felt like a tiny magician who had just pulled off a trick he had practiced twice, failing the first time. Pulled it off, he did.

He had to get back out there, had to find a reason to visit that town again, see the faces, check their heart rhythms. What else might have occurred that he hadn't planned on, what side effects? The color change was one thing, but as a doctor he felt a twinge of remorse that he may have altered other bodily functions, like longevity. A scary thought. One he didn't like to consider.

But the color change. Interesting. Interesting enough to him that he brought the papers into Mr. Pearson's office the next day, spread them out, and asked Pearson what he thought.

Pearson read over the columns, gazed at the before and after shots, shook his head in bewilderment, and looked back to Martin.

"Amazing. The same town, you say, where that Franklin had the nerve to pass off bad property? The same, you say?" He reread the words, studied the faces in the pictures, then sighed. Always sighing. Why the sigh?

"It's intriguing to me as a researcher," began Martin, circling the desk and pointing to various pictures from the clipping, "that many of these people are active sexually. Do you see? Many of these faces are thirty to forty years old, some fifty, but still active, some sixty, still active, I guess. More time on their hands, you know?" He blushed a bit when Pearson glanced up at him.

"What I'm saying here, and this Blake says so, too. None of the oldest people changed color. No old black men got lighter, no old white women got darker. They're not having sex anymore, Mr. Pearson. No sex. No contact." He let his words sink in as he went back around the desk and sat down.

"What are you getting at, doctor?"

"AIDS research, Mr. Pearson. We have a community here of actively normal people, they copulate, right? And the ones that are getting it on, excuse the vernacular, are changing color. They're not HIV positive, don't misunderstand me, but a change, a major change has occurred in them, one that might just suit our purpose, to find a damn cure for this virus." There. He'd said it, preposterous as it sounded even to him. What link? What scientific garbage.

"H-m-m-m. You may be onto something, Schoenfield, may just have a lead we might grasp. Can you get away (he was fully aware of how easily Dr. Schoenfield got away, what with his trumped up funerals). Say, take a week or two and check this out? Never say you're from here, the word might get back to my brother, and he is pissed at that whole town. Really cost him to pay to move that heavy equipment. Someone has to pay, you know, that's the way. While you're gone, can I let you in on another little piece of news? Keep this under your hat. We're being considered for a sizeable government research grant, very nice money, from old Uncle Sam. Millions, we hear, to go toward this research. AIDS has captured the imagination of every red-blooded American now. Kids getting it really makes everyone dig deeper." He rubbed his hands together and waved Martin off, rereading the clippings and fairly wallowing in the fact that Martin may just have given him a feather to wave.

Martin stopped at the CSR's desk, to ask her to forward his messages to the Days End Inn in Pond Ridge, Missouri. She interrupted her chat with a friend, put her on hold, and looked at him blankly.

"Now don't tell me, Dr. Schoenfield. A widowed aunt, desperate and on Social Security as her only means of survival, has passed away at the Days End." She snorted and shook her tightly sprayed hair, which failed to move. "Oh, really now, Doctor. Come up with something new, won't you?" She laughed as she went back to her visit, and Martin wrote out the name and address of the inn and laid it on her desk.

# Chapter Thirty-Eight

*I don't love you and you don't love me*
*La,la. La,la,la,la,la,la.*
*I don't care what you do every night*
*I don't care how you get your delights.*

*Eric Clapton "Promises"*

John Cheevers was packing his clothes, settling them into his mother's worn suitcase, fumbling with the latch to lock it when a shadow crossed the bunkhouse door. He glanced up, expecting Arlon, back from fishing. It wasn't Arlon. It was Marilyn, with Bory resting on her shoulder.

"Knock, knock," she said, not knocking at all. She swung into the room and rested her leg on a chair, settling Bory against her, and the baby waved and watched lint floating through the air.

"You caught me packing," John said, sending his eyes back onto the pile of shirts he had not been able to fit in. "Next week I'll be at the academy, and if I'm lucky, I'll be out in twenty-four weeks and have a real job. How do you feel about that?"

She brushed back her long blonde hair, and it seemed even blonder over her satiny brownish skin.

"What do I think about that? Since when did we agree to disagree over a good opportunity for you? I'm not the one to say what you want to do with your life. Beech says it's a good move for you, a way to get out of here, if that's what you're wanting, and I wish you well, John. I've always wished you well." She shifted the baby on her shoulder and started to leave.

"Well, what's to become of you and Bory if I leave?"

"My being here has nothing to do with you, John. I'm here because of your mama's caring for me, and I owe her for that. I'll always owe her. She is almost like my own, and Bory wouldn't be here if your dad wasn't a better midwife than old ugly Ms. Tubbs. Ugh! To think she almost touched my son!"

"So you don't give me any credit for being here for you, putting up with this crap I hear running around, that Bory's mine. That hurts, Marilyn, that hurts me. I never touched you, and you never talk about that football player no more. You never say you was raped. Why is it you don't give that tale no more?"

She stood in the doorway, and gazed out into the yard, shielding her eyes and shifting the baby on her chest for the walk back to the house. The long walk that she had taken to see if he would hold her, kiss her, love her, let her into his life. A foolish idea, she knew. John Cheevers, smooth and tall and handsome in his mulatto skin, he didn't need her. Then why she paused and let the tears start, she only wondered at.

"That song's sung out, John, that's an old tune and a sad memory and I don't let any sadness into me anymore. I may not have graduated yet, but next year I will graduate, you hear, you smug ass!" She whirled and ran up the path, little Bory bumping along.

"Well, whatever," he called after her, watching her jeaned bottom jiggling up the path. You sure ain't lost your baby-gettin' fat. You got a hunk to lose, sister. He smiled to himself at his little buddy Marilyn playing with him. He knew better. She just playing, like old times.

He swung his suitcase under the bed and sat down to retie his shoe laces. Funny she'd cry over nothing. Women are funny about that crying shit. Hadn't he done right by her? Hadn't he brought her home and hadn't they all cared for her? What with all this color changing going on, nobody should have noticed. But he remembered the mean looks in town. He shied away from after school friends, said he was too busy. Too busy because he didn't want those faces staring at him, wanting him to come clean about him and Marilyn. There was no him and Marilyn, and in his mind, it wasn't likely. Not that he didn't like her, he had always liked her. Even when she got pregnant, he hadn't turned from her. Yeah, he had dreamed about kissing her and holding her, but he knew that was not right. She was white, and he was so plainly black.

But he wasn't that black anymore, he realized, getting up and staring at his face in the bunkhouse mirror. He was the same as she was if his eyes didn't trick him. They were both the same now. Did that change things?

Damn that girl! Messing with his mind. He was for sure going to tell her not to mess with him. He stormed up the back steps, slid past Cloteria and her doll cradle, and shouted, "Marilyn!"

His momma met him in the kitchen, setting out plates and forks, raised her eyes and looked at him as if she didn't know him, shouting like that. "Quiet your voice, your dad's restin'. Why you yellin' like that?"

"She made me feel I done her wrong, like I owed her something, and I don't owe her nothing, Mama. I been putting up with blank faces and cross looks for months now, and I never said nothing, never said boo. But she acts like she belong here and I'm the outside one."

"Marilyn dint mean that, if she said it, which I doan think she did, John. She just feels you brung her here, an' if you goin', she goin', too. That's all she means, nothin' more." Gloria kept folding the napkins and moving the plates, like they were entertaining royalty.

"She going to. To where is she going? Seems we took her in, were her family, loved her and Bory, and now she's going? How did you know that?" He held the back of the worn maple chair in his hands and pressed down. "How you think you know what that girl is thinking?"

"'Cuz she told me, told me right up front, that she wanted to be with us, but if you left, you wouldn' be comin' back, an' if you wern't comin' back, then she'd go, too. That's what she said. Said she'd go to Days End an' get back in school an' raise Bory by herself." She dreamily moved the lone candle in the middle of the table, eyed it as if it weren't quite right, moved it again and stepped back to watch her handiwork.

"Mama, something's not right. She can't just take our baby and trollop off. To her mom, right? The mom that didn't want her when she thought the boy was mine. How can she do that, just up and leave us, not be with us anymore?" He relaxed his grip and walked around the table, circling Gloria admiring the newly placed candle. "How do you figure, Mama? What's the deal?"

"Ast her, doan be puddlin' with me," responded Gloria, turning her back and opening the oven door to look at her chops sizzling.

"I will, if that's what it takes, I will!" he responded, crossing the hall and knocking on Marilyn's door, his door, dammit! Did she forget whose bed she'd taken over?

Marilyn opened the door, and let him in, and he fumed and strutted and got his words together. He thought about a better way to say it, and he raised his arm, as if to a waiting throng, but she stood and waited before his posturing.

He glanced at the bed and saw the suitcase and cardboard box, saw her things and Bory's tossed in swiftly. Knew she meant it, knew she was going and no turning back. Mama was right. Marilyn was out of here when he was. Why that, when Mama had been the one she loved? Why turn against Mama because he was leaving, to get a leg up?

Marilyn picked up Bory from the cradle and offered him to John. "You hold him a minute while I finish up?"

He accepted the baby and snuggled his face against the golden hair, and the boy relaxed against him, pushed his head against his neck, and John was caught off guard. Not with Marilyn, not with anything else except the feel of this weight in his arms.

"Marilyn, just 'cuz I'm going off to the academy, going to school to earn a living, don't mean you can't stay here. This is your home; we all love you."

Marilyn stopped with her hands on a blanket she was folding, stopped and looked at him. "It's family love you talk about, and I know family love is strong, but I'm not a kid anymore, John. I need to get a life of my own, find a husband and a job, find some roots for myself. If it's not here, then maybe I'll find it some other place, but I got to look."

John wondered what she was saying. A job? A husband? Marilyn dating and going to bars, letting guys snuggle up against her? Holy waters! No way!

"Now just think on this a minute, just slow down and think on this. I don't want you leaving here until I get back, you hear? You stay with Mama and Dad. The kids would miss you a lot, and you know that's not right, just going. Promise me this. Stay until I'm out of school, and when I get back, you and I can decide what's best for you. Will you let me have that worry off my mind?"

She reached for Bory and he gave him to her reluctantly. She smiled at him and said, yes, she'd listen to him, wouldn't leave until he came back.

"Well, then, that's settled between us. That's settled. And it was easy, wasn't it? You don't have to get all huffy and rush off. Cool down, Marilyn, let me be in charge."

She smiled over Bory's head, and the smile was so sweet and sincere that he leaned over and kissed her forehead. "All's well. Let's go eat."

He led Marilyn and Bory out to dinner, and Beech was sitting at the table, raring to go into those pork chops, but Marilyn sat the baby in his punkin seat, washed her hands and Cloteria's, took her time moving the candle, so she could see John better, helped serve the mashed potatoes and gravy, took her time before she sat down. Gloria pretended not to notice, let the girl do her thing, but she saw her boy's eyes flitting after Marilyn's every move, saw the gleam and the hope, saw the dream, and she knew before anyone else did that they'd never lose Marilyn.

# Chapter Thirty-Nine

*You may say I'm a dreamer,*
*But I'm not the only one.*
*I hope someday you can join us.*
*And the world can be as one.*
*A brotherhood of man.*
*Imagine . . .*

*John Lennon "Imagine"*

Southwest flight number 457 bore down on Lambert Airport, and Martin held his thoughts in for a moment. Never could do that, he admired, bring a skidding plane in on a dot. Maybe I can sew an arm back on and pray for nerve function, but darn! Those boys in blue can land these hunks! To them I'll leave my blue suit, he thought jauntily, hitting the aisle in front of the crowd. Not hanging back this time. He had miles to go before he slept . . . now, who was that poet?

It was after eleven before he drove down the highway, crossed into the two lane, and pulled over the railroad tracks and into Pond Ridge. All the lights were low, folks either settling in for the night by the TV or getting ready for bed. He turned the rented Taurus into Days End, and was surprised at the changes. The lot could now hold twenty cars, not the three he had seen on his last visit. He locked the car, slinging his duffle over his shoulder. The front looks different, he thought, and he went out into the deserted main street and peered at the front. Yes, the front was all different now, glassed-in and homey looking, with wreaths in the glass and candles and signs about opening hours and cappuccino on call, all hours, for the desperate ones. He smiled. He wondered if Ms. Tandy would remember him. He wondered if he dared even knock at this late hour. But this was Pond Ridge, not New York, and he rattled the frame with his loud knock.

Voices came from within, female voices, tittering and laughing, and the door swung open. A tall spare woman, maybe the lady in the *Bugle* picture, he guessed, met his gaze.

"Hi! Dr. Schoenfield, an old patron, coming to beg your indulgence, being this late and all." He slipped his duffle to the other shoulder and paused, his foot on the threshold.

"Well, it is later than we usually take guests, Dr. Schoenfield, but maybe . . ." and she turned as Tess Tandy rounded the archway.

"Dr. Schoenfield! It is you again, isn't it? Come on in, let him in, Joan. He's one of us."

How he had become one of them was beyond him, but he allowed himself to be dragged into the dining room, relieved of his baggage, shoved down into the sofa, and handed a very nice cup of Kahlua-laced coffee. The face of Tess Tandy beamed at him, well aglow with a few well-laced cappuccinos before he got there.

"Well, you're back, and I was just sayin' to Donn Forest, not more'n a week ago, whatever happened to that good-looking doctor?"

Martin blushed in spite of himself, or maybe it was the heat of the fire coming from the grated hearth. He only sighed, a trick he had learned from Pearson, and smiled. His words came quickly, something he should watch, he reminded himself, but his words followed his mind, and his mind was fast.

"Almost passed you by, with the slick new front and new sign. This isn't the same place; things have changed around here. I hope that means you're doing well."

"Doin' well? Hell, we have a bank account that'd blind your eyes, doc, blind your eyes! With my new help." She graciously waved her hand to Joan. "We are cracking the bean counters. That's what they call 'em, those accountants, bean counters. We made seventy, seventy-five, a day last week, and that's not all reported, so don't you go askin' any more about our prosperity deck." She laughed and rocked in front of the fire.

"So besides your new help, Joan is it?" and she beamed and nodded. "So besides your new help, what has changed?"

"Don't you read the newspapers, doc? This town is gone darkie, now don't take offense, Joan. Darkie we've become. And richer for it. Ain't that a hoot an' a holler? We got darker and richer! It's kinda funny, 'cept it ain't so funny. The white folks seem to be bearin' it better'n than the black ones. But who's to say? We all changed here in Pond Ridge, Masoureye."

"I noticed you were darker, and I did see some pictures in the magazines, but I can't believe it's happened. What do you think caused it?" He really wanted to know the locals' feeling on what could have caused . . . it.

"There's all sorts of theories going round," interjected Joan, sliding forward and sitting by the hearth. "Lots of people believe it was a real miracle. Something God sent down to warn us that the time of being equal, and really equal, not just equal, you know, under the law."

"And don't we know how equal that's been," shot in Tess. "You catch a white brewer's son raping a woman and he gets off scot free. You catch a black man lifting a white woman's purse, you see how equal he gets it, gets thirty in the hard time pen, or the judge ain't doin' his job." She lifted her cup and took a swallow. "I'll tell you how equal it's been. It ain't been equal at all, but now, at least here in Pond Ridge, it's equal. We don't have no squawks, and you know why? Because we're all the color of the coffee we serve, dip it up and serve it out every morning. Eighty-five cents a cup and the folks come by every morning for their cappuccino, because those damn Cyclone fences . . ."

"Cyclone Water Purifiers," corrected Joan.

"Well, those damn gadgets Donn been pushing didn't do the folks one bit of difference. We didn't buy one, hear me, not because we don't believe in Donn and clear water, but we don't need the extra cost right now when we're just getting rolling." She sat back and sipped her drink, nodded for Joan to continue, if she had anything more to add. Joan straightened her back and looked directly into Martin's face.

"We don't know what happened, but the church-attending people, and that makes up about all of us, black or white, we believe it was a miracle. And I think I know what got it started." She turned and picked up the fireplace tool, shoved a log over, and sat back to admire the sheen of sparks flitting up the chimney.

"You may not believe this," she turned to Martin, setting the tool back against the stone, "but I think God said yes to my daughter, my daughter, Marilyn, and he said no to my husband, a self-satisfied bigot by anyone's account. Now, shush, Tess, don't you go defending him. He isn't worthy of my defense or yours. The pot's calling the kettle black here. He was a lousy husband, a faithless pawn of a church he didn't have the heart to believe in. That church, that's a good one, and the people that came to us, asked for our help, deserved a bit more than a creeping vacant soul of a pastor. They deserve better, and from all I hear, and didn't you hear, Tess? Sam Walters preached on Sunday, Mrs. Talbot called me, and oh, by the way, she said she'd bake for us, if we give her a day's notice. And we should, Tess. Get her cakes. She's better than we are at the pastries."

So it had moved to pastries, and Martin knew he had to get some sleep before the drugged coffee brought him to a heap by the fire. He set his glass down, said he'd like a room, and wouldn't it be just fine if someone would show him around in the morning, let him get a feel for this town if he was going to open a practice.

"You really think you might come here, join us in our bubbling kettle of brown genes?" Tess giggled, and Joan nudged her to be quiet.

"Second floor has one room left, 204, so you take that one, Doctor. And forgive us if we got a little open. These are just our thoughts, mind you, just our thoughts. But God did play a card here in Pond Ridge, or I have no faith at all," added Joan.

He tumbled into the quilted Victorian bed, felt sleep come over him so quickly that he thought he may have died, but he felt his heart beating and knew that something wonderful was going to happen. Something that made sense for losing Amelia and Micah, for seeing Claire and Luther shut down their home of eight years and move to a small, cramped apartment, saw him doing what he always envisioned for himself: a life inside science. He wanted them to be over the scope for one minute, so they could see all the colors he saw, see all the magic he could bring to them if they would only see with his eyes.

A woodpecker woke him, tapping and hammering on the wooden sides of Days End, and he rolled out and showered in the bathroom distinctly tinged with copper. The lines all gleamed with the glow of copper and the faucets were rounded porcelain, plainly outlined "hot" or "cold." He raised the window shade, still in his towel, gazed down on the street, and a woman passing caught his eye. He wasn't sure if it was a dream or his first waking moment, but he loved the way she walked, strutting in her high heels, nicely-turned ankles, nicely-turned face, smiling at the people who passed her. That smile. He had seen that woman before. Knew that woman. But where?

Breakfast was crowded, and the attention he'd received the night before was transferred to the customers clamoring for their cups of cappuccino and croissants, smiling and grinning as they left for work with their treasures in their bottomless bags of hope. He slipped into the kitchen, and, seeing the ladies busy, made himself a sad little cheese sandwich and sat munching it when Joan came back for another tray and saw him sitting there on Tess' stool, no less.

"Busy morning, doctor, got to feed the flock. Cash register keeps chim, chimming, and we are flowing. Stick around, though. I want you to meet my grandson." She swept out of the swinging door, and Martin helped himself to more free coffee, and wondered how the other over-nighters were faring. Surely they watched out for their over-nighters.

He wondered about them, got off his stool and peered into the dining room. The couples seated all looked happy as larks, sipping their coffee, and a brave one asked Tess for a little "something extra," and she bravely carried the bottle of Kahlua out to his table and slid in an ounce of the coffee-flavored demon. The man smiled and slipped her two dollars, which she demurely shoved down her shirt.

They're good, Martin chuckled, these ladies are good. He didn't need to see any more of them. Tomorrow they would make it, make it just fine. He waited for Joan to come back, tell him about this grandson she had mentioned. He really wanted to get on out and do some scouting of his own, but his mind said to relax: let the ladies lead. Always a mama's boy, he did just that.

The crowd waned and Joan swung through the door to set her tray down. She went to wipe her hands off, settling the big tray against the sink. Washed her hands and brushed back her wavy brown hair.

"Now here we are, Dr. Schoenfield, just you and me, and believe me, I need you to help me as much as you think one of us might be a good guide. My grandson is with some great people, great people, can't fault them one bit, but the baby's never seen a doctor, never had an exam or a shot, and he's way past that time. Don't they start those shots early? It's not that they don't care. They just need a nudge, you follow? I don't want Bory to get sick. He's so beautiful, Doctor, he's just cream and muffins and all that he should be. But if he had a problem, and I know you'll tell me, I want to know. We want to be there for him, if he has a problem."

"Do you suspect a problem?" Martin asked, moving his coffee cup off the counter and over to the sink. "Why should there be a problem?"

"He was the first of all the mulatto babies that have come since. He was the first, and this town fairly ripped itself inside out over my daughter and the Cheevers boy. It hurt a lot, right then, to admit that Macy had been right, but when the new babies all came in . . . you know, mixed, then I did a turn, I did, saw my own body change, and I cried over that. Not for being darker, God knows that's not what I cried over, but the idea that she started this, my Marilyn, started this miracle that swept this town, and will go everywhere. Leastways," she paused, wiping her eyes, "leastways, I know that he's here and he's perfect and I want him to be whole and I need someone to go look at him, tell me I'm not wrong."

"Can you leave right now?" he asked. "Ask Tess if we can shoot on over, and I'll take a look at him." Her eyes worshiped him for being so ready, so glad, to go with her. She loved this slender doctor, and if she'd been twenty years younger, she would have fought his wife for him, she promised, but she knew the years couldn't come back to her, and knew Martin Schoenfield probably had a beautiful wife and children. They must look like him, if they're lucky. She nodded and hurried out to talk to Tess at the cash register, just adding up the morning's sales and beaming with good will. If Joan Stewart had asked her to go out and dance naked in the street at that moment, she would have, so full of happiness was she over the morning sales. She nodded enthusiastically, went back to counting her money, and Joan came back to him with yes on her face.

"Yes! We're outta here! Let me make a pit stop and you throw some sandwiches together. Turkey in there from last night, some slaw left over, grab that peach cobbler. It'll fit fine in that cooler by the door. Be ready in five." She ran for the stairs, tearing off her apron, and pulling her hair net off on her way up.

Martin wrapped up the meat in foil, and laid some bread out, smearing it with mayo and sliced onions over it. He pressed the pieces together and wrapped the meatless sandwiches in waxed paper, storing them in the cooler with the bowl of slaw and the cobbler perched on top. Drinks they could get on the road, he figured, or drink well water, if it was Cyclone purified, a chance he was willing to take. Got to hand it to Donn. He was in on this change big time. More power to him. He did have the right idea, only the wrong reason.

Joan came down in white slacks and a red tee shirt, wearing a bow in her hair and not looking at all like anybody's grandmother. Martin wondered at her change, decided she might be offended if he said she looked cute, maybe like he was putting the move on her. When would he learn the right words to compliment people? What were the right words?

"You look cute," he blurted, and Joan laughed.

"Cute as a button, that's me." She grabbed the cooler, made a line for the door, and he called back to the silently counting Tess that they were leaving. Tess shouted a hearty, "Have fun!" and they were out the back and into the Taurus.

Martin slid into the driver's seat and Joan stored the cooler on the back seat. They shot out of town, leaving the settled ways behind them. Five minutes later they turned in at the Cheevers' marker, an old pine with a hand-painted sign "Cheevers Place" nailed to it. They drove down the path and up a hill and came down again into the front yard. The log house was freshly varnished with green shutters. Flowers were growing abundantly around it, and Martin saw a neat-looking garden behind it. There was a barn with a bunkhouse slung on the side. The place looked loved and clean. No shack here. He had his test tubes in the trunk, and he knew before he left, he knew he would be able to get several samples of the water.

Gloria Cheevers came out on the porch as they pulled up, and she waved at Joan and came down the steps to hug her.

"You back an' with a beau! Lan' sakes, you movin' fast, girl. Let me see that love ribbon." She turned Joan's head and touched it. "Mighty pretty on you, an' for your man here, I guess." Gloria turned and took in the handsome white man in one glance. Green eyes, he had, sparkling green eyes, and, my, didn't she like the color green and the lips that smiled back at her. Go for it, Joan, make some light for yoself.

"Well, we're not quite promised," she giggled. "But, oh, heck, Gloria, this is Dr. Schoenfield. He's thinking of opening a practice in Pond Ridge, sorta curious, I guess, about our color change, but a doctor, nonetheless. Could he check Bory over, make sure he's fine? Would that be okay with you and Marilyn?"

"Well," Gloria paused, sticking a needle and thread up on her shoulder, "I ain' the boy's mama, but she be right inside. You best ast her."

Gloria led the way, shooing a chicken off the porch with a gentle hand, and opened the screen door to let them pass. Bory was in a punkin seat, staring at a mobile dangling in front of him, trying to get at it with his hands, but he only swung them aimlessly. He was only a few months old. He would get better at it, his determined eyes showed. Joan looked to his mother, her baby, her Marilyn, sitting on the floor by a huge unfinished quilt. Marilyn got up when she saw who it was, held her arms out to her mother, who gratefully held her. Martin stooped down beside the blonde-haired boy, who recognized a face, and turned his head. He got up and watched Marilyn lift him easily, heard Joan's voice telling Marilyn that Martin was a doctor, and could he examine Bory, make sure he was okay. Marilyn stiffened then, held him closer.

"There's nothing wrong with my baby," she started.

"I can see that," Martin laughed. "Just want you to know that I'm here to check him over, see that he's got everything functioning, his hands and feet and heart. Babies need to get their shots, too, and I can get those for him, so he'll never be sick with smallpox or whooping cough. Now you wouldn't want that, would you?"

Marilyn shook her blonde head, held him closer, then changed her mind and laid him down on the floor. "See? He can almost roll over by himself. Whoops!" She caught him as he started to arch his back. "Now that's normal, isn't it?"

"Very, very normal. Let's get a feel of him." Marilyn stripped off his tee shirt and little diaper, and Martin rolled the baby over and checked his spine and reflexes. The baby squirmed on the rug, took to bellowing over this attention, but while he was crying, Martin looked in his throat, felt his skull, and neck, unclenched the fists and straightened the thumb. He picked him up then, held his head against the baby's chest, and listened to the heart and lungs. All seemed healthy, but the baby chose that moment, suspended over Martin's uplifted face, to let out a warm stream of urine that got Martin right on the shirt before he hastily turned him away.

"The other way!" Gloria yelled. Martin turned the baby toward Marilyn and away from the quilt. Marilyn caught it full in the face as she advanced with an outstretched diaper. Gloria moved to check the quilt they were working on, and Joan was doubled over laughing when Marilyn tugged her wetted hair and laughed, too.

"Doc, you're gonna have to improve your quilt-side manner, or you'll never make it."

"Marilyn, you might just be my nurse one day, so practice that move. We might be needing it." They washed up and redressed Bory, letting him watch them from his punkin seat, his feet kicking and his eyes once again fixed on the mobile hung on the handle.

Gloria made fresh tea, and they had a cup with her. Martin told Gloria he needed to see the folks on the Settlement, too, introduce himself, let them know there'd be a new doctor in town. Gloria set her cup down and looked at Joan.

"You tell him I can get him on Settlement? Ain' no way I know those folks close enough to ride on in with a white doctor in tow. You need Beech. He be the only one they let come sailin' in with a stranger. An' Beech ain' home till three, so you got lots of time to stay. Want to help in the garden, Doctor, or feed chickens? Gather some eggs? Marilyn ain' been down yet today, an' we got some brown layers that have mostly double yolks. Joan, you need to get out of those whites an' get some real pants on."

It was close to one before they finished up Gloria's weeding and egg gathering, admired the neat bunkhouse and rubbed Clara's nose. Joan was happy in the belted trousers from Beech, and happier still when Marilyn let her carry Bory out to the field to look the sky. Martin stayed behind and laid out the sandwiches, slicing the turkey between the onion and the mayo, and cutting the neat sandwiches in quarters, to share all around. Gloria added lettuce from her garden, and Marilyn stopped her quilting to run to the spring house for a stored bottle of milk. Joan brought back three huge fat red tomatoes from the garden, but Gloria had some cold and sliced already, so these three got set in the fridge for supper. They ate together on the porch, off tin plates, while Bory took his nap, going down like a sailor in a sinking ship. Squawked and wailed for more attention, but Marilyn told him, "Quiet time, Bory," and he fell asleep like the angel he was.

"You washed up in the kitchen, Doctor, but we got a bafroom here, if'n you need to use it." She said this with a certain pride in her voice, said it to make it point clear that this was no backward family he was dealing with. They knew how to live.

"Ma'am, begging your pardon, but I took care of that little detail all by myself, out behind the barn." Gloria laughed at that, slapped her arms with glee. She liked this man. Liked everything about him. Joan's brought a good man here. Hope he stays, she dreamed. Hope he stays to bring us all better health and longer lives. With John coming home in less than a month, no more of this weekend, rushing in, rushing out, after they'd just hugged hello. If John was home and the doctor was in town, well, they'd be getting up in the world.

The time passed easily on the porch, sipping lemonade and trading stories. Martin had the freshest ones, stories they'd never heard about hospitals, and submarines, and Navy life. Joan told a few, about some of the parishioners she'd met, funny stories of twisted faith and hopes that would never be realized. How she had made them believe in those dreams, she didn't remember. But she knew she had helped when Macy was busy elsewhere, wherever Macy would go.

It was well onto three when Marilyn heard Bory waken, and she slipped in to nurse him in the bedroom. Joan went for more ice cubes, letting the screen door bump her dungarees in closing so as not to slam. Martin and Gloria sat side by side on the top step, enjoying the gentle wind and fragrance of the flowers, when Gloria spotted Beech's pickup churning down the lane. A wicked little smile crossed her lips, and she moved closer to Martin, and whispered in his ear. He looked startled, drew back and stared at her, but she grinned and nodded, so he nodded, too. He would do it, just because she thought it was funny.

She snuggled closer to Martin, laid her curly head on his shoulder, and painted on a face of rapture. Martin, playing his role as she had asked behind her giggle, watched the truck pause, then shift gears, and roll quietly to a dead stop in front of the porch. Beech took off his hat, and opened the truck door, settling his boots in the grass. The two on the porch seemed unaware of his arrival so lost were they in their mock closeness.

Beech put his big foot squarely on the bottom step, and when they didn't move, he brought it down louder. Gloria turned to him with a faked look of surprise, and she rose and said, "Oh, my, you home so soon? Where the afternoon fly? We was just speakin' of you, dear husban', the words just fell from my lips that my precious one be home soon." She kissed his cheek, and eyes turned to steel stared at Martin.

"Who be you?" he asked, setting Gloria aside and going up one more step. "Who be you, that you come aroun' my place and'sit by my woman? You think you got the right to do that? Turn a pretty woman's head? You be gone, son. Gone!" Martin rose to his feet, pressed his hand against his heart, and the words didn't exactly come from Gloria, her part was over, but he felt an actor in him, and he wanted to see how it played.

"I, sir, am the one come to take Ms. Glory away from this all. I come to take her onto Sain Louie, make her my bride. I see great things for us, and I do so dearly love her, that you know she'll up and run with me." Beech looked confused, turned to Gloria smothering her laugh behind her hand, and he turned back to Martin. Martin couldn't hold it any longer, let his hand fall from his chest, and leaned against the railing as he laughed.

"Beech, Beech, we just pullin' you! Damn fool, I luv ya, an' nobody's goin' to sweep me off." She wiped her eyes and put her arms around Beech. Joan came back on the porch with the bowl of ice, saw the three standing laughing, leastways two of them, but Beech joined in as soon as he saw the joke was on him.

"Had me goin' there, son, had me goin'. You almos' got to the head-choppin' block, you know? One more minute an' Glory would have bin fryin' you up for my dinner." He laughed and nuzzled Gloria, who shook him off, and went back up to the porch swing.

"Sit here a minute, Beech. This the new doctor in town, Miz Joan's friend, an' they want to get out to the Settlement today. How 'bout jumpin' in my nice clean shower an' changin' into somethin' clean? Run 'em out. By the time you back, I'll have supper on, an' we can snuggle later." She winked at this promise, and Beech fairly fled to the bathroom.

"Tha man know a good thin' when he got it. An' he sure got it!" She winked and sailed that old porch swing back against the house. A good thump, then she laughed and settled back to float.

Beech, restored by the shower and fresh jeans and tee shirt, waved Joan and Martin toward the dusty truck, even started to clear paperbags and workclothes off the passenger seat. "The Taurus is a rental. Come on," urged Martin and Beech slipped into the driver's seat, as he knew the way, and drove Joan and Martin away from the waving arms of Marilyn and Gloria. He liked this young man, liked the cut of him, liked the joke, too, but he vowed he would catch that tricky Glory before midnight, and make her keep her promise.

They took the rented Taurus over the back way, brushing the underside over some ruts it wasn't built for, but cut a mile off the trip if they'd gone the long way round. Joan held onto the seat with both hands as they hurled along. Too fast for this trail, she said to herself, but Beech was driving, and no way was she going to speak up like a pastor's wife. No more preaching, she vowed, clinging to the upholstery.

"You need to see the head man, Theopolis Franklin, he be the one who has the say over here. Nobody from Settlement gonna come to you, less he say you be the man. That's how these folks is, mighty touchy. An' they all Black, Doctor, the shade never reached 'em. Why they not got lighter, only God knows, but get ready for some real Africans here." He chuckled and drove slower as he crossed over the fields and came into Settlement land.

"See, back here, they got no fences. No need to. They know I be a friend, they know I bring their strays back if'n they cross. I even bring back some of their kids if I see 'em scooting out the back way. He rules tight, that man. No man watches like he do." Beech met a pair of tracks and led the Taurus into the rutted path. "They all still be in the field, early as it is. These folks work, doc, work like you wouldn' believe a body could. They sweat an' groan under their load, but ain' these pretty fields? Doan they have a view of that river?" He stopped on the crest of the hill, and Martin saw the river shimmering between the trees. Joan tenuously let go and peered, too, before Beech shifted to first and started moving ahead, too fast for her.

They passed several men bent to the soil, who only glanced at them, and then raised to their full height. How the word got down that quick to the main man no one knows, but when they rounded a curve, a man stood in front of them, not a hundred yards from the car, and Beech braked quickly to avoid hitting him. The car rested against his outstretched arm, and the hand stayed on the hood one long minute while the face above the arm surveyed the driver. The stony face melted at that moment, and one Theopolis Franklin came around to lean on the jam as Beech rolled down the window.

"Out puddle jumpin', Beech, or you drinkin'?" The eyes in the deeply-lined black face showed a knowledge of life and people that made Luther's face come to Martin's mind. This man could be Luther's daddy, he realized, watching the face next to Beech's.

"We be out scoutin' for a place to build a new hospital, for the new doctor in town. This is Dr ... I doan even know your name." He turned to Martin, who held his arm across Beech's chest, and met the hardy grasp of the old leader.

"Schoenfield, sir, Martin Schoenfield, and glad to meet you." The man held his hand a moment, then stood back.

"A doctor, huh? 'Ospeetal, you say? They be needin' some lookin' at in town, that be where you need to start, doc. Not up here. We doan need no doctor, we all fit and fine. What we need is 'bout two more nice days of harvest time, then let the rains come. Thas what we need," he said, gazing out over the land.

"Stop down now, Theopolis. Time's a changin', an' this man can do things to hep all a us. Keep an open mind, now, let the sun shine on your behind."

Now, not too many people spoke to Theopolis about his behind, but he liked Beech Cheevers, thought he made a good back entry guard for the Settlement. Liked the man who worked and took care of his own, even some that wasn't his own, if that white girl be still there. Only not white no more. No, all dipped in cocoa. All them next door and down the hill. All losing their color, or picking up some. A shame. Turn your back on God and you lose it. Stone must be albino by now.

"Where the sun doan shine ain' your business, Beech, but I see you got a lady wit ya. You better shunt on down to the house, or my woman gonna be fit an' tied for bein' stuck wit a slug."

"Get on in," urged Beech, and Martin moved to open the door and give the man his seat.

"No way. I bin up since seven, got shit on my feet, an' field on my body. I walk. You ride on. Tell Aunty we got company, which she for sure gonna see when she sights on ya." He set off then, striking his gait toward the lowlands, and Beech turned the Taurus up and over the center rim, and settled it back down for a few yards before he jauntily left the trail and followed Theopolis through the field. The man waved them on, and they sped past him and down the field until they came across a path that led in front of a huge white Victorian home, pristine and elegant in its two stories, with a widow walk on the top and gabled porches sweeping the front and sides.

"My gosh, I've never seen such a neat house. It's perfect! Is that their house?" breathed Joan, staring out the back window at the Corothers place.

"Naw, that's old Stone's house, or the old Corothers house,

whichever. Old Stone was Theopolis's nephew, and he inherited this place, but sold out to Uncle Theo when he felt his feet itchin' for bigger thin's. Wanted to play the games, dint take ta being black and grounded. He be one jet setter, thas what Glory tells me, he be gone from Pond Ridge."

Martin's eyes took in the sweetness of the place, the lawns neatly trimmed, the porch freshly painted, the windows sending off reflections of their cleanness. "They keep this as a shrine, or does someone live there?" he asked Beech.

"No one lives there, but they use it for meetin's, an' the kids use the book part of it, an' they youssta like to come up for ice cubes, but all the Settlement got 'lectric now, all them shacks got 'fridgerators." Beech followed the lane between the fruit trees, the fragrance filling the car: peach, apple, and plum. Martin rolled the window down and the smell filled the car. Joan let the smell fill her senses, let it all slide as she breathed in the fragrance. Even getting used to the bumpy ride, the too fast ride, by her measure.

"Why ever leave this place?" she said, putting their thoughts into words. But the shacks, she leaned forward. Why in shacks?

The "shacks" she soon saw as they curved around the last breast of fruit trees, were not shacks at all, but lovely white bungalows, nestled in a circle around a pond that shimmered in the late glow of the sun. She saw two boats out on the acre of water, saw the neatly trimmed yards and garden patches, all fenced and painted, saw the porches on each home festooned with hanging vines and flowers. Some shacks, she murmured, envying these people the rich earth they plowed and owned, envied their yards and swept paths. They had a beautiful home, she sighed, and Martin, in the front seat, heard that sigh, and joined his with hers.

"This is heaven or God doesn't know about it, one or the other." They stopped in front of the first house, and no one came out to greet them. Beech honked the horn and no one appeared.

"Seems Miz Franklin ain' about, or ain' wantin' no visitors. What say we just drive aroun' the pond, say hello till Theopolis catch up?" That's what they did, driving the slow path, slow for once, noticed Joan, until they saw a child running toward them. Beech braked the car and waited for the child to come running up to the window.

"It's Crissy," she cried, catching her breath from the running. "Danny's wife has a baby comin', and Miz Tubbs ain't here, and all the folks down at Milbornes."

"A baby, you say? Crissy Milborne's baby? Coming now? No

wonder Miz Franklin ain' to home." Beech watched the child's pointing finger, and he spotted old Theopolis' wife, Aunty, as they all knew her, waving on the next porch down. He brought the car down by the porch and shut it off. "Deaf, she is. That Crissy be the deaf girl."

Aunty scurried down to the car, fairly dragged Beech out of the Taurus. "Lan', I thought we never see no help. Thank you, Beech, fer comin'. If'n anyone can hep her is you. Come on in, get washed and take a han' here." She bustled Beech up on the porch and he held back, saying, "No, ma'am, I jes' lucky that time, but my luck with birthin' shot isself that night."

She stared into his face, her bird-like look almost resettling his plans to dive under the porch, but Joan stepped in. "Is there a problem? Is the woman all right?"

"How all right you think she be, two days in labor, an' her water broke, an' no baby an' shitload of pain? How you think she be?" Aunty Franklin didn't know Joan Stewart from Queen Lizbeth across the Ocean. Didn't know why this white woman in man's pants dared stick her nose in.

"Maybe we can help, get her to the hospital. We have a car and we're here and able to help." The woman seemed sincere to Aunty, but Aunty was not up for moving anybody off the Settlement into the hands of those white folks or mulatto folks, such as they was, lessen Theopolis said it was right. And she saw his head coming up over the crest of the hill, coming down between the fruit trees crying with their juices.

"No one leaves here less my husban' say it to be. He comin'. We wait for him to say." She stood and watched for the slow tread of Theopolis to catch up to them.

Martin had stayed by the car, hadn't touched the front step, when Joan turned to him.

"Martin, they need a doctor, I think. Would you?"

# Chapter Forty

*Waving hair and ruby lips,*
*Sparks flying from her finger tips*
*. . . See how high she flies*
*. . . She got the moon in her eyes*

*The Eagles "Witchy Woman"*

Aunty Franklin, watching the slowly approaching Theopolis, turned her gaze then on Martin. "A doctor you brung? Whyn't you say you gotta doctor? Get up here, young man. Get up here!"

His moccasined feet skipped up the stairs, and he was grabbed by Aunty Franklin. The others were shoved back, and in her strong grasp he was propelled into the front room.

"Whyn't you speak up, boy, when I was jabberin'? Whyn't you say you be a doctor?"

"I didn't think you wanted me to intrude, Mrs. Franklin. This is your home, your place of living. I can't just jump in and insist you do things my way." He looked steadily into the wise eyes, saw them change in their hardness, saw the tears start at the corners, and felt her arms encircle him.

"We done our best, Mister Doctor, we done our best, but Tillie an' I, we ain up to this. We doan know what to do." She pressed her forehead against his chest as she spoke.

"Then let me look at Crissy, and maybe we can decide what's best. How's that? Let's just take a look and see." He set her back and tried to resume a natural physician stance.

What he saw made him blanch. A room, small and tidy, settled with a bed and a dresser, all right out of a catalogue: maple spindles and Wal-mart spread. The young woman, lying black and shiny in sweat, eyeing him from the bed, with an older woman, rag in her hand, touching her brow. Ever hear of a hospital and prenatal care? Where have you been?

"You got a bathroom?" he asked Aunty, and she pulled him back and into a doorway. The bathroom was neat and tidy, except for the pile of wet towels spilled in the tub behind the pink shower curtain. The room was female, he noticed, no sign of a man, what with the tweezers and the curlers and the mascara on the sink. His eyes rested on a plastic holder: wave clamps, they called them. To get a Marseilles look. Close-crimped waves, like the tootsies in the twenties. He picked one up and squeezed it, the pressure causing the teeth to open, the release letting the teeth clamp down. Women, he mused, what they do to be beautiful. He washed his hands quickly and brushed the water over his face. What next? Oh, yes, he smiled. A medical opinion. That's me. Doctor Martin Schoenfield. Late of the Navy. Currently with the Pearson firm, finding the cure for AIDS, he is. That Martin Schoenfield.

He approached Crissy with Aunty hard on his heels. Watched her eyes grow round with fear, let himself sit by the bed.

"Beech tells me she can't hear, so let her know who I am, however you do that." Tillie brought up a tablet and scribbled "docter" on it, and Crissy's eyes grew soft and glazy. She nodded, yes, yes, her eyes said, let him help.

Martin touched her then and felt her swollen distended abdomen, smiled at her, and said with his eyes, I won't hurt you, and felt below her vaginal lips for the head he expected to find. But he found nothing with his fingers. Nothing. This was further up, he estimated, he needed to go in further.

His pullover clung to his sides and the sweet scent of Bory's urine still clung to his jersey. He needed to get into this, he realized, knew he had a job to do, but somehow it had fallen on him so quickly, so finally, that he regretted being here at all. They had lived without him before he drove in today in that stupid car. They would live, all live without him if he just turned and said, "Sorry. Can't help."

He turned to Aunty behind him, and Aunty's hand reached out to him, and he wished, he wished at that moment he didn't touch it, but he did touch it, and the heat that came from her fingers, the fire that ran up his arm and into his chest, scorched him so badly that he went ablaze.

"Get Joan and Beech in here!" he commanded, the fire filling his lungs and belching out heat he wanted to stay with him always, or get away from medicine forever. Aunty ran off on her old legs, and Joan and Beech came in from the crowded porch, for it had become crowded. All the folks on Settlement came down to sit and wait for the baby to come, and the blankets were spread and ice tea was being handed round. A good old welcoming in for Danny and Crissy Milborne's first baby.

He pulled the two of them aside in the living room, said they needed to stay on with him if he started this, made them swear they would stay by him, and they both swore they would stay by him, not knowing at all what they were swearing to.

"I think she's breech, that's my thinking right now. That baby's bent against her will to push him out. I bet she's spent every ounce getting him down, and babies don't come out sideways. Now that's just what I think." He watched their faces and Joan nodded, yes, yes, but you can do it, you're a doctor. That's what doctors do. Beech paused a little longer, hung his head, and said he knew about breech.

"Sometimes those lambs just get turned 'round, not knowin' which way be out, an' a man's got to hep 'em sometimes, turn those babies, so they fine the right path. I turn a calf for Clara, an' that baby was a poorly sight, but she make it an' with one leg broke, she make it. Crissy goin' to make it, too. I be born breech, my mama say. The old midwife felt me up there an' she cried out, 'It be breech!' an' my mama, who wasn't too smart but wise, I think, she thought she heard 'Beech' an' she closed her mind on any other name. Beech I was an' I be."

He watched while Martin paced and then, to Beech's surprise, Martin put his arms around the two of them and held them in an embrace. Now, Beech wasn't much on this man huggin' thing, but he held Joan and Martin and felt a heat from the man's body he drew back from.

"Let's go, doc. Let's just go." Enough shilly-shally. He got Glory waitin' and just up to midnight. Go, doc, go.

Go he went. He went back to Crissy and asked Tillie to slide her around cross ways on the bed. He called to Joan and Beech to bring in footstools or hassocks for Crissy's feet and they rolled them in by the bed. He placed each of her feet on the stools, and centered her bottom right on the edge of the mattress.

"Support her back," he commanded and pillows were shoved under her and Crissy was raised up. "Tillie, stay by her. We're ready to get our baby!"

Crissy moaned in her labor and let herself sink into a place where no one ever touched her, no one would come near her again. Martin surveyed the battle zone, found himself without tools or allies, found himself at the mercy of what God had unceremoniously dumped on him, and he hated it. Hated it that this woman went through nine months of pregnancy with no help, no vitamins, no check up, no measurements, no weight control, though she was thin, Martin realized, bone thin with this big stomach. A plus if this came to that. What that? What in hell could he do if it came to that?

Have to go in further and see. To go in vaginally and not know for sure. Martin left the room, leaving Joan and Beech to tend to the plumping of pillows and the ice chips, ran into the bathroom and pulled open the cabinet behind the door. Alcohol. They had ethyl alcohol. Hydrogen peroxide. They had a bottle. He held it to his face. Great God. They had something to help him. And bleach. A gallon of bleach and he needed it.

He stripped off his blue pullover, threw it into the tub, and glanced at that shower curtain. Why he saw it differently now, he didn't know, but the shower curtain drew him in, wanted to wrap around him. He scrubbed his hands, called for Joan to come in and pour the peroxide over his elbows and wrists and fingers. She did it, watching him scrub with a nail brush, watching him rinse and hold his hands high as if he were in an operating theater for hundreds of med students.

She watched him walk through the living room in a white vee-necked tee shirt and jeans, his hands up in the air, and she ran ahead and opened the screen door. He went down the steps, holding his hands and arms up to the dying warming rays of the evening sun. The folks from Settlement, waiting for news of the baby, only stood up and watched him with his raised arms, and they powerfully feared at that moment. They wished they hadn't come to see Jesus. A white Jesus, they always knew he might be white, raised his arms with the sun behind him, and some said he asked them to go home and feed their families; others swore he never said a word, only turned and went back to that white lady by the screen door. But some said Aunty wanted to kiss his feet. And that was no lie.

In the kitchen was a blistering kettle of boiled water; the steam kept hissing off the open kettle of boiling, rolling water. Martin stood over the steam, let its vapors fill him and heat him, and he turned back to the bedroom and began his journey into frontier medicine. He crouched before the spread legs, let his hands touch her thighs, be used to his touch before he ventured to slide his hand into her vagina, and keeping his slender hand flat, he managed, only barely managed, to reach up far, far into her, and touch the child. For it was a child he felt, the ridge of the spine meeting his fingertips, the spine. The damn spine is there, laying all spread out and cross ways. A large spine, not a little baby.

He brought his hand out, went to wash, and poured peroxide over it. He looked in the mirror and his dreams of sitting in front of a microscope vaporized before his eyes. This is not me, he felt, heat or no heat, this is not me. Dwayne's face flowed before him, a face he had not seen in years of looking for it, a face he only glimpsed as it slid by the mirror and was gone. Claire came in front of him, holding a wreath, and he wiped his eyes from the tears that flowed. Oh, God, why now? Why do they expect me to run a miracle? I can't run a miracle. I shouldn't even be here. Damn Pearson and AIDS. Fuck this! He turned and looked at the pink shower curtain, and in his anger and rage he jerked it down, tore it off its curly plastic hangers, swirled it under his feet and stomped on it. Some doctor. Can't even get a baby here. Some doctor. He looked at himself in the mirror, and the face wasn't his anymore. It was Luther's.

"What's your problem, boy?"

"My problem? My problem is this lady needs a hospital and surgery. Her problem, not mine, Luther. Don't be mixing up her problem with mine. I don't have any problems. Never had any problems. This lady's got a problem. It's not my problem."

"Then get your white ass outta there. Get in that rented Taurus and have that Beech drive your ass outta there."

"You know Beech?" Martin said to the mirror. But Luther was gone. Martin looked in every corner of that mirror, but Luther was gone.

Everyone I cared about is gone, he murmured, everyone. Amelia's gone, Micah's gone, Dwayne's gone. What the shit am I doing here, fumbling through this life? No life. The Navy. The school, the books. My scope. All gone. The shade isn't what I'd hoped. Look at these people. Back in the thirties, these people, thinking they got it all made.

"You got nothing!" he screamed at the mirror. "Fucking nothing!"

"Martin?" The soft voice behind the door had to be Joan's, the sworn-in member of the team. "Martin?" she asked again. And he remembered Amy saying his name, just like that, urging him to come out and be part of the family again after he'd failed at some task, let his parents down. Ah, Amy, how he wished he could just roll onto a blanket and hold his sister, let her carry him for a while, hold her and cry by her side. Amy, now Mrs. Ned Baker. He hadn't sent a gift. He needed to send a gift.

"Be there, be there," he called out. He opened the door, and all the faces he needed were in front of him: Amelia, Micah, Claire, Luther, and Dwayne, even Amy tugging on his hand and pulling him out. They were there for him. "You two, Joan, Beech. Scrub those hands!"

They all were there when he went back to Crissy, there with him when he settled his ear against her swollen side. They listened with him for the faint heartbeat that he judged wasn't the mother's, knew by the sound that the baby was slowing, had to be slowing.

His legs went out to the porch, and the worried-looking man sitting on the swing had to be Daniel Milborne. He raised his eyes to Martin and asked, "Is it a boy or a girl? I don't care, tell Crissy, I don't care, jus' tha she be whole and fine, and Crissy be back to me."

"Well," Martin began, "we don't know as yet, but it seems we might need some help later on. Think you can drive the old Taurus to town and get the State troopers to give us a header, lead us over to the hospital in Farmington, lead us the fastest way?"

Daniel leaped to his feet, said he'd be back in a minute, but Martin knew the ways of the police. May not listen to this black son of a bitch. That be the way.

"You wait one minute." He went back to the bedroom, took the tablet next to the sentinel, Tillie, and scribbled out that Dr. Martin Schoenfield needed an escort from the railroad tracks at Pond Ridge to the Farmington Hospital, and that better happen. He tore off the sheet and gave it to Daniel, handed over his driver's license for good measure.

"Wait one minute, Daniel, this is important, almost as important as the trooper." Martin skipped down the steps, weaved through the blankets of the patiently waiting neighbors, headed for the rented Taurus, and popped open the trunk. He rummaged for the test tubes he had brought for the water samples, located one, and ran back up to the house. "Be one minute, you wait."

He got a cotton ball from the bathroom, picked up a pin, grabbed the alcohol and opened it as he headed back into the bedroom. He asked Crissy for her hand, and very swiftly he pricked her finger and let the drops slide into the tube. He squeezed her finger, got a little more, then stuck in the stopper and laid her hand on her chest.

"Joan, swab that finger again. Pinch it. She won't need a Band-Aid." No. God dammit, she won't need one Band-Aid. She'll need a ton of Band-Aids before I'm through here.

Martin ran back to the waiting Daniel, handed him the tube. "Now don't break this, Daniel, this is the sample that the hospital needs. When we get there, she's gonna need blood to bring her back up; they'll need to know what type, you know, what brand she needs. You understand?"

"Like A, B, or O?" answered Daniel.

"Exactly! Like A, B, or O. Or negative, but we'll discuss that possibility later. What are you?"

"I'm A", he answered, the keys in one hand and the test tube nestled in his shirt pocket.

"Good, good. Now two things again and I'm counting on you. Send the cop back to us, then you get on to the hospital as fast as you can. Give 'em the blood, and tell him we're bringing in a home-grown C-section. Home grown. Tell them that, nothing more. Okay?"

"Okay," he breathed out, and ran for the car, turned the key in the ignition and shot out of the lane.

Hope we get a good cop, Martin mused. The course was set.

"Folks, if you don't mind, we'll be asking you all to leave. That baby won't be here until tomorrow, but Mrs. Franklin will come tell you about it. Much obliged for you being here. I speak for the family. Go on home now and have your suppers." They obeyed, of course, long used to obeying the white man, picked up their blankets and jars of tea and shambled off, saying good luck and God bless you and not wanting to leave at all. But the white man had spoken, and the echoes coming down through the years didn't take the force out of it. He watched them go, and put one foot at a time in front of him, slowly, as he went back up the porch steps.

He alone knew the risks, the loss of blood, the possible chance he'd lose them both, but he didn't stop. He ran to the bathroom and got those wave crimpers, and he found a straight edge razor and a scissors, and he dumped them all in the boiling kettle in the kitchen, tossing in a bone-handled skinning knife from the drawer. He poured bleach over a towel, digging his nails into the wetness, praying it would get his hands and nails clean enough.

"Fork 'em out, Aunty, fork 'em out and lay 'em clean and straight, on a cookie sheet lined with foil. Wipe it down with alcohol if you can. Cotton balls and alkie in the bathroom."

He checked on Crissy, saw her contractions had continued unabated, as if they were doing some good. His ear against Crissy's stomach picked up her heartbeat, and he checked the seconds ticking off, ticking off a full minute. One hundred. Up a bit, but within normal range. He moved his ear down further and tried to catch the baby's usually faster one. But this baby's heart was going slow, slow as his mama, and Martin knew the full meaning of that slower beat.

"The cookie sheet!" he shouted, and Aunty obliged him, setting the sheet on the floor by his side. "Now," he said. Time it fast.

Beech touched his shoulder. "What you doin'?"

"I'm going in, Beech." He laid the bleach soaked towel over Crissy's stomach, and nodded at Tillie, who moved the damp cloth in slow circles.

"How you doin' that?"

"Fast."

And fast he was going to be, timing his moves so quickly that even if she bled more than he figured they could handle, they still had time to get her to the hospital. For without that hospital, she wouldn't have a chance. The baby, yes, but not Crissy Milborne.

One. Two. Three. Who's behind the zebra tree? Is God laughing or Dwayne crossing his fingers? He stood in the space between Crissy's legs, and did a quick verbal assessment.

"This baby's going to die if we don't go in now. That's for certain. And the mama may die, but I think she'll make it, if we all pull together. Listen up, Joan, Beech, I need you. When you cut, you bleed. That's what you got to watch for: the bleeders. When you see a bleeder, clamp down on it. We got seventeen major bleeders here in the stomach. Use your clamps to cover two if you can, otherwise go for the one that's pumping the hardest. They won't be hard to miss. They'll look like cooked macaroni with blood jumping out."

Martin didn't know when the right moment to start hit him, but the timepiece in Luther's house resounded in his mind, and he made his first slice with the razor at about six chimes. Crissy didn't move, didn't utter a sound, and he was across her lower body with that razor, slitting through that finely stretched bronze, and he stopped.

"Clamps, people, clamps time." Beech slipped his hand in on the right and Joan, faltering at first at the sight of blood, Holy Jesus! So much blood. Martin stopped to help them get oriented, stayed their hands, fed a new clamp to Joan.

"Scrub nurse, Joan. Watch for the bleeders. You'll be fine." His voice sounded sure of himself, and his voice filled the room. Tillie stared at him, kept wiping Crissy's head until she pushed her away. Crissy was over with the wiping and the ice chips. She wanted this over, and her eyes urged him to get going. She was fine, just fine. No pain at all.

Joan checked her nausea level, swallowed, and nodded. "I'm here, Martin. Know that I'm here." He glanced at her in the red tee shirt and Beech's trousers held up by a belt. Her being here meant a lot. And Beech. If they hadn't been here, he doubted he would have been, and certainly not to try this. Aunty took that moment to leave the room, let her hand guide her way as she touched the wall, and slipped in beside Theopolis sitting in the quiet living room.

"How it be?" he asked, touching her hand.

"It be over soon," she said, not wanting to tell him at all about the razor and the blood.

The pulsating body, sliced open before Martin, had several other layers to attack, and he talked as he sniped with the scissors. "See? All encased, all neatly hidden, behind the fasciae and the uterus. Watch that one, Beech. Get that one. Good. Got that one. How're we doing on clamps?" No one spoke. No one could count.

He checked his watch: one minute gone. Fast. Down to the uterus and good time. He slit the vascular sac with the blade, shifted to the scissors and zigzagged across its muscular ridged surface with a speed Amelia would have envied. Fast I am, damn fast, and hopefully fast enough. No more cutting. Time for tug and pull; less blood that way. Knives cut vessels: tugging moves them.

"Help me here, people, help me hold the uterus open. Don't have any more clamps, damn, why don't we have more women who want waves?" He was giddy at that moment, his hands washed in blood, his watch no more than a smeared memory. No gloves, no light to see decent by, but he felt the baby in his hands, and his hands felt the cord around the neck, the cord that would have tightened if they'd tried to turn him. He handed Joan the scissors and twisted the baby out half way. The umbilical cord had to be clamped.

"Joan, would you donate your hair bow?"

"My bow? You want my bow?" she stared at him, thinking he had completely lost it.

"I need that barrette part attached to it."

"It's all together," she mumbled, pulling it out of her hair. He snapped the barrette onto the cord about six inches from the baby's stomach, red ribbon and all.

"Scissors again."

Joan slapped the bloody shears back in his hand. He slipped his finger under the cord, cutting it free, and wrenched the big limp baby free. He watched the uterus now, watched it screaming blood out of every vessel. Too much blood. And two more clamps, he noticed.

"Beech, do your thing! Get this boy going! I got all I can do to sop up this mess." He had to be sure, before he made his final cut, had to be sure that this baby would live. For if it didn't, the uterus had to be saved, at all cost. But if the baby was alive, was breathing and alive, well, one live child is better than a dead one, and a mother soon to be. The whole cavity was brimming now, too full.

"Towels!" Tillie pulled a clean stack up on the bed, and Martin pressed them into the cavity. They were filled all too fast, and he pressed in a fresh one, felt several bigger vessels and held them in his fingers. Joan had attached the last two clamps, and stayed on in there, holding two cut vessels in her pinched bloody fingers. Martin's eyes were closed, but his hands were massaging the uterus. Why now she could only wonder, but the blood flow seemed to slow. It was that uterus doing most of the bleeding, she realized. She gazed into Martin's face, so close to hers, but he wasn't watching her; he was watching Beech with the baby.

Beech grabbed the baby, and held him in wonder. Held him one second before he had the sheet in his hand, swabbing out the little mouth. He held him against his shirt, slapped his back, and when he didn't respond like Bory had, he got mad, definitely got mad. He wiped harder in that mouth, and he blew into that tiny nose and he wiped up the snot and blew again. A shudder went through the baby's body, and Beech said, "Doan you dare shudder when I want a cry!"

He pushed that baby, way over his shoulder, and cried out, "You be my cross to carry if'n you go!"

The baby jerked and Beech wiped out the mouth again, blew in the nose again, and the cry was heard over the Settlement.

Martin knew this was a mess, a mess of slit tissue and hastily clamped blood lines. The light was so poor; he hadn't even thought to ask for a flash light, but he did now. He surveyed the wreckage. Blood was everywhere: on the walls, the bed, the floor; great clots were slowly dripping from the torn uterus. Crissy seemed above all this. She stirred and held her arms up for the crying baby, as if this was how it was supposed to be.

"Keep the baby, Beech," Martin said firmly. Beech did, rocking it against his chest, allowing Joan to settle a towel over it. "Hold her shoulders down, Tillie. Crissy, lie still," he spoke, holding the light against his lips. She nodded and laid back into Tillie's arms. "Tight, Tillie, very tight." Tillie pressed her weight down, and the pinned Crissy only moaned softly and let herself be held. Joan let her hands slip from the vessels she'd been pinching shut, and held onto Crissy's leg for comfort and support. She was ready to collapse.

He checked each clamp, moving several to better use. Watched the flow and saw it out of control. One last answer, and he knew he had to do it. His fingers found the connecting tissue and main vessels supporting the uterine blood and oxygen. His only usable tool, the slender skinning knife, was brought under the organ, and he severed the tissues and vessels. The uterus was large, and he pulled the organ out and dropped it to the floor. He held the pumping cut ends still attached to her body, pressed a fresh towel in, so he could clear his way, and started moving clamps. The towel was replaced and the arena of the battle looked drier, with no further bleeding of any great amount. Stabilized. Held off for now. If only they had more clamps, more ladies who wanted their hair in crimped waves, he might have saved it. But the saving of it, so badly torn and probably never to heal enough to hold another child, might mean a loss of blood from that engorged pumping station that would end her life.

"Joan, get me those clamps from the uterus." She stooped in response that she ever after would wonder at, and picked over the bloody mass, pulling out seven clamps, handed them to him. He used two of the clamps on the severed ends. Fast. Nothing leaking so far. The only answer, the path he'd chosen for her. He pulled the fasciae together, used two, and pinched the surface skin together, left, right and center, with the three remaining.

"We're going, folks." He straightened up, his front covered with blood. They wrapped Crissy in a quilt and the baby in a blanket. Daniel was back by the door in the rented Taurus. He nodded at Martin.

"Wouldn't pay me no mind till I give him your note and driver's license. Bastard of a fool. We goin', right? We goin?"

"The tube, Daniel, what did you do with the tube?" Martin felt fear run over him.

"He took it, took the tube. Said he'd get it over to the hospital. He called another car, said they could lead us in. They got more'n one, doc." He seemed proud to say that. Like he had it all figured to get back here with Crissy.

"We're going, Daniel, but Beech is driving. I'll be with your missus and we'll see you tomorrow." He ran down the steps to open the door for Beech, carrying Crissy, and Joan came behind, carrying the now quiet baby, snug and secure in her arms.

"What it be, a boy or a girl?" Daniel called out to them.

"Damned if I know," shouted Martin, sliding in and nudging Beech to step on it. His hair-brained clamps were no substitute for real medicine, and he damn well knew it.

# Chapter Forty-One

*It's nature's way of telling you, something's wrong.*
*It's nature's way of telling you in a song*
*It's nature's way of receiving you*
*It's nature's way of retrieving you*
*It's nature's way of telling you, something's wrong*

*Spirit "Nature's Way"*


The trooper, setting the tube on the seat, had watched the Black boy back the car in a swift U-turn and race out of town. Should give him a ticket, speeding like that, but he relaxed in the seat, and started the engine. Run it over. What's it going to hurt? Nothing much going on, anyway. Zip on over and earn my good merit badge. Black blood, he pondered. Black blood in that tube. Looks like plain old blood to me, but that can't be right. Gotta be different: thicker or darker or something. C-section, the boy had said. Home-grown C-section. What the hell those niggers up to?

He pulled out the yellow-lined paper, and read the scrawled note from this Schoenfield. Sounds like a Jew. God, what's this country coming to? The driver's license he flashed his pen light on showed a dark-haired green-eyed white man, tan, but no darkie. White as Jesus. But not his Jesus, and there he drew the line. Can't accept Jesus as the son of God, you better find a boat back to Israel.

Just for the kicks of it, and not because he felt he had to hurry, he flipped on the lights and the siren, and tore out of town like he was on an important mission. He passed the cars pulled over for him, and he felt a wonderful surge of power, a big thrust he liked to feel, flooring that state car, eatin' up the gas, and him never paying a dime for it. He chuckled as he sped along, grinned at himself in his trooper's hat. Made it on slim chance. But holy Jesus, I made it, he smiled.

He slid into the emergency entrance at the hospital in Farmington about six thirty, killed the lights and the siren. Quiet, the sign read. Yeah, I'll be quiet. Fun over now. Get this done.

Picking up the tube, he placed it in his shirt pocket and opened the door. An orderly lounged against the back entrance, smoking a cigarette. Black, he was. Tall and slender in his greens. The man nodded. The trooper nodded. That's all I want from them, he thought, pushing in through the door. Just a nod and nothing more.

He'd been here many times, and tonight was not the rush-rush he sometimes handled. No, tonight there was no hurry. Just drop off the sample, leave the stupid message, and head out.

"Whoa, Sue, how you doing?" The nurse looked up and smiled, moved her board aside, and rested her hands under her chin on the desk behind the counter.

"Why, Occifer, how cute of you to ask." They joked a minute or two, played the little game between the man in uniform and the woman in uniform, played it as if they didn't know they would like to get into each others' pants.

"You here on business, or should I call this a date?" She batted her eyes and laughed.

"I guess it's business, kinda monkey business, if you get my drift." He pulled out the tube and handed it to her. She accepted it and rolled it in her hands for a minute.

"Let me guess." She closed her eyes. "Love potion number nine? Did I get that right?" She laughed again and slid the tube into a wire holder.

"Name, please. What name should I put on the label?"

"Schoenfield, I guess. I don't have any other name. Just Schoenfield." He pushed away from the counter and headed back out the door.

She stood up then and said, "Got someone coming in? What's the sample for?"

"Beats me. The nigger just said 'home-grown C-section', like I was supposed to know what he meant. Your guess is as good as mine." He swept on out, the door shushing behind him.

A joke's a joke, but the nurse behind that desk in emergency sensed something coming. She glanced at that tube, reached over and picked it up, and found herself running back to the lab. Terror had seized her. They had an incoming, and that jerk didn't know an incoming patient from his ass. She ran into the lab, shouted for the technician. A black man peered around a floor-to-ceiling shelving unit. "Hi, Sue. Need me?"

"Raymond, run type on this, pronto, and get it back to me. We got a botched abortion coming in!"

A botched abortion would have been a pleasure, she admitted ten minutes later. A botched job could be saved. But the girl carried in by the black man, the girl in the blood soaked quilt, wore the scars of a longer battle. Exhaustion haunted her eyes, her skin was pulled tight against the pain, and Sue rang for the resident and helped the man lay her on a gurney.

"What happened?" she asked, slipping the stethoscope over the girls' heaving chest. "Tell me, for God's sakes."

"The girl's had a baby, a C-section. Baby was breech. I got it out. Thas all."

Thas all. She'd heard it a hundred times. Thas all, and the blacks dumped their messes on them here, and she was supposed to be Florence Nightingale and make it all well. Kiss their wounds and they'd heal. Well, this has got to stop, this butchering and neglect. Why bring them in now when the door was open before? Why bring them bleeding and half dead?

The back room doors swung open and the resident came bustling through, took the scene in with one gasp. "Call floor. Get a room set up. Abdominal, I'll bet, and a mess." He checked Crissy's eyes and felt her wrist. "Set up drip, and call fluids for whole blood. This lady is in bad shape." He eyed the black man, settling himself back against the wall, saw the blood on his pants and on his hands. "You stay near, fella. We need some info, okay?" Beech nodded and turned in relief when he saw Joan coming in the door with Martin after parking the car.

The resident eyed the two whites with a suspicious glare. Whites. How do they figure here? No time to fool with it. He pushed the gurney into the rear room, set up the IV himself and slid the needle into Crissy's arm. She moaned and turned to look at him. "It's okay, miss, I'm a doctor and you're in good hands now. Rest there."

An orderly came in from Fluids, handed him a plastic pouch of blood, the right type, thanks to Sue. The man glanced at Crissy and his soul turned in his body. Why black? Why she have to come in like this and be black? He paid his rent, fed his kids, helped his wife with the laundry. Why she have to be black? It ain't fair, these folks bringing us down. Not fair.

"I want to start another line on you, other arm, please. There. Now, that didn't hurt, did it?" He hung the two bags and touched her face. "You'll be fine. Just fine. Now what's all this wrapping around your middle? Can I take a look? I can? Good." He cut the soaked bloody sheet from around her middle, and for one moment he wanted to join his brother in the investment business. The naked belly had hair curlers closing the cut, and if his imagination let him, he knew there were others below, or she'd be dead by now. His breath came out in one blast.

"You are one lucky gal, miss, one lucky gal. We'll take care of this." He pushed the gurney out and went down the hall with it. Sue ran beside him, saying the baby looked great, wasn't that good news? The elevator door slid open and he guided the gurney in.

"Get Stansfield up to help. This is bad, Sue, real bad. See if you can rouse Dr. Kim."

She stayed back in the hall, only said, "Call Reed on the baby?" The last thing she saw as the door slid closed was his face next to the woman's ear.

"Keep breathing, just a little longer. We'll help you. Hang on," he whispered. But the words were never heard.

እ

The lights flicked on in the operating room. The scrub nurses went about their duties and assisted the doctors into immaculate blowzy suits. Hands were scrubbed, nails polished with brushes. Gloves slipped on and snapped in place. Masks came up and the first doctor came in and stood by the resident's side.

"Whata we have, Cal? Abortion? Appendix?" The older surgeon, close to retirement and not used to these dinnertime interruptions, waited for the answer. The resident only lifted the gauze pad over the abdomen and watched the other man's face. It didn't change.

"You got her down on the shot? She went down that easy?"

"She slipped into that shot like that's all she needed. We could do this on that shot, believe me, after what she's been through." The resident was fuming, wanted the surgeon to scream all mighty at the mess they had to face, but the older Korean doctor, Tae Kim, only touched his covered head and said, "Get anesthesia in. I want her way down. BP okay?" Cal nodded. "BP okay, we go in and see what we see."

How can he be so fucking cool, glared Cal, watching the man look at the drip and check the charts the nurse was showing him. How to be so cool when some stupid black ass had carved up this woman, let her almost bleed to death. He never hated blacks as much as he did right then, even knowing he had a few black friends. But these blacks, that would do a woman like this. He had no time for them.

The anesthetist came in, bright-eyed over her mask, set up and swept the dials to the proper level. She sat and waited on her stool until she was needed. Cal waited for Dr. Kim to saunter back over.

"You call anyone else to help?"

"Yeah, Stansfield."

"Stansfield's in Kentucky at the family reunion. It's just you and me, Cal, so let's get going."

Dr. Kim nodded to the anesthetist, and she nodded back. She started to release the gases so carefully mixed, so lightly kissed with sweetness and ether. Crissy slipped further under, the shot had been a blessing, she realized. If only they knew. She had her baby, though, she swam with that memory. Daniel had a baby.

Cal started removing the hair curlers, and he nudged Dr. Kim who only grunted back. See this mess we got? He wanted the other man to acknowledge this bloody deed, but Dr. Kim only slid his hand under Cal's and removed curlers and slipped on real clamps, never missing a one. He's good, the old fox. Cal had to admit it. Good. They entered the cavity, and found the space empty of the uterus they expected to find, the uterus with its still attached and clinging placenta, the umbilical cord still snugged against it. It simply was gone, the last two wave clamps told them.

"Emergency seems to be over," Dr. Kim mused, searching for fresh places to set clamps. She doing okay?" The anesthetist nodded. The scrub nurse, Tucker, watched them closely, watched the hands moving in the gloves, from one spot to the next, checking, clamping, observing. She hung another bag of blood and checked the fluid drip on the second bag. Used more than 400 ccs. Close, very close.

"Strong. She's right on target. Better'n target. This gal's got a life of her own!"

Dr. Kim seemed happy with that.

"You take off now, Cal, you got rounds and I got chicken waiting on the barbecue, but that can wait. I'll finish up here. You've done the main job." Cal easily assented, gave it up, and moved away.

"Everything okay then? Tell the people waiting she's going to be all right? That okay with you, Dr. Kim?"

"Go for the glory, friend. Tell 'em you got everything fixed." He bent back then to the suturing, and Tucker handed him the threaded needle, all ready, made it so nice. So nice when they knew what they were doing. He reattached blood vessels, smoothing the planes of muscles close to their original pattern, hoping the nerve endings would find their proper home again. He hemmed up the fasciae, humming along, got handed a new already threaded needle, and went up with it, as if he were conducting a symphony, and he almost heard music as he slipped that needle through the black skin, sewed and sewed and nipped and tucked. He wanted to bite off the last stitch, but she was there in front of him, clipping it, and he sat back.

"We did all right, Tucker. You're good help to old hands." The nurse brushed him off, setting the instrument tray aside, counting sponges and clamps, wondering what they would do with the hair crimpers. Damn smart, she figured, whoever buggered this one. Damn smart. And they worked. Some of her people, though, some of her people, well . . .

The anesthetist eased off her pedal, closed down the jets, rose and asked, "You done for now, Dr. Kim?"

"I've been done a long time ago, but I wouldn't have missed this one for anything." She smiled and went through the double doors.

"So what's your guess, Tucker? What hand played here? This was no slop job. Someone knew what he had, and I bet it was dry breech, dying in there. Who led his hand in this? You find out, and I want to meet that woman or man. That person should be a doctor."

"But, Dr. Kim, no doctor did this, no man in his right mind would try this. This was a mistake. Someone who watched too much TV or read a book about what animals do in the dark, now come on, Tae," and she used his first name in the quiet of them being together. "This girl was close to death when they brought her in. No doctor would lead her down that street. No way. No doc."

"You wanna' bet? I'll tell you this." He slipped his hat off, and walked with her to the swinging doors. "I'll bet a damn good man had a hand here, and if it turns out I'm wrong, Mrs. Kim will fix you and the mister a supper fit for kings. And throw in an egg roll."

"Dr. Kim, we got chores to do, and a lady that needs us. Get, now, and I'll hold your wife to those egg rolls."

৯৯

The resident, Cal, did not stop and wash up before he went to Admitting to face off with the black face and stupid white faces he'd seen. He'd had enough of this garbage dumped on him. He knew he was mad, knew he was a little wacko at that point, but he had a right to be. Those damn niggers! Trying to save a buck on medical care, then coming in a charity case. For sure this was a charity case. Let Kim explain that to accounting, but let these folks see his bloody scrubs.

He was roaring inside, setting his words up to be physician-like, patronizing-like, letting them know they were stupid but never saying the words. The words hummed in him as he hit the ground floor and turned into Admitting. Yeah, all there, lined up like dunces. The fools. Probably not one among them finished high school. White or black.

Sue caught his arm and motioned for him to step inside. He looked back at the anxious faces, loved to see those anxious faces, but

Sue ran the show here and she tugged him along. Dr. Reed, neat and smart in a yellow jump suit, was sitting up on the admitting room table, and in her arms was a baby. She nodded at Cal, put the baby down, and reached for her coat.

"Wanted you to know he's okay, but I think we might watch him close. He did suffer some deprival during birth. I'm not saying he's going to be retarded, but my best guess is, this boy will be slow. But isn't he lovely?" She traced her hands over the sleeping child, let her eyes rest on Cal, saw his anger, and stopped.

"Cal? Snap, snap. What's got you so down?"

"We just saved the mother, thanks to Kim, I'm not that good." There was no use arguing with Martha Reed over his shortcomings. "It just makes me mad, that's all. You say the boy's gonna be slow, and I respect that. You're probably right. But, fuck it, this shouldn't have happened. Why should that boy be slow? Why should his mother be upstairs, recovering from a big mess? Oh, Martha, you wouldn't have believed it! Hair crimpers, they used. Curlers were on the veins. How they missed a major artery is a mystery. Luck, I guess. But come on, let's get real!"

Sue watched the two facing off, and she picked up the baby and headed down to the nursery, but not before she showed him around once more to Joan, Beech, and Martin. She winked. "You all did fine," she whispered. "The mama's going to be fine, too." She whisked her bundle down the hall to the elevator.

Martha Reed shrugged her shoulders as she slipped into her windbreaker. "Cal, it won't change as fast as you want, but we have to say we got them this far and they're both living. We can't ask for much more out of life."

Cal wasn't through, had to get one more dig in before she got away in her car.

"And I'll bet she's a single parent, no daddy, just another case for the county to pay out our tax dollars on. Whatchya wanna bet, Martha? Single parent. Single parent and black."

Martha turned back to stare at him, letting her fingers rest on the swinging doors. "We get white in here, too, Cal, plenty of white farm girls, and city girls, too, with real parents. They get pregnant, too, they get help for their kids, free milk and food stamps, free places to stay. Those whites get it, too, and some by choice, choosing an easy way. Have a kid. Feed off the State."

"It isn't the same," floundered Cal, losing the argument.

"No, it's not the same. Those white clinic freebies had plenty more opportunities given them then these blacks have had. We forced them into their situation. Forced them."

He thought he had her on that point. "How forced? Who forced these black women to raise kids on their own?"

Martha shook her head. "It started way back, Cal, way before we were born. You take a family off a boat, you separate the husband and wife and child, you send the man, under chains and the whip to one place, 'cause he's strong and young, you send the pretty wife off to another place because the plantation owner likes her legs, you pull the child from his mother and sell her to a family for kitchen help. What did they do, but want to live? They had to live, that was what it was about. To fight back meant to die. They went the only way they could, and they were dragged into it. Beaten into it. A man who got lucky and got to keep his wife by his side only saw that same wife get called up to the big house on a warm night, and he knew it wasn't for dusting. What do you think happened to any Black man who stood up for his missus' body? Do you think he lived to hoe another row of corn?"

Cal only stared at her, his mouth hanging open. He had no response.

"We created the single-parent family, and now we're paying for it." She nodded, and left him staring after her. He followed her out, saw her stop and shake hands with the three people sitting in the plastic chairs before she waved at him and went out into the night.

Some of the sting ran out of him, and he approached the three more subdued. They all three stood when he came up to them, stood in respect for the man who had saved Crissy. They knew she was saved, thanks to Sue's hurriedly whispered words. Knew they hadn't killed her. Knew the baby was safe. They were safe.

"Sorry to hold you up, things got a little hectic there, but it looks like your little mama is going to make it. She looked real good before I came down, real good. Dr. Kim is with her, and while I could have gone in alone, it's always better to have a backup." Not a blink ran across his eyes. He stared at them, moved himself into a chair, and stretched out his legs. "Dr. Kim is finishing up for me," he explained, gazing down at the blood on his pants. "Good man. Will help me anytime."

The three sat down, Joan to Martin's left, Beech to his right. Beech didn't take in too much of the man's words. He only watched his eyes. Shifty, those eyes.

"Now we need a background here, a little story to put on the chart, about how all this happened."

Joan looked at Martin, and Martin, ready to speak, was looking at the resident when he felt the pressure of Beech's hand on his leg.

Beech faced the doctor and started talking.

"This be the way it came down. We from Settlement, up over Pond Ridge, our own place. We keep close to oursell's, use the midwife an' home remdies more'n we use 'ospeetals. Thas always been our way an' we dun fine, till now. Ms. Tubbs, she be the midwife, she left 'fore she knew we needed her, an' I come in from the fields an' foun' this chile all doubled up, with her water broke an' no one to hep. No one about. Alls at work. So I knows this baby doan jess fall out, my fingers tell me that, so I feel her heart an' I lissen for the baby an' he goin' slow, real slow, an' that ain' good. I see calfs come out after bein' pulled, an' they doan come out so good. We put a bullet in dem. But we doan put no bullets in babes, not if'n we can bring 'em out clean."

Beech stood up, and Martin watched him. Martin's mouth opened to speak, but no words came out. What was this about? Why was the man lying? He had nothing to lose.

"I got some water boilin' an' found all the stuffn I think I need an' I just slit her open an' used those clamps she have. To stop the bleedn. Cut out the baby holdin' part, that was just a pumpn an' pulln on her strength, had the baby up an' breathed into an' he shore seemed happy to be here. He shore did." Beech smiled down at Cal as he spoke.

"But these people. How did they get into the picture?"

"I dint know these folks 'til I stopped dem on the road, checkin' for homesites they was. Seems they had a car an' a good heart, seems they want to hep me out, me an' the girl. I done what I could. They done all they could."

"I see. Well, mister, you did all right with your farm training. Did all right. You might just have brought her in when you found her."

"No truck, no horse, no way I coulda brung her this far," and no blessing to leave from Theopolis. "She be dead, an' that babe, too."

"I see. Well." He rose and they struggled to their feet. "Well, just let this be a lesson to you. Get over here for clinic on Thursdays. Free clinic. We give shots and advice. This is all provided to you people. Spread the word, won't you? Over here we got real doctors." He left them and moved up the hall, never offering his hand.

"Can we see the girl?" Martin called out to the retreating back.

"Tomorrow," came the answer, and the doctor was gone.

The three went out onto the parking lot, and Beech slipped in to drive without being asked. He turned the key, the ignition caught, and Joan, sitting in back, gazed at the blankets and towels beside her. It had seemed like a nightmare, but now it was over. They were fine, fine, and she felt so good about being a part of it.

Martin wasn't so easily placated. He turned to Beech as they pulled out of the hospital entrance and started back to Pond Ridge. He watched the man, bent on steering the car, and keeping his speed down.

"What was that all about?" Martin asked.

"That was a turn in the road, doc, just movin' the car along."

"I don't mean that, and you damn well know I don't mean that. What was that cockamamie tale you told?" Martin shifted in his seat, and watched Beech's profile in the driver's seat.

"Well, givn I had 'bout ten secons to spin that yarn, I think I did purty good. I tol it like I 'membered it. I got a bad memry, thas all."

"You got a damn poor memory, all right, damn poor. What the hell was I doing there at all? Didn't I do anything?"

"Not on the recor' you dint. You dun nuttin but get me here, an' Miss Joan swear to that, doan you, Miss Joan?" He watched her face in the rearview.

"Can't find no fault with that story," she responded, sitting up and placing her hands on the men's shoulders. "Nice back here. I can talk to both of you."

Martin twisted in his seat, and saw the smile on her face. He looked back at Beech's broad grin, and he started to laugh, great whooping peals of laughter. They saved his butt, he suddenly knew, glancing out the window at the dark trees running by. They saved his license when he knew he would have lost it if the truth got out. My license. He slumped back with a great smile on his face. Thought he was so smart when the truth would have ruined him. Beech Cheevers was a whole lot smarter than he was. He glanced at the speedometer.

"Ease up, Beech, you'll get us a ticket."

"Doan need no ticket tinigh', got an invite, an' I bes' get back 'fore she change her mine."

Martin watched the man driving and heard Joan's little giggle.

"You wanting to get back to Gloria, right?" Martin said.

"Some thin's wort' stayin' up fer, doc, an' thas wha' I hopin' fer. Tha everythin' stay up tinigh'!"

# Chapter Forty-Two

Joan slipped into Days End, lugging the cooler, at about ten. The place was quiet and she hated to do it, but she needed Tess tonight. Wanted her to share her day's events. Lord, what a day! She'd have to soak in the tub an hour to get the blood out from under her nails.

She opened the fridge with her grimy hands, and saw the blood on Beech's pants. She loved to see it. Touched it with her fingers and wanted to laugh and dance around the kitchen. She found a new bottle of Chardonnay, pulled the cork in the light from the opened fridge, stood again in the light from the refrigerator, and couldn't help it. The wine got poured and she drank a full glass standing in that light, found an extra glass, shut the door with her foot and carried the two glasses and bottle up the back stairs.

"Tess!" she called, and Tess opened her door and stuck her head out. "Shush. We got guests. What are you yelling about?"

"Oh, Tess, I've just had the most marvelous day, the most marvelous!"

"You don't look all that marvelous to me. You look dirty, and what's that on your pants? Where did you get those pants?"

"Due time, my friend, due time. Grab a glass and pull on your ears. You'll never believe this!" Tess started a tub for her, and Joan started talking, and she couldn't sit still; she paced, drank some wine, kept talking, talking, walked out of the clothes and into the water, and Tess was wide-eyed by then, sat by the side of the tub while Joan soaked one hand, then the other, keeping one free for the wine glass.

❧

Beech drove down the familiar lane to his own place, saw the light on, and Gloria sitting in the porch swing. She got up when she saw them coming, ran down the steps and into the headlights. Beech got out and went round to her and saw she was crying.

"Where you bin? Miz Franklin sent Daniel down hours ago, an' they said you got the baby, but, Lord, man, you lef us sick here, worryin' about Crissy an' the baby. What happen?"

"I 'splain, nip in your worry, woman. Start me some supper an' turn on the shower. I stink tinigh', an' this one night I wanna smell good!"

"What you mean, smell good? How I care how you smell? I so glad you back, Beech, I worry haf to death over alln you. An' you, too, doctor. You, too," she said to Martin, getting in behind the wheel.

"Go easy on him, Miss Gloria. You got one worn-out stallion tonight." Martin ducked into the car and felt the slap on the hood, saw Beech grinning in the windshield as he backed out and headed back to town. Too late to try to find the track across the fields to the other folks in the dark. The good news would have to wait until morning. Good news always kept. Bad only ran fast. He needed a shower and bed. And a time to pray before he slept.

The words were already forming in his mind, words he ran over and mumbled to himself as he turned into Days End. The back door was left open for him, and he found the light, switched it on. The house was quiet, only the sound of a tub running upstairs, and he saw no one, but knew someone had remembered him. The chilled glass of Chardonnay was on the counter, and a neatly printed paper sat against its lip. Congratulations, it read, bet they call him Martin. I luv ya. Tess.

And Martin it was. Martin Beech Milborne. Big as life and half as slow as Martha Reed expected. He came home from the hospital with Crissy on the seventh day, all wrapped in new clothes and the finest blanket Tess could find. Thirty dollars that blanket cost, and worth every penny. They were all celebrating, and Theopolis was the proudest of all, being named the godfather. He took special pleasure in sending a cashier's check to the hospital for the whole amount.

ð❧

Paulette heard about the baby, heard it from Dr. Schoenfield's lips when he came in to cash a check. Beech was the hero of the day, for that was the story that got sent around. Two babies he'd brought in, and not a diploma on the wall.

No diploma on Miz Tubbs wall neither, Luretha grumbled, no paper sayin' she should be doin' this work. Two babies he done stole off me. Maybe I jes set it off, she figurd, fine another bizness, a bizness where folks doan go off an do crazy stuff wit razors an such. Summun need to bring that Beech Cheevers back to what he was. Lay those ties. Shift that load. Mine his own bizness an not go meddlin'.

Joan floated on air for the next two weeks, no pin could have stopped her floating. She filed for divorce in Farmington, laid the papers down herself, and walked out owning the house, the contents, and the bank account. Macy Stewart never showed, stayed crawled into his mother's womblike house, rarely showing his face except for meals, which he loved. His mother looked on him with disdain, fed him more, to satisfy her urge to blow him up and send him into the atmosphere.

Martin Schoenfield left the blessing of Martin Beech Milborne by Sam Walters to be conducted without him, in the hallowed halls of First United Church, formerly led by the obviously absent Dr. Rev. Stewart. Missus Walters, in her red hat and clicking heels, found the new parsonage to her liking, and Joan left it just the way she had. Signed the house over to the Walters and the Church. Oh, she took some pictures and the rest of her clothes, kept a favorite table that would look good in Days End, but for the most part, the house was only a hollow memory that was gone for her, and she couldn't have cared less. She took a nice deduction on her income tax that year, being so generous to the Church, almost forty thousand, and that more than wiped off any taxes Tess had to pay, now that Joan was a partner in the new corporation.

The old house Sam and his missus had filled with love, and not much else, stood vacant until fall, when a breathless Marilyn told Gloria that John had asked her to marry him. Now how that happened is worth telling...

She saw the lights flick on in the bunkhouse at dusk, knew Arlon had flipped the switch. She hadn't heard a car drop John off for the last weekend before he was finished at the police academy. Good for him, she admitted, letting the curtain fall back. So he's almost finished and so am I. For being here. He said to wait 'til he got back; then they'd decide what to do with her. Like she was some plastic blow-up woman. Completely disposable. Well, I'll show him how disposable I am. Mr. Hot Shot police guy. He's not telling ME what I'm gonna do.

Marilyn moved to pick up Bory and go out to help Gloria with supper. Her hair was brushed back into a chignon, but a few wisps hung in front of her face, and she blew them out of her eyes impatiently.

"I got it," said Gloria, bending over the oven. "Go call the kids." Marilyn put Bory into his punkin seat, and reached for her sweater. The evening air carried just enough of a chill to remind everyone that winter was soon arriving. She walked quickly to the bunkhouse and let herself in. Arlon and John were sitting on the edge of John's bed. They both looked up guiltily when she came in. Marilyn was surprised.

"John, you're home! I didn't hear you come. Who dropped you off?"

"I walked in from the road. Needed some time to think about some stuff." He had his hands together between his knees, and Arlon was staring at those hands. He looked up into John's face.

"I think I'm shovin' off," he mumbled, sliding off the bed and heading out the door. He peered back in just once, smiled and shut the door.

John stood up and he did look so nice in his own clothes. He looked nice in his uniform, too, don't get me wrong, Marilyn argued with herself. But I like him best when he's just come up from the spring, and his hair is wet, and he's got a towel around his neck, his top part is all bare, and his arms look so nice and strong, and he has a tiny mole on his shoulder...just once, to hold him just once, and demand he kiss her. Just once.

"So I was thinking," continued John, moving around the bed and holding one hand behind him, "I was thinking maybe in the snow, maybe right here, maybe just Reverend Walters, and you know, some folks from around, some of the guys from high school, for sure. . . whatdya think? I mean, I don't have to know tonight, you can think it over."

"Think what over?" demanded Marilyn, snapped out of her reverie.

"About getting married. That's what we were talking about, Marilyn. About you and me."

"You were doing all the talking. I wasn't talking, was I? Did you see my lips move?"

"I asked you to marry me, but I don't have to know right now." He stood three feet from her in his green sweatshirt and khaki slacks, stood with a patience she could only admire. He waited for her answer.

She shrieked as she barged into him, knocking him flatly surprised onto the bed. "Whoa, whoa, wait, I got something behind me. You're gonna break the box." He pulled out the little gray satin flip-top jewelry box, and held it in front of him in both hands, as a tiny offering to her. Marilyn went to his side then, held his hand with the little box, and closed his fist over it. "I don't care what's in that box," and the tears started to fall on her cheeks. "I only care that you're holding my hand, John. That means more to me than any diamond in the world."

"Then I should have saved my money, I guess," and he started to put the box in his pants pocket. Marilyn pushed him back on the bed, rolled over on top of him, and stared down into his face. "John Cheevers, if you don't kiss me right now, I'm never gonna wear your ring."

He obliged her nicely, bringing her face down over his, kissing her forehead first, then her nose, and finally, taking his time, he brushed his lips over hers, back and forth, then kissed her fully and tenderly.

No surprise to anyone short of a blind man. They were as perfect together as they always were. They had Sam marry them quietly, and no one was more delighted than Gloria. The Walters' home came alive with women crawling over the baseboards and wiping down the walls. Missus Walters may be many things, they whispered, but she wasn't much on dusting.

❧

The familiar airport at Newark came up in front of Martin's eyes as he gazed out the airplane's clean oval. Newark. Back home, but not home. No home. Just Newark, with its dying synagogue. No place here for me, he realized, Pearson better go for my idea or I'm history. My life's in Missouri, he realized. Everyone except Luther and Claire were in the Midwest, and he knew he had to bring them there, too. They belonged there, not in an apartment in the Bronx. Weren't there air conditioners to fix in Missouri? Surely they had to need another good man.

He slept in late in his small apartment, rustled up a breakfast of instant coffee and a frozen bagel stuffed in the back of the freezer. Ate it dry, he had no butter or jam, but it filled him up. He had lost his appetite for anything except finishing his plans. The plans were slowly forming in his mind, the plans for his life and the future. He didn't see it there in the east. Go west, young man, go west.

The CSR saw him coming in, and she didn't vocalize her snort, but her eyes shifted to her memo pad and wrote down the time of arrival. Martin nodded to her, and went toward Mr. Pearson's office when he was stopped at her utterance.

"Dr. Schoenfield, I really think it might be best if we observe a few rules of civility here. Normally you ask if he's in and can he see you, then I do the connection. You follow?" She turned in her padded chair, and eyed him from the brushed frame of blue eye shadow. Her hair was sprayed and teased into an unmoving uplifted coiffure; her short hands, with fake polished nails, laid gently on her keyboard as if she had only a moment to straighten him out before she started an opus. Her fingers ran the company, and Dr. Schoenfield only had to get the message and get on board.

"Mr. Pearson's in, Tracy, I called him from my home, and he's most interested in what I have to tell him. He said to come in as soon as I'd rested, so that's what I'm doing, only following orders."

She sniffed as if she'd caught a bad odor, shifted her fingers to different keys, but didn't press. "This time, okay, but next time, do show a little respect and some manners. This is Pearson Pharmaceuticals, not Missouri, and here we do things a little differently."

"I'll try to remember that, Tracy, the next time."

"Best you do." She turned to answer the phone, and her face went into a smile, and she said to wait, and put the caller on hold. He had already started to open Pearson's door when she sent off one last salvo.

"And your aunt? How did everything go at the poor soul's funeral?" A smirk twisted her painted mouth, and Martin took in a breath and answered her.

"The funeral went fine. Aunty Doris never had much kinfolk, only a lot of money, but darn her! We found out she left everything to a group of black lesbians holed up at the Days End, and it was sordid, let me tell you, Tracy, sordid. The rooms, the clothing, all this I had to settle before I came back to peace, joy, and civilization. Now when you have time, I want you to know about how these women get younger women into their fold, some of them no more than twelve, and the pictures . . ."

"I think I've heard enough about your aunt's way of life. That's disgusting, Dr. Schoenfield, how you could be related to such a woman is beyond me. And you actually went out there to settle her affairs?"

Martin nodded.

"Poor judgment, doctor, very poor judgment. You need to stay at your job if you wish to keep it, and let your relatives, and their numerous funerals, just get on without you."

"I think you may be right, Tracy. If I ever need a friend to help me find the right way, I'll know I can turn to you."

"Well, that's better, doctor, much better. Go on in, Mr. Pearson apparently expects you, and I have an urgent call waiting." She shifted off hold, and leaned back to hear her friend begin another story, having to do with her poodle's continuing diarrhea problem.

Not as urgent as mine, Martin smiled, opening the door and greeting Mr. Pearson, rising to shake his hand.

"Martin, good to see you. Been in the field a week, have you? Lots to tell me, I'm sure." He went back around his desk and sat down. Martin pulled up the side chair and easily found his words.

"The people are all as reported, chief. All gone from their former color. How that happened is the guess of the century, but the newspapers have caught hold of it, and some of the bigger names are coming down to take a look: Oprah Winfrey is planning a special, Diane Sawyer wants a slice, and Barbara Walters is scheduling a special on this phenomenon on ABC, right at Christmas. Playing up the miracle angle. It's big news, Mr. Pearson, big news, and I finally figured out a way that we can get involved. By the way, did you get that grant we spoke of before I left?" Money. Everything revolved around money. The color green swept over black or white.

Mr. Pearson sat back in his leather swivel and posed his fingertips together. "Got it, and more than we hoped. Neat package, no strings. Just go for the virus. Let's just see them take it away, slow as we seem to be going. No one loses those grants from Uncle Sam unless they're real baboons."

"Like dumb niggers?" Martin interjected.

"Exactly, my friend like the standard wood pile sort. Nigger in the wood pile. There isn't going to be any niggers in this wood pile if you get my drift. We're all above board here at Pearson Pharmaceuticals, and I mean to keep it that way."

Martin cringed at the term, felt himself want to roll over that leather desk and choke Pearson, but he kept his anger at a hum, turned his hasty nature into a mold to work for his goal.

"Everyone's going to be diving for Pond Ridge, but I've made some very valuable contacts, and I think if we move quickly, we can cut them off, get the recognition this firm deserves."

Pearson rolled forward, all ears, and Martin laid out his plan.

"Our primary publicized concern is for the welfare of these

people, stripped of their intended color. We need to let the public, black and white, know that as the protector of the people's health, our goal is to study this situation, find its medical and physical root, and let the healing of Pearson Pharmaceuticals assist these people. That's my plan for us, Mr. Pearson, to be the forerunner in the battle, which began as the AIDS battle, and now may be linked to this pigment change."

"Amazing, Schoenfield, simply amazing, and I think you've hit on it. God. The press we'd get, jumping in there and doing something. What do you propose doing?" he asked blankly.

"Build a hospital, right on the site. Let it be an open clinic for the afflicted, let it be pay-as-you're-able for the willing, let it be pay up-front if you have medical insurance, but let it be a clinic, and hospital, and teaching arm to some very deprived people. Use that grant money or part of it to get this crusade going."

"Martin, you've hit on it, to feel the pulse and integrity of this company so early on. You had me worried, and I apologize for doubting you, when you left us so early for what some said were trumped-up excuses, but I'm not a man to judge others. No," and he waved his hand in deference when Martin began his protest, "no, let's just let the past slide. What you did with your time is more than balanced out by what you've brought me today. A clinic, a hospital, a research center, right in the Midwest." He leaned back in his chair and swiveled to take in the view from his window.

"Sir, I have never . . ." began Martin.

"Slide, Martin, let it slide. Let's talk money here. How much to do this, how much do you figure we'll need? Got to run it through the board of directors, the lawyers, public relations, but I'll have my way."

Martin paused and collected his thoughts. Money. He wants to talk money. We're talking a building design, acquisition of land, cost of construction, and outfitting the building with the latest in medical research technology. For there'd be a shiny spanking new chrome and glass lab with an electron microscope, or he was taking his football and going home. We're talking some major bucks on a civic planner, engineers, architects, laborers. We're talking money that takes time to figure, and can't be just shot from the hip.

"Two million eight would cover it," came back the voice from Martin's throat, and he almost looked over his shoulder to see who prodded him to say it. Was Luther playing his tricks? Was Theopolis shifting the coins? Did Aunty stretch out her hand? Where did the message get its wings?

"Two million eight." Pearson frowned, and pulled himself over his desk. Two million eight the man comes up with, without knowing the amount of the grant, already signed, sealed and vaulting toward him. One third of the grant this man suggested using. And the publicity for his company! How could that ever be balanced against so small an investment? How to handle the press? How to manage the slides, the presentations, the projections he wanted to give the public? He'd have to give in, he knew in his heart that he would have to, have to hire a projection image enhancing firm to set this off right. Martin couldn't do it, he knew nothing of Internet and slick glossies and releases done on time. Who to use? The man his brother had used, his investor brother in St. Louis, what was that name? Kon-Por Overview. Ah, God, it will work, he planned, let this happen for us. And they could use his brother's construction connections, even get that lawyer Mackey to draw up the legal part. They'd need a Missouri lawyer.

"Well, you have my go ahead, doctor. Get the building going, find a site, keep in touch with me, so I'll know where to send the publicity people. We'll need to use every resource to keep this thing grounded."

"Sir, I know how valuable the work here is, know it may seem like I'm deserting the ship and going off on a raft, but if this building and the details of getting it outfitted and up and running, if this isn't watched real close, we could go over budget. I think if I moved out there, just rented a cheap room, nothing fancy, maybe even board and take my meals in as a cost-cutting measure, I could keep my eye on things, move 'em along. Now that's just a thought."

"Mighty big sacrifice, doctor, take a whole slice out of your life here. Up to a year on the project, and then you'd be stuck for a while, stuck until we could send in a replacement or find a doctor in that area to run the show for you, so you could come back east. Hate to push you to that." But if it will save me money and get us good press, I'll slaughter one Jewish lamb.

"One last important thing, chief, and I know you'll agree with me. We need a top-notch person here, a base person to field the calls, answer the questions, keep this from bogging down. We need a liaison person here, if I'm to go back to the field, and I know that's what you want, to have me go back, and I will make that sacrifice, chief, give up my comfortable life here in Newark to get it done. Can I ask another sacrifice from you? A big one, a huge one? Can I impose on you? No, I've pushed this as far as I can."

"Ask it, doctor, you've already made the biggest sacrifice, to go back to the Midwest. Anything else I can only bow down to."

"I need Tracy to run the ropes from here. Now, I see how

much she means to you, know her contribution here, but I could only ask that she be assigned exclusively to my team. We'd roll, Mr. Pearson, know how we'd roll if Tracy were on our team!"

"She's been with us fourteen years," Mr. Pearson reasoned, "been here through thick and thin."

"Then doesn't she deserve a chance for the limelight?" Martin slipped in.

"Hate to spoil that for her, she's such a devoted employee, and you say you've kinda singled her out because of her skill?" Pearson wanted affirmation that Martin found some intrinsic value in a woman he had little time for, and less respect, but she dutifully showed up and did her perfunctory chores with grumbling and breaks that he found abominable.

"She's my choice, and I know I'm not wrong. The woman has the feel of the people in her, lets it stay hidden, but she can be a great asset to me, and to the company. Have you ever thought about the wasted surplus of material we have stored on Second Street in the warehouse? Imagine how good that torn Naugahyde and corroded chrome would look in a charity clinic! Using what we have, struggling to give what we got. Great image. Image of our forefathers. They wouldn't accept more than Salvation Army in Pond Ridge, feel it their civic duty to be proud of recyclables. Missouri's the land of yard sales and micro buses. And if anyone can pull it together, it's Tracy, with her love of people and her desire to get the job done, and as cheaply as possible."

"You say we can save some money here, using our castoffs to line that hospital?"

"Positively. That figure I gave you, that two million eight, that only factored in with the use of those stored cabinets and lamps and desks. Otherwise, it would shoot over three five, mind, that's just an estimate, according to my people."

"So you've talked to others, is that what's happened? I'm not just here for the decoration and blessing, doctor. I make the big decisions. How, exactly, can Tracy be useful?" For if Schoenfield could find it, he'd have her out of there in an hour. Milda from the secretarial pool was better at half the salary.

"She could be our commander of used material. The warehouse on second that houses about the most worthless bunch of castoffs this company has accumulated in fifty years: lamps, tables, desks, filing cabinets. Perfect for our project. Those folks in Missouri don't know diddley squat about new things. They like old things, keep worn out refrigerators on their front porches like old friends. They think

Naugahyde comes from real leather. They fix things with duct tape if they want them to last. We could go through that storehouse of treasures, save thousands of dollars and get a double-dip at tax time. You paid for it once, it's depreciated out of its life's use. Now you sell it, and it becomes a cost to the new project. Any money you make you give to the AIDS project back here specifically. I think it will work, but only if someone as gifted as Tracy rules the project from here."

"You've got her, Schoenfield, and my best wishes as well. Send her in on your way out. Let me know how I can help. Don't just think I'm a rubber stamp sitting here."

"Chief, I could never think that."

Mr. Pearson chuckled and clasped Martin's shoulders warmly. As they walked to the door, Mr. Pearson suggested an architect he knew, and Martin filed that name at the back of his rolodex. He already knew who he was going to choose. There was no doubt about it, the project had been whirling in his head for long enough to have made this well thought out selection drop into place. Planning, that was the key. Lining it out and examining it, picking out the flaws before the seam of the fabric fell apart. An architect was too important not to have been selected mentally, and for good reason, long before the idea for the building took form.

He stopped at Tracy's desk and asked her for the yellow pages. She leaned forward and Martin noticed a large bulge of waist under her expensive Liz Claiborne silk blouse. Punching hold, she looked up at him in exasperation.

"Really, Dr. Schoenfield, cutting in like that when I'm on the phone." She shook her head and nothing moved. Martin wanted to ask her what kind of hair spray she used. He wanted to analyze it. They were looking for the screen to keep AIDS out, a shield of protection. Be a good joke if it was in hair spray all along.

She tugged the yellow pages out of a drawer and slapped it firmly on the floor. He graciously picked it up, and laid it on the corner of her desk. Her mouth fell open as she scooted herself back on the wheeled chair, out of his way. So stunned was she at his behavior that she thought for a moment of going into Mr. Pearson and lodge a sexual harassment complaint against Dr. Schoenfield. He had come frighteningly close to brushing her thigh when she pushed herself back.

"Oh, Tracy, good news for you. Real good news. This isn't your desk anymore. You're up for a job move, and no one deserves it more than you do. Mr. Pearson said to come right in, and my heartiest congratulations to you." She rose and went quickly into the sanctuary.

Martin flipped to architects, shut his eyes on the page, and ran his finger down the list for five seconds, opened them to look to see who had gotten picked. Ulmer and Osaka. Small size print type. No address, only a phone number. He reached over and pressed in line three, heard a voice, went to line four, heard a voice, hit five, no voice. He punched up Ulmer and Osaka.

"Brad Ulmer," came the impatient, snappy voice.

"Have you ever designed a clinic-like building?" asked Martin.

"Once, out of Legos," he quipped.

"If I wanted to build, say, a three-story building, native stone on first, cedar laid diagonally on second and third, with celestory windows, about twenty-seven of them. Fireplace in the waiting room. Four public baths on each floor. Fourteen semi-private rooms with a full bath. A metal lined X-ray room. An isotope isolation area centered in the basement, under twelve feet of substone . . . How much to design that building?"

Now there were some things Brad Ulmer did fast, and some things he did slow, but this shopper was just chewing on his arm, killing some time. You don't call Ulmer and Osaka for the plans for a three-story medical building, for chrissake. He was hungry for work, but he wasn't stupid enough to take this joker seriously. He'd give him a price all right.

"I can do that in an afternoon, sir, no problem. My fee is two hundred dollars an hour for original planning time. The drawings themselves, depending on how many copies you require, are seventy-five dollars each, with an origination fee of one thousand dollars. If I'm required to make any sketch adjustments, for changes you request, my consultation fee remains the same, two hundred dollars an hour." That should hold him.

"I just wanted to know the bottom line, Brad. I'm not a cook, don't feed me the recipe. What's an amount you'll start with, just rounded to a safe estimate?"

Brad smiled and looked at the phone. He looked up at Han Osaka, bent at his laptop, watching him and listening. Brad twisted his finger in the air at his ear, whirling it in a circle of craziness. He'd made one hundred and fifteen dollars this week, Han had done a little better, four hundred and ten, but Ulmer and Osaka, three years out of college and working out of Osaka's bungalow, were going down before they got up as independents. These prank calls didn't help, wasted his time and patience. The lanky twenty-seven-year-old, losing his hair and his car if things didn't turn around, decided to stay with his first joking menu.

"Well, let me punch this up, sir. Dedee, dedee, dedee times four plus . . . oops, wrong button. Hum-m-m. Looks like that comes to

$3,150 dollars, sir, and a real bargain."

"Sounds good to me. How much up-front?"

Brad sat up a little straighter. "We always ask for . . ." and he watched Han move his hand across his throat, "half down, balance on final engineer's approval of the plan. Additional cost for consultation, as I said, that would have to follow, were we needed."

"When can we meet?"

"We're jammed up today, sir, tight as a drum." Brad watched Han stick out his lower lip a little, then grin, nod his head and bend back to his work. Some joke. Funny world. Too much time on his hands, that funny guy on the phone.

Han heard Brad give the guy directions to Han's house near Independence Park, heard him say ten o'clock tomorrow would suit them, and Brad hung up the phone.

"Strange guy. Almost sounded like he meant it." Ulmer cleared off his desk, and just because he had nothing else to do, just because he hadn't completely dismissed the guy as a quack, he opened his Macintosh for the day and set up a new screen. Dating it, running the architects slug lines by one keystroke, his mind became filled with the stones the man had said would make up the walls of the first story. The wood, the rafters, the ceiling; he shifted to a second screen and ran up the wall with the chimney, all solid field stone with some pink granite sliced rough. He flushed up a backup screen, started his functional material list. The hospital rooms he went into descriptive detail over: the oxygen jet portals, the steel cabinets. Walk through it, Ulmer. Which way do you want this door to open?

Han made them both some lunch, rice and salmon cakes, and they ate it out in the pleasant but tiny backyard. They had built a deck together on the front of the five-hundred square foot, one story bungalow, had really put some thought into it. It was more than just a flat surface for eating barbecue. It was an advertisement for them, finished just last month, but no one knew who it was that had built it because they didn't have the money yet for a sign. But it looked beautiful, even the pebbles shimmered in the low pond filled with goldfish. The ponds, three of them, had almost invisible steel filamented urethane mesh covering them, in case a child or pet should walk around the deck (circling the front about fifteen feet from the house) and somehow fall in. These pools were deep, so the fish could stay out throughout the deep cold of an east coast winter. And one was heated.

Brad's mother, an avid gardener, had known which plants would work well and which fish, too. She encouraged them to go the extra expense, make one of the smaller ponds for salt water fish.

"Oh, Brad, the color! If you could have those colors slipping through the water. And don't paint the walls. Leave the sides rough and gray. Throw in some stones and branches. They love to have obstructions. It makes them stronger, keeps their scales polished. You are putting lights in the bottom, aren't you? Imagine this at night," she mused, walking the completed deck and gazing down at her son and Han digging in about three feet of wet Newark clay. "This will be so beautiful, I can't believe it!" Tears filled her eyes as she looked down at them.

"Believe it, Mom, believe it," Brad groaned, not liking this physical part at all. The best exercise he'd found was raising his wrist to sip at the end of the day, but he kept a watch on that. His dad had died that way, solidified liver, the doctor told his mother. Said it was so hard you could have skated on it.

Mom was good-hearted enough to pay for all the fish and the lights. Without her, they never could have finished. Brad kept up his end of the bargain: lived in just the basement of a four family flat she owned, paid her rent when he had it, and did all the heavy work.

After lunch, he went back to work on the blueprints for the clinic, stayed much later than his usual knock-off time. Somehow he had gotten fired up over this project: he called a friend with a big firm who gave him a couple pointers on the X-ray room and isotope isolation chamber. That firm built hospitals, and the friend's voice was just a tad curious about Brad's questioning. He gave him the answers, though, knowing they wouldn't do Brad any good, were just the questions any curious architect might ask a more experienced, better heeled associate.

# Chapter Forty-Three

*I said too much, I said it all.*
*That's me in the corner.*
*That's me in the spotlight . . .*
*I said too much,*
*I haven't said enough.*

*REM  "Losing my Religion"*

Martin had his man, he could tell by the sound of Brad's voice. He pressed the intercom into Pearson's office, and the man said, "Pearson here." Martin asked how he could get a draft for $1,575 dollars for the architect. "Have Milda get it for you," responded the chief, rubbing his hands together in delight that Martin could act that fast. So Tracy had heard that final toll, knew her new job, whatever it was, would keep her lights on and her new car payments paid up. If working under the rude Jewish doctor was it, so be it. Her title pleased her: Liaison Representative. No offer of more money, and she hesitated to ask, hard as jobs were to come by.

Martin found Milda by touching the phone button marked Pool; she came right up to Mr. Pearson's office, a plump sweet lady with a nice laugh. She said she'd be back with the check in a minute, and it was only five before she handed him the envelope.

"Milda, mind the store for Tracy, will you? Don't go back to the pool. Mr. Pearson needs you up here, and be sure when you talk to him, be sure to ask him for a raise, say, forty per cent." She nodded and smiled, sat on down in Tracy's chair and attacked the stack of correspondence Tracy had never gotten to start, much less finish.

"Mr. Pearson is opening a hospital in Missouri. Building it from the ground up. To study those people who have had a color change. You read about it?"

"You'd have to be asleep not to have heard about it. Makes that O.J. mess look like small potatoes. Is that what we're doing, trying to find a cure?"

"That's it. Oh, and get the names of the people in St. Louis, the contractor and lawyer Mr. Pearson wants to use. He'll draft the letters or tell you what to E-mail, fax, whatever. Details, that's all. Details. You okay with this?"

She beamed at him, pulling Tracy's chair in closer to the keyboard. "Nothing ever felt so right, doctor."

He left her to go clear out his desk, tell the others he was going back out to Missouri, and they gave him a look of understanding sympathy. How they found out why Martin was going, and for how long a time, was not Martin's problem. Pearson could tell them however he chose to after getting Kon-Por in on the plan. Wasn't Martin's job. He prided himself on staying out of other people's business.

He called his apartment manager, said he had to leave, break his lease. Send the amount due to Pearson Pharmaceuticals, in care of Milda. The packing took less than an hour. Let them keep the damage deposit and pay a clean-up crew to come through. Now that he had decided to go to Pond Ridge, he didn't want any delays. One more day, just to get the architect going; one more day to stay in Newark or not to stay in Newark.

He called the airport and heard a flight was leaving every forty minutes for New York. It was best he keep moving, see Amy and her new husband, maybe even Jane, but most certainly Claire and Luther. Time, though, was his enemy. His watch said one o'clock. His travel bag was already packed. Why not? Spend the night in New York, jump around and see them all. He was very short on sleep, but much shorter on time with them once he headed west to Missouri.

The answering machine at Amy's was malfunctioning, it clicked and clicked, rang some chimes, then went dead. He tried the Hauk's, and Claire's musical voice sang out that they were out, leave your name, we'll call you back. But I won't be here, Martin fumed, setting the receiver down. Jane. His last hope.

Jane's battery of phones would never run out of room. He was just piping in his message when her delighted voice cut into the recorded message. "Martin, it's you! How are you and when are you coming to see us? Amy misses you, and she's having a baby . . . oops! Maybe I shouldn't have said that, she wanted to be the one to tell you. Pretend you don't know, okay?"

"No problem," Martin replied, delighted inside that he'd be an uncle. Probably never be a dad, so why not be happy over being an uncle?  Little squirt will be cute, too; Martin could picture a tiny girl with Amy's face and round eyes, sitting on his lap. "How's today work for you? I can be there in an hour."

"Today would be grand. Know your flight?"

"Just decided to come five minutes ago. I'm moving to Missouri, Jane, gonna be a midwife in Missouri. No, really, my firm is building a hospital out there, to help the people with the skin color change. You know about it?"

"God, doesn't everyone? I mean, for real, weird, very weird. Very extraterrestrial. How long you going to be out there?"

"I've closed my apartment; which reminds me, I need to call a mover. Can you put up with a little company? Call the Hauks and Amy. Bring in some pizza and beer. Host me a little send off?"

"I can do better than that, Martin. I'm no slouch in the kitchen. You don't see me complaining about throwing on a few extra plates. I've got a dishwasher, a stove, an icebox." She paused. "Call me when you get in. I can be there in a jiff."

The taxi shot him to the airport, he charged his ticket and felt himself being frisked by the metal detector. It seemed the plane was up and down before he read one word of the magazine in his hands. The man next to him, watching his face, said, "Grab a little nap?"

"Must have," Martin responded, shaking his head and rubbing his eyes. "Been up all night. Working on taxes for clients. Tough job, this money grind."

"You an accountant? I got a couple questions if you got a minute. Plane's just coming down. If I had a place I was fixin' to sell, but not really gonna sell, like I just would like it to seem . . ."

Martin raised his hand. "Stop right there. I didn't say whose taxes, or who my clients are. How does the name Internal Revenue grab you?"

The man's eyes grew as round as his mouth as he nodded. "Thanks. I'll shut up." They taxied in without further comment.

Jane was there in ten minutes, sweeping up to passenger pickup at just the moment he came out of the airport entry. He had called her from the gate, got a cappuccino and not near as good as Tess'. A young man handed him a card: I AM MUTE. CAN YOU GIVE ME TEN DOLLARS? New York, New York. Martin shook his head, pulled out his pen, and turned the card over. He wrote on the back: I HAVE AIDS. CAN YOU GIVE ME TWENTY? The man backed away so fast that he almost tripped. He turned and ran away. Martin wondered if he might just have something there. Have a whole bunch of those cards printed up. You could sell those in New York and in California and come out with a nice profit.

"Martin, you look wonderful," Jane complimented. "That Missouri must bring out the farm boy in you. Is it really okay out there, for you, I mean?" On the ride to her condo, he did indeed reassure her that he had found a real reason to be happier, found a place where he could make a difference, not the exact one he'd built his dream on, but close. Very close.

When they went up in the elevator, Martin holding his travel bag on his shoulder, military style, wearing his moccasins and jeans, same old pullover, and Jane, in a sleek red jump suit with a purple Nehru jacket, very trendy, very in at that moment, got a few stares from the elite sharing the ride. They chatted easily, about the weather and Thanksgiving and the Holidays coming. Would he be coming back for the Holidays? Somehow he knew one New York Jew was going to be dragging in a Pond Ridge Christmas tree this year, singing carols with the Walters flock if they had anything to say about it. He knew there'd be celebrating in Pond Ridge this year; the new hospital going in was going to be a boon. A place for the high school graduates not able to afford college to find work at whatever they could handle. They'd need maintenance people, they'd need aides and practical nurses. Some RNs might get their start there. He had big plans, big plans.

The condo door was open and the living room was a flood of brilliant green. Everything had been changed. The walls were in green leather, soft and misty. The chairs were redone in different hues: emerald and turquoise and mint. Martin gazed in surprise. What had occurred to Jane, to her way of looking at colors, that she mixed all these shades?

"You like?" she asked, pulling off her purple jacket, and tossing it in a chair the color of jade.

"I love. Not that it wasn't lovely before, but now it's smashing. Why the color change? Amy said you like subtle around you; last time it was all hushed, and now it's screaming!"

"Oh, Martin, it's not screaming. Don't use that word screaming. I didn't use red, did I? Now red would have been screaming." She headed for the kitchen. "Come on, let's have a drink."

"Can I take my shoes off? I want to feel this stuff with my bare feet."

She giggled. "Yeah, strip naked and roll on it if you want."

Martin slipped out of his mocs and socks, reached for his pullover, and she burst out laughing. "Martin Schoenfield, stop right there. You're terrible, just terrible."

He followed her into the clean bright kitchen, and before he saw her he heard her.

"Martin!" It was Amy, standing in front of her husband, his name slipping Martin's mind. Seated on a stool like the queen she was, all Black and African with her hair in a maze of beads and braids, was his Claire. And big Luther was right beside her, sitting not quite as easily on a stool he felt perched on, his great shoulders covered in a white shirt and wearing a vest, he was. Everyone got a warm hug; they stood in a circle and wrapped themselves around him, touching each other or

Martin. They were all equally at one in that circle of love for their Martin. He stood in his bare feet and wanted to dance with happiness, but a fox trotter he wasn't, nor a jitter bugger or waltzer. They were all talking at once, Luther holding the back of Martin's neck as they chatted. Looking into his face made Martin want to crawl into his arms and rest there, suck up some strength for the path ahead. He wanted so badly to thank him for helping with Crissy's baby, wanted him to know that maybe without all of them, things might have been different. They all had made him what he was. He was part of them.

Cheese was served, and corks were popped, Martin serving as the maid in his bare feet. He heard he had long toes, heard he had the whitest feet they'd ever seen, heard so much about his feet that he kept them bare, just as a challenge to new comments. They were drinking, nibbling, and laughing when Martin saw Jane look up. A woman was standing in the doorway to the kitchen, younger than Jane, short curly blond hair and nice freckles across her nose. She smiled at the gathering.

"I go to work and you have a party!" She came in and kissed Jane on the cheek, started shaking hands all around, never missed a beat. Got an extra glass, and helped herself to some champagne. Martin had held her hand just one moment, heard her say "Diane" and he liked her, liked her a lot. Jane was lucky to have this woman as a friend. What else there was, he didn't care. He was never one to get involved in other folks' business. He sidled over to Amy and her husband, now moved to the living room couch, shook the man's hand again and crouched down on the floor in front of them.

"Amy, I'm so happy for you. So glad you're fine. Anything you want to confess to me?"

"Oh, Martin, big mouth told you, didn't she? I hate her. Well, it's going to be a girl, and we're going to call her Katherine, Ned's mother's name is Katherine. Are you disappointed that I'm not calling her Amelia?"

"Hardly. Katherine's a beautiful name, but let me pick the middle one. Will you let me do that? How do you like Nedilia?" They watched his face, lower then theirs, and they smiled.

"I like it, don't you like it? Sounds like a flower. And original! Claire! Come here, Martin's given our baby her middle name." Claire poked her braided head around the archway.

"Nedilia. What do you think?"

"I think it sounds kind of Black," she quipped, and she went back to help set the table for supper. Martin rolled on the floor then, got his earlier desire fulfilled without stripping naked. He rolled on the rug and laughed so hard Luther came in from checking the furnace filter to stand over him.

"You got a problem, boy?" The same thing he'd said from the mirror at Crissy's.

"I don't have any problems, Luther. I'm just happy, that's all. Can't a man be happy?"

"Don't get drunk on me, son. I need a checker game out of you, so straighten up." Martin did straighten up, sat like an Indian monk with his legs crossed. Sat mute with his arms across his chest for a good two minutes. He would have kept it up longer, but the bell sounded and two men were let in by Luther, and Martin got to his feet and went into the kitchen. They followed him, setting down assorted Styrofoam containers and a white cardboard service box. Jane bustled around with Claire by her side, Diane handling the opening and oohing and aahing over the roast beef, sliced honey-soaked ham, minced salad with green olives, hunks of fresh cheese, a basket of frosted grapes. Claire winked at him when she saw the grapes. The memories, oh, the flooding memories. French bread, wheat bread with oatmeal crusted on top, croissants and scones, and blueberry jam. A feast they had.

"Told you I was good in the kitchen," Jane whispered, nudging his ribs. Over dinner, Martin gave them a brief rundown on his assignment, gave them some background as they chewed the beautiful food, let them see his face get heated up when he told them about Beech and the babies he'd helped with. They listened and nodded, Claire and Luther rapt over his words.

"Why didn't that Settlement go light?" asked Claire.

"I may find out. And if I don't, it doesn't matter. Seems most folks down there want to be the color God gave them. Maybe that's what the lesson is all about." He forked in more salad, smeared blueberry jam on his scone, and took a big bite.

"So where in Pond Ridge is your hospital gonna set?" asked Luther, wiping his mouth and pushing himself back from the table.

"Beats me, but it'll find a place. By Wednesday, there'll be a place for this clinic. You mark my words."

❧

He spent the night on the Hauk's couch, driving with two of his favorite people to the little apartment off Newcastle. "Not as nice as we had it, but we got more black friends here, and that makes it better for us." Sad for having to say that, sad that the whites didn't know what they were missing.

Before they turned in for the night, Claire tossed him the argyle shawl. "Stay warm, son. And sleep as late as you can. Luther'll get you up in time for your flight. Eight, right? We got Aunt Martha to wake us." Only the Hauks would give a clock a name.

Sleep did come easily. The smile on his face stayed with him all night, for it was still in place when Luther nudged him and said, "Seven bells. Up and at 'em. We got some traffic to fight."

Luther won the fight, ducking in and out of work-directed commuters from the Bronx. He dropped Martin at the passenger leaving lane, shook his hand in his big one, holding Martin's a bit longer than usual. "You say you might be needing an HVAC man at that hospital? You say they gonna run air through that building? You say that?"

"Most likely, Luther, building's gonna be modern, even if it is Missouri and parts of it are rustic. Why? You thinking of coming west, old man?" He slid out of the door, pulling his bag up to his shoulder.

"I'll give it some thinkin'," Luther said, reaching over and shutting the door. Martin watched him pull out and speed off in the old van. Martin raced for the flight, barely slipped into the last seat available on the plane. He buckled up and sat back to run the last day before his eyes. A great day. One of the best in his life. How he wished Dwayne could have been there. The only really obvious missing piece. Amelia and Micah were ready to move on to God's next plan for them; he knew that in his heart. Good lives. Fairly long lives. Some die younger than they had.

He got a taxi to take him to the Osaka bungalow. The taxi driver whistled when he saw the front deck. "Neat, now that's neat," he uttered, and got out with Martin to walk the deck and watch the fish gliding through the pools. "Ain't it pretty, Mister? Ain't they beautiful? Look, that's a black swallower, that's a salt water fish. And there's a sculpin. Man, these are good pools, makes you want to stop fishing for food, and just grow 'em to enjoy 'em."

Martin paid the man, and the driver stuffed the tip in his pocket and didn't say thanks or have a good day. Before he left, Martin said he wouldn't be long, would the man mind waiting, off the meter, and run him back to the airport. The man was still standing on the deck when Han Osaka opened the front door.

"Good morning," Martin called. "I'm here to see Mr. Ulmer about the plans." Han nodded, disbelieving at first that the funny man on the phone actually had come. He had told Brad to ease back on his drawing and drafting, ease back on listing material that would never get used. He liked to see Brad working, he knew he had great ideas, but he didn't want his partner to be crushed, didn't want to see the look of disappointment and longing.

"Tea?" asked Han as they passed through the tidy kitchen.

"Later," answered Martin. Han nodded, picked up his cup, and led the way down the basement steps. Brad looked up from his work, saw the handsome dark-haired man with green eyes, and his heart almost stopped. The man had come. He actually had come. Oh, great God, thank you. Thank you for this. Not time wasted, no, not at all. Time well spent. He was up on the roof with the building, laying out the heavy timbers, and suggesting slate if the budget allowed. Why not? Until that moment it had only been a dream. It wasn't his budget, anyway. He had let his dreams flow into that structure.

They shook hands, and Martin sat by Brad's side, heard him talking about wood and plaster, headers and tie ins. He heard all the words but understood few of them.

"Could I see what it might look like?" asked Martin.

Brad flipped the screens, zeroed in and tapped a key. The screen came onto the most wonderful building Martin had ever imagined. So quickly his mind had pictured it, then lost its image, but now, in front of that Macintosh, he saw his dream come to life under Brad's eye and hand. Some of Frank Lloyd Wright's work had been blended in, the clear shape seemed to blend in with the trees and shrubs Brad had drawn in.

"Well, what do you think?" Brad breathed. "Fast, I admit, I've done this fast, but it still looks good, feels right to me. What do you say, Dr. Schoenfield? Can I keep going?"

"Looks like you're finished, Brad," and the doctor got up. Brad's heart slumped in his chest. Finished, and only twenty-seven. Finished, the man said. Fucking lot he knows. He can't do more than bilk patients on Social Security. I'll show him who's finished. He rose as the doctor did, was all set to fire a parting remark he hadn't thought of yet, when the man opened his briefcase, and handed him an envelope.

"For your time, Brad, for your time. Thank you. We'll be in touch." He fished in his case for a business card, tossed it on the keyboard. Disrespect, Brad flared. Don't you dare touch my keyboard. Touch my Mac. Martin touched his forehead with his fingers in his parting salute.

Yeah, right, Brad said to himself, sat back down and fingered the envelope. The guy gives him a token for his work, hours he'd spent on this, and it was good.  Good as anyone else could get it in twelve hours on a Mac.  He ripped the envelope open as Han came back down from letting Martin out.  He pulled out the check and stared at it.  It wasn't for the two hundred dollars he had expected to see.  No, it was for half the finished job, half the job!  He was hired!  He threw the check in the air and ran to hug Han, spin Han around.

"My tea, my tea!" warned Han.  He set his cup down, pushed Brad back as he was dancing and yelling.  He pulled the check from under a prancing foot, and it wasn't a moment before he was whooping and yelling just the same.

એ

It wasn't all whooping and yelling in frenzied joy back on Second Street in Newark that morning.  Tracy had driven right to the warehouse, pad and pencils in hand, her laptop comfortably situated on the passenger seat.  Survey, Dr. Schoenfield had left instructions.  What do we have?  Won't take a minute, she reflected, then back to the main office.  Set up a place in a new location.  Where that was, she wasn't sure.  She hadn't stopped to read the rest of the E-mailed message to her, only printed it out and stuck it in her purse.

She locked her BMW and clicked up the walk in her Donna Karan light blue suit, her Liz Claiborne blouse, neatly made imported Italian shoes.  Perfect nylons for a Liaison Representative.  She unlocked the door with the key left with Milda at her old cubicle.  That fat witch will wish she'd never sunk her big butt in my rolling chair.  She'd get her comeuppence.  Tracy had accepted the key from Milda's plump hand, had noticed the 'in' basket was empty, a vase of flowers sitting on the counter.  "Good luck," Milda had called out as Tracy spun on her heels without a word back.

She fumbled for the light switch, and the gloom of the small windowed warehouse bore in on her.  Fifteen minutes, tops, she figured.  Run through it.  She eyed the tangle of pushed back and upside down tables and chairs, all covered in a layer of dust.  She sneezed, wiped her nose with a Kleenex from her purse.  There was the neatly folded E-mail she hadn't read.  May as well do it now, she reflected, wiping her nose again.  Nasty place.  Fifteen minutes, tops.  She brought the message closer to her blue shadowed eyes, read a few moments, and then gasped.  No way, she stormed, no way this will happen.  But she did follow the line of the message, did take the elevator to the second floor, and turned on the brilliant fluorescents. The room was a flood of brilliance, outlining every piece of discarded and worn office furniture churned over by Pearson Pharmaceuticals in fifty years of being in business. Stuff dragged from the last plant location. Her worst fears were affirmed when she opened the first doorway off to her right, glanced in at the old bathroom with a pull-chain toilet. Very old. This must have been the first building on this site; too sturdy to tear down, and too outmoded to use for offices or labs, it had been resurrected, and called by the employees in blue uniforms, "The Grave." She sniffed her nose and shut the door. Stunk, it did. Very nearly stunk of standing toilet water.

She read on in the E-mail, let her eyes run over the words, "and you'll find a very adequate and nice work station behind the next door. Hated to see you shuffling back and forth between the main and the worksite. I thought it more prudent to put you close to your mission. I hope you find the office to your liking. Special effort was put into it."

She smiled a twisted smile, and moved to open the door mentioned in the E-mail. The handle was grimy, old, and corroded. It almost broke loose as she twisted it. Inside, the light was good, the desk in the middle clean and smart, a phone sat on one corner, a typewriter in the middle. That looked adequate, she thought, but the rest of the room, the crowded-back unswept rest of the room made her cringe. Packing boxes of old correspondence were stacked to the ceiling. Old chairs were set against them to keep them from tumbling down. An ancient non-working icebox flashed its yellowed front at her. This is a mistake, she realized, a cruel mean-spirited joke. She couldn't work here under these conditions. The name plate on a highly polished piece of walnut stared at her. She bent to read it: Liaison Representative. She sent it spinning off the desk, and ran through the hall, stumbled in blind tears on the elevator's lip, sent herself down, down to first.

# Chapter Forty-Four

*Some they do and some they don't*
*And some you just can't tell.*
*Some they will and some they won't*
*With some it's just as well*

*Super Tramp    "Goodbye Stranger"*

Aunty Franklin sat and rocked Martin Beech Milborne to sleep.

"Na na na," she heard Crissy say. You be spoilin' him, Aunty, her smiling proud face spoke.

"Lans, thas what they fer, fer spoilin'. If rockin' gonna ruin 'im, then we'd all be ruint, I from a rockin' fambly. Rockin' soothes his tummy, it does."

A horn tooted outside the Milborne bungalow, and Crissy ran to the window to pull back the curtain. The day was cold and gray, winds blowing in from the fields, but she felt that toot.

"Na na neigh!" she cried, running to open the door.

"How you know tha toot? One toots the same as anudder." She wrapped the boy tighter against the cold that might creep in once the door was opened. How she know that toot? Deaf, she was. Deaf but smart.

Dr. Schoenfield came running up the steps, pulled off his cap and rubbed his hands together. "Damn, ah-h-h, darn, it's cold. We're gonna get snow, aren't we? Aren't we, Crissy?" Crissy shut the door, missed his lips, only gloried in him coming to visit her. She loved this man, almost as much as her Daniel, she loved him. He turned and she pulled his jacket off his back, fairly dragged him to Aunty's side. She pointed at her baby, and Martin got down on his knees to look again at him. He was perfect, dark tight hair and pursed lips, sleeping in a filled-out chubbiness Martin could only wonder at. A miracle, this baby. His miracle come true.

He rose and faced Crissy. "He's beautiful, Crissy, just beautiful. And he's so healthy!" She knew that, she only pulled up her shirt and showed him her full breast. Martin paused, watching her happy face, baring her chest to him like a warrior. Her doctor. Her reason for being alive. She would show him anything.

"Good, good, I'm so happy for you," he said, rounding the words and watching her eyes. The baby stirred and whimpered, Aunty gave him up to the mama, and she spread her empty hands in her lap.

Crissy sat on the couch, held the boy on her breast, and Martin sat down by Aunty's rocker.

"Aunty, I got a problem, and maybe you can help."

"Will if'n I can. Might old to be your lady if that be the problem, but I giv' it a go." She laughed and rocked at Martin's blush.

"Wish it were that simple, just you and me running off, but Mr. Franklin would have me caught and skinned by sundown if I nabbed you."

"Theopolis? He cain't catch us, if'n we ran real fas' an' hid in a wood pile."

Martin laughed and picked up her wrinkled hand. He kissed it, and she felt a flush run clear through her. She tingled in her tummy, she did, with that kiss of his.

"Aunty, I'm moving myself to Pond Ridge, want to start a clinic to help people, people like Crissy," and he nodded toward her and the baby. "Do you think you can help me?"

"Wha kinna hep you be needn?" she asked, bending forward and resting her hand on his shoulder. He kissed that hand again and she was his. He felt it in the warmth of her hand on him.

"I need a corner of Settlement to build my hospital on, just a smidge you'll never miss. The part by the front gate, that's all rock, Aunty, nothing will ever grow there. Ask Theopolis. He'll tell you. No top soil. Nothing. I have this plan, and a man you'll like drew up some pictures of it, and it'll fit right in, you won't even see it until you're in it."

He sprang to his feet, started pacing in front of her, wearing his faded pullover and jeans, feet in boots. He looked down on her, and she faced him square up with her eyes.

"Take part of Settlemen'? You cain't be thinkin' right, Doctor Shone. No white's gonna own any of Settlemen'. This be our lan, you know this be our lan, no way, uh uh. You be askin' the wron' whore to make tha move. You be kissin' on the wron' woman." She turned her head and rocked hard, setting her feet against the rug and shoving hard. "Uh, uh, no way. Theopolis niver let you near dis place if'n he knowed what you plannin'. Take our lan, woud you? Thas what this kissin' 'bout? Take our lan?"

"Only a corner you'll never miss, Aunty, but that corner'll fill up this place with well people, people with no sickness medicine can't heal. Girls like Crissy won't ever have to go through what she did with us so close by. And we won't be hammering you, Aunty. We'll stay to our side. Won't walk the fields or chum with the people on their own land. No. That won't happen," but he wished, silently, that it might.

"I hearred 'bout 'nuth of this crap," she spat, and got up from the rocker. She pulled on her shawl, wrapping it around her head and shoulders. "Nigh', Crissy," she leaned into her face.

"Nigh," Crissy answered, pulling the woman down for a kiss. Aunty kissed the baby, too, let herself out on the porch, snugging the door tight behind her. Martin slumped into the rocker, rocked and thought, and rocked and thought. His plan had not met the ears he had prayed would help him.

Aunty stumbled down the steps, caught her breath, and struck off for home. That man! The very beef of him, comin' onto her, an her married an all. A swine he was, and thas no laughin'. Take part of Settle, run it over with white folks, thas what that Jew boy 'bout. Not true to hisself, not true to us. Smoky green eyes. Snaky tongue of a kiss. Almos' pulled her in, he had, wit tha smile an' tha nice smell on his white body. She trudged up the hill, the shawl pulled tight in her twisted hands. Cold. It be gettin' cold. Theopolis be home by now, waitin' on supper. All done, all tidied away for the bring out. That Theopolis. He be so high on tha man, spoutin' how tha man be a Jesus cum back. Tha man be a thief, furs stealin' Crissy's baby sac, den comin' to rape the lan. Shos what you know 'bout folks, slipin' in an' stealin' wha' ain' theirs.

She slipped a little in the mud as she hurried along, felt the ground meet her once when she tumbled down. Hurt misself, she cried, but the hurt didn't come from the tumble. The hurt came from inside, and Aunty knelt in the path between the bungalows and the Corothers house and prayed. Tears streamed down her creased cheeks. Help me, God, she said, lift this cloud.

What I doin' this far? I dun past my own house. Let it slip by me in my thoughts of this. She got back up and fairly stumbled down the hill, entering the house, and sending the cold blasting across the room.

"Shut the door, Mother, you be lettin' in old Jack Frost." Theopolis was sitting in the front room, reading the paper, and listening to the radio. He had his pipe by his side, and he lingered over it as he lifted, puffed, then laid it back to rest. It never went out.

She set up her shawl on the post, brushed her hands through her finely-wired hair, and went to use the toilet and wash her hands. She fussed over dinner, setting out the best china and silver, and Theopolis eyed her from over the paper.

"Where the problim be, woman?"

"Ain' no problim of yorn, ain' no problim you kin handle. I handle this one. You be comin' in an' eatin' now."

They ate in silence, and Theopolis lit up his pipe, waited for the cup of coffee she always brought, but she seemed out of sorts tonight, so he fetched it himself. She stood by the kitchen window and stared out into the night.

"I not be lickin' this cream off'n the spoon tonigh'. I be jes layin' it on your white." She turned from the window and watched him, her lovely man, ready to lay down that mark on her linen.

"You doan dare."

"I dare, lessen you tell me what up wit you. Why the dada eyes, the funny look-see? You got someone else you be wantin'? Is tha what this 'bout? I gettin' too old for you, is tha what those tear marks 'bout?"

She laughed at the thought, tossed her dishrag into the sink, and came back to the table. "Is 'bout Settlemen'. Is 'bout our lan. The doctor wans me to giv 'im the rocky corner, to build a doctor place. Whites be comin' in, I jes know they be whites, crawlin' all ovah us, ruinin' our place wit they trash an' they tin homes on wheels. Swell ovah us an' crowd us out. I fear tha happn to us, Theopolis, fear tha a whole lot. Thas my fear, thas the tear marks you see. I bin cryin' ovah this, now you knowed 'bout it, too."

Theopolis leaned for his pipe, brought it back to his mouth. He stirred his coffee, moving the sweet cream through the mocha brew. He sat a long time without speaking, rubbed his chin, and scratched his head.

"Tonigh' less pray on it, Mother, less just pray on it. Mornin' bring the ansa. Afta the dark passes. Mornin' always bring new hope."

They shut off the radio and the lights early that night. His hand on her side calmed her. Blessed Lord, show me the way. Please, God, show this blind lady some light. She glided into a troubled sleep and in the dream that ran before her frightened eyes, there were no whites running over Settlement. She saw Crissy running, running with the baby, and the baby had a pork chop bone stuck in his throat. Now how that be, she wondered in the dream, but she could only watch the girl running, running toward the rocky corner of Settlement. She screamed for help, but no one heard her. They told her it would be so snuggled and hidden that they wouldn't be able to find it, but it wasn't there at all. It just wasn't there.

Aunty Franklin jerked awake. Theopolis slept on by her side, but she got up and walked through the house, paced through the house. Felt the house wasn't so important anymore. Thought the house might just blow away, but they'd get another. But they only had one Crissy, the dream warned, and one Martin Beech Milborne.

"I takin' care of it," she said to Theopolis as he paused for his kiss the next morning. "I lissen up real good las nigh', an' I got the true messg, real clear it come, an' you doan be standin' in my way."

"Niver," he said, pulling on his hat and grabbing his walking cane. "Niver stood in no wimmens way an' thas a fact. Do your thin', mother, do your thin'. I be by you."

*. . . against your skin so brown . . .*
*And I want to sleep in the desert tonight*
*I'm already standin' on the ground.*
*I found out a long time ago*
*What a woman can do to your soul.*
*I got a peaceful, easy feelin'*
*I know you won't let me down.*

*The Eagles "Peaceful Easy Feeling"*

Aunty Franklin got a ride into town on the school bus, the kids rowdy and excited to have Theopolis' wife on board. They were moving around and acting unruly, so she stood and tol them all to hush or she'd crac' 'em and they listened. No one wanted Aunty mad at them.

"A lady to see you," Joan spoke through his door, "and she looks like she means business." He tumbled out of bed, thinking for a flash that the good-looking gal at the bank, that Paulette, may have stopped by. He ran into the shower, scrubbed down, and dressed quickly in his jeans, pullover, and almost new boots.

He ran down the stairs a few minutes later, slowed his step as if to appear casual, and saw Aunty Franklin sitting on a stool by the kitchen island. Joan and Tess were carrying breakfast out to customers, but they slipped Aunty a cappuccino, which she was sipping with some pleasure when he slipped in.

"You be talkin' 'bout somethin' I doan know much 'bout, Doctor Shone. You be talkin' an' kissin' an' I dun missd the words for the feelins I got. I missd the big pitccha 'til God spoke out to me. Now you let me get on." She had seen Martin wanting to hold her, let her know that she had a right to refuse him, had every right in the world. He knew he had tried to win her over, swoon her a bit, but his cause was for their own good, he knew it in his heart. They needed him, they just didn't know how much.

"We all owns Settle, we owns it, 'cept for the note at the bank, an' we makin' that, Stone's gif' to us, but a small pay for all we got outta that deal. I be a owna, too, we be seventy-eight strong, so I be ownin' one-seven-eight of that place. We got 1,080 acres, an' I decide this mornin', jes up an' decide tha the part thas mine is the corna by the gate. You know tha corna?"

Martin nodded his head, the rocky corner, the one she'd said no to. He knew that corner, had seen it in his sleep, the big dozers aiming for that corner that wouldn't be his, the questions and looks, the remembrance of the bad water deal. Now why weren't they still asking about the water? Because Settlement had stayed black? Not a word from Pearson about the water. But Pearson didn't know the lay of the land. Didn't know the origin of the water here. Didn't know it came from two different sources. Settlement, with its clear spring fed ponds. Pond Ridge, dragging into the twentieth century with its hundred year old well. But Martin hadn't told Pearson where it would be, hadn't known for sure where the clinic would fit in. It has to go there; come on, Aunty, give a little.

"I know that corner," he answered, wishing that corner was his.

"Well, tha corna be yorn." She said it so simply and matter of fact that Martin sprang to kiss her hands and her cheeks and her lips. Kisses rained over her, and Joan, carrying in dirty coffee cups, backed out and told Tess to just wait a moment.

"What's going on?" Tess whispered, holding her tray, and trying to peer into the kitchen.

"Martin's sprung a leak and is kissing old Mrs. Franklin. Oh, wait 'til Theopolis hears about this! We gotta find him a girl closer to his own age, Tess. This is too funny to be real!" They stayed by the door, helped a few latecomers to the crumbs and heated up coffee, but they stayed their ground outside the kitchen. If Martin wanted to kiss a lady twice his age and black to boot, that was not their business. But they paced and wiped up the tables, stood and waited until they saw Mrs. Franklin come by the front window and cross to the post office. They saw her look both ways, and nice as you please, went on over and took a big mouthful off the public fountain. She wiped her mouth with enormous satisfaction, and went on up to the grocery store where they saw a sulky pull in, and Daniel helped Mrs. Franklin in, and snapped the horse to attention with a whistle. They went on out the front way, and never looked back.

Tess and Joan entered the kitchen with their trays, nonchalant as all get out, setting the trays down and passing by Martin sitting in a dreamy state. He was perched on the stool by the island, stirring the unfinished cappuccino in Aunty's cup, and he looked up as they kept brushing around him, trying to get his attention, dying to know what was going on. He picked up the cup and started to leave and go up the back way.

"Martin," Joan spoke, afraid he was just going to leave them hanging.

"I love that woman," he said, and he ran up the stairs away from them. They stared at each other, wondering what to do next, besides the dishes and dusting. Thanksgiving coming, they babbled, let's talk about turkey. Oh, Christmas is coming, where should we put the tree? They babbled and avoided the real topic, the topic that coursed through their brains. It's not possible, they both thought.

"It's not possible," they both mouthed to each other at the same moment.

They kept a tight lip on it, never spoke about Mrs. Franklin again. If she was Martin's fancy for the cold nights ahead, well, they weren't going to make no judgments.

"What do you think she looks like naked?" Joan asked Tess while they were snuggled together in one bed, enjoying their late night wine.

"Joan! I'm shocked at you, speaking about such things. I'm really shocked! What's a body to do with it if the feelings are there? If Martin loves Aunty Franklin, then that's his choice, and hers, too, if she's still alert enough to make the choice." They rolled then, in laughter, went off the bed on either side, and giggled like children. Weak and exhausted from laughing, they turned to their own beds, Joan slipping the latch and saying good night. She shushed down the hall in her fuzzy slippers, and only put her ear against Martin's door for a moment to hear the sound of his laptop pounding away. Writing love verses, I'll bet, sighed Joan. Poor Martin. The ways of the heart are not for the wise. Children and fools, only children and fools fall in love.

❧

Milda back in Newark was a true champ. When they found that Tracy had left them, left them very suddenly and with a week of vacation coming, plucky Milda picked up the reins along with the bent Liaison Representative's plaque, set it back on the desk in the Second Street warehouse, came in on Tuesdays and Thursdays with her jeans on and a cleaning bucket. Milda split her time between the warehouse and the slinky clean recep desk. She got all the work out in three days, anyway, was bored by the hush-hush slowness. She liked the warehouse, asked Mr. Pearson if she could buy an old lamp with a Victorian shade, tassels and all.

"My gift to you, my dear." Pearson was no fool; he knew a good worker when he saw one. He liked Milda and her ways. "Keep me posted," he'd call out as he left for business lunches. He was never

~ 333 ~

there to read her lists of usable items, cleaned and waiting for a new home. Never there. Always on the go. He's big, and I'm just a spoke in the wheel, but she kept the wheel going, sending letters to Dr. Schoenfield in Pond Ridge, asking him when they'd be ready for the really neat stuff she'd dug up.

ॐ

Aunty Franklin had some talking to do, to let the old man know that the Settlement was going to be short about fourteen acres, come tax time.

"Now, run this by me one mo time, Mother. Real slow. You say you givin' yo share of Settlemen' to the whites? You say you givin' it to the whites? Whoa, whoa, we doan be givin', we be gettin'. We be gettin', we give long nuff, we give til no givin' left. Stone be givin' but Stone be takin', too. An' he one a us, lease he was. Let them buy, Mother, let them buy, that be the way."

"How much I ask?" Aunty asked him, touching his neck, and snuggling a kiss on his ear.

"'Bout thirteen hunnerd an acre seem square wit me. Tha seem fair to you?"

"Tha seem fair to me. But they wantin' the gate posts, too. I dint figur' on sellin' the gate posts. Seems they aught pay for them, too, if'n we sellin'."

"Make it a round twenty, woman. Tha 'bout cover it." He liked it when she touched his ear with her mouth. Nice feelin' ran down his good leg. Thas a powerful feelin'.

"Now I be out my share of lan', what I gonna do?" She rubbed his hair with her fingers.

"You move on ovah to my lan', missy, come on into my shack." Theopolis pulled her into his lap.

"But a big man like you, he mus have a missus, what she say, when you brin' me home for kissin'?" She cuddled against Theo's chest.

"I be the man in my house," he stated, getting to his feet, cradling Aunty against his chest. "Tha woman doan like you, my new gal, tha woman go!"

ॐ

Martin always expected to have to pay for the land. Being she "goin'" to give it to him, he anteed the price, told Pearson flat-out they wouldn't budge for less than fifty thousand.

"Fifty thousand!" blurted the chief. "For rock land? What are those niggers trying to pull? That's rock hard crap growing shit land they got, tell him five and no more." He wondered at the unfairness of it all: trying to help those poor folks, bring in needed medical care, set up a nice place for some of them to find jobs and get off welfare, and what did he get for his trouble? A knife in the ribs. The grant had dwindled down too fast for him, too fast to get much interest. Schoenfield moved a little too fast for him. Slow that boy down, he mused. How to slow that boy down. That Porsche Frances had wanted and the bracelet of diamonds to go with her new mink had set him back. Time to pause, good doctor, and get a better handle on your spending.

"I've wheedled them down to fifty, chief, and Mackey says it's about the best we're gonna do. He knows the head man of the tribe, old Theopolis, knew him back when they thought the water was bad. But this water is so good, chief, I never tested such water. I been drinking it every day, and my sex life . . . Oh, I'm sorry, I shouldn't have said that, really sorry, chief, way out of line. But I think the water here is the source of my renewed . . . shall we say, vigor?"

Pearson leaned onto his desk at hearing Martin's ambling words. Renewed vigor? The damn water?

"And if I'm correct, we could have a new line out in the Spring: Erectus Bubbling Bottled Water. Know just the man who can peddle it for us. Donn Forest. We got a gold shaft we're plumbing, chief. A real shaft."

Pearson nodded yes before he spoke into the receiver. "Sounds like you're onto something, Schoenfield. Keep me posted. Call Milda about drawing up the check. And keep track for me, if you don't mind, being a scientist and all, about your renewed vigor. Graph it for me and send it over. I'll speak to the board as soon as I hear your . . . ah, stats."

Got it! Got it for them! God, he was glad he was crafty, glad he was the craftiest man ever born. Was that his Jewishness running the deal? Was this all about being a Hymie Goldstein? No, it has to be deeper than faith, deeper than religion. Deeper than not eating honey-soaked ham. What was it, then, that drove him to these tales that worked?

"I am man, hear me roar," he sang out in the shower. Tess, passing his door, pressed her ear to catch the words he was singing loudly. He's got it wrong, she wanted to say. God save poor Mrs.

Franklin. She didn't know what she'd gotten going here. Tweak a lamb's tail and you get a lion. Poor, poor, frail Mrs. Franklin. She thought of passing on her secret to the only man she knew would understand: Rev. Sam Walters, but he was so busy with his grown congregation, taking in the mission on Front Street as part of his work, feeding the ill and aged his wife's tasty soup, for as bad a housekeeper as she was, nobody could touch Missus Walters' soup.

# Chapter Forty-Six

*Farewell to arms*
*Rest in peace*
*May the reign of freedom be released*
*We can't just walk away*
*We're all sharing this earth*
                    *at the end of the day.*

*E-L-P "Farewell to Arms"*

The dozers and cats and dumps chugged through Pond Ridge just as Paulette Pardine was going over to Days End for lunch. She hadn't been there in a while, trying to save her money for the course she planned to start. She wasn't sure what she'd be taking through the mail, but it sure had to be better than sitting at home nights watching Grady laugh at TV and her mom grading papers. Her grandma was about her only source of fun, and the stories she'd tell, about being barefoot and walking to school fourteen miles, it was always fourteen miles, cracked Paulette up.

"Now, gran, it couldn't have been fourteen miles, and you but five. Tell me you're joking."

"You callin' me a liar, 'cuz if you is, I stop talkin' wit chu at all. We Blacks had a row to hoe, an' no shoes, an' no mules neither, the men pulld dem rakes, doan you be tellin' me what chu doan know nuttin 'bout. You wit your bleached skin. How you gonna 'splain dat skin to Gawd Ahmighty on Judgment Day, huh? How you gonna 'splain what you gif away?"

"Gran, we were having fun, don't let's talk about that."

"Sick 'bout it, ain' ya? Sick 'bout whacha los. Well, thas a good thin', Daisy, thas a good thin'. Be sick 'bout it. You young. You got to carry tha bleached out hiny of yorn many mo days. My black backside goin' in the grave wit me. Thas the powerful truf of it. My butt is jes like Gawd Ahmighty made it, no bleachin' dun here. No ma'am. Doan belief in it, doan wan it, no way."

Paulette dressed that morning in slacks and a white turtleneck sweater from a catalogue. She didn't need to really get dressed up for the bank, but she always looked nice, smelled good, kept her bobbed hair clean. Hard for her with that hair, all kinky and living like it had a mind of its own. Powerful hair, Granny called it, doan be knockin' your hair. Why, when I be a girl . . .

So when she decided on lunch and walked down the sidewalk

to Days End, she never meant to see anyone special, never meant to step aside for the man in jeans, wearing boots and a parka against the wind. She didn't know why she did it, but when she saw Dr. Schoenfield, the man she'd cashed checks for, she didn't want to be in his way. She nodded and stepped into the street as he passed, smiling and nodding she did, and came back up after he passed.

He came after her at that moment, grabbed her arm, and turned her to face him. She was cold in the wind (her coat wasn't even buttoned over her sweater), it was a short walk. Her face must have looked startled at his holding onto her. He looked angry, confused, hurt.

"Why'd you do that?" he asked, his green eyes flashing anger.

"Do what? What did I do?" she asked, pulling her arm out of his gloved grip.

"Get off the walk like that."

"I thought I might be in your way. The walks are kinda narrow with the snow shoveled on the sides. I just thought I'd be the one to step aside." She held her hands against her cold ears.

"If it was too narrow, I'd have been the one to step aside. Don't you ever step aside again!" He turned and went fiercely on his walk, crunching his boots down on the packed snow.

Well, I never, thought Paulette, letting herself into the warmth and closeness of Days End. What a goose, acting like that. A doctor and a moron. Just what this town needs. Grabbing women on the street for being polite. No manners. A boor. Bad temper.

He had seemed so nice at the bank, so much a gentleman, asking her about how she felt physically after her skin got lighter. They all asked that, all her newly-darker white co-workers. How do you feel, Paulette? Isn't it nice? It's harder on us, they pleaded. It's real hard on us, but you got it good. You got lucky, girlfriend.

She ordered a bacon-lettuce-tomato on wheat toast, no mayo, and sat stirring her hot tea. Tess sat for a minute, told her she looked beautiful in that white sweater, and Joan asked her to come by Sunday, help them put up the tree.

"Martin's bringing a huge one, we picked it out Friday. We're going to decorate the tree for Thanksgiving in gold and brown, with gingerbread turkey cookies, and give 'em out. Then we can keep it watered and it's humid enough in here to have it stay fresh for Christmas, too. It's a beautiful tree, only one side has a big flat space, but we can turn that side to the corner. Nobody ever has to see it. Settlement said we can come in and cut it. Wasn't that nice of them with all they got going on? The hospital is going in, you heard that, didn't you, Paulette? Dr. Schoenfield is going to be with us forever, we hope."

"Lessen his lover has to get him out of town," shot in Tess, laughing on her way back to the kitchen. She knew the whole story now, but they still liked to laugh about it.

So he has a girlfriend, so why would I care anyway, fussed Paulette. But the hospital was for sure coming in, and it might just be a break for her. The bank was dead end. Twyla Tharp could have toe danced on the counter, and the president wouldn't have noticed. Banking is not my field, she sighed, biting into the sandwich. Maybe nursing might be.

She turned in her chair by the window when Martin's face peered in through the frost at her, watching her chew. She was taken aback at the man in the parka, peeking in on her. The nerve! The nerve of this man! Nervy enough to come right on in like he owned the place, hug the ladies, and hang his parka near the fireplace. He stopped and talked to several other diners, but came right back to stand by Paulette.

"May I sit here?" he asked.

"I'll be done in a minute," she mumbled with her mouth half full. She'd throw that sandwich in a bag and eat it back at the bank before she'd sit with him.

"I don't want you to hurry on my account," he said, sitting down and folding his hands on the table. His eyes were so green, with straight brows and curled up lashes. Skin on his cheeks looked pink from the weather beneath his tan. The black hair had grown into curls again, and he knew he had to get over to Margaret's Salon for a trim. "Please," and he reached over and touched her hand as she was laying her napkin down. "I may have been abrupt out there on the street, and I apologize for startling you, for that I'm sorry. But for telling you to stop what you were doing, never do it again: that's what I won't say I'm sorry for. A lot of things I'm sorry about, but that isn't one of them." He looked out the window. She watched him out of the side of her eyes as she grabbed her coat. Fresh snow had started to fall, and she was going to be late if she didn't hurry.

Tess stopped to clear, and Paulette felt in her coat pocket for the five-dollar bill she'd stuck there, but it was gone. She pulled the pocket lining out. Where did it fall? She looked under the table. Martin looked, too, sensing her embarrassment.

"Catch us later, Paulette. Some kid'll be happy to find that in the snow. An early present." She laughed as she wiped up, asked Martin if she could get him something, but he shook his head, watching Paulette go out the door and past the window through the flakes.

"Should have given her a scarf," Tess mumbled. When she

looked up again, not one minute later, Martin was zipping past the window, pulling his coat on, and he had a scarf in his hand.

The bank president saw the smiling Paulette come in the door. His eye ran up to the clock. Three minutes late. She'd hear about this, and right now, he decided. Uppity she is, especially now that she's lighter. Well, he'd darken her mood some. He hated tardy and moved forward to tell her, but coming in behind her was the new doctor in town, the Jewish doctor. A clinic in town. One small savings had been opened already, but the president knew that lots more money was tied up in New York and New Jersey banks. Maybe some of that can come back here if I play my cards right, he plotted. They might help him get back to his correct color, too, while they're at it. Very, very different reception he was getting at the golf course in Farmington.

Martin was shaking hands with Ms. Pardine. Now why that? She should stay in her place, serve Settlement like she was supposed to. He'd have to talk to her about that, about taking over for him when it came to important future depositors.

"Dr. Schoenfield, nice to see you again," beamed the president of Pond Ridge Bank. Florid, hair thinning, nattily dressed, smelling of a bit too much cologne, for men like the president didn't call it 'after shave' anymore.

"'Fraid I kept your Ms. Pardine late at lunch. Hope you don't skin her alive over it." Martin nudged the president, and the president nodded to Paulette to get back to work, he'd take over. Ms. Pardine at lunch with the doctor? Whose idea was that, he wondered.

"She's been pestering me, pestering me, every time I come in," started Martin, following the bank president back to his paneled office and closing the door himself. His voice was quietly confessional, like something besides money was involved. Oh, she wouldn't, she wouldn't, moaned the bank president internally. "I kept saying no, I'm happy with who I'm with, but she just kept it up. She's persistent, that one. That lady gets what she wants."

Sex, they'd had sex. Probably at lunch, up in his room at the Days End. The hussy, thought the president. The brazen hussy gets lighter and starts after white men. Always did like 'em anyway, if the rumors were true. Went road housing with 'em, reported the teller in the third cubicle.

"I'll speak to Ms. Pardine, doctor. Know that I'll handle this."

"No, that's just it. I want her handling me. I want her to be the only one handling me. I'm moving a money transfer tomorrow, for the construction escrow, and I want her to run that money for me, from here. I don't have the time or brain she has for this stuff. My bank in

New York could do it, but Ms. Pardine spoke so highly of you and the way you treat folks, well, I said, he's the kind of man I want to do business with."

He shook hands with the bank president, and winked at Paulette as he left through the gleaming glass and brass. Teller number three peered over the top of the separator.

"Got yourself a new white boy, Paulette?"

"Just a friend," Paulette responded. She went back to work, tallying up interest and counting out change, but for some reason, her hands felt lighter at their task, her heart felt joyous, and her mind was filled with the image of eyelashes on those green eyes.

# Chapter Forty-Seven

*Anytime you feel alone, just raise your hand,*
*Pick up the phone.*
*Tap in my number, there I'll be.*
*If one day your star don't shine,*
*I will give you some of mine*
*Cuz they could fall so easily.*

*E-L-P "Footprints in the Snow"*

The contractor and engineer were out on the site, holding the plans from Ulmer's first floor, shielded from the wind by a canvas lean-to. Later, when the cold cut in, they'd need two trailers for the men to use. His men weren't going to shit in no Porta Potties with their asses stuck to the seat. Not out in Missouri December, the contractor vowed.

The excavation part was over. Small units of explosives had stirred up the animals just one day while the men loosened the rock. The huge machine had rumbled in and set the rock up and aside in its huge teethed lift, like a ballerina that man handled the gears. They admired his work, stood like an audience at a field event. The hole left from removing the rock became the huge basement. They graded and leveled, put in the concrete bunker for the isotope room, setting red flags on rods at the corners to mark the place. Pipe was laid, electric lines sketched out, ironworkers laid out the steel rods for reinforcing the basement floor, and they prayed for a warm day to pour. Foundation men set up their forms. Now if only the weather would cooperate. It did.

The crew of masons came in, and the contractor knew with the weather coming in so fast, and so unpredictable in Missouri, that his best move was bringing in a second crew from St. Charles that was on a church. The church could wait, he figured. Hospitals took precedence. Heal the sick, the mission message ran, then you can heal the soul. Twelve masons. Working with a cement truck on duty all day, the hose and temperature keeping the sludge from settling as it tumbled in the huge drum, the contractor knew he couldn't run that way for the whole job. Too cold, too much cement ready too soon. The men would be hurrying to use it, and the work might get sloppy. The contractor knew a good design when he saw it, and the structural engineer approved of the change as well. They went back to the little electric cement mixers, putty, putty. Each mason had two helpers, to lift the stones and keep him fixed with just the right slump of cement. And to make sure the work was uniform, these masons being as big a group of prima donnas as the ironworkers were, the contractor shifted the masons around every day, and shifted the helpers the other way. No man worked with the same men throughout the job; no cement mix, never quite the same anyway, stayed in just one area. The engineer liked the method, felt it enhanced the building's structural integrity, named it "Patchwork," and that's how the clinic got its nickname.

"How's things going on Patchwork?" "Hear Patchwork's coming up to five feet." "I got a job running cement on Patchwork."

Theopolis didn't go near the place, stayed as far up the hill as he could. Aunty walked over every day and watched the men work, sometimes standing in the lean-to when the wind was strong. Thanksgiving was coming, and the wall was almost finished. It stood like a fort. Holes left in it for the ready-made sashes to slide into, then caulked around the uneven stone. No other way. They voted out covering the caulk with flashing or trim boards. Ulmer had a fit back in Newark when the word got back to him that they were considering covering even two inches of that rock face. He couldn't just say no. They'd want a reason. "No. Factor: future maintenance. The trim will fall apart in thirty years; the rock will last forever."

The old gate posts from early Settlement were sent to a refinisher, who, for the life of him and a paycheck to encourage him, found nothing wrong with the weathered wood just as it was. Walnut, he knew. Walnut will do that for you. The posts measured ten inches straight through, were uneven at knots, but smooth and silky to the feel. Just dull, they were. He air brushed them, loosened the dirt and tiny bits of moss, then ran three coats of urethane over them and set them to dry. The contractor cut the side lengthwise off each post, the mill told to run that sucking blade in at about three inches on each one. Each post now laid flat on the bed of the mill truck, its lost member laying on top for now.

Skilled carpenters came in next to set the posts, flat side against the studded-out front opening. The part they had cut off one post became the lintel; the other post's backside became the threshold. Because the top was convex and someone might trip, the engineer asked the architect to design an inlaid box to display the log and still let people walk over it safely. Brad designed the seven-foot long coffin for the slab, made it four inches high to cover the curve and twelve inches wide to cover the width. He suggested copper and brass fittings for the edges, designed the box of high impact scratch-proof urethane, which cost as much as the metals. He had so much fun designing that threshold that he forgot to bill them the hours. Han Osaka and Brad Ulmer had more work than they could finish. Their design for the clinic on Settlement, much to their surprise, won them New Architects of the Year Award. They had a nice banquet in Paterson at the Elks Lodge.

They had another hospital to design, and Brad let Han take over on this one. Wanted Han to get his part in, his also excellent ideas. Straighter lines, shifting walls on tracks, lights on tracks. Han liked everything on tracks. His designs were clean, efficient, and maintenance-free. The clinic he designed was a two-story black jewel. All outside was black. All inside was white. "In the lobby," he said to Brad, "in the lobby they will have a shrine to my mother, only I'm not telling them that. I'm asking them if they want my plan, to have a table by the pool in the lobby, and on that table have a single glass building block, filled with white and black marbles. And in the vase," he told Brad, "always an orchid or an iris. Always a purple flower."

Martin spent more time at the bank than he really needed to, spent hours at the bank, staring at Paulette's hands moving over the figures. No matter what she said, he thought she was brilliant. No matter what he did, she felt he could do no wrong. Others knew that about each of them. They just forgot to tell each other.

Until tree-trimming time. Aunty Franklin was asked to come for Settlement, and anyone else she cared to bring, so it surprised no one standing by the freshly-cut tree in Days End to see her, Crissy, Daniel and MBM (Martin Beech Milborne seemed a little long for a baby), smothered in shawls, come sliding up to Days End in a sleigh, no less. Where they'd found it, and who'd sharpened and soaped the steel rails, no one asked, but they all went for rides that day, and anyone in town who wanted to give a dollar to Sam Walters' mission on Front Street could get one, too. Beech and Gloria came in from their place in their truck, tires wrapped in chains, brought Arlon and Cloteria, all bugeyed and scrubbed up so bright their foreheads looked like silver plating. Gloria brought the cookies for the tree; Tess and Joan had so much else going, they hadn't said boo when Gloria offered. "Only if we can pay for the ingredients," Joan said. "Agreed, fair nuff," Gloria said.

Marilyn, big with another child on the way, came with Bory and John in his police car. John was gorgeous in that uniform. His creases were so sharp Cloteria pretended they cut her when she hugged him. Missus Walters came in her hat with a feather, clicked in wearing little brown high-heeled boots, and Sam Walters, Reverend Sam, came in carrying a stock pot of soup. He filled a room when he entered.

"Sam!" Tess called out first. "How are ya?"

He set the pot down, raised his hands to the ceiling, and called out, "I'm above ground, ain't I?" They all laughed at him, mingled and talked, brushed snow off the children slipping in and out for dollars for the sleigh ride. Mr. Blake from the *Bugle* brought his wife and they set up a portrait camera, and anyone with five dollars for the mission . . . yeah, they knew the song.

Paulette had bought a fuzzy new sweater from the catalogue. It was peach-colored, and she thought to herself after she tried it on, how stupid to buy a peach-colored sweater in the winter. Red or green or black or another white one. What was I thinking? At least it was a scooped neck, showed her nice bronze skin didn't end at her face. She pulled on black stirrup pants over long underwear that morning. It was cold for the day before Thanksgiving. The snow had fallen earlier in November, and now it banked in the streets, and the only one plowed was Main Street in front of the grocery store, the post office, the bank, Days End, and the other small businesses that sprang up after the color change hit. Everyone knew about Pond Ridge, Missouri. Tourists came through and visited the place, and spoke with the people, and the ones that were smart, they charged five dollars for a picture of themselves before they changed. Then they charged another five dollars for the after shot, which the tourist had to take himself. Becky and Marjorie opened a little photo shop together, and business was booming, what with Grady Pardine doing all their running and setting up some before and after packets for the tourists who didn't really want to talk to these people.

Paulette had seen the sleigh going by, pulled by a huge plow horse from Settlement, its shaggy fetlocks brushing the snow at each step. Steam blew out his nostrils, and the gelding looked warily back at Daniel, him holding the whip up over the horse's rear, more for effect than that he was gonna hit him.

Where was my whistle? I would do it for a whistle. Don't be laying that whip on me.

Clarice and Grandma offered some money to Grady to ride the sleigh, but he said no, he paid his own way. From his photo packet project. He'd be paying his own way, ladies, and thank you very much. Clarice had her stuffing to make, and Granny just sat by the window and waited for that old sleigh to pass again, so she could wave her sprightly hand. But now this Paulette of theirs, this Daisy girl she had, well now, didn't she look the picture coming down the stairs. Clarice wiped her hands on the towel and watched her daughter. Granny took her in, too, smelled her 'fore she saw her.

"You in luv, Daisy, I can smell ya from here. Bring 'im in, less see this boy yo all luv."

"What does she mean, Paulette, you in love? You didn't say you were in love, didn't say a word to me." Clarice felt left out, left out and Granny in.

"Mama, that's just Granny. She's just doing her talking and dreaming and running off at the mouth. Granny, you stop that now. We'll send you out to live on Settlement if you don't behave." She went in to lean down for her kiss. Granny pulled her face down between her hands. Clarice watched the two of them from the doorway, her towel slung on her shoulder.

"Uncle Remus say dat Old Brer Rabbit got throwd in the Briar Patch. Said, no, no, not dat patch. But Brer Fox, he lissen, he mean, he throw that rascal rabbit high into tha patch, to sizzl' on the thorns. Bleed him on the thorns. But, Daisy, I ain no rabbit, but I is sayin' no, no, jes hopin' you let me go out to Settlement."

"You want to go to Settlement?"

"'Course I wanna see it. Fun ta see only black faces for once. An' smilin' an' well off."

"Well, Gran, get your leggings on. I'm going to walk up to Days End, reserve some time for that sleigh to come get you personal, and we're going to run you through Settlement. I gotta ask, though, but I'm sure the answer will be yes. I know someone who can get in."

Clarice helped her mother up, and once on her feet, Gran got around pretty good. Paulette got her coat and mittens, left Granny shuffling through the closet for her warmest. "Bye, Mom, I love you."

"Be good," Clarice called back. She watched her mother rummage in the old hall closet, and smiled as she went back to her rosy kitchen.

It was almost four. Martin had stood by the window near the tree, occasionally hanging a strung turkey cookie, looking up the street toward Paulette's, frequently having his picture taken with Crissy, or Beech, or Cloteria, who had a mad crush on him. He'd spent over a hundred dollars on sleigh rides and portrait shots, pulling out his worn leather whenever a new poser slapped Blake on the shoulder.

"Whatever happened to Tom Sweet?" Martin asked, remembering Tom was having a time dealing with his new shade.

"I think he went to Washington," Blake said. "Doing some speech writing for the NAACP, last I heard. Making up words for their side, his side now. Our side," he reflected, glancing at his hands. "Funny, isn't it? Sometimes I just get to laughing over it and I just crack up. Say, heard you got a water bottling plant planned for the outer edge of Cheevers' place. Their water that good?"

"Best water around. Beech and two others can run it; Donn

Forest says he'll sell it, helped his vigor, he said."

"His vigor, you say?" Blake rubbed his cheek and gazed on over at Linda clearing up plates and lifting them over the seated heads. That might just be a nice thing for Linda. Me with vigor. "You get me a bottle, doc. Put it on a tab."

It was almost five, and Martin still didn't see her. The sleigh was pulled in so the horse could be fed and watered. He eyed the way he thought she'd come, but he turned away just as she rounded the corner on Main Street.

"Miz Franklin's in the kitchen, Martin, if that's who you're looking for." Tess stood by him, watching Daniel hold the grain bag up to the gelding's nose. "That Daniel better get in for a bowl of soup himself."

"I'll tell him," Martin said, catching his coat off the hook and picking his way through the fifty some people eating and laughing and drinking some wine, but there Joan drew the line on giveaway. If they wanted some wine, fine. They'd all be walking home anyway, 'cept for Beech, and if he drank some, Gloria would handle the wheel. Beech sure did like those apple-rum kisses of Joan's. Reverend Sam liked a little port now and then, and Linda Blake favored Liebfraumilch, and they roundly discussed bouquet and texture and firmness of grapes, passing their glasses to each other, trying to change a mind. Others were sharing stories about Patchwork going up. One man said they got a body buried under it for luck; he had seen the marker himself, right under the basement.

"They said it was dead injun, put there for luck."

Martin saw her coming then, and his heart went out to her, picking her way through the snow, trying to keep her slick boots from pulling her down. He watched her approaching the horse and sleigh from over the gelding's neck, his eyes just at the right height. She came up to the horse, saw his legs before she saw whose they were. She turned Daniel into Dr. Schoenfield real fast.

"Want a ride?" he asked. She nodded, yes, and Martin ran in to get Daniel out of the warm kitchen.

"You got two riders, Daniel," said Martin, pulling out his thinning wallet. He was out of ones and fives, and he slipped Daniel a ten spot. "You keep this for you." Daniel smiled and pocketed the bill.

They swooped to pick up Granny, coming out to be lifted off the snowy porch by Daniel, and placed between her Daisy and a good-looking man with flashing eyes. Clarice waved a towel from the living room window by the rocker. Happy for her mom. So happy.

"You be the one," Granny said, settling back under the fur robe to look him over close.

"I be the one," he answered, laughing, whatever she meant by that. The sun was setting behind them as they drove through town in the jingling sleigh, all cozy and laughing as the flakes kicked up by the horse stung their glowing faces. Granny whooped when they ran over a ridge, fairly danced on her black bottom on the seat. They cut through a back way and up into Settlement just as the men were coming out to stretch before going up to milk and feed. Snow covered the snug bungalows, and young people were playing and throwing snowballs, and they all looked warm and cared for. Lights were just being switched on, and the sleigh pulled up past the barren fruit trees and over the hill, past the still whiteness of the Corothers house, down the hill to Martin's corner. Paulette and Granny could not believe the way that hospital was coming. They had only just heard about it, but to see it, all rocks neatly in place on the first floor, and a second floor going up fast as the carpenters could work in the cold of late November.

They circled the fields and went as far as a good view of the slowly moving Mississippi before Daniel glanced back at Martin and saw him give him the nod. They cut back to the main road and came back into town that way.

"Granny, you come in and have a cup of soup with us. We'll get a ride home from someone here, everyone's here." Granny nodded, her bright eyes taking it all in: the street and the lights and the warmth coming from Days End. Some folks were just leaving, nodded pleasantly, called good night as they headed on foot to their homes. Others stayed inside, hating to leave this good company, sipping wine and soda, eating cheese and crackers Joan brought out to fortify the stragglers. Mr. Blake insisted on taking a picture of Paulette with Granny, then one with Paulette, Granny, and Martin, still in their wraps. Tess nudged Mr. Blake, and he said for Paulette and Martin to get one alone. They tugged out of their wraps, and stood shyly side by side in front of the fireplace, smiling at the camera.

"Closer together," said Mr. Blake, focusing his shot. Sam Walters lifted his great head to watch the two of them, and he smiled. He raised his wine glass in a toast.

"You look good together," he called. And they did.

Days End felt happy to have its rooms so full. It felt the warmth seep into its old wooden walls, felt the sting of winter on the outside, but inside it was snug. The place started to clear out about ten, and the last two they had to round up and move out of the kitchen were Aunty and Granny, sipping cappuccino at the island. They looked like two wise old birds perched there, nodding and gabbling, speaking of things only they understood. Beech had been into his cups a little more than usual, so Gloria drove her family home. Daniel had taken Crissy and MBM home in the sleigh. He'd gotten them settled before he came back down to run anyone else out to their places. He hated to park it, could hardly wait for Christmas when he could run the riders up and down. Fun. He'd had so much fun. Oh, please, let it snow for Christmas.

Granny and Aunty wanted to ride home together. They sat under the fur robe in the dark and marveled at the shimmering street lamps in the snow, flakes floating down and sending beams of split color into their aging eyes. They held hands under the cloak, murmured that they would stay in touch, now that they'd found each other. Clarice opened the door to Daniel, waved him in carrying Granny, for the path was slippery, and she didn't need no broken bones at her age.

Back up on Settlement, he carried Aunty in, too, and Theopolis opened the door to his blushing bride. Daniel unhitched and watered the steaming horse, wiped him down with a burlap sack, and gave him extra oats in the sheltered barn. He could hear cows shuffling outside in their lean-to, felt the straw get up under his pants leg, pressed his face against the horse's warm side, could hear the echoes through the great body of the grain being crunched by molars, and Daniel said his evening prayers early.

Sam Walters carried their empty but clean stockpot out to the van he'd gotten for the Church. He settled the pot and came back to lift Missus Walters off her feet.

"Slick out, you be hangin' on to me." They sounded the horn as they pulled out of sight toward their wonderful new parsonage. Ladies from the Church came and cleaned it once a week, and it was a good thing, they murmured to each other. Soup she understand. Good old lye soap for scrubbin', she has missed hearin' 'bout.

Close to twelve now, and Tess and Joan shushed them up when they tried to help with the clean-up.

"What clean-up? We been cleaning up all night as we went along. Kitchen is fine, you just sit and stay warm by the fire. Should I call for Freddy to get you a cab, Paulette? Slick as it is, don't want you falling on your walk home alone." Tess smiled at them with a deadpan look on her face.

"Oh, I think I'll be fine," she answered. Tess and Joan moved into the kitchen, checked out their clean-up, got their evening wine, and crept up the back stairs to Tess' bedroom. No boarders tonight, so close to the biggest feast of the year. Everyone was with their loved ones, far from Days End. No one went to a bed and breakfast for

Thanksgiving, and they knew they would have a nice day off for a change. Tess rummaged through her old eight tracks, found just the one she'd been thinking about, and slid it into the machine.

Martin had wanted to touch that fuzzy sweater all night. When she stood before the fire and leaned to put a log in, he saw the fire-light shining through each tiny soft hair woven into it. She smelled so good sitting next to him, kind of close but not close enough. He should tell her she smelled good, but that sounded kind of personal. He would have to think about how nice she smelled and how he would tell her about that. You don't just turn to a beautiful lady beside you in the fire-light and look like a fool. He'd have to work on those words.

"You smell good," he said, biting his tongue and correcting himself too late. He was always doing that, he realized. People must just wonder if he had good sense, blurting things out.

"Thank you," she answered.

They sat back together, watching the fire, and a soft song drifted down from upstairs. It was Elvis' voice they picked up, an oldie: Love me tender, love me true, never let me go.

"Never did think he was that great a singer," Paulette spoke, "but I like the words."

Martin paused, put his arm around Paulette's shoulders in that dreamy sweater, and pulled her nearer. "How do those words go? The ones he just sang?"

Paulette turned her face to his and repeated the words, her heart a little out of control. "Love me tender, love me true, never let me go." He watched her lips, and put his index finger on her chin.

"I think I can remember it. Thanks for helping."

"You're welcome," she said, wondering if this would just end now, and he would let her walk on home alone. He moved away from her, and she wanted to catch him, and pull him back, but she sat stiffer and let it go. Those green eyes were moving away. She wasn't quite light enough, she figured, in spite of his nice words about black people fighting for themselves. Nor did she see that her nice smell had gotten her a man she knew she had fallen in love with. He moved to the fireplace, threw in a log, and watched the crispers float up the chimney.

"Stand up, please," he asked, and now she knew the whole truth. Now the coat would be put on, now she'd be pushed out the door with a wave for a good bye. Keep yourself up, don't let him see what you're feeling. She stood and Martin reached to put his arms around her. He gently pulled her toward him, and she found her mouth pressed against his neck.

"I'm only going to do this once, and never ask me to do it

again."  He knelt in front of her stirruped legs, over long underwear, and looked up at her face.  In his best voice, long unused to singing, he tried to sound good.  He really tried, but Paulette had to admit the voice wasn't real good at singing, but, oh!  She heard the words as he knelt on the rug in the fire-light.

"Love me tender, love me true ... never let me go."

# Chapter Forty-Eight

*Down this road we've wandered
for so many years
With every step we take, we take.
We can tear down all frontiers
Make no mistake*

*E-L-P "Farewell to Arms"*

They made love that night in front of the fireplace on Days End's woven cotton rug, and Martin held her so snug and warm against his furry chest. She snuggled in and breathed his scent. No lotion could ever do that to her. It was his skin and hair she smelled, and it was a smell she wanted to have surround her for life.

Heavy snow started coming in at about two, great feathers of it floated through the night air from God's split pillows. Clarice had turned in after tucking her glowing and babbling mother under her quilts, but she woke about three, and went to see the empty bed of her daughter. No fear clutched at her, no premonition of something gone wrong. The snow must have held her at the inn. Tess and Joan would put her up. Tomorrow would be fine, she sensed, slipping back under the woolen covers. Tomorrow is going to be Thanksgiving, and that bird better be good.

The day was sparkling and crisp, the snow had filled all the footsteps of the revelers, and no traffic moved. Tess made coffee in the kitchen, poured two cups, and thought to check the fireplace. No one had put water on it last night, and they always did. She saw the two asleep together, their arms wrapped around each other, Martin's parka and Paulette's coat covering them as they slept. Tess backed out quietly so as not to wake them. She put a few cookies on the tray, placed the cups of steaming coffee, set a small bottle of Kahlua on it, praised God for miracles, and hurried up the back way in her robe to kick at Joan's door.

The storm had passed them by, the forecaster from St. Louis said over the radio, but it had dumped on Pond Ridge real good. Just about everyone was snowed in for the time, but no one was more pleased about it than Martin and Paulette. They told stories, sang songs, baked Tess and Joan a peach cobbler. Paulette got word to her mother by way of a boy coming by for shoveling, gave him a dollar to scoot over, and tell her mom that she was safe at Days End, and the phone was out or she would have called. All the phones were out in the lower half of the state, but the two new lovers could not have cared less if the world had fallen out of the universe.

On Thanksgiving afternoon, the four of them pulled on their warmest clothes, and walked the few blocks to see about another feast they would share. He had all the feasting he could handle for now; just thinking about her legs around his back drove him wild with new desire for her. That water must be working, he reflected. Need to get those stats updated. This time they won't have to be made up.

Paulette decided she didn't need a ring or anything to flash. She told him quietly to save his money, the future needed savings, not wasteful splendor. He agreed entirely, kissed her hand, and said to let that be her ring, and they were content with it. Martin knew he had no extra funds for the kind of ring she should have, knew that his love for her would be her greatest joy, and hers for him. Gold and diamonds aren't necessary, he realized. They only show the world what you have and how much you value it. The world didn't need to know what he had. Good judgment. Well thought out.

❧

"It's huge!" gushed the teller in the third teller's cubicle. "Just huge!"

Paulette let it stay in full view as she guided her hand over her work. She loved the ring, the big showy handmade two-carat stone in the broad gold band. It was a work of art, a treasure, the nicest thing she had ever dreamed of owning.

Martin had done some praying about this, had reasoned that you only find a queen once in your life, and he had been lucky enough to find two. One he couldn't get to because he knew Luther would tear his arms out of the sockets and throw them in the Hudson River. But this one, so like Claire in some ways, so much herself in others: this one was for him. When he told them over the phone that he was in love, they both talked to him at once, handing the phone back and forth.

"Now I got a favor."

"Anything, son, anything," said Luther, and he heard Claire in the background singing "anything, anything."

"We need a wreath for our door, a big one, a perfect one. I want one like you used to have, Claire, for our front door."

Claire was back on the line. "I'll start tonight. Does your girl like pink? Or white? Is she a posy or a tulip? Martin, I'm dying to see her. Paulette. I can just see her."

"She's beautiful, like a creamy rose, " explained Martin.

"Do you need any money?" offered Claire.

"Naw, I'm fine. I'm even saving some," he added.

When the big square wreath box arrived, neatly-wrapped with a return label embossed in silver, Claire Richworth Hauk, he had to smile. Claire didn't have a middle name, only an initial. She'd made that name up. Boy, he didn't like to see her making things up. Something he'd never do, make things up. Have to speak to her about that. He ripped the box open, tore off the tissue paper and sank back on the chair by the Christmas tree and started to cry at the utter splendor of it.

🙙

The streets cleared up, and new lumber was trucked in daily to the hospital site. Paulette worked on at the bank, squirreling every penny away for a wedding dress and a lovely reception. They hadn't picked the day, but she thought spring would be lovely. Maybe the folks on Settlement would let them use the old Corothers place for the event. She'd ask Granny to ask Aunty who'd have to twist old Theopolis around to the idea, but she saw the house now as a lovely spot to have a wedding party. Maybe even get to stay overnight, spend their wedding night on the hill over the Mississippi. They'd have to find a place to live, a grand place, befitting the jewel of a wreath.

Patchwork was up to the high-ceilinged roof. The plywood was nailed, sealed, and coated. Black paper spread and smoothed. A crane lifted the slate up, and craftsmen, brought in special for this part, started setting the pieces down for a roof that would last forever. Brad Ulmer spent his vacation walking around the site, checking the walls with the engineer and contractor, going over every inch of it. He made a few adjustments and forgot to bill his hours. He stayed at Days End, slept in the room down from Joan's, liked these folks so much that he wondered if going west hadn't been such a bad move for the frontiersmen.

The inside was yet to be finished, but the biggest part was over. Teams of medical people, advisors and specialists, spent a weekend suggesting and changing some things, but for the most part, Martin had his way, and Ulmer's original twelve-hour draft held water. The big units for the HVAC were craned to their nestling spots on the roof, ready for their wires and water lines. The contractor had let those units be supplied by Marlo Coil in St. Louis. They came in with the second lowest bid, but they stood behind their units, and agreed to set up the connecting contractors at a lower price. Man, wouldn't these blow the socks off Luther, he thought, walking around in the snow, staring up at those units on the roof. Lord, we getting us a hospital.

The laptop fell into Paulette's hands about this time, and she ran through Martin's hastily typed-in notes, tried to make some sense of his figures.

"How do you know where you are, money-wise? I must be stupid, but I can't figure out your column work. All I see are those draws at the bank. What method were you using?" She gazed at him over her mom's kitchen table. Her brown eyes were direct, cool, and sincere, but she was all business now. When it came to his business, she didn't footsy under the table. Now in bed, that was different, but when she pulled on her clothes, she became a woman of the world.

"Borrow from Peter to pay Paul, borrow from Paul to pay Peter," he teased, a little embarrassed that he really didn't know where the balance sheet was.

Pearson Pharmaceuticals sent out an inspection team to see the building, and Milda got her first plane ride ever, and her first TWA skyway meal. She loved it. All her hard work had paid off, she realized. Hard work always did. She had really found some notable antiques stuffed away in the warehouse. When she took over the grubby office, Mr. Pearson had remodeled it, put in a modern bath, and replaced the doors. How did Martin expect Tracy to stay on in that grubby workplace? He rubbed his hands and left to meet his wife, feeling pretty peppery these days. That water sample sent to him by Donn Forest was doing its turn on him.

The team went through the nearly finished clinic building, and Milda did some mental sketches about what would work where, and she found a place for almost everything. Some things wouldn't work, but they were all crated up and ready for the move, so she left them on the trucks. Most of the cleaning people came down from Settlement, at Martin's request, to earn five dollars an hour apiece, waxing and buffing and dusting. Good late winter work, and the money was theirs, not Settlement's. They still held all their money in the joint account, but now Theopolis was tired of the trek to get grocery money for the Hodges or the Slaters, dental money for the Bridges, college money for the Hobbs girl. He was plain sick of the trips to the bank to get Paulette to write out those money orders. From then on they each, and on their own, drew out what they felt they needed, but they had to bring a paper by to Aunty, stating how much they took and why. Aunty kept a shoe box for these receipts, and once a month they'd sit together, and she'd read them to him. Not that he couldn't read. He could read if he went slow, liked to hold a paper while he smoked his pipe. It was that writing he hated. All those marks he would have to make if'n he learned. He knew he could, but it jes didn't seem worth the while to him.

The folks went cautious with the money, knowin' he was lookin' over his shoulder at them receipts. Even that careful, they hadn't budged that old mortgage more than three thousand dollars. It had hung up there, big in front of them, until the thirty thousand Aunty had put up to get the principal down. Over seventy thou they still owed, and many wanting to see the place paid off fore they left for the next pasture. How to get that down?

The question needed some discussin', for the answer might come through Granny by way of Aunty. The two had to stay in touch, but with no car for either, and no phone on Settlement, there was no way. Aunty rocked over that a long time, bit her lip deciding, but called up the phone company and said to bring an outside phone up to the Settlement and wire her in.

The redwood and solid glass-doored beacon stood by the side of the lane past the Franklins. It was there for a mergency, she 'splained to the folks who came up to check it out. They wondered if they really wanted the intrusion, but she said it was for calling out, like a mergency, like a pork chop bone stuck in the throat, and that shut 'em up.

"'Course if'n ya need to call out, it jes cos a quarter, an' you can get as fer as Farmington. This be our gif'. Theopolis an' I is payin' for this." First Theopolis knew of it was that night when they were coming back from milking, him and Hodges, saw the little light on in the ceiling of the booth. They opened the door and checked it out.

"We got us a phone," Hodges admitted.

"Looks dat way," grumbled Theopolis, waving to Hodges as he left for his own place. Theo dragged his bad leg up the steps. Damn leg. Cursed damn thin'. He pounded on it, shook it, and it acted like it didn't want to wake. Other foot, other one was okay most times, but it tingled in the night till he had to get up and slam around the floor till it quieted. The one leg on me that's not lettin' me down is my love leg. When tha son of a gun starts goin' to sleep, I be gone.

Aunty opened the door to his stamping. Before he even had a chance to unbutton his coat, she had an idea. "You know, my man, we ain' bin up to the Corothers place in a lon', lon' time. The Millers an' Daniel keep it up an' we doan even get to 'joy it. Les go 'joy it." She packed a hamper with their dinner, all ready to serve, and they trudged back up past the phone booth, and the fruit trees, and into the yard of the big house. Theopolis carried a flashlight, and the two picked their way over the melting snow until they came to rest on the front porch.

"Set a spell, woman, my leg's gone numb."

"Not the little one, I 'ope," she giggled.

"Naw, my lef one. Need to work it a bit, need to work dat kink out. Maybe I walk down an' make a phone call, no, that be too far, all the way to town. My, my, I wisht I had a phone place, righ' here, righ' on my own lan, righ' here on MY lan." He looked at her little face staring up at the stars. She didn't say a word.

They opened the house and walked through the sweet-smelling rooms. All fresh and nice. Theopolis knelt and started a fire. The room came to life and warmth as they had their picnic in front of the fire. When it was nice and cozy, Aunty slipped out of her clothes and helped Theo out of his, untying his boots for him, sitting naked in front of him, serving his feet. He kissed the top of her head. Later, after they'd held each other's bodies and found a freshness they hoped they could always have, they danced a little in front of the dying embers, a slow song that warmed them as they each turned their bottom to the fire.

"My turn to dance on the warm side," Aunty said, and they'd twirl. His butt cheeks got cold. They had no furnace going, a waste for such a short time in the house.

"My turn by the fire now," and he warmed his back end nicely.

"You be a marshmallow," she cackled, pulling on her stockings and skirt. "We had a good ole time tonigh', old man, you be a good lovah, I evah tell you dat?" She smiled at him.

"No, you nevah once tol me dat. How I be good?" He wanted to know, he really did. He had no idea what good might be. His clothes found their way over his body in the dark. The words, woman, say those words, so I be knowin'.

She blew out the candle, pulled the fireplace screen shut over the dying coals, and moved to get her coat and shawl. "If'n I tol you now, you be up all nigh' practicin', an', man, you already worn this ole lady out!"

# Chapter Forty-Nine

The technician adjusted the lamp, fried the solder in place, and moved his eyes behind the goggles to the last three wires. Movers, shippers, electricians, HVAC men and women were swarming over Patchwork. Five days it had taken Paulette, five long days while he nibbled a hangnail and paced. Five long days it took her, her whole vacation time, but the president of the bank waived it. Good man. Good plan.

She shoved back her glasses and looked up to him, standing over her. "You're over. By three hundred thousand. Over, Martin. That means over."

"I know what over means. Who knows I'm over? Are you the only one that knows I'm over? Does the bank know I'm over? Does Pearson know I'm over? Shit, we're all over, the fuckin' government's over, and who squeaks?"

"Watch the mouth. I'm a good Christian girl."

He moved to hold her, press her hair against his face, and smell the sunshine in it. He ran over. Everyone runs over. He'd just apologize, say he was sorry, let them take it out of his salary for the next umpteen years if they decided to keep him on. That was fair. Fair to Pearson, his benefactor here. That was the right thing to do. Good judgment, Martin. He could almost hear Tracy speaking those words. But she was right. Right is right.

The double crews hit the site under floodlights. "What goes?" asked the engineer of the contractor. "Why we up and running at double time?"

"Thought you called it, Mike."

"I didn't call it."

"Then who did? You think Pearson called it? Must have been Pearson. I'll check with Dr. Schoenfield, he'll know."

"Pearson wants this finished, so I had no choice. I have to follow orders." That satisfied them. The bill would be paid if Pearson Pharmaceuticals was behind it. The contractor brought down the rest of the St. Charles church construction carpenters, finishers, floorers. If the Union kicked, they'd settle an amount on them, but the men didn't mind the overtime, didn't mind the work on Settlement. Every one of them liked to be working on something that was simply beautiful. It was beautiful, and to a man they vowed they'd bring their family back to see it, and with any luck at all, each man could find the screw he'd placed, or the joint he'd seamed, or the ceiling he'd dropped.

A quiet fell over Patchwork when the cleaning people came in to start. The men and women with the hand tools that they owned only slid them into their pouches, hitched up their pants, and headed out for the long drive to wherever they had come ten hours before. The technicians and medical equipment people left in silence, and felt sorry that the week had run by so fast. They were finished. Pearson had his hospital. And it was beautiful. Like an old home, it was beautiful. Milda's hand had filled the rooms, already stuck with the solitary cold sterile-looking necessary life-giving equipment. She filled up the rest of the vacant space with antiques and dressers and old couches, worn rugs, and rockers, lamps with Victorian shades of every hue: lavender shades and misty silver sateen, velvet balls bobbling in their happiness in being cleaned and needed once more.

Martin walked through the hospital with some of the Settlement people. They marveled at it, and his pride swelled his chest.

"And this is the operating theater."

"What's showin'?" quipped Aunty, and he hugged her.

"I can show you an X-ray," and he did, slipping the plastic over the light field.

His lab he didn't show them, not because they wouldn't understand, he knew they'd understand, but because he wanted to go through it alone the first time. Simply stupid, he knew. Why alone the first time? What did it matter? Alone, with someone else. But he had settled on seeing it alone for the very first time, and he had thought it out, and decided it was best that way, following his well-reasoned judgment. Alone, he said. The first time I set foot in that lab, I'll be alone.

They loved the lab! Were amazed at the racks of solutions and bottles and decanters and stoppers and Bunsen burners. They stood around the microscope and Martin explained its function, cast a picture on the white wall of a slide he just grabbed and slid in. No one spoke, so impressed they were with his lab. They wandered back down the hall, took two elevators to first, and said good night in the lobby. The people who lived there would walk over the hill to home, and Martin would head back to Days End for a good night's rest.

Just as he was locking the door and setting the alarm, a boy of about sixteen ran back from the group and touched his arm.

"I forgot to say thanks," he breathlessly got out, a little winded from the run back. "You gave me an answer tonight, Dr. Martin. I want to go on that scope of yours. I know now what I want to do."

"Glad you saw something you liked. I love the scope, too, Tony, is it?" The boy nodded happily. "Never scrimp on a cheap scope, Tony. Always get the best." His eyes saw the dark path through the fields that the boy must traverse alone, and Martin didn't want that for him. Wanted the boy with a dream to be safe.

"My car's down here. Jump in! I'll run you over home." Tony climbed in the rented car; would Pearson die when he got that bill from Enterprise? Martin hoped not, looking back at part of his dream as he gunned the Taurus over the broken ground. Out over the ridge, past the Corothers house, dark and silent, down the lane between the barren fruit trees, past the red and glass phone booth, and around the pond to the last house. Tony slipped out, said thanks, and ran up his stairs. Like that kid, Martin mused. Like that boy.

It was well past the hour of dropping in, but he couldn't help it. He wanted to thank Aunty and Theopolis again, wanted to tell them how much they had done for him, bringing the Settlement to him. Not polite to come knocking without an invite, barge in on others, set off their private time with his worrisome staying. Too late to stop. Not good judgment.

He rapped on the door and Theopolis opened it. He looked weary tonight, shaky tonight, and Martin wondered over that. Theopolis was the rock of this place, not even seventy. He had many more powerful years to live and walk these fields, watch over his land, watch his people prosper. But tonight his face was tightened with a stretching over the cheeks, a pull that drew Martin in.

"Mr. Franklin, you're not well."

"Nailed it, doc, I ain' at all well. Aunty not here. She run on pass to see Crissy an' Daniel. I hungry but food doan las long. I eat more an' I sweats. My feets, they the worse of it, they tingle an' they go to mush on me. I stomp 'em wake an' lays down, but they hop at me agin, they hip-hop on me."

"Let me check you over, Theopolis." He moved easily to the man's first name when he was a patient. He had seen the sturdy Mr. Franklin up on the hill, watching them build the hospital, but now he was needing some looking at, and Martin rolled up his sleeves and went to wash his hands. Theopolis was slouched on the couch, stamping his foot occasionally.

"You don't mind?" Martin asked, feeling the man's arms and wrists, pressing his ear against Theopolis' back, not waiting for permission. Martin had his answer. Or he hoped he did.

"Can you pee for me?" asked Martin.

The old man's eyes flashed open, and he stared at Martin. What kind of son of a gun would steal a mother's birth sac, rob them of their land, an' then ast for his pee? A quirk, he is.

"I doan pee for no one but misself." He crossed his arms, stamped his irritating foot a moment, and stared back. Martin knew what was wrong, knew he could help him, but he had to be sure.

"If I can get rid of the stamping, and the sickness, get rid of the hunger that you can't feed, what can you give me?" Martin asked, crouched by Theopolis' feet. "Come on, man, what can you give me?"

"We got some money," Theopolis said, in tears, pain, and worry. "We give you all some more money. Thas what you wan', doctor. Thas what you wan', ain' it?"

"I don't want your money, Theopolis. I want to help you. I got a test I can run. I can run it tonight over at Patchwork. You got a sickness I can cure!" Martin stood and paced in front of the stamping Theopolis. "Please, sir, please let me help you."

Theopolis saw no other way. He was sinking, and he couldn't find the way back up to the top of the water. He was dyin', he thought, I be goin' tonigh'. Pee, he wants. A pee he says he needs, to fix me up. I get 'im his pee, an' then he let me be.

Martin got his urine sample in a clean pickle jar. Theopolis was told to sit tight, drink water, and keep his feet up till he got back.

He raced up the lane, through the fields, past the dark house, and swept down to the hospital. He turned off the alarm and entered, carrying the pickle jar of urine as carefully as a crystal glass. The specimen lab! Where's the specimen lab? His mind was rushing as he went mentally through the plans Ulmer had shown him; he rushed mentally through the building, and remembered. Second floor. Back part. He went up in the elevator and raced down to the lab, flicked on the lights, and unscrewed the lid on the pickle jar. Why am I shaking, he asked himself. I know what it is, has to be. But the doctor in him made him say this time you pause. Don't hit that man with insulin when that may not be it. Might not be hyperglycemic.

He scrambled through the boxes, finally located the litmus paper, and stuffed three narrow strips into the jar. The color said it all. Theopolis was a hyperglycemic diabetic. The color told him everything he needed to know.

Sure now, sure of what he had, he went back through his mind for the meds room. Where is the meds room? This floor, he knew, but which door? The signs weren't on the doors yet, but he lucked out on his third try. He pushed the cartons around on the floor, found the unopened syringes, went for the refrigerator, and saw the stash he had ordered, ordered ahead of time, trying to overspend before they found out and stopped the ride. Oh, God, thank you for making me rash, brash, and rude. He slipped four samples into his pocket, grabbed four syringes from the hastily ripped carton, and raced back out into the night.

The Taurus pulled the hill like a trooper. It had no choice. Martin slammed to a stop and met Aunty at the door. Her face was pinched with worry, her hair out of its bun and strewn on her forehead. "Doctor Shone, oh, praise God, Doctor Shone! You here! He be so quiet, he just layin' there on the floor. Oh, Lord, Lord, doan take my Theo! Doan be so bad to me!"

Martin pushed her aside and tore Theopolis' shirtsleeve back. He raised the vial, inserted the needle, and sucked that precious juice down. He burped the needle, slid it gently and firmly into that old man's skin, and pushed. He tossed the syringe, raised Theo's head, and cradled him. "Not now, old man, not now. Not when we' re so close!" He laid his head on Theo's chest, and heard his heart thump, thump, slowly but then faster. He watched Theo's eyes open and the man turned to look up at his face. Martin felt a shudder go through his body, a weakness fill him, and he wanted to roll over and pull his legs up and sleep from the weakness. His hands were shaking now; they hadn't shaken a few minutes ago, hadn't shaken over that shot.

Aunty swooped into Theo's arms and he held her: shush, mother, shush, shush. He felt his strength returning, felt it rippling through his deprived blood, started to get up, then sagged back to lean against the couch. Martin crawled up on the couch, mumbled to Aunty to put these in the fridge, handed her the remaining vials, and felt sleep knock him down.

Theopolis watched him sleep, found his own legs, and they moved. He held the wall and moved around the room. He felt good. He wasn't hungry, just tired. His feet didn't hurt. He looked in the mirror by the door, and Aunty, coming in from the kitchen, saw him touch his face. He looked at her and smiled.

"Dat man can haf all the pee he want, in my book!"

# Chapter Fifty

*Miles away*
*The light in the distance looks miles away*
*Going back to the Holy Land*
*Last night your anger was born again*
*Carry the torch in your heart*
*And your anger on the vine*
*Still buried in your pride.*

*E-L-P "Burning Bridges*

Mr. Blake thought the occasion of the first person treated at Patchwork deserved a front page article. He wrote the story himself on his old typewriter, and sent it down to the typesetter. He called Martin to see if a picture of the man was available, and Martin said he'd find out.

"Like to get one or two of the hospital, too, turn this into a feature issue." He had always dreamed he would be a great reporter and writer, never thought he'd end up in a town turned cocoa to live out his life. A good story, he thought. Maybe the whole thing's a good story.

Martin had driven Theopolis to the hospital in the morning, got him into the lab to take a sample of his blood, and get him on the right dosage. He had slammed the old man last night. He prayed he would never have to do that again. He needed to get staffed, Theopolis' emergency being only the first. He looked over all the applications that Paulette had given a cursory weeding. There were a lot, and more would be coming if the *Bugle* got them some attention.

He needn't have worried. Kon-Por Overview was up and running with the hospital, he just hadn't the time to stop and look. Paulette shrieked at him to come look at the TV, and he saw a walk through before his eyes of the whole hospital. Clarice brought home some *Newsweek* magazines, five copies she'd grabbed before the rest were snatched up. Kon-Por Overview lived up to their reputation.

Pearson had been keeping a close eye on the money going out, but the last few weeks Milda had slacked off, and couldn't seem to find the current figures. When she did finally get them all together, he blanched. Two-million-eight, Schoenfield had quoted him, and now this bottom line of three-million-two-hundred! He roared and ranted at Milda, stormed around the office like a banshee while she quietly slipped out. He asked himself over and over: Why me, Lord, why take this out on me? All that grant money that was left was going to be used for its intended purpose. Why, why, he stormed. It wasn't fair. It just wasn't fair. No bonus this year, no trip to the Orient like he had promised Frances.

Frances, for all her love of luxury, actually felt more at peace with herself than she had for a long time. She started to go to the gym and work out, gave up smoking, changed her hair color to a shimmery and very flattering Titian red. She liked her body again, liked her life and her husband. Oh, man, did she like her husband! Frederick had turned into an insatiable lover, and Frances loved him for it. That Missouri bottled water held the charm. She knew it was the water, and no one would be able to tell her otherwise.

Word gets around, and the President of the United States, grasping at any straw to show his appeal to the people, insisted that his secretary get the president of Pearson Pharmaceuticals on the phone. That man had shown enormous courage to get that remote hospital and research facility going. Some fat cats just sat back and never busted their buns. The call was placed, and Frederick Pearson was staring out the window at his dream vacation slipping away from him for now when Milda tapped on the door, rather loudly.

"I don't even want to speak to you right now, Milda. I am quite upset over this extra cost, quite upset, as you knew I would be."

"You have a call, sir."

"Well, handle it. That's what you're paid for." He turned back to the window.

"It's the President, sir," she said timidly.

"It can't be the president, Milda. Let me show you." He went to his desk and pointed to the plaque. "President. See? I'm the president."

"Not of the United States," she said proudly.

For it was the soft drawl of President Clinton when he picked up the phone, and Milda had been smart enough to set the recorder on. Kon-Por could do wonders with this call, she knew.

"Oh, I couldn't, sir, simply couldn't accept another grant at this time. There are so many other needs to fill, so many other companies needing your help . . . yes sir . . . if you say so, sir. Five million would help us reach our goal by the year 2000. I will, sir, and you take care. Thank you, sir. And say hello to the missus for me."

"Milda!" he screamed in delight. "We got it! We got it! We got our money for the . . . AIDS research! We will prevail over it. I just know it now with the caliber of men like Dr. Martin Schoenfield. Thank you for prayers answered!"

All sorts of prayers had been answered, and Theopolis Franklin was wise enough to know that he was walking, talking, eating, breathing because of one man's care. It was only because Martin cared that Theo was here. How to repay the man? How better than to have a good talk with the landowners of Settlement and decide to keep things even.

Spring had returned to Pond Ridge, and the earth smelled of opening flowers and rich green grass. The cows even mooed in a throatier way, shifting over the hills, munching the goodness of it. Baby pigs snuggled under the sows, the bull bellowed to let him get on with his stud work, double-yoked eggs seemed to spring out of every brown shell. Martin's name sake, little MBM, was walking and babbling, and Crissy had learned how to give Theopolis his daily shot. That and a differently good diet was all he needed.

Marilyn and John Stewart had a baby girl and the new obstetrician in town, not Martin, delivered her. Martin ran the research part mostly, seeing a few patients, like Theopolis, who wouldn't see anyone else. They had patients come from as far as St. Louis, people from Ste. Gen and St. Mary's were regulars. They had four doctors now, and five registered nurses. Many of the older women on Settlement worked in the hospital as clean-up people; they never had the training to do much else. Tillie was the first patient they lost; she died at ninety-eight of heart failure after chasing chickens with MBM and laughing too hard.

Brad Ulmer came back to see his building all finished and found it much to his liking. He also found Reverend Macy Stewart's ex-wife to his liking, and, after refusing him at first, because she was twelve years older, she went back with him to Newark and opened a bed and breakfast. Tess missed her friend, missed her dearly, but there'd be another friend; she knew she only had to be one to have one.

The town had grown up some over the change of color. Grown in size, but more in spirit. Neighbors watched after each other in Pond Ridge. Neighbors don't turn their back on the folks next door. Reverend Sam held down the religion for all of them, stirring them to reach out, grasp the good life they were given.

"And doan be droppin' that 'F' outta life, doan be leavin' that behin' and sayin' you can't be havin' no fun 'cuz that's not the Bible way; who says that's not the Bible way? You take away that 'F' for fun, and you doan got life. You got a lie."

It had to be, just had to be. The phone call he had prayed for.

"We're coming, Martin! Luther says we can come! Oh, I'm so happy I can't stand it!"

"Then we'll wait to get married, so you can really be part of the family," decided the happy Martin.

He spent his time staffing the hospital and clinic, found a man to come and clean the scope and keep it humming: Tony. A nurse practitioner came over from Farmington hospital on her day off and taught child care and nutrition for the people who came. And everyone seemed to be coming. Patchwork had become the new Days End, but here they got more than croissants and cappuccino. Here they all learned how to take care of their bodies and the children of the future. Dr. Martha Reed extended her patient care to the children of Pond Ridge and the Settlement, and she became richer emotionally for it. She knew she had a gift. Now she was positive it was doing some good.

Cal, the young resident who had assisted Dr. Tae Kim in saving Crissy, was late one night to the hospital in Farmington, and he did a stupid thing: he darted between two parked cars just as the trooper who had delivered Crissy's blood sample, brought to him by Daniel, was waving good night and blowing Sue a kiss. If his head had been working as fast as his foot, he could have seen the young man in greens hold up his arms to ward off the blow; if he hadn't ducked to slip on his trooper's hat, so he'd feel powerful, he might have been able to step on the brake and not hit him so hard that they found his shoe in the next aisle and his stethoscope on top of a truck. The trooper was cited for involuntary manslaughter. He trooped no more. One small step backward for medicine, two giant steps forward for mankind.

Martin raised his eyes and caught Theopolis walking by in the hall. He got up and went after him, calling him back, and Theopolis turned and came back into the small-but-elegant, antique-appointed room.

"Walk righ' by ya, dint I? Fancy man, all sealed off. No wonners I couldn' fine chu."

"Ask, Mr. Franklin, and ye shall find. On your way to have your pee checked?" Martin waited for a roar.

Theopolis only chuckled, slid into the chair by the desk, and handed Martin a paper bag. Martin leaned forward from his chair and opened it gingerly. A frog or a squirrel might be jumping out, as silly as this old man had gotten in his new-found health. He pulled out a shirt, a badly ripped and wrinkled shirt. Martin wanted to thank him for the gift, but he paused.

"I don't think it'll fit me, Theopolis, but thanks for the thought."

"It ain for you to wear, doc, it ain yorn. It be mine, an' tha shirt be my favrit, my very favrit. You dun tore the hell off of it, send it to the trash. You owe me a shirt, doc, you know, times as they are. I needs a new shirt, an' as youse the one dat tore it, well, I be here to get you buyin' me a new one." He sat back in the visitor's chair and crossed his legs.

"You can't be serious," but he saw the old man was serious as hell.

"I wants a new shirt, thas all. Thas not too much to ask of ya."

"Okay, okay. What size do you wear? I'll buy you a shirt, if that's what you want. A shirt you got. Now are you happy?" The worlds between them seemed to be widening, and Martin wondered if he hadn't found a people who really didn't understand at all.

"I wears a sixteen half neck an' lon in the arm. An' I wants it today."

"Today, you say? Well, let me just rearrange my schedule: skip that surgery, leave the nurse to handle the checkout on the newborns. Oh, yes, I can do that for a silly shirt."

"That be my favrit shirt," Theopolis repeated, watching Martin.

"Okay, okay, you win. I'll go buy the shirt."

"Thas better," said Theopolis, rising. "Now you fessin' up to you bad way wit dat shirt."

Martin stood, not sure if he should shake Theopolis' hand or his head, but he shook the offered hand, and sat back down to watch him leave.

"Oh, an' one more thin'," Theopolis said, coming back to the desk. "This be for the care ya give me. This be for the care." He tossed an envelope on the desk.

"I told you that you owed me no money, Theopolis, we went over that."

"This ain money, Doc Shone, this be from all a us." He left the room and shut the door. Martin smiled and opened the envelope, but his smile turned to a straight line, and he sat up and read the papers over and over.

The White house, the house with the porches, the house that stood empty and quiet and clean. The Sylvia Corothers house. Given to him, he read through tear-streaked eyes, given. Deeded to him and the amount due on the note still part of their burden.

No way to say thank you, no way to tell him that what he had done he would have done for any man or woman in the world. No way to salvage his torn curtain of false pride at his feelings over the shirt. God, he cried, pressing the shirt against his chest.

è⋏

The news rippled over Pond Ridge and the Settlement as if a bird had picked up a seed, eaten it, and sent its droppings over every house and store.

Paulette couldn't believe it, simply couldn't believe it at all. The house. The house she'd only wanted for one day and night; that house was going to be her home.

"Well, I tol ya, an' ya jes dint lissen. That be the man." Granny rocked in her superior knowledge, rang up the phone on Settlement, and sent the boy who picked it up to fetch Aunty one more time today.

Claire was delighted with the news that Martin had found them a home so fast. She spoke into the telephone. "And the rent, Martin, how much is the rent?"

"Three hundred a month," Martin replied, and Claire whooped with joy.

"Easy, we can do that easy. And you say that house is near you and Paulette?"

"We're going to be right over you," Martin replied.

Claire figured that must be Missouri talking, right over must mean next place, or over the hill and down a piece. Right over. Come on over, that must be what Martin meant.

Right over meant right over. Red rover played no part in this. When Claire saw the Corothers place, she screamed in delight. She grabbed Luther and hugged him, and sashayed all over the house. Too big, for us, she admitted to herself. Too big. We'd be fine with one floor. Used to one floor.

Paulette ran them around in the still-rented Taurus; they took in the town and tracks and the side streets. They went over to Settlement and asked if they could sit by the pond. Hodges said it'd be his pleasure. She brought Luther and Claire to meet her mother and Granny.

"You here!" Granny said, rising on her own out of her rocker. She looked at Claire in the archway, saw the hair and eyes and the color, she saw it all and tears rolled down her cheeks. Claire looked at Paulette, who only shrugged her shoulders. Clarice watched her mother and wanted to go forward to help her, but Claire was there before her.

"Yes, I've come. Were you waiting for me?"

"Oh, I bin waitn' on ya fer so long, I think you forget me!" cried Granny. Claire held Granny in her arms and Luther went out on the porch. Claire stroked Granny's head, set her back down on the rocker seat, and crouched at her feet. Granny touched Claire's face, her eyebrows and lips, touched the very soul of her.

"You be here," Granny said.

"I be here," Claire answered.

Granny passed that night. She never had a tube run up her nose, never had a shot in her arm. Never saw a bad thing happen after she'd seen the face of Africa and home.

After the simple funeral, well-attended and overseen by Pastor Walters in a yellow robe, Settlement allowed Granny to be buried on their land, in their little designated cemetery. Aunty made that happen for her friend.

On Thursday, after the service and the callers left them to each other, they sat in Clarice's kitchen, over a bowl of soup dropped by for the supper by Missus Walters. They discussed the living arrangements, and Claire and Paulette, like a mother and daughter new-found, hugged each other in happiness. Martin broke the news.

"Now we won't be crowding you, living upstairs. We are mostly gone, and feel free to come up when you want. We want you to feel the house is yours, except we do need to send some money Settlement's way, that's why I said the part about the rent, Claire." He watched Claire let her hands fall from Paulette's shoulders.

"What do you mean, no rent?" She watched Martin twisting in his chair.

"I mean, I lied to you. I knew you would never come if you thought you'd be living free. You've been paying your dues for so long, you'd run from this unless I got you out here to see it. There isn't any rent, Claire. This place was given to me and Paulette."

Claire looked to Paulette, who only nodded.

"These folks give you this, scot free?" she said. Luther went out on the porch.

"Free. No burden to us, just to them. They still got a mortgage," said Martin.

"How big?"

"Oh, I don't know, Claire," said Martin, standing and walking around the table. "Maybe ninety, maybe more. Why?"

"Luther and I have some money. We were saving for a house, and we got the Goldstein money, still set aside. We could cut that mortgage way down, way down, if we went to the bank."

No amount of cajoling and reasoning would keep Claire from her goal. Why give the man at the bank all that interest when they were making so little on their savings? Better to get that note down, let them all breathe easier, let the gift be passed back.

So it was that Theopolis got a monthly notice with an unexpected entry. Forty thousand had been put against the balance and he damn well knowd it wasn't Stone what done it. Now, how that be, those banks so good with their figures? How that be, he mused, watching Aunty setting up the tomato stakes out in the garden. That lady be part of this, he figured, that Black Queen old Martin done brought in for the magic.

The wedding date was set: August the eighth, and the town bustled with the news. There would be no hand-delivered invitations, no envelopes to return with the love stamps stuck on. The *Bugle* ran the invitation: come one, come all. Bring a covered dish. Grab your lady. Settlement is hosting a wedding, and you better be there.

No one missed. Dresses were sewn up quickly, hair was restyled at Margaret's Salon, Days End was kept busy with reporters and out of towners asking about the wedding and could they come? They'd seen the invite, was it for them? Tess assured them the invite was for everyone, but bring food, she yelled after them.

Paulette was radiant as she came down the staircase of Porch House, her name for Sylvia's long-lost home. Her skin and hair and eyes flashed her loveliness and happiness as she met Rev. Sam Walters, wearing his finest flowing red garment, compliments of the closet of the late forgotten Dr. Rev. Macy Stewart. The robe fit him just fine.

The notion of the day was to say your own vows, not let the words be read to you, but you read to the word. Martin and Paulette had practiced this over and over, had said this would sound good, that might be better. Why not let the words just come when we're up there? Why not just say what we feel?

"I love you, Paulette, I want you to be my wife and hold you for as long as God wants me to," he breathed over her veiled face.

She lifted the veil and spoke back to him.

"My love has found a place to stay in. It will stay in your heart, your hands, your lips. I love you, Martin Micah Schoenfield, and you'll never be sorry you married me today."

And those were their vows, and it seemed right enough to the listeners. Rev. Sam nodded his approval and asked for a show of hands, anyone who could say this man and this woman should not be joined in holy wedlock. The quiet he expected started as quiet, but it became a roar of approval instead, a roar of laughter and holding and sweeping the couple from the living room of Porch House. It lasted through the early evening, lasted through the quieting of the young ones into blankets by the fruit trees, lasted through the ringing of the phone in the red and glass box. It lasted until they all dropped into sleep on the grass, all those without a real home on the place, turned into a hum that settled over the unwashed plates and the melting ice. There must have been seven hundred people coming over Settlement that night, and the music and laughter, the spinning feet and the swishing dresses over the grass, set a rhythm going. The saints must have been awakened at the din, must have looked down and said that noise must stop, but when it finally did quiet down, it seemed too quiet upstairs. They missed the music.

Violin and dried gourds; harmonica and washboard. Bare feet slapping on the painted porch. Whether it was that night, or the night after, or the night after that, Paulette didn't know. She only knew that Martin's seed was growing in her, and she blushed with joy.

# Chapter Fifty-One

*The walls come tumblin' down*
*The walls come rumblin' down*

*John Cougar Mellencamp*
*"The Walls Come Tumblin' Down"*

"Do these have to go, or can I pitch 'em?" Martin asked, standing over a box of books.

"Look through them. Some might be Dwayne's. I'll keep his books. Some might still work at Porch House." The open library. Didn't have to be open, but more and more lately the young people would stay out of town, turn off the TV, and come by to visit with Claire, read in the quiet den, and visit with Luther. When they weren't at the house, they'd be slipping into the hospital to load the trash or carry in supplies. They loved Patchwork, thought it was neat to have a place so important be part of their home. The families who hadn't money or time to build their places, and had rented in the town instead, came back to claim their portion. Four new homes were going up on the second pond.

Paulette and Luther had stayed behind, letting Claire and Martin fly back to New York for the last boxes, the close up of the apartment, the utility shut off.

"Inorganic chemistry," read Martin off the book's spine. "How's that strike you? In or out?"

"Let me see." She held the book, was flipping through the pages when a paper fell to the floor. She picked it up and unfolded it, slipped on her glasses and held it to the window. Tears filled her eyes and she leaned to the wall.

"Christ, now, why now?" she wept. Martin went over and put his arms around her. He plucked the note, and a chill ran through him. Fuck! Dwayne's last note, the note Martin had stuck away so long ago, in a place he had forgotten, hoping the note would never be seen. Stupid, stupid of him not to have burned it that night.

She turned to him in anger and frustration.

"You knew, didn't you? Knew what was wrong with him? Why didn't you tell us? Why didn't we know? We were his parents, for God's sake. We had the right to know!"

"Claire, Claire, I didn't know, didn't know anything then. I just knew the note could wait, could not be important for then. Christ, what could I do then but what I did? He was dead, dead in front of me, and you were dead to me, and Luther did what he could, we all did what we could, but the note didn't help, didn't help us."

Tears ran down her face, cut into the lines around her mouth. She licked at the tears.

"What track is he talking about? He says he got off the track. What in God's name did he mean? We gave him our best, Martin, loved him so much. Did we fail him? Did we get him off this track?"

"I don't know for sure what he meant. I can only guess what happened."

She wiped her eyes on her sleeve, licked her lips, and sat down on a chair left behind for the Goodwill. "You have a guess. A guess. Well, that's mighty comforting. You have a guess."

He thought about it, felt it wasn't right to jump to a conclusion he could never prove. Knew in his mind that the past was past, and no good could come of digging it up again. Let this pass. Claire was strong. She didn't need to know any more.

"I think someone molested Dwayne when he was a child." There. He'd said it, the words only confirming what he thought was true.

"Who?" she asked, standing, her eyes round and staring.

"Oh, Claire, it's just a wild hare of mine. I spoke with Petey, and he said there was a counselor Dwayne was afraid of, a man who touched the boys, wiped their . . . their . . . you know, wiped them off after going pee, and straightened their pajamas, told them silly stuff. I had a creepy feeling that maybe this man molested Dwayne. That's all, that's all I can think about what might have happened."

"And that may have turned him, you think, turned him against us and let us sit by and lose our son?"

"He was a kid, Claire, a little boy alone at Scout camp. What did he know?"

"Who was the fucker?"

"Claire! This is exactly why I didn't want you or Luther to see that message. Off the track can mean a lot of things. If Dwayne was hurt, yes, I can see your argument, but we can't prove that, this was twenty years ago. We got to look at this realistically."

She wiped her face on her sleeve again and faced him.

"If some son of a bitch hurt Dwayne, I don't care if it's a hundred years ago. I want his ass!"

"We're almost finished up here, Claire, we have a flight out to St. Louis at nine. There's no time to do anything now."

"There are other flights, Martin, other planes leaving New York every day, and I am not budging if you think you know who that creep is. I want him up for this, want him to be put away. God, Martin, he could still be doing it, still be hurting little frightened boys. I read about it all the time, and it makes me sick. Sometimes it's men of the cloth! If Luther knew about this, he'd tear the man apart!"

Martin watched her earnest face. She meant it. She could be heavy to pull onto the plane, dragging and kicking. Not anything he wanted to try. She was dug in, and he had no way out except to follow up on what he feared and dreaded for the past years. A confrontation with a molester.

He wanted her to know, that as much as he would like to see that man stopped, that the chance of trapping him into an admission, a chance of proving his guilt, a chance to see him stopped in his professional life, knocked out for good, were slim. Let's just let the past be the past. It won't bring Dwayne back. But he knew deep inside he had to try.

"Call the airline and change our tickets. Let Luther know we had something come up so he won't come up to meet us. Tell him we'll call when we need the ride from St. Louis. Book us into a motel, Claire, a double room is fine, or get two if you feel more comfortable with that. I'll start out right now to track this man."

"You know who he is, don't you?"

"I may. I may not, but when I know for sure, I'll call you."

She made reservations at the Holiday Inn, got their number, and Martin slipped it into his pocket. It was Saturday, and he needed to find out as much as he could as fast as he could. Now that he knew he was going to do it, he hurried, fearing that each moment he waited, after having the specter raised again, another boy might be suffering with guilt.

He used the phone and called information. Glen Haven was in the book. He got the church's number and dialed.

"Glen Haven," chirped the cheerful woman's voice.

"Reverend Townsend, please," he asked brightly.

"May I ask who's calling?"

"Dr. Schoenfield, Miss, moving into the area, my wife's out looking at homes right now, but I wanted to find a church close to where we decide. We feel the church is the heart of the community."

"Oh, so like Rev. Townsend you sound. I'd turn you right over to him, but he's tied up right now, with one of our boys. Do you have children, doctor?"

"Yes, twin boys, eight years old and they're a handful for us. Full of gumption and get-at-it. They need a hand to keep them under control, you know what I mean? My wife and I are both doctors, and the boys seem to need a lot of activity to keep them going."

"Then they'll love our pastor. He's very fond of boys, understands their problems, spends as much time with the church's boys as he does with his own girls."

Well, that's a relief. The man was married and had girls. So much the better. He may have straightened out. This whole thing might just die here if Mick Townsend had turned his thoughts around. Maybe he had begun to hear his own message, really helped the people of his church.

"May I speak with him for a moment, just get a feel of the man?"

"Not when he's with his boys. He has a crusade he started when he came here. He calls it his One On One, a boy for a man. Rev. Townsend handles the eight-year-olds, others take the younger and older kids. He works best with the eight-year-olds. How important, those development years, don't you agree? He's in session with one of the boys now, and he's asked never to be disturbed for any reason when he's doing his crusading."

"I couldn't agree more. Is it possible, seeing my boys seem to fit right into his plan, that I could visit with a few of the boys in his program, see for myself how they like it?"

"Not a problem." She paused, shuffled some papers, and gave him the names, addresses, and phone numbers of three eight-year-old boys in the One On One.

He rang up the first number, and being Saturday, the parents were home. Sonya McDougall responded immediately to his request, asked him to stop anytime, they were all home, and so happy to have him as a new neighbor.

Martin kissed Claire goodbye, leaving her with the final clean-up of the apartment. She kissed his cheek, held his hand in a tight grip, and said, "Good Luck."

The taxi brought him to a sweeping subdivision of two-story and split-level expensive homes, professional people with big mortgages. He got out at 1306 Sycamore Glade Court Drive and asked the man to wait. He nodded and clicked off the meter. Martin handed him a ten for his courtesy.

Sonya McDougall was slender and sweet, her dark hair in a ponytail, and her body in a running suit. "Just caught me running out, Dr. Schoenfield, but so nice to meet you. My husband is here, so he'll introduce you to Wynn, and you two can have your chat. Winthrop! Ta, ta!"

Winthrop McDougall was a pleasant man in his thirties, casually dressed in slacks and a Colt's tee shirt. He shook Martin's hand, and let his other rest on the nicely turned banister.

"Wynn, boy! Come on down here, you have a church visitor!"

A small dark-haired boy, slight for his age, came hesitantly to the top of the staircase and looked down. When he saw the stranger, he came down quickly and offered his hand to the man. Manners. Good training.

"This is Dr. Schoenfield, Wynn, coming to live in this area. He has two boys, it was two, wasn't it, Sonya said twins. Boy, I bet that was rough." He smiled at Martin and looked back at his son.

"He's a Jew," the boy stated simply. The father would have crawled under a rug if he hadn't installed wall-to-wall carpeting.

"You got me pegged," Martin laughed. "Yes, I was born to a Jewish family, but I married a Lutheran girl, and for the sake of our children and our love, we decided to find a meeting ground for our faith."

The boy nodded, seemed to understand.

"And what I'd like to know is this. Would we be happy with your church? Are you happy in it? I hear Rev. Townsend is good with you young men, One On One, he calls it."

The boy's face turned a shade whiter; Martin saw it change.

"I like it just fine. Can I go now?" He glanced at his father, and Winthrop waved his hand, and the boy fairly ran up the stairs and back to his room.

Winthrop scratched his chin, looked at Martin, and winked. "Most times we can't shut him up, but lately he's gotten quieter. I think this Rev. Townsend has a hand on him, settling his spirit down to be more reflective. We hope so. He was bouncing off the wall a year ago before Townsend got his hands on him. Good man, taking so much of his time for our kids. We have a busy life, and Reverend just slips in, and takes charge, and everything seems to be getting quieter."

"Amazing," said Martin. "And other parents are seeing the same thing?"

"Oh, my, yes. You need to speak to some of them. Maybe they'll give you another endorsement here."

"The church secretary suggested Reed Taylor and Zeke Clawson. You know those folks?"

"Right down the lane and up over Church Park Hill Place. Don't mistake it for Church Park Hill Court. That's a cul de sac. Remember Place and you'll be fine."

"Would I be pushing my luck to use your phone?" Martin asked.

"Heavens, no, grab this one or sit down in the kitchen. I was just getting ready to barbecue. Sonya loves her run, but she likes supper started when she gets back. The duty of us liberated men, right?"

Martin smiled in agreement, and sat down at the comfortably appointed island to make two calls: one to the Clawsons on the aforementioned Place, Court, Cul de Sac; the other to the Taylors residing on Buttercup Spring Point Lane. God, I'd hate to be delivering mail out here, Martin thought, tapping in the first number.

A man's voice came on the phone, and in the background Martin heard the shrill voice of a child and the lowered reasoning tones of a woman. "Hello?" came the voice. "Hey, will you two pipe down?" He spoke again. "Sorry, kids, you know, trying to run the show."

"Hi," he said brightly. "I got your name from Glen Haven and I'm new in this area, trying to settle on a church for my family. I understand you're a member of Glen Haven."

"No other place like it. You'll know as soon as you come down that drive that you'll find peace at last. It takes a long time, but once I laid my eyes on Pastor Townsend, and he laid his eyes on my son, I said to myself, now there's a man who can change things. Haven't been disappointed yet."

"That's good to hear, on top of the McDougalls' praise. Could I just stop by, meet your boy? I have twin sons, about eight, and they're a handful for my wife and I. We seem to be going against the boys so much of the time, us both being doctors and damn busy running the boys here and there, trying to give them good direction, but the time, man, the time seems to get away from you."

"Know that feeling well." He paused and turned and asked for quiet again. He continued. "Stop on by, we're up the lane from Sonja and Win, over three drives and down the hill."

Martin checked his watch. Three thirty four. Time to keep going. Time to see them all and decide if his hunch was just a poof of smoke or if he had found a real problem.

The Taylors were snugged into the end of the lane, and the cabbie said, yeah, he'd wait, and Martin waited till he clicked off the meter before handing him another ten.

"Reed! Come on in here and meet a new church friend!" The boy peered around the corner of the TV room, cautiously looking out, but when he saw it was a stranger he came forward. His hair was as brown as his eyes over the tanned little face, and he looked up at Martin.

"You the man with two twins?" he asked.

"Yep, that's me." Martin watched his face turn from his dad, and back to the TV room. He seemed to want to go away, but he wanted to stay, too. He moved his feet in his tennis shoes and toed the carpet.

"Your sons might not like the church here so much." His father reached over and grabbed his arm, and sent him up the stairs with a good spank on his bottom. Mr. Taylor came back down and apologized.

"That kid. One day he's all up and happy. One week later he's spouting off crap like that. Gave my wife a hassle today over going on over for Rev. Townsend's quiet time with him, his One On One. The boy's just hard headed, and I tell my wife she gives in to him too much, lets what he thinks rule this roost. I'm not about to let that happen. Kids need to hear "no", and if Rev. Townsend takes the time to coach these kids, and slow them down to enjoy what they've got, well, then the kids better catch on, and damn quick!"

Martin nodded agreement. "May I use your phone?"

Mr. Taylor agreed and went back into the TV room where his wife was watching an Egyptian tomb being opened on cable.

One last call, and this would be it. If he didn't pull a rabbit out of the hole on this one, he was forgetting the whole thing. Life was too good for him to spend this much time on conjecture, and the twenty years since Dwayne had possibly been hurt fled by in Martin's mind. He realized the kids looked a little timid, a trifle wary, but he was a stranger. Why wouldn't they be hesitant? But Reed saying his twins might not like it. Was he warning him? He decided not to call the Clawsons at all, just stop by.

The Clawsons resided in an even more elegant home, up on Buttercup. They had three acres, a swimming pool, and a basketball court. Martin slipped the cabbie another ten and the man smiled. He would sit here all day with his meter shut off if this crazy man kept giving him ten dollars for dead time.

Martin checked his watch. Four thirty eight. They could still make that flight if they hurried, but he knew they had changed the plan, had gotten the room, charged it to Pearson Pharmaceuticals, and he sighed and walked up the long drive. This plan he was working out, this plan that was supposed to bring in a child molester, was not going as great as he'd hoped. The McDougall kid had stopped talking and gone upstairs. The Taylor boy, a nice kid, had said his sons might not like it, and he'd gotten a swat for his honesty. Well, it was time, Martin figured, to pull out the plugs and the game and the disguise. It was time to show some power.

A boy was on the drive, shooting baskets that had no chance of making it, standing his ground and pitching them up; his style was all wrong. He was flinging the ball hard and to the left and right, never aiming it right. He stopped when he saw Martin, looked scared, and then relaxed. He walked toward him with the ball held against his chest.

"Hi," Martin said.

"Hi," said the boy, holding the ball and looking at Martin curiously.

"I used to play ball, and I was pretty good. I can show you how to drop that ball in easier than you can believe."

The boy watched Martin as he took the ball and dribbled it in. "See? Get in real close, then spin like this," and Martin did a half turn and came back. "Then they think you don't know what you're doing, they follow your spin, but you move off, this way" and Martin took one step, and sent it flying. One hand over the other, cradling it, lifting its weight, throwing it up, and dumping it straight through the net.

"Wow!" said the boy, who must be Zeke Clawson. "You are good at that!"

"Ah, not just good, I'm the best. Could have been the best, they said, but I went to the police academy instead, got my feet down to earth." He tossed the boy the ball and moved to leave. The boy caught up to him.

"Shoot some more with me. I can't get a game up, and I shoot by myself 'cuz nobody's my age."

"What about Wynn and Reed? Don't they play ball with you?"

The freckled face turned to him, and Martin went to his knees. "You're friends with those boys, right? You talk, right? What do you talk about? Do you talk about Mr. Townsend?."

The boy was frightened, stood back from Martin, and held the ball against his chest.

"I'm a cop, I told you that," Martin stood up, "but I'm here to say hello, throw a few balls with you, and then tell you about Wynn and Reed."

The boy nodded, clutching the ball.

"Well, I've just come from talking with those boys, and they told me some things about Mr. Townsend that seemed wrong to me, seemed mighty wrong, so I sent a police car to Glen Haven, and they put a chain on the Reverend's hands, and he's not going to touch anybody anymore. He's a bad man, Zeke, but I want you to know that he won't bother your friends anymore; he won't touch anybody."

The boy's mouth fell open. He screamed and spun and threw the basketball down the drive, where the cabbie jumped out to nab it.

"He did it!" Zeke screamed. "He did it to me, too! He said

he'd," and the words choked in him, "fingers. She's my sister. She's a baby. Cut off her fingers, he said. I can't let that happen, can I?"

Martin got up and put his arm around the shaking child. "The police have him, son. He's never going to cut anyone's fingers. He was trying to scare you, make you be quiet, because he's a sick person. The police have him, and we won't let him go."

Zeke clung to Martin's hand, and wiped his face with the other. "Tell Mama and Dad. Tell them. Never make me go back over there."

"There is no going back over there. The man's in jail, big bars in front of him. You told the truth. And Wynn told the truth, and Reed told the truth. Always tell the truth, Zeke, and you'll be fine."

Three irate and questioning parents met at the Clawson's, upset with the disturbing news that their sons had been pawns in a sick man's game. They tossed it around, grew angrier, and the one man in the group who saw what to do, did it. He called his high-priced attorney, who listened quietly, spoke with the only levelheaded person there, a Martin Schoenfield, and he knew what he had to do. The attorney made a few calls and got the ear of the power he needed.

"Help me on this, Florence. They've got him nailed, and we can't just let him stay out there doin' it. He could have a kid with him right now, right under the nose of the parents. Get me an order tonight. A search and seizure. Let the prosecuting attorney know, and he can get those cops in there fast. I know you need his okay, please, Florence, just ask for it. I don't want any stone left unturned, no handle for them to creep this guy out the back way. When those officers hit the door, I don't want a refusal to admit. Get him picked up. Make sure it sticks. I swear this is for real. I want him picked up."

Judge Florence Harper didn't bend to many such requests she received on a Saturday night at home, sizzling her burger and reading on the porch. No, she liked her time away from the bench to be her time away from the bench, but she listened to the attorney who had always played fair with her way of doing things, and did just what he asked. She called the local prosecuting attorney, said he had her seal on this, and he drew up the papers and hand-carried them to the police chief of the environs around Glen Haven, and asked him to send his men on down and pick up the Rev. Mick Townsend for questioning. Just questioning. He wasn't about to hold this man more than a few hours, let him get his mouthpiece in to deny his innocence, then the matter would be over. Just pick him up, he ordered. And the boys in blue spun their cars around and headed to the drive above the church of the One On One Crusade.

The officers pulled in quiet, no lights or noise. Two of the men circled the building on foot, acting as if they had a mad gunman under siege, and two others approached the door of the parsonage. Accessibility had been Townsend's motto, always be near, and near he was to the church. His nicely laid out five levels had rooms below rooms; had a room for ping-pong and a room for greeting the flock, had a room for guests to stay over if their weary feet needed his counsel. He had a room for everything, and his One on One room, well, that left very little to the imagination.

When the surprised Mrs. Rev. Mick Townsend opened the door to the men in uniform, she was stunned. She stood back without a sound, and let them check through the rooms; quietly they walked, finding doors unopened, and peering in to check. They moved down through the house while the poor woman stood with her daughters clinging to her skirt, and she shushed them and went on to feed them supper as she had been doing. Perhaps a prayer would help, she pondered, spooning the potatoes. Perhaps Mick has a lost soul that he tried to help, and now they have come looking for that lost soul. She knew it wasn't really Mick they were looking for. She knew in her heart that God wouldn't let him down, this man who had been so careful with her body that he only touched her twice, and each time the fruit had bloomed. A saintly man, her Mick.

The search was thorough. The place was absent, as far as they could tell, of the elusive Rev. Townsend. Maybe God just swooped him up into protective custody. They chuckled, relaxed by the ping-pong table by the blaring TV. It was then, after shutting it off, that they heard a noise of muffled squealing. Other men might have shuffled off that noise, other men might have said, I'm dreaming here, but the officers, red in the face, knew that sound and didn't like it. It was hand over mouth they hated, face against sweating back, the sound of holding down and shutting out, the sound of covering up something that shouldn't be happening at all.

When they found the panel off the ping-pong room, found it and broke it down with their shoulders when they couldn't find a way to make it slide open, they only stood in the torn doorway and gasped. A man spun toward them, screamed at them to leave; he was about the Lord's work, leave me, he cried, but they didn't leave him. He was garbed in a flowing yellow church robe with the front open, and the bareness of him underneath was all too obvious. His green sash was tied in slip knots over the metal handles of a gymnast's horse. The slim wrists of a small redheaded boy were in those knots, and his shocked eyes only barely focused on them.

They grasped the man's agitated flailing hands, slipped

handcuffs on him, and brought them together in a click. He was pushed before them against the ping-pong table.

Another officer, come lately to the scene, figured this must be the one that needed bringin' in. He swept his great arm around the sweet Reverend, held him tight, and whispered in his ear. "We be goin' upstairs."

"To God?" asked the bemused man,

"I sure as hell hope not," said the black officer.

# Chapter Fifty-Two

*Ain't nuthin like a live man
In the dead of night . . .*

*Kristina Olsen
"Live Man in the Dead of Night"*

"They got him?" asked Claire, flinging open the motel room door.

"Buttoned," answered Martin. "He had a kid with him when they went in, and more proof those folks don't need. He can't squirm out of it. What happens to him is up to them and the hereafter, but for now we've done what we came to do."

"I only wish," said Claire, slumping onto the bed, "only wish he knew what he did to us."

"He's sick, Claire, very ill. What he did twenty years ago, he's forgotten. Telling him now wouldn't mean a thing to him."

"Then you didn't actually see him, did you?"

"God, no, Claire, I never want to see him."

But see him they did the next morning on the plane, saw his slouched figure and haunted scared eyes, saw him in the newspapers that bore the blaring headline: Shepherd Accused of Fleecing Flock.

It was only later that they read that Rev. Mick Townsend had been sentenced by a grand jury to a mandatory twenty-five, with five years off for good behavior. A mandatory twenty he had to do, and by then he'd be in his sixties, and maybe some of the men in prison would change his tastes. They read where the Reverend's wife had joined the congregation in their effort to support him, clear his name, but the photos that were shown, and the statements of the sons of the McDougalls, and the Clawsons, and the Taylors shut that effort down.

They arrived back in St. Louis on the noon flight, and reliable Luther was there to meet them. Claire leaped into his arms and clung to him as if he was her earthly link. Martin drove back with Claire and Luther sitting with their heads together, and the old Taurus kept adding up the miles. He smiled at the odometer. Some day he'd have to simply go in and buy this car. There was no way around it.

Life settled back to a normal speedy pace. Porch House got settled in, the boxes so carefully packed by Claire opened up in a new home, their home. Shelves were filled and the dusting and cleaning began. Patchwork was thriving, and Martin got the clinic running without him, getting to spend more of his time in the research lab with

Tony when he got in from school. The kid was so smart, noticed Martin, smarter than he had ever been at his age. Watch this one, Martin decided. Help him get there.

Amy picked this time, in spring, to say it had been high time since she'd been invited, and Claire and Paulette checked their busy schedules and said June, come in June. They wanted Amy to see the trees in full bloom, the new calves and piglets, the contented bull resting up his used parts, and the grass around the place growing and cut and trimmed. They wanted all the flowers in, and the porches with their gray paint hosed down and spotless. Windows all sparkling and the widow's walk on the roof freshly painted with black enamel.

"Cat" Nedilia Baker was shaky on her plump legs, but she did try a few steps, then sat herself down. MBM tried to tug her up, but she crawled to the safety of her father's arms.

The folks on Settlement all came on the invite, and they brought food in the heat to be set in the fridge. Clarice came in Freddie's cab, and old Freddie stayed around behind Mrs. Pardine almost the whole day, but she paid him no heed under her blush. Tess came with the Walters, and for the first time in memory, they didn't bring the soup pot. Rev. Sam had a van full of watermelon instead, which got tied up in an old badminton net and set to cool in the spring. Aunty and Theopolis came, and the Hodges, the Millers and the rest of them, some working on their new places up on the second pond. Town had worked for a while, but they were mighty happy to be back with their own. How they figured Martin and his family from the east were part of their own, they didn't stop to worry over.

Ned and Amy fit right in, slipped the new kids gum and peppermints, fed the animals, and walked the land.

"Gorgeous," Amy breathed as she strolled with Martin. "It's like out of the Wyeth painting, only there's no one crawling up the hill." She paused and threw a rock at a tree. "I brought you something, kinda late, I know, but I've been saving it for you."

"Just you being here is present enough," Martin said, slipping his arm around her and heading back to the house. "I like Ned. You are lucky to have a man that fine."

"And you're not lucky to have Paulette?" He grinned. "Martin, we're both so lucky, I only wish Dad and Mama knew how this turned out."

"Oh, they know, they know. They have to know, or we wouldn't feel this good."

She liked that answer, and skipped into the house to bring out a wrapped painting. She slid the large paper-wrapped frame over to him, and he sat on the top step and unwrapped it carefully. It was the one he'd wanted so long ago. The antelope running across the painting filled him with pleasure.

"It's too much, Amy, I can't accept this. It must be worth a lot with what your work is bringing."

"This one isn't for sale, Martin, it's for you." He rose and hugged her with one arm, the other clutching the painting in its gold frame. Paulette came over to look at it, and she liked it, too, without understanding why it meant so much to her husband. If he liked it, that's what she liked. Until it came to bill paying. There she said how it was, and he went out on the porch most times, to sit with Luther and watch the stars.

But today there were no stars, far too early for stars or lightning bugs. The day was hot and humid, and the ladies waved their newspapers and fans, and the drinks went round, plenty of iced tea and wine for the brave. Too early for food, they just enjoyed watching the kids playing in the waving sprinkler on the sloping lawn.

Martin paraded his picture around the porch for everyone to admire, then he slipped into the house with it, to set it by the armoire from Micah and Amelia, now nicely centered between the tall west windows. In the center of the library room stood the old roll-top oak desk where Claire sat with the children and told them stories, and sent them home with books and hugs. Luther had set up a woodworking and fix-it shop off the chicken coop, and he explained wiring and circuits and air conditioning to the eager young men not bent on medicine.

Theopolis had wrestled Katherine Baker out of her father's protective arms, and set her down to teach her to walk. She gazed up at him, touched his face, and went for Aunty across three steps. Aunty grabbed her and kissed her, sent her back on her stumbling legs, and before long, she was so good MBM came and planted a kiss on her for a reward. Claire captured that moment on the camcorder, sent the lens swooping over the porch and the gathering, almost forty people, black and white. This is color, she reminded herself; this film's in color.

Paulette was heavier with the baby, she moved slower, but her smile was as quick as it had always been. When Martin came back outside, she let him help her sit on the top porch step to watch the kids laughing, soaked through, running in the sprinkler.

"That does look cool," Paulette said, moving her hand to her back. "Wish I was out there running with them."

"You do, now?" responded Martin. "Now how can we explain to our child that his mother just slipped in the grass in her eighth month, went sprawling, and no place to land but her stomach? And that's why his head has a flat side to it?"

Paulette giggled. "Then you go run for me. You do the grass dance."

"Me? Why me? There goes MBM heading for it. Crissy must be watching something else." But Crissy was watching MBM just fine. She leaned on the railing with Daniel and watched their boy with his hands held out to the spray for the wave of drops. "Let him do your grass dance."

The water did look refreshing, and Paulette nudged him again. He pulled off his moccasins and socks. His long white toes wriggled on the step.

"You got the longest toes," she laughed. "Martin, you got the feet of a white monkey. You could climb trees with those long toes." She laughed so hard she laid back on the porch, and he took that moment to roll against her for a kiss. Their heads laid side by side on the clean gray porch floor, and he kissed her gently.

"I love you, Paulette," he murmured.

"Not as much as I want you dancing in the sprinkler," she answered.

He leapt off the top step and ran toward the water, rolling up his jeans as he went. Paulette rolled up to sit and watch him frolic with the kids. He played with the spray, ran his face and hair into it, and shook off the big cool drops. He shook all over like a damp puppy flinging the drops, the wetness covering him, chased the screaming delighted kids, came back soaked and happy and let his hair drip on her. She laughed, they all were laughing at their crazy doctor, and Gloria Cheevers tossed him a towel. He went into the house laughing, rubbing his hair. His body felt so cool and good as he ran up the stairs to their bedroom to change out of the wet things. So cool and wet and clean. Kids got it made, he smiled. Stand out there in the water and everything gets washed clean. Please, God, never let any of this change.

The sun was dropping down as Daniel went to turn off the sprinkler and grab MBM. The kids were stripped and dried and sent off in clean shirts and shorts. The women went in to set up the food, and the heat came back over the fields. Luther dragged out an old attic fan, and set it up in the yard, facing the porch, and the breeze blew back and forth, back and forth over their bodies as they ate and talked and shared stories.

"God left me over for one more day," Martin heard Hodges say as he came back on the porch in his clean jeans and tee shirt to grab the plate Paulette had fixed for him. "Thas why I be a leftover." The soft laughter filled the porch as the sun slid down to evening.

One more day. He chewed his chicken and beans and forked in the slaw. God, I got it so good.

Ariel Claire Amelia Schoenfield was born in late summer after the party at Porch House. She weighed six pounds and fourteen ounces, and she was a perfect eighteen inches long. The young obstetrician in Pond Ridge, who worked with Patchwork, delivered the baby a rock's throw from Porch House. Luther insisted on nicknaming her Cassie, for short.

She was only four days old when Martin took her from Paulette's arms and tightened her blanket around her. Martin knew she was too young to take on such a long walk. Babies needed to stay by their mamas. Babies didn't need to be exposed to all that sun and light and hot air. The people of Settlement would want to be touchin' her, be wantin' to hold her and rock her against their breasts, kissin' on her. No, not a good idea. Skip that scene. Leave her up where she belonged. Good judgment.

He and his Cassie stopped at Aunty and Theopolis' house first.

*Because so many made requests for recipes found in this book, we have asked the Days End people, Tess Tandy and Joan Stewart, Gloria Cheevers, Missus Walters, Claire Hauk, Paulette Schoenfield, and Jane to share them with the reader.*

## Tess Tandy's Blackened Fish

Pick out several nice cuts of white fish. Defrost. Sop up the moisture. Roll in blackened fish seasoning and set aside. Get an old iron frying pan, preferably black iron, and slip in a pat of butter. Run that heat up high til its sizzling. Slap the fish in and soundly let it cook on the skillet one to two minutes. Turn it once, gently, for it'll be flaky even then. Sprinkle more seasoning over it. Put a dot of real butter from Settlement on each piece and turn off the heat. Cover the pan tight with foil or a plate. Let sit and hum while you fork up brown rice or wild rice and butter beans make a nice side dish.

## Missus Walters' Minestrone

Start out as best you can with what you got. If you don't have fresh carrots, zucchini, celery, green peppers, fresh picked peas from Pond Ridge, grab a bag of frozen oriental vegetables from the store. We ain't all lucky enough to have Settlement over us. Same goes with the matoes. You ain't got fresh ones? Get a can of whole tomatoes, about a size 2 ½ and pick up some Italian flavored cans at the same time.

Get a nice size pot out, a stock pot they calls 'em. Come get one a mine if'n you ain got one. Get a clean quart sized milk bottle, fill it wit fresh water (Cyclone Purified Water works best). Pour the water into the pot and start adding things, things you got. Add those vegetables all cut up nice and small, or add the frozen oriental ones. They do just fine. Break up some pieces of sghetti, about a good handfull. Add some bouilion cubes, chix flavor if'n you ain got stock boiled down. Toss in some dried basil and some of that italian oregano. Slice in a whole bunch of nice fresh mushrooms. We pick ours, but store bought'l do. Chop up about two big handfuls of skinny zuchini, wit their skins left whole. Any meat'd do but if'n you got some cooked chicken, slice that in now, bout two cups I'd say. Any meat'd do, but make sure it's cooked and cooled down. Slice in some matoes now, or add the Italian ones or the plain old canned whole ones.

Simmer that nice and bubbly for a time. Let it suck in good, keep that old heat low, and stir it onct or twice, to move those flavors in. That be good soup. This be good for three days if'n you keep it cold in the ice house

## Claire Hauk's Blue Cheese Dressing

Three tablespoons nice wine vinegar
Twelve tablespoons good oil (canola is best for the waist)
Three tablespoons Worcestershire sauce
One-half teaspoon fresh ground mill pepper
Crush up fresh garlic and spill it in
Crumble in some blue cheese and shake it up
Nice

## Paulette's Chili

Two pounds of meat, beef, diced up and browned nicely
Add three pounds canned tomatoes if you don't have fresh
Chop up two nice feeling onions and one green bell pepper
Add some cooked pinto beans, or a can if that's what you got
Crush up two cloves of fresh garlic
Put in a big spoonful of chili powder
Add some black pepper, fresh ground
Add one teaspoon of cumin, and a smash of cilantro, if you got it fresh
Add some salt if you like, but add the best thing now: jalapenos, two, diced up will finish it nice. Let this simmer for a day if you got the time to look in on it, or put it in a crock pot, turned low.

# Gloria Cheever's Best Biscuits

Sift two cups of nice white flour. Shake in 'bout three teaspoons of baking powder toss in some salt. Sift it all together, nice and light. Cut in bout third cup of stiff shortening or lard. Make it mealey. Add bout three-forts cup of Clara's milk. Stir well.

Flop it out onto a floured cloth. Punch it round a bit, til it feel right. Take the old rollin' pin and flatten it out some. Maybe half inch. Take a water glass and stamp out dem biscuits quick like. Slide em on a cookie sheet and lift'em into an oven poked up hot, say 450. Watch 'em Dey sneaky. Ten minuts, twelve minuts . . . the time do move

# Joan Stewart's Evening Kisses

Heat three cups of apple juice, not cider
Add two-thirds cup triple sec. Add one-third cup rum
Toss in a cinnamon stick.
*You'll have the breath of an angel and pleasant sleep*

*Oh, and this one, the one Macy would never touch:*
One can beef bouillon. Keep the can. Use it for the measuring.
Add one-fourth can Worcestershire sauce
*Isn't that safe? Isn't that a pastor's drink?*

*Now for the fun, the way Brad likes it.*
Add one-half can Vodka, preferably Sky. Add one can V-8 juice
Two dashes of lemon pepper and the juice of a lime, squeezed dry.
Stir and enjoy.

# Jane's Manhattan Honey-Soaked Ham

Locate a good deli.
Call him when he's in.
Order up three pounds of nicely trimmed baked honey-soaked crispy crust ham.
Have it delivered.
Put it on your MasterCard.

*Another new book from Black Oaks Publishing to look forward to...*

## Shrooms by Judy Hogan

An enchantingly beautiful woman. . . a black cat. . . a fatal mistake. . .
Both the author and the character learn the price of rejection in this
intertwining of two-tales-in-one. . . Mushrooms and Murder . . . a
stubborn black social worker who hides two white kids. . . a marked
child. . . an unfortunate nurse who was in the right place at the wrong
time. . . a lawyer with a heart, who forgets to bill his hours.
     You will meet them all in *Shrooms*, and you won't forget them!

**Visit our web site at www.csss-inc.com/blackoaks
for more information on upcoming projects and other books.**

---

### BLACK OAKS PUBLISHING ORDER FORM

*Please feel free to make as many copies of this form as you and your friends need!*

Please Print or Type

| | |
|---|---|
| Name | |
| Street Address | |
| City, State, Zip | |
| Daytime Phone | |

\_\_\_ Copies of "The Shade" by Judy Hogan @ $16.95 each = _____

Add $3.00 per book for sales tax, shipping, and handling   = _____

Send your check or money order for $_____
TO:    Black Oaks Publishing
          P.O. Box 803
          Hillsboro, Missouri 63050

---

### FOR ALL CREDIT CARD TRANSACTIONS
call our St. Louis Distributor, CSSS at 314-645-6080 or 800-275-4055